MW01132183

STEPHEN KING

NEVER FLINCH

A NOVEL

SCRIBNER
New York Amsterdam/Antwerp London
Toronto Sydney/Melbourne New Delhi

Scribner
An Imprint of Simon & Schuster, LLC
1230 Avenue of the Americas
New York, NY 10020

First Scribner hardcover edition May 2025

Interior design by Kyle Kabel

Manufactured in the United States of America

1 3 5 7 9 10 8 6 4 2

Library of Congress Control Number: 2024055988

ISBN 978-1-6680-8933-0
ISBN 978-1-6680-8935-4 (ebook)

For Robin Furth,
with love and thanks for all your hard work

NEVER
FLINCH

Trig

1

March, and the weather's miserable.

The Straight Circle meets in the basement of the Buell Street Methodist Church every weekday from four to five PM. It's technically a Narcotics Anonymous meeting, but plenty of alcoholics also attend; Straight Circle is usually packed. It's calendar spring, has been for almost a week, but in Buckeye City—sometimes known as the Second Mistake on the Lake, Cleveland being the first—actual spring comes late. When the meeting lets out, a fine drizzle is hanging in the air. By nightfall it will thicken and turn to sleet.

Two or three dozen attendees gather near the butt can by the entrance and light up, because freebasing nicotine is one of two addictions left to them, and after an hour in the basement they need that hit. Others, the majority, turn right and head for The Flame, a coffee shop a block down. Coffee is the other addiction they can still indulge.

One man is stopped by Reverend Mike, who also attends this meeting and many others on a regular basis; the Rev is a recovering opioid addict. In meetings (he attends two or three every day, weekends included) he introduces himself by saying, "I love God, but otherwise I'm just another fiend." This always gets nods and murmurs of approval, although some oldtimers find him a bit tiresome. They call him Big Book Mike for his habit of quoting (verbatim) long passages from the AA handbook.

Now the Rev gives the man a soul shake. "Not used to seeing you around these parts, Trig. You must live upstate."

Trig doesn't but doesn't say so. He has his reasons for going to meetings out of the city where recognition is unlikely, but today was an emergency: hit a meeting or drink, and after taking the first drink, all choices would be gone. He knows this from personal experience.

Mike puts a hand on the other man's shoulder. "In your share, Trig, you sounded upset."

Trig is a childhood nickname. It's how he introduces himself at the start of meetings. Even at out-of-town AA and NA, he rarely speaks other than that initial identification. In tag-team meetings he mostly says, "I just want to listen today," but this afternoon he raised his hand.

"I'm Trig, and I'm an alcoholic."

"Hi, Trig," the group responded. They were in the basement instead of the church, but there's still that revival meeting call-and-response. Straight Circle is, in fact, the Church of the Crashed and Burned.

"I just want to say that I'm pretty shaken up today. I don't want to say any more, but I had to share that much. That's all I've got."

There were murmurs of *Thanks, Trig* and *Hang in there* and *Keep coming back*.

Now Trig tells the Rev he's upset because he found out he lost someone he knew. The Rev asks for more details—pries for them, actually—but all Trig will say is that the person he's mourning died in lockup.

"I'll pray for him," the Rev says.

"Thanks, Mike."

Trig starts away, but not toward The Flame; he walks three blocks and climbs the steps to the public library. He needs to sit and think about the man who died on Saturday. Who was murdered on Saturday. Was shanked on Saturday, in a prison shower.

He finds a vacant chair in the Periodicals Room and picks up a copy of the local paper, just to have something to hold. He opens it to a page-four story about a lost dog recovered by Jerome Robinson of the Finders Keepers Agency. There's a picture of a smiling and handsome young Black man with his arm around some kind of big dog, maybe a Labrador Retriever. The headline is one word: **FOUND!**

Trig stares through it, thinking.

His real name was in this same paper three years ago, but no one has made the connection between that man and the one who attends out-of-town recovery meetings. Why would they, even if there had also been a picture of him (which there wasn't)? That man had a slightly graying beard and wore contacts. This version is clean-shaven, wears glasses, and looks younger (quitting the booze will do that). He likes the idea of being someone new. It also weighs on him. That is the paradox he lives with. That, and thinking about his father, which he does more and more frequently these days.

Let it go, he thinks. *Forget it.*

That is on March 24th. Forgetting lasts just thirteen days.

2

On April 6th, Trig sits in the same Periodicals Room chair, staring at the feature story in today's Sunday paper. The headline doesn't just speak, it shouts. **BUCKEYE BRANDON: MURDERED PRISON INMATE MAY HAVE BEEN INNOCENT!** Trig has read the feature, and listened to Buckeye Brandon's podcast three times. It was the self-proclaimed "outlaw of the airwaves" who broke the story, and according to Buckeye, there was no "may have been" about it. Is the story true? Trig thinks that, given the source, it must be.

What you're thinking of doing is crazy, he tells himself. Which is true.

If you do it, you can never go back, he tells himself. That's also true.

Once you start, you must keep on, he tells himself, and that's truest of all. His father's mantra: *You have to push through to the bitter end. No flinching, no turning away.*

And . . . what would it be like? What would it be like for *him* to do such things?

He needs to consider some more. Not just to get clarity on what he's thinking of doing, but to put a space of time between what he found out courtesy of Buckeye Brandon (also this feature article) and the acts—the *horrors*—he may commit, so no one will make the connection.

He finds himself remembering the headline about the young man who recovered the stolen dog. It was simplicity itself: **FOUND!** All Trig can think about is what he's lost, what he did, and the amends he must make.

Chapter 1

1

It's April now. In the Second Mistake on the Lake, the last of the snow is finally melting.

Izzy Jaynes gives a one-knuckle courtesy knock on her lieutenant's door and goes in without waiting. Lewis Warwick is tilted back in his chair, one foot resting on the corner of his desk, hands loosely clasped on his midsection. He looks like he's meditating or dreaming awake. For all Izzy knows, he is. At the sight of her he straightens and puts his foot back on the floor where it belongs.

"Isabelle Jaynes, ace detective. Welcome to my lair."

"At your service."

She doesn't envy him his office, because she's aware of all the bureaucratic bullshit that comes with it, accompanied by a salary bump so small it might be called ceremonial. She's happy enough with her humble cubicle downstairs, where she works with seven other detectives, including her current partner, Tom Atta. It's Warwick's chair that Izzy lusts after. With its high, spine-soothing back and reclining feature, it's meditation-ready.

"What can I do for you, Lewis?"

He takes a business envelope from his desk and hands it to her. "You can give me an opinion on this. No strings attached. Feel free to touch the envelope, everybody from the postman to Evelyn downstairs and who knows who else has had their paws on it, but the note should maybe be fingerprinted. Partly depending on what you say."

The envelope is addressed in capital block letters to DETECTIVE LOUIS WARWICK at 19 COURT PLAZA. Below the city, state, and zip, in even larger capitals: CONFIDENTIAL!

"What *I* say? You're the boss, boss."

"I'm not passing the buck, it's my baby, but I respect your judgement."

The end of the envelope has been torn open. There's no return address. She carefully unfolds the single sheet of paper inside, holding it by the edges. The message has been printed, almost certainly on a computer.

To: Lieutenant Louis Warwick
From: Bill Wilson
Cc: Chief Alice Patmore

I think there should be a corollary to the Blackstone Rule. I believe the INNOCENT should be punished for the needless DEATH of an innocent. Should those who caused that death be put to death themselves? I think not, because then they would be gone and the suffering for what they did would be at an end. This is true even if they acted with the best will in the world. They need to think about what they did. They need to "Rue the Day." Does that make sense to you? It does to me, and that is enough.

I will kill 13 innocents and 1 guilty. Those who caused the innocent to die will therefore suffer.

This is an act of ATONEMENT.

Bill Wilson

"Whoa," Izzy says. Still being careful, she refolds the note and slips it back into the envelope. "Someone has donned their crazy pants."

"Yes indeed. I googled the Blackstone Rule. It says—"

"I know what it says."

Warwick puts his foot up on the desk again, hands this time laced together at the nape of his neck. "Elucidate."

"Better for ten guilty men to go free rather than for one innocent man to suffer."

Lewis nods. "Now for Double Jeopardy, where the scores can really change. What innocent man might our crazy-pants correspondent be talking about?"

"At a guess, I'd say Alan Duffrey. Shanked last month at Big Stone. Died in the infirmary. Then that podcaster, Buckeye Brandon, blowing off his bazoo, and the follow-up piece in the paper. Both about the guy who came forward to say he framed Duffrey."

"Cary Tolliver. Got hit with the cancer stick, late-stage pancreatic, and wanted to clear his conscience. Said he never intended Duffrey to die."

"So this note isn't from Tolliver."

"Not likely. He's in Kiner Memorial, currently circling the drain."

"Tolliver making a clean breast was sort of like locking the barn door after the horse was stolen, wouldn't you say?"

"Maybe yes, maybe no. Tolliver claims he fessed up in February, days after he got his terminal diagnosis. Nothing happened. Then, after Duffrey was killed, Tolliver went to Buckeye Brandon, aka the outlaw of the airwaves. ADA Allen says it's all attention-seeking bullshit."

"What do you think?"

"I think Tolliver makes a degree of sense. He claims he only wanted Duffrey to do a couple of years. Said Duffrey going on the Registry would be the real punishment."

Izzy understands. Duffrey would have been forbidden to reside in or near child safety zones—schools, playgrounds, public parks. Forbidden to communicate with minors by text, other than his own children. Forbidden to have pornographic magazines or access porn online. Have to inform his supervising officer of an address change. Being on the National Sex Offender Registry was a life sentence.

If he had lived, that was.

Lewis leans forward. "Blackstone Rule aside, which really doesn't make much sense, at least to me, do we have to worry about this Wilson guy? Is it a threat or empty bullshit? What do you say?"

"Can I think it over?"

"Of course. Later. What does your gut tell you right now? It stays in this office."

Izzy considers. She could ask Lew if Chief Patmore has weighed in, but that's not how Izzy rolls.

"He's crazy, but he's not quoting the Bible or *The Protocols of the Elders of Zion*. Not suffering Tin Hat Syndrome. Could be a crank. If it isn't, it's someone to worry about. Probably someone close to Duffrey. I'd say his wife or kids, but he didn't have either."

"A loner," Lewis says. "Allen made a big deal of that at the trial."

Izzy and Tom both know Doug Allen, one of the Buckeye County ADAs. Izzy's partner calls Allen a Hungry Hungry Hippo, after a board game Tom's children like. Ambitious, in other words. Which also suggests Tolliver may have been telling the truth. Ambitious ADAs don't like to see convictions overturned.

"Duffrey wasn't married, but what about a partner?"

"Nope, and if he was gay, he was in the closet. *Deep* in the closet. No rumors. Chief loan officer at First Lake City Bank. And we're *assuming* it's Duffrey this guy's talking about, but without a specific name . . ."

"It could be someone else."

"Could be, but unlikely. I want you and Atta to talk to Cary Tolliver, assuming he's still in the land of the living. Talk to *all* Duffrey's known associates, at the bank and elsewhere. Talk to the guy who defended Duffrey. Get *his* list of known associates. If he did his job, he'll know everyone Duffrey knew."

Izzy smiles. "I suspect you wanted a second opinion that echoes what you already decided."

"Give yourself some credit. I wanted the second opinion of Isabelle Jaynes, ace detective."

"If it's an ace detective you want, you should call Holly Gibney. I can give you her number."

Lewis lowers his foot to the floor. "We haven't sunk to the level of outsourcing our investigations yet. Tell me what *you* think."

Izzy taps the envelope. "I think this guy could be the real deal. 'The innocent should be punished for the needless death of an innocent'? It might make sense to a nut, but to a sane person? I don't think so."

Lewis sighs. "The really dangerous ones, the ones who are crazy and not crazy at the same time, they give me nightmares. Timothy McVeigh killed over a hundred and fifty people in the Murrah Building and was perfectly rational. Called the little kids who died in the daycare collateral damage. Who's more innocent than a bunch of kids?"

"So you think this is real."

"*Maybe* real. I want you and Atta to spend some time on it. See if you can find someone so outraged by Duffrey's death—"

"Or so heartbroken."

"Sure, that too. Find someone mad enough—I mean it both ways—to make a threat like this."

"Why thirteen innocent and one guilty, I wonder? Is that a total of fourteen, or is the guilty one of the thirteen?"

Lewis shakes his head. "No idea. He could have picked the number out of a hat."

"Something else about this letter. You know who Bill Wilson was, right?"

"Rings a faint bell, but why wouldn't it? Maybe not as common as Joe Smith or Dick Jones, but not exactly Zbigniew Brzezinski, either."

"The Bill Wilson I'm thinking of was the founder of AA. Maybe this guy goes to AA and he's tipping us to that."

"Like he wants to be caught?"

Izzy shrugs, sending him a *no opinion* vibe.

"I'll send the letter to forensics, much good it'll do. They're going to say no fingerprints, computer font, common form of printer paper."

"Send me a photo of it."

"I can do that."

Izzy gets up to go. Lewis asks, "Have you signed up for the game yet?"

"What game?"

"Don't play dumb. Guns and Hoses. Next month. I'm going to captain the PD team."

"Gee, I haven't got around to that, boss." Nor does she mean to.

"The FD has won three in a row. Going to be a real grudge match this year, after what happened last time. Crutchfield's broken leg?"

"Who's Crutchfield?"

"Emil Crutchfield. Motor patrolman, mostly works on the east side."

"Oh," Izzy says, thinking, *Boys and their games*.

"Didn't you used to play? At that college you went to?"

Izzy laughs. "Yeah. Back when dinosaurs walked the earth."

"You should sign up. Think about it."

"I will," Izzy says.

She won't.

2

Holly Gibney raises her face into the sun. "T.S. Eliot said April is the cruelest month, but this doesn't seem very cruel to me."

"Poetry," Izzy says dismissively. "What are you having?"

"Fish tacos, I think."

"You *always* have fish tacos."

"Not always, but mostly. I'm a creature of habit."

"No shit, Sherlock."

Soon one of them will get up and join the line at Frankie's Fabulous Fish Wagon, but for the time being they just sit quietly at their picnic table, enjoying the warmth of the sun.

Izzy and Holly have not always been particularly close, but that changed after they had dealings with a pair of elderly academics, Rodney and Emily Harris. The Harrises were insane and extremely dangerous. It could be argued that Holly got the worst of it, having to deal with them face to face, but it was Detective Isabelle Jaynes who had to inform many of the loved ones of those who had been victims of the Harrises. She also had to tell those loved ones what the Harrises had done, and that was no night at the opera, either. Both women bore scars, and when Izzy called Holly after the newspaper coverage (national as well as local) died down, asking if she wanted to do lunch, Holly agreed.

"Doing lunch" became a semi-regular thing, and the two women formed a cautious bond. At first they talked about the Harrises, but less so as time went by. Izzy talked about her job; Holly talked about hers. Because Izzy was police and Holly a private investigator, they had similar, if rarely overlapping, areas of interest.

Nor had Holly entirely given up the idea of luring Izzy over to the dark side, especially since her partner, Pete Huntley, had retired and left Holly to run Finders Keepers singlehanded (with occasional help from Jerome and Barbara Robinson). She was at pains to tell Izzy that Finders didn't do divorce work. "Keyhole peeping, social media tracking. Text messages and telephoto lenses. Oough."

When Holly brought up the possibility, Izzy always said she'd keep it in mind. Which meant, Holly thought, that Iz would put in her thirty on the city police force and then retire to a golfside condo in Arizona or Florida. Probably on her own. A two-time loser in the marriage sweepstakes, Izzy said she wasn't looking for another hookup, especially of the marital variety. How, she said to Holly during one of their lunches, could she come home and tell her husband about the human remains they had found in the Harrises' refrigerator?

"Please," Holly had said on that occasion, "not while I'm trying to eat."

Today they're doing lunch in Dingley Park. Like Deerfield Park on the other side of the city, Dingley can be a rather sketchy environment after dark (*a fucking drug mart* is how Izzy puts it), but in the daytime it's perfectly pleasant, especially on a day like this. Now that warm weather is on the come, they can eat at one of the picnic tables not far from the firs that circle the old ice rink.

Holly is vaccinated up the ying-yang, but Covid is still killing someone in America every four minutes, and Holly doesn't want to take chances. Pete Huntley is even now suffering the aftereffects of his bout with the bug, and Holly's mother died of it. So she continues to take care, masking up in close indoor situations and carrying a bottle of Purell in her purse. Covid aside, she likes dining *al fresco* when the weather is nice, as it is today, and she's looking forward to her fish tacos. Two, with extra tartar sauce.

"How's Jerome?" Izzy asks. "I saw that book about his hoodlum great-grandfather landed on the bestseller list."

"Only for a couple of weeks," Holly says, "but they'll be able to put *New York Times Bestseller* on the paperback, which will help the sales." She loves Jerome almost as much as she loves his sister, Barbara. "Now that his book tour is over, he's been asking to help me around the shop. He says it's research, that his next book is going to be about a private eye." She grimaces to show how much she dislikes the term.

"And Barbara?"

"Going to Bell, right here in town. Majoring in English, of course." Holly says this with what she believes is justifiable pride. Both Robinson sibs are published authors. Barbara's book of poems—for which she won the Penley Prize, no small hill of beans—has been out for a couple of years.

"So your kids are doing well."

Holly doesn't protest this; although Mr. and Mrs. Robinson are alive and perfectly fine, Barb and Jerome sort of are her kids. The three of them have been through the wars together. Brady Hartsfield . . . Morris Bellamy . . . Chet Ondowsky . . . the Harrises. Those were wars, all right.

Holly asks what's new in Blue World. Izzy looks at her thoughtfully, then asks, "Can I show you something on my phone?"

"Is it porno?" Izzy is one of the few people Holly feels comfortable joking with.

"I guess in a way it is."

"Now I'm curious."

Izzy takes out her phone. "Lewis Warwick got this letter. So did Chief Patmore. Check it out."

She passes the phone to Holly, who reads the note. "Bill Wilson. Huh. You know who that is?"

"The founder of AA. Lew called me into his office and asked for my opinion. I told him I'd err on the side of caution. What do you think, Holly?"

"The Blackstone Rule. Which says—"

"Better ten guilty go free rather than one innocent suffer. Blackstone was a lawyer. I know because I took pre-law at Bucknell. Do you think this guy might be in the legal profession?"

"Probably not a good deduction," Holly says, rather kindly. "I never took a law course in my life, and I knew. I'd put it in the category of semi-common knowledge."

"You're a sponge for info," Izzy says, "but point taken. Lew Warwick at first thought it came from the Bible."

Holly reads the letter again. She says, "I think the man who wrote this could be religious. AA puts a lot of emphasis on God—'let go and let God' is one of their sayings—and the alias, plus this thing about atonement . . . that's a very Catholic concept."

"That narrows it down to, I'm going to say, half a million," Izzy says. "Big help, Gibney."

"Could this person be angry about, just a wild guess, Alan Duffrey?"

Izzy pats her palms together in quiet applause.

"Although he doesn't specifically mention—"

"I know, I know, our Mr. Wilson doesn't mention a name, but it seems the most likely. Kiddie fiddler killed in prison, then it comes out he maybe wasn't a kiddie fiddler after all. The timing fits, more or less. I'm going to buy your tacos for that."

"It's your turn, anyway," Holly says. "Refresh me on the Duffrey case. Can you do that?"

"Sure. Just promise you won't steal it from me and figure out who Bill Wilson is on your own."

"Promise." Holly means it, but she's engaged. This is the sort of thing she was born to do, and it's led her down some strange byways. The only problem with her day-to-day workload is that it involves more filling out forms and talking to bail bondsmen than solving mysteries.

"Long story short, Alan Duffrey was the chief loan officer at the First Lake City Bank, but until 2022 he was just another loan department guy in a cubicle. It's a very big bank."

"Yes," Holly says. "I know. It's my bank."

"It's also the Police Department's bank, and any number of local corporations, but never mind that. The chief loan officer retired, and two men were in competition for the job, which meant a hefty salary bump. Alan Duffrey was one. Cary Tolliver was the other. Duffrey got the job, so Tolliver got him sent to prison for kiddie porn."

"That seems like an overreaction," Holly says, then looks surprised when Izzy bursts out laughing. "What? What did I say?"

"Just . . . that's you, Holly. I won't say it's what I love about you, but I may come to love it, given time."

Holly is still frowning.

Izzy leans forward, still smiling. "You're a deductive whiz-kid, Hols, but sometimes I think you lose your grip on what criminal motivation really is, especially criminals with their screws loosened by anger, resentment, paranoia, insecurity, jealousy, whatever. There was a monetary motive for what Cary Tolliver says he did, of course there was, but I'm sure other things played a part."

"He came forward after Duffrey got killed, didn't he?" Holly says. "Went to that podcaster who's always digging dirt."

"He claims he came forward *before* Duffrey was killed. In February, after getting a terminal cancer diagnosis. Wrote the ADA a confession letter and claims the ADA sat on it. So he eventually spilled everything to Buckeye Brandon."

"That could be your atonement motive."

"He didn't write this," Izzy says, tapping the screen of her phone. "Cary Tolliver's dying, and it won't be long. Tom and I are going to interview him this afternoon. So I better get our lunch."

"Extra tartar sauce for me," Holly says as Izzy gets up.

"Holly, you never change."

Holly looks up at her, a small woman with graying hair and a faint smile. "It's my superpower."

3

Holly is in her office that afternoon, filling out insurance forms. She sees the futility of hating big insurance companies, but they are definitely on her Poopy List, and she *loathes* the ads they show on TV. It's hard to hate Flo, the Progressive Insurance lady—not in the least because Jerome Robinson once said, "She looks a little like you, Holly!"—but it's easy to hate Doug and his silly Limu Emu, and Allstate's Mayhem Guy. She detested the Aflac Duck . . . who has been mercifully retired, along with the GEICO Caveman (although it's not impossible that both duck and caveman will make a comeback). As an investigator who has worked with adjusters from many companies, she knows their big secret: the fun stops once a claim, especially a big one, is lodged with the company.

This afternoon's forms are from Global Insurance, whose TV pitchman is Buster the Talking Donkey, with his irritating hee-haw laugh. Buster is on every form, grinning at her with his big (and somehow insolent) teeth. Holly hates the forms but is delighted to know that in this case Global's Talking Donkey will soon be on the hook to reimburse for a cache of jewelry taken in a home invasion. Sixty or seventy thousand dollars' worth, minus the deductible. Unless she can locate the missing gems, that is. "So who's the donkey's behind today?" Holly says to her empty office, and just has to laugh.

Her phone rings, not the one for business calls but her personal. She sees Barbara Robinson's face on her screen.

"Hello, Barbara, how are you?"

"Great! I'm great!" And she sounds it, absolutely bubbling over. "I've got the most wonderful news!"

"Your book hit the bestseller list?" That would be fine news indeed. Her brother's book peaked at number eleven on the *Times* list, didn't quite make it into the top ten, but still not bad.

Barbara laughs. "With the exception of Amanda Gorman, poetry books don't chart. I'll have to be content with four stars on Goodreads." She pauses. "*Almost* four."

Holly thinks her friend's book should have *five* stars on Goodreads. *She* certainly gave it five. Twice. "So what's your news, Barb?"

"I was caller nineteen on K-POP this morning and scored two tickets to see Sista Bessie! Hasn't even been announced yet!"

"Not sure I know who that is," Holly says . . . although she *almost* knows. Probably would know if her head wasn't stuffed full of insurance questions, all subtly slanted to favor the company. "Remember, I'm getting on in years. My knowledge and enjoyment of popular music pretty much ended with Hall and Oates. I always liked that blond one."

Also, she has zero interest in rap or hip-hop. She thinks she might like it if her ears were younger and sharper (she misses many of the rhymes) and if she were more attuned to the streetlife serenades of the artists Barbara and Jerome listen to, people with exotic names like Pos' Top, Lil Durk, and—Holly's favorite, although she has no idea what he's rapping about—YoungBoy Never Broke Again.

"You *should* know, she's from your day, Holly."

Ow, Holly thinks. "Soul singer?"

"Yes! That and gospel."

"Okay, I do know," Holly says. "Didn't she cover a song by Al Green? 'Let's Stay Together'?"

"Yes! It was *huge*! I karaoke that one! Sang it live at the Spring Hop when I was a senior."

"I grew up listening to Q102," Holly says. "Lots of Ohio rockers like Devo and Chrissie Hynde and Michael Stanley, but they were white. There wasn't much Black music on the Q, but that version . . . I remember that one."

"Sista Bessie's kicking off her comeback tour here! At the Mingo Auditorium! Two shows, both sold out, but I have two tickets . . . *and backstage passes*! Come with me, Holly, please say you will." Wheedling now: "She does some gospel, too, and I know you like that."

Holly certainly does. She's a big fan of the Blind Boys of Alabama, and the Staple Singers, especially Mavis Staples, and although she barely remembers Sista Bessie, or most of the music from the twentieth century's last decade, she loves that good old solid-gold soul from the 60s, people like Sam Cooke and Jackie Wilson. Wilson Pickett, too. She tried to go to one of the Wicked Pickett's shows once, but her mother forbade it. And now that Mavis Staples has crossed her mind . . .

"She called herself Little Sister Bessie in the eighties. I used to listen to WGRI back then. Tiny AM station, went off the air at sundown. They played gospel music." Holly only listened to GRI when her mother wasn't home, though, because many of those groups, like BeBe & CeCe Winans, were Black. "I remember Little Sister Bessie doing 'Sit Down, Servant.'"

"That was probably her, before she got like totally famous. The only record she made since retiring was all gospel. *Lord, Take My Hand.* My mother plays that one a lot, but I like the other stuff. Say you'll come with me, Holly. Please. It's the very first show, and we'll have an awesome time."

Mingo Auditorium has bad associations for Holly, ones having to do with a monster named Brady Hartsfield. Barbara was there, but she wasn't the one who clobbered Brady; that was Holly herself. Bad associations or not, she can't refuse Barbara anything. Or Jerome, for that matter. If Barb said she had two tickets to see YoungBoy NBA, she would have said yes. (Probably.)

"When is it?"

"Next month. May thirty-first. Plenty of time to clear your calendar."

"Will it be late?" Holly hates late evenings.

"No, not late at all!" Barbara is still bubbling, full of happiness, which cheers Holly's day up considerably. "Starts at seven, it'll be over by nine, nine-thirty, at the very latest. Sista probably doesn't want to stay up late, she's old, got to be pushing sixty-five by now."

Holly, who no longer thinks of sixty-five as particularly old, offers no comment.

"Will you come?"

"Will you learn 'Sit Down, Servant' and sing it to me?"

"Yes. Yes, absolutely! And she's got a great soul band." Barbara's voice drops to what's almost a whisper. "Some of them are from *Muscle Shoals*!"

Holly doesn't know Muscle Shoals from a muscle strain, but that's okay. And she still wants to make Barbara work for it a little. "Will you also sing 'Let's Stay Together'?"

"Yes! If it gets you to come, I'll karaoke the hell out of it!"

"Then okay. It's a date."

"Hooray! I'll pick you up. I've got a new car, bought it with my Penley Prize money. A Prius, like yours!"

They talk a little longer. Barbara tells her she hardly sees Jerome since he came back from his tour. He's either doing research for his new book or hanging around the Finders Keepers office.

"I haven't seen him the last few days, either," Holly says, "and when I did, he was kind of mopey."

Before ending the call, Barbara says (with undisguised satisfaction), "He'll be mopier than ever when he finds out we're going to see Sista Bessie. Thanks, Holly! Really! We're going to have an awesome time!"

"I hope so," Holly says. She adds, "Don't forget you promised to sing for me. You've got a very good v—"

But Barbara is gone.

4

Izzy and Tom Atta take the elevator to the fourth floor of Kiner Memorial. When they get out, arrows on the wall offer them either Cardiology (right) or Oncology (left). They turn left. At the nurses' station, they flash their badges and ask for Cary Tolliver's room. Izzy is interested to see the momentary flash of distaste on the duty nurse's face—a pulling-down at the corners of the mouth, there and then gone.

"He's in 419, but you'll probably find him in the solarium, soaking up the sun and reading one of his mystery novels."

Tom doesn't mince words. "I've heard pancreatic is one of the bad ones. How long has he got, would you say?"

The nurse, an old vet who still wears head-to-toe white rayon, leans forward and speaks in a low tone. "His doc says a matter of weeks. I'd guess two, maybe less. He would have been shipped home except for the insurance coverage, which must have been a hell of a lot better than mine. He'll slip into a coma, and then good morning, good afternoon, goodnight."

Izzy, mindful of Holly Gibney's pet peeve about insurance companies: "I'm surprised the company didn't find a way to wiggle out of it. I mean, he *did* frame a man who got murdered in prison. Did you know about that?"

"Of course I know," the nurse says. "He brags about how *sorry* he is. Seen a *minister*. I say crocodile tears!"

Tom says, "The DA declined to prosecute, says Tolliver's full of shit, so he gets a pass and his insurance company gets the bill."

The nurse rolls her eyes. "He's full of something, all right. Try the solarium first."

As they walk down the corridor, Izzy thinks that if there's an afterlife, Alan Duffrey may be waiting there for his one-time colleague, Cary Tolliver. "And he'll want to have a few words."

Tom looks at her. "What?"

"Nothing."

5

Holly pulls the last of the Global Insurance forms in front of her, sighs, grabs her pen—these forms have to be filled out by hand if she wants a chance at finding the missing trinkets, God knows why—and then puts it down. She picks up her phone and looks at the letter from Bill

Wilson, whoever he might really be. It's not her case and she'd never poach it from Isabelle, but Holly can feel her lights turning on, nevertheless. Her job is often boring, there's too much paperwork, and right now cases—good ones, engaging ones—are thin on the ground, so she's interested. There's something else, too, even more important. When her interior lights come on . . . she loves that. Adores it.

"This is not my business. Shoemaker, stick to thy last."

One of her father's sayings. Her late mother, Charlotte, had a thousand pithy aphorisms, her father only a few . . . but she remembers every one of them. What is a shoemaker's last, anyway? She has no idea and quashes the urge to google it. She does know what *her* last is: filling out this last form, then checking pawnshops and fences for a bunch of jewelry stolen from a rich widow in Sugar Heights. If she can find that stuff, she'll get a bonus from Buster the Talking Donkey. *Which he'll probably poop out of his butt*, she thinks. *Very reluctantly.*

She sighs, picks up her pen again, puts it down, and writes an email instead.

> Iz—You'll know this already, it's pretty obvious, but the guy you are looking for is smart. He talks about the Blackstone Rule, which isn't in an uneducated man's vocabulary. I believe the innocent should be punished for the needless death of an innocent might be a cuckoo sentiment, but you have to admit it's a nicely turned phrase. Balanced. All his punctuation is perfect. Note the use of colons in the heading and how he uses Cc in reference to Chief Patmore. In the old days, when I was doing office correspondence, that stood for "carbon copy." Now it just means "also sent to," and is commonly used in business. Suggests to me your Bill Wilson may be a white-collar guy.
>
> Now as to that name, Bill Wilson. I don't think he picked it out of a hat. (Assuming he is male.) It's not impossible that he met the murdered man, Alan Duffrey, in AA or NA. (Also assuming it's Duffrey the letter-writer is on about.) You might be able to reach out to someone who goes to those meetings. If not, I have a source who's in NA and quite open about it. He's a bartender (of all things), six years clean and sober. He, or someone you can tap, might be able

to spot someone clean-cut and well-spoken. Someone who might even have said something in a meeting about Duffrey, or "That guy who got stabbed in prison." The anonymity aspect of AA and NA makes this a long shot, but it might be possible to locate the guy this way. Slim chance, I know, but it's a line of investigation.

Holly

She puts her cursor on the send button, then adds a few more lines.

PS! Did you notice he misspelled Lewis Warwick's first name? If you catch someone you think might be your man, don't ask him to write his name. I repeat, this guy isn't stupid. Ask him to write something like, "I have never liked Lewis Black." See if he spells it Louis. You probably know all this, but I'm sitting here with nothing to do.

H

She reads this over, then adds **PPS! Lewis Black is a comedian.** She considers this and decides Izzy might think that *Holly* thinks Izzy is stupid, or a cultural illiterate. She deletes it, then thinks, *She really might not know who Lewis Black is*, and puts the line back in. These sorts of things torture her.

Bill Hodges, who founded Finders Keepers, once told Holly that she over-empathized with people, and when Holly replied, *You say that like it's a bad thing*, Bill said, *In this business, it can be.*

She sends the email, and tells herself to get off her buttinsky (that one's all Charlotte Gibney) and start looking for the missing jewelry. But she sits where she is a little longer, because something Izzy said is troubling her.

"No, not Izzy. *Barbara*."

Holly is computer savvy—it's how she and Jerome bonded—but she's old-school about appointments and keeps a datebook in her purse. She hunts it out now and pages through it until she gets to the end of May. There she has written *Kate McKay, MA 8 PM. Maybe?* MA standing for Mingo Auditorium.

Holly goes to the movies fairly often since Covid abated (always wearing her mask if the theater is even half-full), but she rarely goes to lectures and concerts. She thought she might go to the McKay lecture, though. If, that is, she didn't have to wait in line too long, and assuming she could get in at all. Holly doesn't agree with everything McKay espouses, but when she talks about the sexual abuse of women, Holly Gibney is right there with her. She herself was sexually abused as a young woman and knows few women—including Izzy Jaynes—who were not, in one way or another. Also, Kate McKay has what Holly thinks of as *strut*. Never having been much of a strutter herself, Holly approves of that. She supposes she had some strut when it came to the Harrises, but that was mostly a matter of survival. Also luck.

She decides she'll sort out the double-booking mystery later. Because she still has a tendency to blame herself for things, she supposes she might have written down the wrong date. Either way, it seems to be her fate to be in the Mingo Auditorium on the night of Saturday, May 31st, and as much as she admires Kate McKay's strut, on the whole she'd rather be with Barbara.

"Jewelry," she says, getting up. "Must find jewelry." The Global Insurance forms can wait until later.

6

Izzy has an idea how the First Lake City Bank chief loan officer should look, maybe from a brochure she got in the mail, or a TV show. Slightly pudgy but well-groomed, nice suit, cologne (not too much), pleasant smile, all ready to say, *How much do you need?*

Cary Tolliver is not that man.

She and Tom find him snoozing in the fourth-floor lounge with a copy of a detective novel called *Toxic Prey* open on his chest. Instead of a natty three-piece suit, he's wearing a tired hospital robe over wrinkled pajamas with Hello Kitty faces on them. His hollow cheeks sport a salt-and-pepper beard scruff. His hair is half-long and half-bald. Plates of yellowish eczema shingle the bald spots. The skin of his face not covered with the patchy beard is so white it's almost green. His body is skeletal except for the bulge of his belly, which is huge. *Like a mushroom ready to sporulate*, Izzy thinks. There's a wheelchair on one side of him, an IV pole on the other. As they draw closer, Izzy realizes that Tolliver doesn't smell very good. Actually, that's not exactly true. Actually, he stinks.

They split apart without talking about it, Tom standing by the wheelchair and Izzy next to the IV pole, which is drip-drip-dripping some clear liquid into the back of Tolliver's hand.

"Wake up, Cary," Tom says. "Wake up, sleeping beauty."

Tolliver opens his eyes, which are red and rheumy. He looks from Tom Atta to Izzy and back to Tom again.

"Cops," he says. "I told that County Attorney everything I know. Wrote him a letter. Fucker sat on it. I'm sorry Duffrey got killed. That wasn't supposed to happen. I have nothing else to say."

"Well, maybe a little more," Tom says. "Show him the letter, Iz."

She takes out her phone and tries to hand it to him. Tolliver shakes his head. "I can't take it. Too weak. Why can't you let me die in peace?"

"If you can hold that book, you can hold this," Izzy says. "Read it."

Tolliver takes the phone and holds it close to his nose. He reads the Bill Wilson letter and then hands it back. "So? You think this guy believes I'm the guilty one? Fine. Even though I tried to take it back, fine. Let him come and kill me. He'd be doing me a favor."

Izzy hasn't thought that "Bill Wilson" might consider Tolliver the one guilty person . . . although she's betting Holly already has. She says, "We want your help. Bill Wilson is almost certainly an alias. Can you tell us who might have written this? Who was close enough to Alan Duffrey to make such a threat?"

Tom says, "The letter might be bullshit, but if it isn't, you could be saving some lives."

"I'm no kiddie freak," Tolliver says, and Izzy realizes he's stoned to the gills. "I told the other cops that. And the DA guy, that fuck. The stuff they found on my computer, I only saved it so they'd believe me. Dumped it, then brought it back when I got sick. Duplicates of most of the stuff I sent to the Duff." When he says *the Duff*, he raises his upper lip in a doglike snarl, and Izzy sees some of his teeth are gone. Those remaining are turning black. He really *does* stink: *eau de piss, eau de merde*, and *eau de mort*. She can't wait to get away and breathe some clean air.

"He had mags as well as the crap on his computer," Tom says. "I've talked to Allen and read the file on the way over here. One of them was called *Uncle Bill's Pride and Joy*. How's that for disgusting?"

"If you did it—" Izzy begins.

"I did, and that fuck ADA Allen knows I did. Sent him a letter in February, after I got my diagnosis. Explained everything. Told him stuff that wasn't in the papers. He sat on it. Duffrey should be out. *Allen's* the guilty one."

"*If* you did it," Izzy repeats, "we don't care how you did it. We care about who might have written this letter."

Tolliver doesn't look at her. He keeps his eyes on Tom. Izzy isn't surprised; when she works with a male partner, male subjects usually discount her. Women do, too.

"I bought the magazines on the dark web," Tolliver says. "Snuck into his house—the basement bulkhead was unlocked—and stashed them behind his furnace."

"Tell us who was close to Duffrey," Izzy says. "Who might have been pissed off enough to—"

Tolliver goes on ignoring her. It's Tom Atta he's talking to, and gathering steam. "You want to know how I got the stuff onto his computer? I explained it all to Allen, but that fuck paid no attention. So once I made my peace with dying—sort of, I guess as much as anyone does—I told it to Buckeye Brandon. *That* guy listened. I sent Duffrey a notice that purported to be from the USPS. Misdirected package. Anybody knows that's phishing, *grandmas* know it's phishing, but this dumbbell—supposedly smart enough to be chief loan officer, but about as smart as a busted light switch—this dumbbell went ahead and clicked on the link. Then I had him. I sent him a zip file tucked in halfway through his tax file. But I never meant for him to die. That's why I came forward."

"Not because you found out you were dying?" Even though this isn't why they're here, Iz can't help herself.

"Well . . . sure. That had something to do with it." He looks at her briefly, then switches his attention back to Tom. "Some of the blame has to go on the guy who stabbed him, right? All I wanted was for him to be on the Register when he got out. That promotion should have been mine. It should have been mine and he stole it." Incredibly, Tolliver begins to cry.

"KAs," Izzy says. She thinks of tapping Tolliver on one thin shoulder to redirect his attention but can't quite bring herself to do it. The stink of him has got her stomach sudsing. "Known associates. Help us out and we'll leave you alone."

"Talk to Pete Young in the loan department. Claire Rademacher, the chief cashier. He was buddy-buddy with both of them. Or Kendall Dingley, he's the branch manager." That doglike lift of the upper lip. "Kendall's dumb as dirt, only got the manager job because his grandfather founded the bank and his uncle runs the Fire Department. There's a park named after old Hiram Dingley, you know. I should have sent Kendall some kiddie stuff, too, everyone would have thought the Duff and the Dingbat were in it together, but I didn't because I'm a good guy. I know you don't believe that, but at heart I'm a good guy. The Duff used to suck up to the Dingbat like crazy. That's why he got my promotion."

Izzy is writing down the names. "Anyone else?"

"Maybe he had friends in his neighborhood, but I wouldn't know about th—" He grimaces and lifts his pregnant midsection. He lets out a trumpet blast of flatulence, and when the smell reaches Izzy, she thinks it's strong enough to blister paint.

"Christ, that hurts. I need to go back to my room. The morphine pump will have re-set by now. Roll my chair, will you?"

Tom leans forward into the stink and speaks low. "I wouldn't piss on you if you were on fire, Cary. If you're telling the truth, you got an innocent man sent to prison and he got stabbed and it took him a day to die. You think you're in pain? *He* was in pain and didn't deserve it. I'd punch you in that grotesque gut of yours, but you'd fart some more."

"My wife left me," Tolliver says. He's still crying. "She took my kids and left me. I did it for her as well as me, she was always bitching about we can't afford this and we can't afford that, and who'll bury me? Huh? Who'll bury me? My brother? My sister? They won't answer my emails. My mother said—"

"I don't care what she said."

"—she said, 'You made your bed, now lie in it.' How shitty is that?"

He lifts his hips and produces another trumpet blast. Izzy says, "Let's get out of here. We've got all he can give us."

"I made a clean breast," Tolliver is saying as they leave. "*Twice*. First to that ADA fuck, then to Buckeye Brandon. I didn't have to do that. And now look at me. Just look."

Izzy and Tom go back to the nurses' station. The old vet in the white rayon uniform is filling out forms. Izzy says, "He wants to go back to his room. He says by now his morphine pump will have re-set."

Without looking up, the old vet says, "He can wait."

7

May, and the weather is beautiful.

Not far from the city is a woodsy suburban township called Upriver. At its northern edge is a little pocket park where a few people are doing meditation poses that might (or might not) be called asanas. Trig doesn't care what they're called. They are looking toward the horizon, not at him. That's fine. He got a burger at a drive-thru but tossed it on the passenger seat after a couple of bites. He's too nervous to eat. The letter he sent to the police was a warning. This is the real deal.

There's a question of whether he can do it. Of course there is. He *thinks* he can but understands he won't know for sure until the deed is done. He killed squirrels and birds with a pellet gun as a boy, and that was all right. Good, in fact. The one time his father took him deer hunting, Trig wasn't allowed to carry a real gun. His father said, *Knowing you, you'd fall in a hole and blow your foot off.* Daddy said if they saw a deer, he would let Trig shoot, but they never saw one, and he was pretty sure his father wouldn't have allowed him the gun even if they had. Daddy would have hogged the shot to himself.

And to break his cherry by killing a man? Trig understands that once he's stepped over that line, he can never go back.

The street running past the pocket park has an amusing name: Anyhow Lane. It's a dead-ender. Trig has been here three times before and knows that the Buckeye Trail passes near the end of the street. The Trail is eighteen miles long. It used to be a railroad line, but the tracks

were taken up thirty years ago and replaced by a wide, county-financed asphalt path that winds through trees and bushes, finally emerging beside the turnpike and ending on the outskirts of the city proper.

There's a little beaten earth square at the end of Anyhow Lane with a sign reading NO PARKING AFTER 7 PM. On each of his previous reconnaissance visits, a dusty Komatsu bucket-loader has been parked there in defiance of the sign, and it's still there this afternoon. For all Trig knows, it's been there for years and may be there for years to come. It will give him cover for his car, and that's all he cares about. Beyond it is a copse of woods marked by signs reading BUCKEYE TRAIL and DO NOT LITTER and WALK/BIKE AT YOUR OWN RISK.

"Hey Daddy, hey Daddy."

His father is long gone, but Trig sometimes talks to him anyway. It's not comforting, exactly, but it feels lucky.

Trig parks behind the bucket-loader and takes a backpack and a trail map from the rear seat of his Toyota. He shrugs into the pack and puts the map in his back pocket. From the center console he takes a snub-nosed Taurus .22 revolver. He slips it into his right front pocket. In his left pocket is a slim leather folder containing thirteen slips of paper. He passes picnic benches, a litter basket full of beer cans, and a painted post with a laminated map of the Trail. He has seen plenty of walkers and bicyclists on the Trail on his previous scouts, sometimes in pairs or trios—no good for his purpose today—but sometimes alone.

Today I may not see anyone by himself, he thinks. *If I don't, that will be a sign. "Stop while there's still time to stop, before you step over the line. Once you're over the line, you can never come back."*

This makes him think of an AA mantra: *One drink is too many and a thousand are never enough*.

He's wearing a brown sweater and a plain brown gimme cap pulled down almost to the brow-line. There's no logo on the cap for a passerby to remember. He walks east rather than west, so the sun won't illuminate the part of his face that shows. An elderly couple on bikes passes him headed west. The man says hello. Trig raises a hand but doesn't speak. He keeps on. About a mile ahead the woods thin, and there the Trail skirts a housing development where kids will be playing in

backyards and women will be hanging up clothes. If he gets that far without seeing someone walking alone, he'll pack it in. Maybe just for today, maybe for good.

Sure, Daddy says. *Go on and flinch, you fucking flincher.*

Trig ambles along, one hand on the butt of the revolver. He'd whistle, but his mouth is too dry. And now, from around the next curve in the trail, comes the solo walker he was hoping for (also dreading). Well, not completely solo; there's a Standard Poodle on a red leash. He always imagined his first would be a man, but this is a middle-aged woman wearing jeans and a hoodie.

I won't do it, he thinks. *I'll wait for a man, one without a dog. Come another day*. Only, if he means to carry through with his mission—all the way through—he *must* include four women.

He's closing the distance. Soon she and her dog will be past him. She will go on with her life. Make dinner. Watch TV. Call a friend on the phone and say, *Oh, my day was fine, how was yours?*

Now or never, he thinks, and takes the map from his back pocket with his left hand. His right is still clutching the revolver. *Don't blow your foot off*, he thinks.

"Hello," the woman says. "Lovely afternoon, isn't it?"

"It sure is." Does he sound hoarse, or is it just his imagination? Must be the latter, because the woman doesn't look alarmed. "Can you show me exactly where I am?"

He holds the map out. His hand is shaking a little, but the woman doesn't seem to notice. She steps closer, looking down. The Standard Poodle sniffs at Trig's pantleg. He takes the revolver out of his pocket. For a moment the hammer catches on the pocket's lining, but then it comes free. The woman doesn't see it. She's looking at the map. Trig puts an arm around her shoulders and she looks up. He thinks, *Don't flinch*.

Before she can pull away, he places the short muzzle of the Taurus against her temple and pulls the trigger. He's test-fired the gun and knows what to expect, not a loud report but more of a snap, like breaking a dry stick of kindling over a knee. The woman's eyes roll up to whites and the tip of her tongue pokes out of her mouth. That's the only horrible part. She sags in his encircling arm.

Blood is trickling from the hole in her temple. He puts the muzzle of the Taurus over the powder-blackened hole and shoots her again. The first bullet didn't come out, it stayed in her darkening brain, but this one does. He sees her hair flip, as if lifted by a playful finger. He looks around, sure someone is watching, *must* be watching, but there's no one. At least not yet.

The poodle is looking up at its mistress, whining. The red leash is puddled at its front feet. The poodle looks at Trig, its eyes seeming to ask if everything is all right. Trig slaps its curly rump with his free hand and says, "Go!"

The poodle jumps and runs twenty or thirty feet down the path, out of slapping distance, then stops and looks back. The leash is a red ribbon trailing behind it.

Trig drags the woman through the bushes edging the trail and into the thin woods, looking both ways until he's under cover. Cars are passing nearby, but he can't see them.

The dog, he thinks. *Someone will wonder why it's out with its leash trailing. Or it will come back. I should have let it go.*

Too late now.

He takes the leather folder from his pocket. His hands are trembling a lot now, and he almost drops it. There's a dead woman at his feet. Everything she was is now gone. He fumbles through the slips of paper. Andrew Groves . . . no . . . Philip Jacoby . . . no . . . Steven Furst . . . no. Where are the women? Where are the goddam *women?* At last he comes upon Letitia Overton. A Black woman, and the woman he's killed is white, but it doesn't matter. He may not be able to leave a name with all his targets, but with this one he can. He puts it between two fingers of her open hand, then turns and makes his way back to the Trail. He pauses, still in the bushes, looking for hikers or bikers, but there are none. He steps out and heads west, toward the parking area and his car.

The poodle is still standing there at the end of its trailing leash. As he approaches, Trig waves both hands at it. The dog cringes, then skitters away. When Trig comes around the next curve, he sees the dog standing with its forepaws on the asphalt and its rear paws in the bushes. It backs away at the sight of him, waits until Trig goes by, then dashes back the way it came, its leash trailing. It will find its mistress and like as not begin barking: *Wake up, Mistress, wake up!* Someone will come along and wonder what that fool dog is barking about.

Because the Trail is still deserted, Trig breaks into a jog, then an all-out run. He reaches the parking area without being seen, slings his pack into the backseat, then sits behind the wheel, gasping for breath.

You need to get out of here. His thought, Daddy's voice. *Right now.*

He turns the key and a chime bings, but nothing else happens. His car is dead. God is punishing him. He doesn't believe in God, but God is punishing him nevertheless. He looks down at the console and sees he left the shifter in Drive when he shut off the engine. He shifts into Park and the car starts. He reverses out from behind the bucket-loader and drives back down Anyhow Lane, resisting the urge to speed. *Slow and steady*, he tells himself. *Slow and steady wins the race.*

The asanas, or sun salutes, or whatever they are, seem to be done. Men and women are chatting or returning to their cars. None of them look at the man in the brown cap as he drives by in his utterly forgettable Toyota Corolla.

I did it, he thinks. *I killed that woman. Her life is over.*

There's no guilt, only a dull regret that makes him think of his last year drinking, when every first sip tasted like death. That woman was in the wrong place at the wrong time (although the right place and time for him). There's a book she'll never finish, emails and texts she'll never respond to, a vacation she'll never take. The Standard Poodle may get fed tonight, but not by her. She was looking at his map, and then . . . she wasn't.

He did it, though. When the time came, he didn't blow his foot off and he didn't flinch. He's sorry the woman in the jeans and hoodie had to be a part of his atonement, but he's sure if there *is* a heaven, that woman is already being introduced around. Why not?

She is one of the innocent.

Chapter 2

1

It's a rainy morning in Reno and Kate wants a newspaper. Not any newspaper, either, but one of the sort she calls "a rag" or "a screed." This particular screed is *The West Coast Clarion*.

Corrie points to Kate's laptop, but Kate shakes her head and flashes a grin. "The *Clarion* is strictly hard copy." She lowers her voice. "The internet is a tool of the deep state. Although the people who write this pile of crap don't mind having the juicy bits posted on social media. Where troubling things like facts and context don't matter." Then, as an afterthought (afterthoughts have a way of causing trouble): "And wear my hat."

"Are you kidding?"

Kate's Borsalino—a kind of fedora, comically large, almost a parody of what the well-dressed *Esquire* man would wear—is a McKay trademark. She wears it to all her events, sweeping it off and making an extravagant bow to acknowledge the preordained storm of applause (plus boos). She was wearing it on the cover of both *Ms.* and *Newsweek*.

"Zero kidding." She's making notes for her upcoming speech at the Pioneer Center tonight. Although the tour is barely underway, this isn't Kate McKay's first rodeo. She's got a basic template, but she's a believer in the Tip O'Neill maxim that all politics is local, and tailors each speech to the town she's in. And the bottom line isn't *Buy my book, now on sale*, because the book is already a bestseller, like the three that came before it. The book is simply the door-opener to her views and agenda. Applause follows, outrage follows, press and TV coverage follow; on to the next city. Which will be Spokane.

"I want to see what garbage they have to say about me. I may be able to use it tonight, but I don't want you getting soaked. God forbid you get sick when the tour's just getting started. It's really coming down out there. I thought Reno was supposed to be *dry*."

Corrie settles the Borsalino almost reverently on her head, cocking it to the left as Kate does. That way it obscures most of her face, thus assuring her of a trip to Saint Mary's ER not long hence.

"That rag will squeal like a stuck pig," Kate says, not without satisfaction. She's looking out the rain-streaked sitting room window on the top floor of the Renaissance Reno Hotel. "But nothing will equal the *Breitbart* headline when we kicked off the tour."

That one had been THE B*TCH IS BACK. Kate had it framed, and by now it will be hanging in the study of her cliffside home in Carmel-by-the-Sea. She called it great advertising. Hattie Delaney, her agent, called it a recipe to bring out the kooks, nutbags, and True Q believers. Kate spread her hands and made a beckoning gesture with all ten fingers—another McKay trademark—and said, "Let em come."

2

Corrie inquires as to where she can find a well-equipped newsstand and is told Hammer News on West 2nd Street should have everything she wants. She calls and asks if they carry *The West Coast Clarion*. She takes the reply—"Does a bear do it in the woods?"—as a yes and sets out.

Is the redhead in the rainhat and belted trenchcoat sitting nearby in the lobby when Corrie asks for directions at the desk? Perhaps looking at a magazine or bent over her phone? Corrie thinks later—tells the police later—she must have been. Must have listened to the helpful concierge giving her instructions, then gone ahead to get in position.

Did Corrie see a woman precede her out of the hotel? She'll say she honestly can't remember. Nor does she care. In the ER she only cares about two things. The first is whether or not she'll ever be able to see again. The second is this: if she can, how ugly will be the face she sees looking back in the mirror?

Those things will be her concerns.

3

The previous year, Corrie was chosen along with ten others to attend a graduate seminar taught by Kate McKay. It lasted two weeks, and those were the best classes of Corrie's academic career. After the last one, Kate asked her to stay so she could discuss something with her. Kate told her that her new book was going to be published in April, and she'd support it with a multi-city tour, beginning in Portland, Oregon, and ending in Portland, Maine.

"I need someone to assist. I was thinking you might like the job. Seven hundred dollars a week. You'd have to make arrangements to finish your other classes a little early. What do you think?"

Corrie was at first so astounded by the out-of-the-blue offer that she was unable to reply. This woman has been on the cover of magazines. She's on TV *all the time*. Even more impressive to Corrie, a child of the social media age, Kate has twelve million followers on Twitter. That's twelve with six zeros behind it.

"Close your mouth," Kate said. "You'll catch a fly."

"Why . . . why me?"

Kate ticked off reasons on her fingers. "When I needed a PowerPoint, you hooked me up. Your paper on Ada Lovelace was well-written and thoughtful. You didn't neglect the fact that she became interested in mathematics because she was afraid her father's insanity might be hereditary. You saw her as a woman, not a goddess. Human, in other words. You ask good questions, and are currently unattached. Have I missed anything?"

Only that I idolize you, Corrie thought, but later she'll come to understand Kate knew that all along . . . and she is a woman who enjoys being idolized. In many ways—Corrie will also come to understand this—Kate is a monster of ego. Her tongue is a Ginsu knife. She's capable of coolly slicing and dicing a commentator who dares oppose her views, then doing a furniture-kicking tantrum over a busted bra strap. She has no off button. She's also balls-to-the-wall courageous. Corrie thought then and thinks now that Kate McKay will be remembered long after most women (and men) of her time will be forgotten.

"No! I mean yes! I want the job!"

Kate laughed. "Relax, girl, it's not a marriage proposal and it won't be glamorous. I might send you out to Starbucks at seven in the morning. Or to Walgreens for Prilosec. You'll have to lug equipment, plug in equipment, sometimes fix equipment—as you fixed that fucking PowerPoint gadget when I couldn't make it work. You'll also spend a lot of time on the phone. Keep a schedule, make calls, concoct the occasional excuse, organize press conferences. The one thing I'll never ask you to do is apologize for me or, God save us, 'clarify' something I said. I don't do apologies, I don't do clarifications, and you won't, either. Now does that still sound like—"

"Yes!"

"Can you drive a standard shift?"

Corrie's shoulders slumped. "No."

Kate grasped her by the shoulders. Her grip was strong. "Then find someone to teach you. Because we're going in my truck. Homegirl doesn't fly, especially over flyover country. I'm a gal of the people."

Corrie went to a driving school and learned. Once she got the hang of using the clutch, it was sort of fun. She liked the instructor telling her, "Relax, young lady. If you can't find em, grind em."

Kate said they would split the driving. There was no need to adjust the seat when they switched, because both of them were about the same height, five-five and change. Kate was a blond, Corrie what her mom called a brownette, but in Portland she went blond, saying it was just for a change. Kate probably knew better.

"When you let your hair down, and from a distance, we could almost be sisters," Kate said as they drove out of Portland, bound for Reno.

Which was, of course, the problem.

4

Corrie walks down Lake Street to West 2nd, Borsalino pulled low. If the woman in the trenchcoat is ahead of her, Corrie either doesn't see or doesn't remember. She can see her destination ahead—HAMMER NEWS OUT OF TOWN PAPERS, the sign reads—when on her left, a woman cries, "Hey, Kate!" Corrie will later tell police that the voice was hoarse, as if the woman had been screaming her lungs out at a rock show.

As Corrie turns her head, she's grabbed by the collar of her jacket and yanked into an alley that stinks of garbage. She stumbles but keeps her feet. She thinks, *I'm being mug—*

The rest is jolted from her mind as she's thrown against the alley's brick wall hard enough to rattle her teeth. *Now* she sees the woman in the trenchcoat: taller than Corrie by a couple of inches, and with bright red hair that can't be natural. It's smashed down under one of those cheap see-thru rainhats you can buy for a buck. Her bag is on a strap over her left shoulder. Her right hand dips into it and brings out a Thermos with the word ACID printed on it in black Sharpie. She lets go of Corrie to unscrew the cap and Corrie is too stunned to run. She can't believe this is happening.

"Here's what you have coming," the redhead says, and throws the contents of the Thermos into Corrie's wide, startled eyes. "Suffer not a woman to teach, or usurp the authority of man, but to be in silence. First Timothy, bitch."

The burn is immediate. Her vision blurs away.

"Go home, Kate. While you still can."

She doesn't see the redhead exit the alley. She doesn't see anything. She can hardly hear her own screams. The pain has swallowed her whole.

5

The first thing she does in the ER when her vision begins to come back—blurry but there, thank God and Jesus and all the saints—is to fish her compact out of her purse and look at her face. Her cheeks and forehead are flushed a hectic red and the whites of her eyes are scarlet, but there are none of the blisters she expected.

This is after the doc has washed her eyes out with a saline solution. It stings like hell. He says he'll be back in ten minutes to do it again. "Whatever she splashed you with, it wasn't acid," he says before hurrying out to deal with another patient.

The second thing she does is call Kate, who'll be wondering where Corrie is. By then she's calmed down a little. Kate is calm, too. She tells Corrie to call the police if someone on the staff hasn't already done it.

Kate arrives ten minutes after a uniformed cop and five minutes before a woman detective. Corrie expects Kate to take charge, it's what she does, but today she only sits in the corner of the exam room and listens. Corrie isn't sure if that's because the lead cop is female. It might be. The detective gets a description and writes it down. She tears a sheet off her pad and gives it to the uni, who leaves, presumably to call it in. The detective has introduced herself as Mallory Hughes.

"The red hair—was it a dye job or could it have been a wig?"

"It might have been either. It all happened so fast. I know that sounds like a cliché, but—"

"Understood, totally understood. If it *was* a wig, they'll probably find it in a nearby litter basket. If someone hasn't filched it already, that is. How are the old eyeballs doing?"

"Better. I'm sorry to have made such a fuss, but—"

"Don't be," Kate says from her seat in the corner.

"It's just that I thought it was acid. It said so right on the Thermos."

"Because that's what she wanted you to think," Hughes says. "Like in a Road Runner cartoon where the box says ACME EXPLOSIVES." She turns her head. "Kate McKay, right?"

Kate nods. She's not taking a big part in the discussion, she's letting Hughes do her job, but her attention is fiercely focused. Corrie has an idea her boss is very angry—it's in her tightly pursed lips and the way her hands are knotted in her lap—but she's showing respect.

At least so far. If she feels that Hughes is fucking up or slacking off, that will change.

"I've read two of your books," Hughes tells her. Then, turning back to Corrie: "The woman who threw that shit in your face, probably bleach, thought you were her, didn't she?" Cocking her head at Kate, whose lips are now so tightly pressed together they have almost disappeared.

"Probably."

"The Borsalino," Kate says. "It's sort of a trademark. It's on all four book jackets and a lot of publicity photos."

"Well, this one is evidence," Hughes says. "You'll get it back eventually, but you'll have to buy another one if you want to wear it to your gig tonight."

From Mallory Hughes, Kate takes this without comment. Corrie wonders again if she would from a man. Kate's not a hater of men, but she's got a lot of push-back in her.

"Are you going ahead with your lecture tonight at the Pioneer?"

"Oh yes. I'd be happy to comp you tickets, if you want to come."

"Working." Then, back to Corrie. "I want you to come down to the station this afternoon and make a statement. You up for that?"

Corrie looks at Kate, who says, "*Early* afternoon, if possible. I need Corrie later on." Simply assuming that Corrie will be ready and willing to do her show-night duties. Corrie supposes there's a degree of diva arrogance in this, but it doesn't irritate her. On the contrary, she's grateful for it. Understands it's Kate's way of saying she assumes Corrie is as brave as she is. Corrie wants to believe that.

"Let's make it one-thirty," Hughes says. "455 East 2nd, not all that far from where you were going when you were assaulted. I'll want both your phone number and email address, since I expect you'll be moving on with Ms. McKay." She doesn't defer to Kate because she's not the victim. At least not this time.

"One-thirty it is," Corrie says.

"If we catch her, you'll have to come back. You're aware of that, right?"

Corrie says she understands.

6

When Hughes is gone, Kate says, "I want you onstage tonight. Are you good with that?"

Corrie feels a bolt of fright at the idea. "Would I have to speak?"

"Not if you don't want to."

"Then okay. I guess."

"You don't mind being Kate McKay's object lesson? Don't resent me for it?"

"No." Is that the truth? Corrie wants it to be.

"I want to take your picture. While your eyes are still red and puffy and your skin is still irritated. All right?"

"Yes."

"People need to understand there's a price for standing up. But it can be paid. They need to understand that, too."

"Okay."

I've become a selling point, Corrie thinks. She sees Kate's willingness to do this, to *seize* this, as a character flaw, but also as a character strength. That it can be both is a new idea for her.

Kate McKay has been called a zealot. She wears the label with pride. On CNN, a pundit accused her of suffering from Joan of Arc Syndrome. Kate's response: "Joan of Arc heard the voice of God. I hear the voices of oppressed women."

She asks Corrie if she wants to continue the tour after tonight. Kate says she didn't want to ask the question in front of the detective.

"Yes, of course."

"Are you sure? Now that you see what can happen?"

"Yes."

"Talking about hate is one thing. Seeing it in action—actually experiencing it—that's a whole other deal. Wouldn't you say?"

"Yes."

"Okay. Subject closed." Kate produces her phone to take Corrie's picture. After looking at the screen, she says, "Muss your hair up. Widen your eyes."

Corrie looks at her, not understanding. Or not wanting to.

"Let's be honest, Corrie. This isn't a book tour, the book would do fine if I just sat at home on my ass and watched TV. It's an *ideology* tour. Otto von Bismarck compared ideology to sausage—you might want to eat it, but you don't want to see it being made. Well, no. He was actually talking about making laws, but same difference. You're *sure* you want to go on with me?"

For an answer she makes Kate's trademark gesture, both hands out and all fingers beckoning: *Come on, bring it*. Then she musses up her hair. Kate laughs, snaps a picture, sends it to Corrie's phone, and tells her what to do with it.

"Then call your parents, hon. They need to hear about this from you before they see it on the news."

7

She's in a shop called Cloth & Chroma, doing what Kate asked with the picture (more embarrassed than ever at the result), when Mallory Hughes calls and says they found the wig. *A* wig, anyway. She sends Corrie a picture. Although the wig is on a plain white background, it brings everything back: the Thermos, the splash, the burn, the sureness that her face was going to melt.

"That's it."

"You're sure?"

"Sure shot."

"Great. Wigs are DNA mines, unless she was wearing a bathing cap over her real hair. If we get a good result and catch her, a cheek-swab match and game over. Have you called your folks?"

"Yes."

Her mother wanted her to come home, ASAP. Her father, made of sterner stuff, just told her to be careful. And to get some protection. He said something he's been telling her all her life: *The bastards don't get to win*.

In the background, her mother cried, "It's not *politics*, Frank, it's her *life*!"

Not politics, ideology, Corrie thinks.

Her father said, "Her life is exactly what I'm talking about."

8

Kate called from the venue and told her to wear a dress. "Look good, hon. And I've got something for you."

When she gets to the greenroom at the Pioneer Center, Kate looks her over, approves of the belted blue knee-length dress Corrie's wearing, and gives her a can of pepper spray.

"Tomorrow I'll get you a gun. Easy-peasy in Nevada."

Corrie stares at her, appalled.

Kate smiles. "Just a small one. Purse-sized. You're okay with that, aren't you? Or not?"

Corrie thinks of the Thermos with ACID printed on the side. Like ACME EXPLOSIVES in a cartoon. She thinks of the woman who thought she was Kate saying, *Here's what you have coming.*

She says, "I'm okay with it."

9

The Pioneer Center seats 1,500, and it's almost packed when Kate strides onstage at seven PM prompt. The speakers blast out Kenny Rogers's "The Gambler." Corrie set that up at Kate's request. There is the usual wild applause, plus the usual lusty booing section. Outside, people are waving signs both pro and con. Inside, signs are verboten. There are men in the audience but mostly it's women-women-everywhere. Some are in tears. Those who have come to show their hate and contempt for everything Kate believes in—plenty of women there, too—boo from a sitting position. Some shake their fists. Many birds are hoisted.

Instead of the Borsalino, Kate wears a Reno Aces gimme cap (which Corrie also found). When it comes to charming the crowd—at least the part of it that *can* be charmed—Kate never misses a trick.

She sweeps her hat off in her trademark deep bow. She's standing halfway between the podium and a cloth-draped easel. It looks like a courtroom exhibit. She takes the cordless mic from its cradle on the podium as effortlessly as a standup comedian about to begin her set. She pumps it at the ceiling.

"Woman Power!"

The majority of the crowd responds. *"Woman Power!"*

"Woman Power, let me hear you, Reno!"

"Woman Power!"

"You can do better, let me hear you! *Woman Power!*"

"*WOMAN POWER!*" the crowd roars, and the boo-birds are totally drowned out. The crowd is still on its feet, some pumping their fists, most still applauding. Corrie thinks, *She lives for this. It feeds her*. Is that a bad thing? Corrie thinks not. She thinks it's that rarity, a true win-win.

When the crowd settles—the boo-birds cowed into temporary silence, which is part of the purpose of the call-and-response—Kate begins.

"You might be wondering why I'm not wearing my trademark hat, and you're probably wondering what this is." She taps the covered jumbo photograph on its stand. "My hat is now in the evidence room of the Reno PD, because it was on my assistant's head when she was the victim of an assault."

Gasps from the crowd. The boo-birds sit stonefaced, waiting.

"She was wearing my hat because it was raining. The assailant—a woman—thought it was me. She pulled my assistant into an alley and threw liquid into her face from a Thermos with the word ACID printed on the side."

More gasps. Louder. The boo-birds look uneasily at each other. Many of them, Corrie thinks, probably wish they'd stayed home and watched something on Netflix.

"It wasn't acid. It was bleach. Not as bad, but bad enough. Look."

She drops the cloth that was hiding the picture, and here is Corrie, red-eyed and blotchy, hair all in a tangle. This produces more gasps, and moans, and one loud cry of "Shame!" The boo-birds, so militant when Kate came onstage, seem to be shrinking in their seats.

"Ladies and gentlemen, let me introduce you to this brave woman. I gave her a chance after this cowardly assault to leave my tour and go back home to New England, but she refused. She means to continue, and so do I. Corrie Anderson, please come out here and show these people that you're all right and full of fight."

Corrie, not feeling a bit full of fight, walks onstage in her blue dress and low heels, hair done in a schoolgirl braid, makeup lowkey. The audience leaps to its feet again, applauding and cheering. No boo-birds now; they don't dare. The crowd is united. United for Corrie Anderson from Ossipee, New Hampshire.

And what does the object of this approving thunder feel? As they say on TV, it's complicated. But she thinks of that one lone voice that cried *shame*, and is that what she's feeling? *That?* Why would she?

Kate gives her a hug and whispers, "You done good."

With that, Corrie is released to go back offstage, and there's no question what she feels then: relief. Kate may crave the spotlight; Corrie does not. If she didn't know before, she does now.

10

Not shame after all.

The applause, that standing O, has clarified her mind, and Corrie finds herself thinking clearly for the first time since the bogus redhead threw bleach into her open eyes and unprotected face. She goes back to the greenroom and calls the Spokane Police Department. The dispatcher switches her call to an Officer Rowley. Officer Rowley is a woman. That's good.

Corrie identifies herself and tells Rowley who she's working for. Rowley knows who Kate is; most women of a certain age do. Corrie tells Rowley that she and Kate will be in Spokane tomorrow. She tells Rowley what she wants and why she wants it. Officer Rowley—Denise—says she'll see what she can do and promises she'll text Corrie as soon as possible. In the course of the conversation they have become, not sisters in arms, but at least chums.

From the audience, faint in the greenroom, she hears the periodic thunder of applause as Kate makes her points. The haters are drowned out.

But it only takes one, she thinks as she ends the call. *I guess I knew that, but now I've . . . what?*

"Internalized it," she murmurs.

It wasn't shame at all. What she felt, standing beside that absurdly huge picture of herself and listening to the applause, was *used.* It doesn't make her angry, but it does make her realize she has to take care of herself. Has to grow up a little. A gun won't do that. Neither will pepper spray.

11

The next day they drive to Spokane in Kate's Ford F-150 Crew Cab, their gear in back under a locked vinyl canopy. Kate is behind the wheel, keeping five over the 70 MPH speed limit, still high from last night. The radio is on loud, Alan Jackson singing about the Chattahoochee and what that muddy water meant to him. Corrie leans over and turns it off.

"I'll keep the pepper spray, but I don't want a gun after all."

"Didn't have time to find one, anyway," Kate says. "We're slaves to the damn schedule now, hon."

"I've made arrangements with the Spokane police to have an off-duty cop with us while we're in town. *He'll* have a gun. The lady I spoke to—Denise—says there are always widebodies who want to earn a little extra cash. You'll have to pay him, of course."

Kate is frowning. "I don't want—"

For the first time in their still-new relationship, Corrie interrupts her. "I'll make similar arrangements as we go along." She gathers herself and says the rest—the bottom line. "If you want me to continue, this is non-negotiable. It wasn't just a threat, Kate. Not some online troll with a potty mouth. The person said, 'Go home while you still can.' She's out to get you, she got me by mistake, and she could try again."

Kate says nothing, but Corrie can tell by the set of her mouth and the vertical line between her brows that she's not even close to happy about this—call it what it is—this ultimatum. Kate McKay doesn't want to be perceived as a woman who needs a man to protect her. It's antithetical to everything she's made a career of standing against. But there's something else as well, and it's pretty simple: Kate McKay doesn't like anyone telling her what to do.

She changes her mind when they check in. There's the usual budget of messages, a couple of bouquets, and five letters. Four are fanmail. The fifth contains a photo of Kate and Corrie eating at an outdoor restaurant in Portland, a day or two before the first gig. They are laughing about something. The F-150 is parked at the curb in the background. There's a note, carefully printed. *You only get 1 warning, so receive it well. Next time it will be you and it will be for real. She who speaks lies shall perish.*

Kate's name is printed on the envelope, but there's no stamp. She asks the desk clerk who dropped it off. The clerk, a pretty young man in a white shirt and red vest, tells her someone must have left it while he was away from the desk. Which probably means on a pee break.

"Don't you have a security camera in the lobby?" Corrie asks.

"Yes, ma'am, we sure do, but it's pointed at the front doors, not at the reception desk. Plus, whoever left it could have come in through the restaurant."

Kate thinks this over, then turns to Corrie. "When is your rent-a-cop due?"

"He'll meet me—both of us, if you want—in the lobby at three o'clock. Before I go to the venue to meet the event coordinator and the bookstore people."

Kate holds up the photo and the note. "Let's show him this. And then get a look at the security footage. See if the bitch made the mistake of coming in the front door."

"Good idea," Corrie says. Now that she's gotten her way, she's back to being the meek (but can-do) assistant.

"Bitch is actually following us," Kate marvels.

"Yes," Corrie says. "She is."

Chapter 3

1

Trig expected bad dreams. He expected to see himself putting the gun to the woman's temple over and over again, on instant replay and in slow motion. The poodle looking up at her as she sagged in his encircling arm, its eyes asking, *What's wrong with my mistress?*

There were no bad dreams, at least that he can remember. He slept right through.

Now he makes coffee and pours himself a bowl of cornflakes. Sniffs the milk, decides it's all right, gives the cornflakes a bath, and sits down to eat. He's stepped over the line and he feels okay about it. Fine, in fact. Best thing to do, he decides, is go to work like any other day, then move ahead with his *real* work.

One down, thirteen to go.

He rinses out his bowl and leaves it in the sink. Pours more coffee into an insulated go-cup and leaves his trailer. It's a nice doublewide in the Elm Grove Trailer Park, which is far out on Martin Luther King Boulevard, just before MLK becomes Route 27 and Upsala County becomes Eden County. Sticksville, in other words.

Mrs. Travers next door is loading her twins into the back of her car. She gives him a wave and Trig returns it. The kids are bundled into identical jackets, because the morning is chilly. They just turned three. Mrs. Travers had a birthday party for them the previous week, outside because the weather was warmer than it is now. She brought Trig a birthday cupcake, which was nice of her.

The twins wave to him, little hands opening and closing. Pretty cute. There's no man in Melanie Travers's doublewide, but the missus and her little bundles of joy seem to be doing all right. Trig guesses she has a good job of some kind in the city, plus what some men call hellimony. Trig would never call it that; he's a man who believes you must pay for your mistakes. His father raised him that way.

Melanie's got a Lexus, not brand-new but of fairly recent vintage, so yeah—she's doing all right. Trig is glad for her. Also glad that he didn't meet her yesterday on the Buckeye Trail. If he had, she'd be dead now. Her children orphans. He follows her in his Toyota out to MLK, follows her as she turns right toward the city. Two miles later she turns left into Wee Folks Daycare.

Trig continues on, leaving the countryside behind. On the radio, the morning DJ is saying last week's warm weather was just a tease, a cold front is moving in and the next few days are going to be chilly. "Bundle up, Buckeyes!" he says, and then plays "A Hazy Shade of Winter," by Simon & Garfunkel.

Trig's stomach is rumbling. Apparently the cornflakes weren't enough. He thinks, *The murderer of a defenseless woman is hungry. A woman who just happened to be in the wrong place at the wrong time. A woman who might have children, maybe even twins with matching coats. The man who did that is hungry*. He's mildly amazed. He stepped over the line, and guess what? The other side of the line is no different. The idea is both terrible and comforting.

He pulls into a Wawa on the outskirts of the city proper and buys a breakfast burrito. Also a newspaper. The stories above the fold are about politics and wars. Below the fold is the headline UPRIVER WOMAN SLAIN ON BUCKEYE TRAIL. Her next of kin must have been notified, because her name is given: Annette McElroy, 38 years old.

Trig reads the story while eating his burrito, which is warm and fresh and tasty. There's nothing in it to worry him. No mention of the paper with Letitia Overton's name on it found in the dead woman's hand. The police will be withholding that piece of information.

I'm wise to your tricks, Trig thinks. He heads for downtown, where he'll put in an appearance at the office and then leave early. Now that he's begun, he wants to continue. No need to hurry, haste makes waste, but he's done plenty of scouting and knows where he can find another innocent, perhaps even two.

The cold weather will help.

2

Holly meets Izzy for lunch, but not in Dingley Park; it's too chilly for that. They eat in a little café called Tessie's, where they get a corner booth and can watch the pedestrians go by. In Love Plaza across the street, a busker in a motorcycle jacket is playing a guitar. *You won't do much business today*, Holly thinks.

Sitting across from her, Izzy says, "Look at you, eating inside just like a big girl. You're coming out of your Covid shell. That's good."

"I'm fully vaccinated," Holly says, looking at the menu. "Covid, flu, RSV, shingles. Life has to go on."

"Indeed it does," Izzy says. "I got the Covid and the flu vaccines together, and they laid me out for two days."

"Better than being laid out in a funeral parlor," Holly says. "What do you suppose an Aussie Melt is?"

"I believe it's lamb with pepper jack cheese and some kind of sauce."

"That sounds quite tasty. I think I'll—"

"Bill Wilson wasn't just a random nut after all. He got one."

Holly lowers her menu. "Are you talking about the McElroy woman?" She also reads the morning paper. She gets it on her iPad.

"Yes. I'm not a hundred per cent sure, but in the high nineties."

The waitress comes. Izzy goes for the Reuben, Holly the Aussie Melt. They both order hot drinks, tea for the cop and coffee for the private investigator. Holly has tried to quit coffee, the caffeine sometimes makes her heart jump, but she tells herself that quitting cigarettes is enough for now.

When the waitress is gone, Holly says, "Tell me."

"It stays between us, right?"

"Of course."

"We held back some evidence. There was a piece of paper in Annette McElroy's hand. Printed on it in block letters was a name—Letitia Overton. Does that mean anything to you?"

Holly shakes her head, but files the name away for later consideration.

"Me either. Tom Atta and I have talked to Cary Tolliver, the scumbucket who framed Alan Duffrey."

"You think he really did that?"

"I do. We also talked to Duffrey's colleagues at First Lake City, the bank where he worked. Every one of them said they never believed that pedophilia stuff in the first place . . . but what do you think they said when Duffrey was arrested and put on trial?"

Holly likes to believe the best of people, and *does* believe there's good in just about everyone, but her time at Finders Keepers has also taught her that just about everyone has a shitty streak. "Most of them probably said, 'There was always something weird about him' and 'I'm not a bit surprised.'"

"You bet they did."

The waitress brings their drinks and says their food will be right out. Izzy waits until she's gone, then pushes her tea to one side and leans across the table. "We're *assuming* it's Duffrey who set this Bill Wilson off, but he could just be a wacko who thinks he's avenging Taylor Swift or Donald Trump or . . . I don't know . . . Jimmy Buffett."

"Jimmy Buffett is dead," Holly feels compelled to add, although she knows Izzy is just making a point.

"Annette McElroy's husband, who's totally grief-stricken, didn't even know who Alan Duffrey *was*, and says he's pretty sure his wife didn't, either. He says they avoid the news as much as possible, because it's all so bad."

Holly can relate to that. "The Alan Duffrey part doesn't matter, though, does it? Wilson said he was going to kill innocents to punish the guilty. If Letitia Overton is guilty, at least in this guy's mind, you need to talk to her."

"No kidding. She's a real person, lived at 487 Hardy, but no longer resides in the city. She and her husband moved to Florida, according to her neighbor. The neighbor thought Tampa, or maybe Sarasota. Her husband got a better job, apparently. Regional manager for Staples. Except it might have been Office Depot or Stats & Things. We're running it down. Might have something tomorrow or after the weekend."

"You've been busy."

"This is a big deal, because the nutbag is promising more murders." Izzy looks at her watch, then around for the waitress. "I've got forty-five minutes, and then I have to re-interview the people from the bank, plus Duffrey's lawyer. Run the name Letitia Overton past them. Also Annette McElroy's name, but that's just busywork. McElroy was a target of opportunity."

"An innocent," Holly murmurs. She tries not to hate anyone, but she believes she could come to hate "Bill Wilson." Only why waste the emotion? It's Izzy's case.

The waitress comes, bearing sandwiches. Holly bites into her Aussie Melt and finds it delicious. She thinks lamb may be the great overlooked meat. As a young woman she went through a vegetarian phase but gave it up after eight months or so. She supposes she's a carnivore at heart. A hunter, not a gatherer.

"You said you knew a bartender who goes to those sober meetings," Izzy says. "Would you be willing to talk to him?"

"Happy to," Holly says.

"But keep it on the downlow. I don't want the brass to find out I'm . . ." What was it Lew Warwick said? "That I'm outsourcing our investigations."

Holly wipes away a little sauce—delicious!—then makes a zipping gesture across her lips. She says, "When you track down Letitia Overton, would you let me know what she tells you? On the downlow, of course."

"Absolutely. I have those re-interviews this afternoon. What are you doing?"

"Looking for stolen jewelry."

"Much more exciting."

"Not really. Just visiting pawnshops." Holly sighs. "I hate that donkey."

"What donkey?"

"Never mind."

3

The northeast part of Buckeye City is called Breezy Point. Here the not-so-Great Lake the city is situated on gives way to shallow polluted water that cancer-friendly oil slicks dye every color of the rainbow. There are few breezes, but when they blow, they bring the stink of mud and dead fish. Breezy Point mostly consists of public housing. These are four- and five-story brick buildings that look a lot like the accommodations at Big Stone, the state penitentiary. The streets all have tree names, which is sort of hilarious because few trees grow in the Breeze. Every now and then, on Willow Street or Mulberry Street or Oak Drive, the pavement splits and mud oozes up. Sometimes sinkholes big enough to swallow a car also open up. Breezy Point was built on a swamp, and the swamp seems determined to take it back.

Far out on Palm Street (a stupid name for a street in the Breeze if there ever was one), there's a dingy strip mall with a Dollar Tree, a pizza shop, a medical marijuana dispensary, a Wallets check-cashing store (where quick loans may be negotiated at outrageous interest rates), and a laundromat called the Washee-Washee. This may be politically incorrect (or downright racist), but the Breezy Pointers who use the place don't seem to mind. Nor do Dov and Frank, a couple of veteran winos who often cruise the strip mall for interesting leftovers and then plant their tatty lawn chairs behind the laundromat on chilly days like this one.

It's 48 degrees in most of the Breeze, but behind the Washee-Washee, it's a balmy 74. This is because of the exhaust from the coin-op driers. It's as pleasant as can be. Dov and Frank have magazines, *Atlantic* for Dov, *Car and Driver* for Frank. These were trash barrel finds from their latest scavenging run behind the pot store. In addition to the mags, they collected enough returnable cans and bottles to purchase a sixer of Fuzzy Navel Hard Seltzer. After a can each, they are starting to level out and enjoy life on life's terms.

"Where's Marie?" Dov asks.

"Lunch break, I think," Frank says. Marie works in the Washee-Washee, and sometimes comes out back to smoke a cigarette and be sociable. "Look at this Dodge Charger. Is that nice, or what?"

Dov gives it a brief look and says, "The fruits of capitalism always rot on the ground."

"What does that even mean?" Frank says.

"Educate yourself, my son," Dov replies, although he is in fact ten years younger than Frank. "Read something that's not . . ."

He pauses as a man comes around the corner of the Washee-Washee. Frank has seen him before, although not recently.

"Hey, man. Didn't I see you at some of those meetings in Upsala a few years back? Maybe the Shine at Noon? I used to live up that way. I'd invite you to sit, but you don't have no chair, and ours—"

"—are currently occupied," Dov finishes. "We'd ask you to share our current libation, too, but unfortunately funds are low and we must conserve."

"That's all right," Trig says. And to Frank: "I haven't been at the Shine at Noon for quite awhile. I guess those meetings weren't for you."

"Nope, I tried it, but do you know what? Sobriety sucks."

"I find it useful."

"Well," Frank says, "it takes all kind to make a world, so they say. Have I seen you around before? Maybe at the Dollar Tree?"

"It's possible."

Trig looks around, confirms that they are unobserved, takes the Taurus out of his pocket, and shoots Dov in the center of the forehead. The snap of the revolver, not loud to begin with, is lost in the steady whoosh of the driers' exhaust. Dov's head rocks backward, hits the cinderblock wall between two of the metal exhaust ports, then drops onto his chest. Blood trickles down the bridge of his nose.

"Hey!" Frank says, looking up at Trig. "What the fuck was that for?"

"Alan Duffrey," Trig says, and points the pistol at Frank. "Sit still and I'll make it quick."

Frank doesn't sit still. He shoots to his feet, spilling his Fuzzy Navel all over his lap. Trig shoots him in the chest. Frank staggers back against the cinderblock, then comes forward with his hands outstretched like Frankenstein's monster. Trig retreats a few steps and shoots three more times: *snap-snap-snap*. Frank goes to his knees, then—unbelievable!—gets up again, hands once more outstretched. They are groping for something, anything.

Trig takes time to aim and shoots Frank Mitborough, who once lived upstate and at one point had almost a year clean and sober, in the mouth. Frank sits down in his lawn chair, which collapses and spills him onto the ground. A tooth falls out of his mouth.

"I'm sorry, you guys," Trig says. And he is, but only in an academic way. Killers in the movies say only the first one is hard, and although Trig guesses their lines were written by folks who have never killed anything bigger than a bug, it turns out to be true. Plus, these two were a drag on society, no good to anybody. He thinks, *Dad, I could get to like this.*

Trig looks around. No one. He takes the folder containing the slips of paper from his pocket and thumbs through the names. He puts PHILIP JACOBY in Dov's hand. In Frank's he puts TURNER KELLY.

Do the police know what he's doing yet? If they don't, they will soon. Will they offer protection to those remaining, once they figure it out? It will do them no good, because he's not killing the guilty. He's killing the innocent. Like these two.

He walks around the side of the Washee-Washee, peeks, sees no one except for a man going into Wallets to cash his check or get a loan. No sign of the lady who works in the laundromat. Once the Wallets guy is gone, Trig walks to his Toyota, which is parked in front of an empty storefront with soaped windows and a sign in the door saying FOR LEASE FROM CARL SIEDEL REAL ESTATE. He gets in and drives away.

Three down, eleven to go.

It seems like a mountain to climb.

When the atonement is complete and the amends are made, you can rest. So he tells himself.

He goes back to his job, little though it means to him.

4

Two hours later, Holly Gibney walks into a drinking establishment called Happy. It's only two o'clock in the afternoon, but there are at least twenty customers, mostly men, sitting at the bar and imbibing their own drug of choice, which happens to be legal. Despite the establishment's name, none of them seems particularly happy. There's a baseball game on TV, but it's got to be an oldie, because the team in the white home uniforms is the Indians instead of the Guardians.

John Ackerly is behind the stick, looking hunky in a white shirt with the sleeves rolled up to show muscular forearms. He comes over to her with a smile.

"Holly! Long time no see. Your usual?"

"Thanks, John, yes."

He brings her a Diet Coke with two cherries impaled on a swizzle and she pushes a twenty across the bar. "No change required."

"Ah! Fine with me. Is the game afoot?"

"Yes and no. Are you still going to meetings?"

"Three times a week. Sometimes four. Dom Hogan lets me off if it's an afternoon meeting."

"He owns the bar?"

"Indeed he does."

"And Mr. Hogan values your expertise."

"Don't know about that, but he appreciates the fact that I always show up straight and sober. Why do you ask?"

She tells him what she wants in short bursts, interrupted by his trips to service various customers. One patron he cuts off. The guy argues briefly, then leaves Happy, looking blue. By the time Holly finishes, she's on her second Diet Coke and knows she'll have to use the women's before she leaves. She refuses to call it the ladies' just as she refuses to call her underwear panties. Little girls wear panties, but her little-girl days are long gone. Holly is totally down with Kate McKay on what Kate calls "the advertising-driven infantilism of women."

When she finishes bringing John up to speed, she says, "If this conflicts with your anonymity vow, or whatever you call it—"

"Nah. If a guy confessed to murder in a meeting and I believed him, I'd beat feet to the nearest police station and tattle my ass off. I think any oldtimer would."

"Are you an oldtimer?"

John laughs. "No way. Opinions differ, but most addicts would say you have to have twenty years in to qualify as an oldtimer. I'm a long way from that, but next month it'll be seven years since I snorted my last line."

"Congratulations. And working here really doesn't bother you? Don't they say if you hang around the barber shop long enough, you'll eventually get a haircut?"

"They also say you don't go to a whorehouse to listen to the piano player. Only here *I'm* the piano player. If you see what I mean."

Holly sort of does.

"And I never cared much for alcohol anyway. I was a firm believer in the idea that things go better with coke. Until they didn't."

John goes down the bar to pour a whiskey, then comes back to her. "If I may recap, you want me to keep an eye out for somebody who's mad this Alan Duffrey got framed for a crime he didn't commit and then got shanked."

"Correct."

"You're pretty sure this somebody is . . . what? Killing innocent people to throw shade on the guilty ones?"

"Essentially, yes."

"That's fucked up."

"Yes."

"This guy has already killed one innocent person?"

"Yes."

"You're pretty sure of that?"

"Yes."

"Why?"

"Can't tell you."

"Police holding something back, are they?"

Holly doesn't reply, which is an answer in itself.

"You think the guy goes to meetings because he calls himself Bill Wilson."

"Yes. And a guy calling himself Bill Wilson, or Bill W., might really stand out."

"He might, but you have to remember there are three dozen NA meetings in this city every week. Add in the 'burbs and upstate, throw in AA, and you're talking close to a hundred. Needle-in-a-haystack deal. Also, Bill Wilson is undoubtedly an alias."

"Undoubtedly."

"Even if it wasn't, people in the Program sometimes use nicknames. I know a guy named Willard who calls himself Telescope. Another guy calls himself Smoothie. A woman who identifies as Ariel the Mermaid. You get the idea. What's your stake in this?"

"None. It's a police case. I just got kind of . . . interested."

"That's my Holly, you're just another addict. Don't take that wrong, most people are riding one pink horse or another."

"Philosophy before five gives me a headache," she says.

John laughs. "I'll give it a shot, because now I'm sort of interested, too. If anyone knows, it'd be Reverend Mike, aka the Rev, aka Big Book Mike."

"Who's that?"

"Kind of a pain in the katookis. The Rev lost his church because he was an Oxy freak, but he must have gotten some kind of pension, because his job now consists of going to meetings all over the city, from Sugar Heights to Lowtown. Also Upsala, Tapperville, and Upriver. But Holly . . . I'd say the chances reside somewhere between slim and none."

"Maybe a little higher than that. People say all kinds of things in those meetings, right? Don't you folks say 'honesty in all your affairs'?"

"They do and most people are. But Hol—it's not lying if you just keep your mouth shut."

This guy might not be able to, Holly thinks, remembering his note. Not to mention his alias. She thinks this guy sees himself as an avenging angel with a flaming sword, and people like that can't help popping off. It relieves the pressure.

She notices a sign behind the bar that shows an orange with a straw sticking out of it. An obviously tipsy hummingbird is hovering nearby. Below the orange it says, EARLY BIRD SPECIAL! YOUR FIRST SCREWDRIVER FOR A BUCK! 8-10 AM!

"Do people really come in for a vodka and orange at eight in the morning?" Holly asks.

"Girlfriend," John Ackerly says, "you'd be surprised."

"Oough." Holly finishes her drink, then goes to the women's room. There's a graffiti on the door of her stall that says, FUCK THE 12 DAYS OF CHRISTMAS.

Someone was having a very bad day, she thinks. *Probably last year, when Alan Duffrey was still alive.*

She's in the act of pulling up her pants when an idea strikes her so hard that she sits back down with a thump. Wide-eyed, she stares at FUCK THE 12 DAYS OF CHRISTMAS.

Oh God, she thinks. *So obvious. I have to talk to Izzy.*

She begins to count on her fingers, lips moving.

Outside John's bar, she calls Isabelle Jaynes. It's a rule of her life that when you call someone with bad news, you always get them. When you call with good news or exciting news, you get voicemail. She's hoping this will be the exception that proves the rule, but it's not. She tells Izzy to call her as soon as possible, then goes in search of lost jewels . . . although right now, jewelry isn't her priority. Duffrey's not her case, but she's got her teeth in it, anyway.

5

Izzy checks her phone, sees it's Holly, and pushes dismiss. *Not now, Hols*, she thinks. The plan was for her and Tom to split up and do re-interviews, asking about Letitia Overton, but as John Lennon once said, life is what happens when you're making other plans.

She met her partner outside the First Lake City Bank, and they were just about to go in when Lew Warwick called. "I'm thinking Wilson may have gotten two more." He gave Izzy an address in Breezy Point.

Now she's standing beside the Washee-Washee with a stout woman named Marie Ellis. The Ellis woman is trembling and won't go around to the back of the laundromat; she says once was enough.

"I haven't seen a dead person since my grammy," she tells Izzy, "and at least Grammy died in *bed*."

Tom is around the corner, photographing the two dead men, the lawn chairs (one collapsed), the cans of Fuzzy Navel, and the container they came in. The forensics van will be here in short order with their cameras and brushes, but it's best to get pictures as soon as possible.

Marie Ellis works as a cleaner, folder, change-maker, and all-around woman of work at the Washee-Washee. The men might have been murdered while she was at lunch . . . or not. Not is an idea that scares her to death. Even empty, the big driers run for five minutes out of every fifteen, she doesn't know why, and they're noisy. If there had been gunshots, she probably wouldn't have heard them unless they were very loud.

She had a Twinkie in her smock for dessert, and once the last batch of clothes were folded, she went around back to eat it and have a smoke, because the drier exhausts keep that area warm. She thought if the two winos weren't there, she could sit in one of the lawn chairs to eat her Twinkie. Only they *were* there, and they were dead.

"Do you know their names, Ms. Ellis?"

"One was Frank. I think he's the one on the ground. The other one was Bruv or Dove or something like that."

"You didn't hear gunshots?"

Marie shakes her head. "Those poor men! Whoever did it could have come in and shot *me*! I was all alone!"

"You didn't see anyone?"

"No. Just . . . them." She points around the corner, then jerks her hand back as if her finger were a periscope that might show her what she doesn't want to look at again.

Tom comes back. "Ma'am, you'll need to come down to the police station at Court Plaza and give a recorded statement, but not until later. Can you do five o'clock?"

"Yes, I suppose."

"For now, you can go back to work."

Marie looks at him like he's crazy. "I'm going *home.* I have a Valium in the medicine cabinet and I'm going to take it." She looks at Tom defiantly, as if daring the detective to contradict her.

"Do that," Izzy says. "Can I have your address?"

Marie touches the loose skin under her neck. "I'm not a suspect, am I?"

Izzy smiles. "No, Marie, but we'll need that statement. Are you okay to drive?"

"Yes, I think so."

When she's gone, Tom says, "Each of the decedents has a piece of paper in his hand. I could make out TURN on one of them. What might be BY in the other guy's. I was tempted to spread their fingers a little but didn't."

"Probably just as well. We'll know soon enough. Is the lieutenant coming?"

"He is." Tom glances around. "Thank God there are no lookie-loos. This is a zombie shopping mall if there ever was one. Of course that means no witnesses, either."

"Including Marie," Izzy says. "You think she's lucky to be alive?"

"I do. And I think she knows it."

Izzy goes around the corner. The body of one sits in his lawn chair with his head on his chest, as if sleeping. The other lies facedown in the weeds, one cracked and dusty loafer against the laundromat's cinderblock back wall. "What a shitty place to die."

"At least they died warm," Tom says. "I brought six corpsesicles to the morgue after that hard freeze we had in January. Two with no IDs. One was a little kid."

"Excuse me a minute."

She goes out to the sidewalk and sees that Holly has left a voicemail. It's two words, just *call me*, but Holly sounds excited.

She's figured something out, Izzy thinks. *Damn, that woman is* so *spooky. Sherlock Holmes in low heels, pastel blouses, and tweed skirts.*

6

Holly finds some of the jewelry she's looking for at O'Leary Pawn & Loan on Dock Street. Being nonconfrontational unless she absolutely has to be, Holly doesn't engage with Dennis O'Leary, who wants to argue and be all poopy, but simply photographs the sparklers and walks out. Let the insurance people take over, with or without police involvement. She'll get at least part of her bonus, and that makes her happy.

Her phone rings as she's getting into her car. It's Izzy. Holly was excited in the women's room, sure she'd nailed at least part of the puzzle, but she has a tendency to second-guess herself, and now she hesitates. What if she's wrong? But Izzy won't laugh at her even if she is, in her heart Holly knows this, and besides . . .

"I'm right, I know I am," she says, and takes the call.

"What's up, Hols?"

"Do you know how many different two-digit combinations add up to fourteen, Izzy?"

"I don't know. Does it matter?"

"Seven, but only if you use seven twice. Six if you don't. And one of those combinations is twelve plus two."

"Stop dancing around it, girl. I'm at a crime scene. Double murder. Bill Wilson's work. Forensics van's on the way."

"Oh my God! He left names?"

"Yes, but we can't read them. They're in the hands of the corpses, who were having a little hard seltzer party behind a laundromat in Breezy Point before this dirtbag showed up and shot them. We'll know what they are after the forensics people get here and do their thing. What are you thinking about?"

"Have you located Letitia Overton yet?"

"No. Soon, I hope."

"When you do, ask her if she was on the jury that convicted Alan Duffrey."

Silence at the other end.

"Iz? Are you there?"

"Fuuuck," Izzy whispers. "Twelve people on a felony-count jury. That's what you're thinking?"

"Yes," Holly says, then hastens to add: "It's only a guess, but if you add in the judge . . . plus the prosecutor . . . you get . . ."

"Fourteen," Izzy says.

"It *could* only be thirteen—the letter isn't clear, maybe on purpose—but I think it's fourteen. Or the guilty one could be Cary Tolliver. That makes logical sense." She thinks that over and then says, "Mr. Tolliver is dying, but it could still be him."

"I'll find out about Overton, also about the names these two dead men have in their hands. You can't say anything about this, Holly. If Lieutenant Warwick finds out I put you in the loop . . ."

Holly runs a finger across her lips. Then, because Izzy can't see that: "Mum's the word. But if it should prove out, the fish tacos are on you the next time we're in Dingley Park."

7

Trig beavers away at work for the rest of the afternoon. He waits for the cops to come and arrest him for the double murder behind the Washee-Washee. He's sure he wasn't seen, yet the idea—the result of too many *CSI* episodes, maybe—lingers, but his only visitor is Jerry Allison, the elderly head janitor in his building. Jerry feels he can drop by for a chat—with Trig, or anyone else—any old time he likes, because he's been pushing a broom and waxing floors here since Reagan was president, as he's happy to tell anyone, and at length.

After work, Trig gets in his car and drives thirty miles to Upsala, where there's a meeting called the Twilight Hour that he sometimes attends.

On the way, a marvelous thing happens: his free-floating anxiety lifts. His sense of doubt about his ability to complete his mission also lifts. Unless he makes a mistake, the police won't be able to find a trail leading to him, even if (*when*) they realize what he's doing, because his targets are completely random. Yes, he knew about the Buckeye Trail, but so do thousands of others. Yes, he knew that those winos sometimes drank behind the laundromat, because he saw them on one of his scouting expeditions after the death of Alan Duffrey and Cary Tolliver's horrible confession on that Buckeye Brandon podcast. There are only eleven to go. It is important to carry through. When he's finished, the world will know that when an innocent man dies, the innocent must also die. It's the only atonement that is perfect.

"Because then the guilty suffer," he says as he pulls into the parking lot of the Upsala Congregational Church. "Right, Daddy-O?" Not that *Trig's* Daddy-O suffered. No; that was the son's job.

I'll wait a bit before taking the next one. A week, maybe even two. Give myself a breather, and give them time to realize the why of it.

In a way that's funny, because it's what he always thought about the drinking: *I'll take a week off, stay sober, just to prove I can do it.* But this is different, of course it is, and the idea of taking time off lifts a weight from him.

He goes downstairs to the church basement, where folding chairs have been set up and the ever-present urn of coffee is chuffing out its pleasant aroma. His upbeat mood holds through the reading of the AA "Preamble," and "How It Works." It holds through the reading of "The Promises," and after the rhetorical question "Are these extravagant promises?" he chants, *We think not* along with the rest. It holds through the chairman's drunkalogue, which follows the usual pattern—rum followed by ruin, ruin followed by redemption. It holds until the chairman asks if anyone has a topic they'd like to discuss, and a burly man—someone Trig knows well, even though the burly man is in the front row and Trig himself is sitting in back—raises his hand and lumbers to his feet. "I'm Reverend Mike."

"Hi, Reverend Mike," the alkies and druggies respond.

Tell them you love God, but—

"I love God, but otherwise I'm just another fiend," Reverend Mike says, and just like that, Trig's upbeat mood collapses. *Maybe it was just a freak rush of endorphins, after all*, he thinks.

It's true that the Rev is apt to show up at any meeting (although rarely this far out in the williwags), always standing so everyone can see him, running his mouth, going on at great length. For him to be at the Twilight Hour just after Trig has killed the two winos . . . that seems like a bad omen. The *worst* omen.

"As Chapter Seven of the Big Book of Alcoholics Anonymous tells us . . ." The Rev then goes on to quote, verbatim, from said chapter. Trig disconnects from this declamation (and judging by the glazed eyeballs he sees around him, he's not alone), but not from the Rev himself. He remembers Reverend Mike catching him after a Straight Circle meeting sometime in late winter or early spring. Saying Trig had sounded upset when he shared.

How had he replied to that?

It was hard to remember exactly, especially while Big Book Mike is still holding the floor and spreading the polysyllables. Hadn't Trig said he'd lost someone very recently? Yes, and that part was all right, only then he'd told the Rev that the someone he'd lost died in lockup.

I didn't say that!

Except Trig is pretty sure he did.

Even so, he'll never remember, and what difference would it make even if he did?

But that was just a day or two after Alan Duffrey died, it was in the paper, and if the Rev made the connection . . .

How unlikely is that?

Very unlikely . . . but unlikely isn't impossible.

The Rev is finally sitting down. The gathering murmurs, *Thanks, Reverend Mike*, and the discussion finally begins. Trig doesn't share because he doesn't know what topic the Rev finally suggested when he finished blathering. Also because he's focused on those broad shoulders and balding head.

Trig is thinking he might kill a fourth one after all before taking some time off. Just to make sure the unlikely doesn't happen. And really, who is more innocent than a recovering addict—a fiend—who loves God?

An unworthy thought comes to him, but it's also an *amusing* thought, and he covers his mouth to hide a smile. *Shutting him up would be doing the recovery community a favor.*

After the meeting, Trig shakes the Rev's hand and tells him how much he enjoyed listening to him. They talk for quite awhile. Trig confesses to the Rev that he's having a serious problem making amends, then listens patiently while the Rev quotes (verbatim) from Chapter 5 of the Big Book: "We must be willing to make amends where we have done harm, provided we do not bring about still more harm in so doing." So on and so forth, blah blah blah.

"I need some counseling about this," Trig says, and watches as Big Book Mike almost visibly expands. They make an appointment for Trig to stop by the Rev's little house at seven PM on the 20th.

"It's near the Rec Center."

"I'll find it."

"Unless," the Rev says, "you think you might drink over it. Then you can come tomorrow. Or even right now."

Trig allows that he'll be okay until May 20th, mostly because he doesn't want to continue his mission so soon. He grips the Rev's meaty arm. "Please don't talk about it to anybody. I'm ashamed of needing help with this."

"Never be ashamed of reaching out," the Rev says, his eyes sparkling with juicy disclosures to come. "And believe me, I won't say a word."

Trig believes this. Reverend Mike is a bore and a windbag, but he's also good AA. Trig has heard him declaim from the Big Book *ad nauseum*, but never a story or even an anecdote about a fellow sufferer. The Rev takes that end-of-meeting command, "What you hear here, when you leave here, let it stay here," very seriously.

Which is good.

8

While the murderer of Annette McElroy, Dov Epstein, and Frank Mitborough is attending an AA meeting in Upsala, Isabelle Jaynes is in her cubicle at 19 Court Plaza, calling Letitia Overton. Tom Atta located her through Overton's ex-sister-in-law, who said she only had Letitia's number because she forgot to delete it from her contacts. She called Overton "that bitch," but the soft-voiced woman who answers Izzy's call doesn't sound in the least bitchy.

Izzy identifies herself and asks where Overton is currently located.

"I'm at the Trellis Apartments, in the town of Wesley Chapel. That's in Florida. Why are you calling, Detective Jaynes? I'm not in trouble, am I? About that . . . thing?"

"What thing would that be, Ms. Overton?"

"The trial. Oh, I'm so sorry about what happened, but how were we to know? Poor Mr. Duffrey, it's just awful."

Izzy has what she called for but wants to make absolutely sure. "Just to be clear, you were on the jury that convicted Alan Duffrey of a third-degree felony, to wit trafficking in pornographic material involving the sexual exploitation of a child or children?"

Letitia Overton begins to cry. Through her tears she says, "We did the best we could! We were in that jury room for almost *two days*! Bunny was the last to give in, but a bunch of us talked her around. Are we in trouble?"

In a way yes, and in a way no, Izzy thinks. Is she going to tell this woman, who did the best she could with the evidence she had, that a woman was found murdered with Overton's name in her dead hand? Chances are excellent that she'll find out eventually, but Izzy isn't going to tell her now.

"No, Ms. Overton—Letitia—you're not in trouble. Do you know who else was on the jury? Remember any of the names?"

There's a hearty sniff, and when Overton speaks again, she sounds a little more in control of herself, maybe because the detective calling from her old hometown has told her she's not in trouble.

"We didn't call each other by our names, only our numbers. Judge Witterson was very strict about that, because of how sensitive the case was. He said in other trials there had been death threats. He mentioned one about a man who killed an abortion provider. Maybe to scare us. If so, it worked. We had these stickers we put on our shirts. Mine said Juror Eight."

Izzy knows that the identity of jurors in high-profile cases—and Duffrey's was front-page news—is often kept from the press, but she's never heard of it being kept from the other jurors.

"But ma'am—Letitia—weren't you called up for *voir dire* by name?"

"You mean the questions they asked when they took our names out of the pool?" Before Izzy can answer, Overton bursts out, "I wish to God I'd never been picked! Or that one of the lawyers had said, 'She won't do!'"

"I totally understand that, Letitia. It's just that the usual procedure is for the court clerk to call out the names of the jurors who might be—"

"Oh yes, they did that, but then Judge Witterson said, this was even before the trial started, that he wanted us to forget our names. Like, you know, when he said a few times during the trial that the jury should disregard what just got said because it was improper for some reason. Although that was very hard to do."

"Do you remember any of the names?"

"Bunny, of course. I remember her because at the end she was the last one holding out for not guilty, and because at the beginning she said, 'I'm Belinda, but everyone just calls me Bunny.' And the foreman, Juror One, said, 'No names,' and Bunny put her fingers over her mouth and popped her eyes in a funny way. Bunny always had a smile or a joke."

Izzy writes *Belinda aka Bunny* on her pad. "Anyone else?" Although she wonders why, exactly, she's asking. The *jurors* aren't the targets, after all.

"There was a guy named Andy . . . another one named Brad . . . I think . . . I'm sorry, that's the best I can do. It was a long time ago. Almost three years. I'm sure there's a list somewhere. Don't you have it?"

"Not yet," Izzy says. "The Clerk of Courts is on vacation, and Judge Witterson says he doesn't remember. He sees lots of juries."

There's a tinge of alarm in Letitia Overton's voice as she says, "Is someone out to get us?"

"No, ma'am, not at all." Izzy is glad to say it. Overton's ex-sister-in-law may think Letitia is a bitch, but based on this phone conversation it's not Izzy's opinion. "I'm going to let you go back to whatever you were doing, but before I do, tell me if the names Turner Kelly and Philip Jacoby mean anything to you."

"Yes, Turner was on the jury. The other one I'm not sure of. Both Turner—he was Juror Six, I think—and Bunny were talkative. She was Ten. Some of the others were more like listeners, you know. Philip Jackson—"

"Jacoby."

"Jacoby, yes, he might have been one of those. More of a listener than a talker, I mean."

"You said it took you two days. Why so long? I would have thought, based on the evidence, it was open and shut."

"Mr. Duffrey's lawyer kept saying that all of the evidence could have been planted. I think he even mentioned that man Tolliver, who wanted a job Mr. Duffrey got. He was very good. The District Attorney—I guess he was actually the Assistant District Attorney—said that was unlikely because Duffrey's fingerprints were found on the magazines that were hidden behind his furnace. Still, there were two or three who thought the case wasn't proved beyond a reasonable doubt. Bunny was one. Number Seven was another one. She was another woman."

"Were you one of the holdouts?"

Another watery sniff. "No. Those images, the ones on Duffrey's computer, convinced me. So, so horrible. One I'll never forget. A little girl with a doll. She had bruises on her arms, Juror Nine pointed those out, but that little girl was still trying to smile. To *smile*!"

Izzy has everything she needs, and she could have done without that last—the bruised girl with the doll. *No wonder they convicted him*, she thinks. *And no wonder he got shanked.* She thanks Overton.

"You promise we're not in trouble? Or any danger?"

"None whatsoever."

"I came down here to start a new life, Detective. My husband was . . . mean. But when I listened to Buckeye Brandon's podcast about how Alan Duffrey was framed, it seemed like that old life was following me. I can hardly eat, thinking about what we did to that poor man."

"It was a miscarriage of justice, Letitia. They happen."

"What is this about?"

"I'm not free to go into details. Sorry."

"I'm going to go back to my maiden name," she says. "I don't like this one anymore."

Izzy says she understands and means it. She's been through bad marriages herself.

She rings off and calls Tom Atta. After she's recapped her conversation with Letitia Overton, he says, "Now we know. Jurors, judge, prosecutor. Pack your bags, guys, Bill Wilson's sending you on a guilt trip."

"What he's doing is so pointless," Izzy says. "The woman I talked to feels plenty of guilt already. God knows how much more she'll feel when she finds out Annette McElroy was murdered for *her* sins. At least her sins in the eyes of this Bill Wilson freak."

"Overton will be an outlier," Tom says. "Most of the others on that jury won't feel bad at all. They'll say they followed the evidence, rendered a verdict, and won't lose any sleep over it."

"I hope that's not true."

But when they finally get all the names of the Alan Duffrey jury, it turns out that it pretty much is.

Chapter 4

1

Although it's nominally a tour for Kate McKay's new book, *A Woman's Testament*, the publisher has had nothing to do with planning the dates; Kate is an old hand when it comes to scheduling, and thus getting the biggest bang for her buck. The dates are far apart at the start of the tour, but they'll speed up, including a few one-nighters. She's told Corrie it's like a prizefight: you feel out your opponent, then move in and start pummeling.

On May 10th, the gig is at Denver's Ogden Theatre, which seats sixteen hundred or so. Corrie has nine AM coffee with the venue's event coordinator, who assures her Kate will fill almost every seat. This is no doubt helped by the fact that there is no actual admission charge (although the book, random copies autographed, will be on sale).

The women have connecting accommodations high up in the Brown Palace Hotel. "Quite luxy," Corrie says. "I've actually got a bidet."

Kate laughs. "Enjoy it while you can. It's apt to be all downhill from here."

Corrie finishes with the coordinator at nine-thirty. She's got a meeting back at the hotel with a bookseller from the Tattered Cover at ten-thirty. The woman will arrive with two hundred copies of *A Woman's Testament* to sign. While Kate signs, Corrie will meet with the security person who'll be with them until they leave town, bound for Omaha. His name is Brian "Bull" Durham. He'll be joined by two more off-duty cops who will be with them from the time they leave for the gig until they're back at the hotel.

Corrie arranged for Durham ahead of their arrival. The extras come courtesy of the Ogden's event coordinator. News of Corrie's adventure in Reno has spread. No one wants the famous Kate McKay attacked (or God forbid, assassinated) on their patch. At three PM, Corrie will be back at the hotel, readying a meeting room for the press conference, where Corrie herself will be asked many questions about what happened in Reno. She would prefer—*much* prefer—to stay in the background, but Kate insists, and Kate is the boss. Corrie tells herself she doesn't resent being Kate's show pony.

It's going to be a busy day.

She'd like to have a few minutes to herself before meeting the bookstore lady—she needs to pee, for one thing—but when she sticks her head into Kate's suite to see if the boss needs anything, she realizes me-time will have to wait a little longer, because the boss is having a full-bore Katie McKay tantrum. They aren't common, and Corrie has discovered they're basically harmless. It's how Kate blows off steam. Corrie tries to not find this annoying or self-indulgent. She reminds herself that Kate is right, men are allowed to holler all the time—when in doubt, they scream and shout—but Corrie still doesn't like it. It wasn't the way she was raised.

"Mother *FUCKER*! Cunt *LICKER*! Bitch *KITTY*! You have to be fucking *SHITTING* me!"

Kate looks up and sees Corrie standing in the doorway, mouth open. Kate tosses her phone on the couch and brushes her tousled hair away from her face with the backs of her hands. Gives Corrie a razor-thin smile. "So how's *your* day going?"

"Better than yours, I guess," Corrie says.

Kate goes to the window and looks out. "Have you ever noticed that the best curses, the most *effective* curses, always center on women and their parts? *Motherfucker*—to commit incest with one's own progenitor—used to be the queen of curses, and even overuse hasn't entirely robbed it of its power. And *cunt*. Is there an uglier word? It's a goddam blunt instrument. Even *cow*, at least the way the British use it . . ."

"How about *cocksucker*?"

Kate waves a dismissive hand. "An equal-opportunity vulgarity."

"*Scumbag*?"

But Kate has lost interest. She's looking out at the Rockies with her hands stuffed deep into the pockets of her Lafayette slacks.

"What's wrong?"

"We lost our venue in fucking Buckeye City. Why are we finding this out so late? Because they were scared. Cowards! Buckeye City cowards! From now on I don't even want to say its name. From this point forward it's just the one that's Not-Cleveland."

Corrie doesn't even need to consult her notes. "The Mingo?" She's astounded.

"Yeah, that's the one. Some soul-singing diva comes out of retirement, and *we* get bumped." Then, grudgingly, "Okay, so it's not just *some* diva. It's Sista Bessie, and she's great. Listened to her all the time when I was a teenager—"

"The Sista? Really? 'Love You All Night,' *that* Sista?"

Kate gives her a sour look. "She's terrific, no doubt, but we still got bumped. Which pisses me off. I can't call Sista Bessie a cunt, but the people who knocked us off the schedule? Them I call cunts! Them I call motherfuckers!"

Corrie keeps all the tour info on her laptop and her tablet, but she doesn't need to go into her connecting room to get either of them. She's got the tour—at least the midwestern part of it—by heart. "They can't *do* that, Kate. I've got a contract. She's a great singer, no doubt, but that date is *ours*! May thirty-first!"

Kate points to her phone, which is half-buried between two couch cushions. "Read the event coordinator's email if you want. Cowardly fucking cock-knocker didn't even have the guts to call me. He quotes the 'extraordinary circumstances' clause in the contract."

Corrie rescues Kate's phone from its semi-internment, taps in the code, and looks at the email from Donald Gibson, the Mingo's Program Director. The phrase *extraordinary circumstances* is there, all right. Now Kate's tantrum seems justified. Corrie's pretty mad herself. The nerve!

"This is bullshit. *Extraordinary circumstances* means a flood or a blizzard or a citywide blackout! Extraordinary circumstances would be if the damn building burned down. It doesn't mean Sista Bessie! It wouldn't even mean the Beatles if they decided to get back together!"

"They can't," Kate says, beginning to smile. "Two out of four ain't rockin no more."

"Well even if they *did*, and decided to play the Mingo! And they're scrapping us for a date we made months in advance? Ridiculous. I'm calling this Gibson person and setting him straight."

"Whoa, girl, slow your roll." The smile is stronger now, and a tiny bit indulgent. The steam has been blown off; thus thinking can recommence. "Sista Bessie's not the Beatles, but she's a big deal. The woman hasn't performed a full-on concert in ten or twelve years, let alone done a tour. She's a legend. Also, she happens to be Black. We got some good press after that bitch scared you—"

"She did more than scare me. That *hurt*!"

"I'm sure it did, and I'm sure I'm being crass, but ask yourself what happens if I enforce my contract, lawyers and all, against Sista Bessie. In a city that's forty per cent Black. How do I look if she says, 'I'm sorry we had to cancel. White lady enforced her contract and took our date.' How will that look? How will it *sound*?"

Corrie thinks it over, and her conclusion makes her angrier than ever. "He knows that, right? This Donald Gibson person knows that."

"You bet. He fucked us at the drive-thru, honey."

He also fucked the people hoping to see you, Corrie thinks, but doesn't say. "So what do we do?"

"Rearrange."

Corrie's heart sinks. She worked hard to fine-tune the schedule, and now Kate wants to trash it. Not that it's Kate's fault.

Putting her hands on Corrie's shoulders, Kate says, "You can fix this. I have total confidence in you."

"Flattery will get you nowhere." Nevertheless, Corrie *is* flattered.

"The event coordinators in most cities will go along, Cor. It would be different if the summer concert season had started, but it hasn't. Most of those halls are standing empty except on weekends. Also . . . we have three days off after Cincinnati, right?"

"Yes."

"Suppose we take those off days in Not-Cleveland instead. We can go see Sista Bessie. How does that sound?"

"It actually sounds pretty cool. Listen, Kate, you've got that presser at five. What if you were to say that, in solidarity with your Black sisters and because you love Sista Bessie's music, you're giving up your date at the Mingo so the Sista can play?"

"If Donald Gibson says that wasn't my idea—"

Corrie is smiling. "Do you think he'd dare?"

Kate kisses Corrie first on one cheek, then the other. "You're good, Anderson. Very good indeed. And I think our new friend Donald will be happy to provide us with house seats for Sista's first show. Do you concur?"

Corrie, smiling more widely than ever, says she absolutely does.

"Plus backstage passes. He better add those." And then, with great satisfaction: "That scumbag."

2

Thirteen hundred miles east of Denver, Izzy and Holly are once more having lunch in Dingley Park. As promised, Izzy buys.

Holly doesn't waste time. "What's up with Bill Wilson?" She adds: "Absolutely on the downlow."

"It's the jurors, for sure," Izzy says. "Targeting them by proxy. Those murdered men behind the laundromat . . . you know about those two?"

"Of course," Holly says, and chomps into her fish taco. "Dov Epstein and Frank Mitborough."

"You really *have* been keeping tabs."

"Buckeye Brandon had the names."

"That busybody piece of shit," Izzy says.

Holly wouldn't exactly put it that way, but understands Izzy's frustration. Whatever sources Buckeye Brandon has in the city PD, they're good. And there was his scoop about Alan Duffrey, of course. "Have you gotten the names of the other jurors?"

"Six of the twelve so far, thanks to what Letitia Overton, Philip Jacoby, and Turner Kelly remember."

"Those three names were . . ."

"Placed in the hands of the murder victims, yes."

"Oough."

"The jurors' names were kept very close because of the nature of the case. The judge actually wanted them to call each other by their numbers."

"Like in *The Prisoner*," Holly says.

"What?"

"A TV show. 'I am not a number, I am a free man!'"

"I have no idea what you're talking about."

"Never mind. Go on."

"We'll have the rest of the names when the Clerk of Courts comes back from Disney World. I reached out to her, but she says the names are locked up in her terminal of the courts system computer."

"Of course they are," Holly says. "The jurors probably don't matter, anyway. They're proxies, as you said. The ones who have to live so they can . . . how did he put it? Rue the day. Judge Witterson was in charge. Who was the prosecuting attorney?"

Izzy swirls a french fry in her ketchup and doesn't answer.

Holly backtracks. "If you really don't want to talk about it, that's okay."

Izzy looks up and smiles. It's a wide one, making her look about sixteen for a brief moment. "You're better at this than I am."

Holly doesn't know what to say. She's flabbergasted.

"Which presents me with a problem. I'm a girl who believes in giving credit where credit is due, but I'm also a girl—"

"Woman," Holly can't help interjecting.

"Okay, I'm also a *woman* who has her eye on the lieutenancy if Lew Warwick retires in a few years. I don't want the bureaucratic bullshit that goes with the job, but it'll help with my pension. Also, I love his chair."

"His chair?"

"It's ergonomic. Never mind. What I'm saying is if you come up with some amazing deduction—like the one about twelve jurors plus possibly two others—giving you the credit could put me in a mess with the department."

"Oh. Is *that* all." Holly waves it away, and then says something so much a part of her that it seems neither ridiculously overmodest nor in the slightest extraordinary. "I don't care about credit, I just like to find answers."

"You mean that, don't you?"

"Yes."

"You like to *deduce*."

"I guess I do."

"Eat your taco."

Holly tucks in.

"All right, here's more. The ADA who prosecuted Alan Duffrey is Doug Allen. He's an up-and-comer with his eye on Albert Tantleff's job as County Attorney when Tantleff retires. He went at this case hammer and tongs, so he *could* be the guy Bill Wilson calls the guilty party. Also, Tolliver claims—*claims*—he wrote Allen in February, fessing up to the frame job."

"Holy gee. Any proof?"

"If you mean did he send an email or even a registered letter, no. Just regular snail-mail. Tolliver could be lying about that. He could also be lying about what he told Buckeye Brandon."

"Do you believe that?"

"No."

"Why?"

"Can't tell you. I have to re-interview someone first, but it'll have to wait for tomorrow, when Doug Allen's out of town at a Republican fundraiser."

"Who's the someone?"

Izzy shakes her head.

"Can you tell me later?"

"Yes, and at that point you can amaze me. Did you find the missing jewelry?"

"Some of it, yes."

"Are you on the trail of the rest?"

Holly looks up from her second fish taco. Her eyes gleam. "*Hot* on the trail."

Izzy laughs. "That's my Holly."

3

That afternoon, Holly's young friend Barbara Robinson gets a call from an unknown number. She answers cautiously. "Hello?"

"Is this the Barbara Robinson who wrote *Faces Change*?" The caller has a deep voice for a woman. Husky. "It says on the flap that you live in Buckeye City."

"Yes, this is her," Barbara says, then, remembering her grammar: "She. How did you get my number?"

The woman laughs—a deep, rich sound that invites Barbara to join in. Barbara doesn't, she's been through enough with Holly not to trust unknown callers, but a smile touches her lips. "Spokeo," her caller says. "It's a website—"

"I know what Spokeo is," Barbara says. She doesn't, exactly, but knows it's one of several sites that put names and locations together with phone numbers. For a fee, of course.

"You might think of going unlisted," the woman says. "Now that you're famous, and all."

"People who write poetry aren't famous and don't usually need unlisted numbers," Barbara says. The smile is more pronounced now. "Especially poets with only one published book under their belt."

"I enjoyed it very much, especially that title poem, about faces changing. When you been in the bi'ness as long as I have—"

"What business? Who are you?" Thinking: *It can't be, it just can't.*

The woman with the rich, husky voice pushes on as if the question merits no answer . . . and if Barbara is right, it probably doesn't. "You get to know people who are *three*-faced, let alone two. I wonder if I could get you to sign my copy. I know it's pretty ballsy of me to ask, comin out of the blue like this, but since I'm in your town, I thought why not try? My mama always told me if you don't ask, you don't get."

Barbara sits down. It's either that or fall down. It's crazy, but who else would call with such a bold request? Who but someone who's used to having all sorts of whims catered to?

"Ma'am, are you . . . this is crazy, but are you Sista Bessie?"

That rich laugh again. "I am when I'm singin, but otherwise I'm plain old Betty Brady. I flew in last night. Band is with me, at least some of em. The rest comin."

"And the Dixie Crystals?" Barbara asks. She knows from Sista's website that the famous girl group from the 70s has also come out of retirement to sing backup and harmony on the tour. This is Barbara's first encounter with fame, it came out of nowhere, and she's finding it hard to catch her breath.

"The girls are s'posed to be in today. I'm stayin at the Garden City Plaza Hotel downtown, and tonight we're goin to start our rehearsals at this old empty place out by the airport. Used to be a Sam's Club, Tones says. Tones is my tour manager. You could come to the hotel, or if you wanted to drive on out and watch a scraggy-ass first rehearsal, you could do that. What do you think?"

Silence from Barbara's end.

"Ms. Robinson? Barbara? Are you there?"

Barbara finds her voice, although it's more of a squeak. "That would be . . . so good." Then adds, "I won tickets to your first show on the radio. K-POP. And backstage passes. I'm a fan."

"Fanwise, right back atcha, girl. Then maybe you'd just as soon skip the rehearsal. It's been a long time for me, and like I say, we goan be piss poor at first. We got two weeks and a little more to get right."

"No, I'll be there!" Barbara feels like a girl in a dream. "What time?"

"We'll start around seven, I s'pose, and prob'ly go late. You wouldn't want to stay for all of it, but there'll be food."

Like hell I won't, Barbara thinks. She finds her feet again. "Sista . . . Betty . . . Ms. Brady . . . this isn't a joke? A prank call?"

"Honey," Betty Brady says, again with that rich chuckle, "it's as real as can be. You come on out to that Sam's Club. Tones and Henrietta—she's my agent—will have your name."

4

When Barbara pulls her Prius into the parking lot of the defunct Sam's Club out by the airport that evening, she feels a pang of anticipation that's mixed with fear. She has a fair amount of self-confidence, but it's still hard for her to believe she hasn't been pranked. How likely is it that a famous person would call *her*, just because she's written a slim (128 pages) book of poems? She can see a couple of Ryder trucks parked near the building, and she supposes those are filled with musical equipment, so yes, Sista Bessie is probably here, but when she approaches the man sitting by the door and smoking a cigarette, what are the chances he'll say, *Never heard of you, lady, get lost?* Barbara thinks the chances are pretty good.

Still, she's not without courage (she thinks her friend Holly has more of that), so gets out of her car and walks to the man sitting on the plastic milk crate. He stands up and gives her a grin. "You're the one she wants to see, I'm thinking. She said young, Black, and female. Barbara Robinson?"

"Yes," Barbara says, relieved. She shakes the man's outstretched hand.

"Anthony Kelly, but everyone calls me Tones. I'm Betty's tour manager. Pleased to meet you."

"I'm in a daze," Barbara says.

He laughs. "Don't be. We're just regular people. Come on inside."

It's a big space full of echoes. There are a few men and women rolling equipment around; a few more lean against the walls, talking. An elderly, thin-faced woman—Sista Bessie's dresser, Barbara assumes—is rolling a rack of glittery costumes to where the cash registers used to be.

Betty Brady—Sista Bessie—is up front by herself, slinging a guitar over one shoulder. The case, battered and covered with stickers, is open at her feet. Dressed in mom jeans and a sleeveless top that strains to hold in truly mighty bazooms, she could be almost any streetcorner busker. Barbara is immediately struck by how broad-shouldered she is. How indubitably *there*.

"Let me introduce you," Tones says.

"No, not yet. Please." Barbara can hardly speak above a whisper. "I think she's going to play. I'd like to . . . you know . . ."

A white woman with a deeply lined face, a yacht of a nose, and too much rouge on her cheeks joins them. "You want to hear her sing. I understand."

Betty is tuning up, or trying to. One of the roadies approaches. Betty gives him the guitar and says, "You do it, Acey. By the time I found out I was no good at this part, I was too rich to quit."

The over-rouged woman says, "I'm Henrietta Ramer, Betty's agent. I don't guess you're the only reason Bets wanted to kick things off in this town, but I think you were a big part of it. She loves-loves-*loves* that book of poems. Has read it half to death. I think she has an idea about one of them. You might like it, you might not."

The roadie hands the Gibson back. Betty slings it and sings "A Change Is Gonna Come," strumming each chord just once. Tones and Henrietta wander off, Tones to confer with an old Black man uncasing a saxophone, Henrietta to talk to the old lady who brought the costumes. They've heard it all before, but when Betty soars to the top of her range, Barbara gets goosebumpy from the nape of her neck to the small of her back.

Two more roadies wheel in a beat-up piano, and almost before it's stopped moving, Betty begins to pound out "Aunt Hagar's Blues." She plays standing up, shaking her bluejeaned butt, getting a rough growl into that otherwise smooth, one-of-a-kind voice. The Black man with the sax claps along and sways his skinny hips. People are walking around, talking, laughing, but Betty ignores them. She's totally into it, tuning her voice the way the roadie tuned her guitar.

Sista goes back to the Gibson. A skinny longhair, Barbara assumes her sound guy, puts a mic stand in front of her and plugs into a power strip. He also plugs in her guitar. Sista doesn't even seem to notice; she's singing gospel now. Amps are put in place. Sound monitors. A few musicians start to wander in, carrying their instruments. The old guy steps up beside her and honks his alto horn.

Sista Bessie pauses mid-verse of "Live A-Humble" to say "Yo, Red, you old son of a gun."

Red yo's her right back, then joins her singing: "Watch the sun, see how steady he run, don't let it catch you with your work undone." Barbara gets the goosebumps all over again. She thinks they're perfect, but perfection is still building.

One by one other members of the band assemble behind her. Two of the three Dixie Crystals come in. One has her hair in Bantu knots, the other an Afro as gray as fog. They see Betty, scream, and rush to her. Sista hugs each in turn and says something about Ray Charles that makes them yell with laughter. Betty hands her guitar off, not looking, just assuming some roadie will take it. The three women put their heads together. They murmur, then launch into an electrifying version of Thelma Houston's "Don't Leave Me This Way" that ends with Red honking away all by himself. They all laugh and Betty bumps him with her bazooms and almost knocks him down. There's more laughter and applause.

Betty starts to say something to one of the Crystals, then catches sight of Barbara. She puts one hand to her chest, then rushes forward, high-stepping over a few electrical cords. "You came!" she says, and takes Barbara's hands. In her state of heightened acuity, Barbara can feel the calluses on the fingertips of Betty's left hand, the one she uses to make the guitar chords.

"I came," Barbara croaks. She clears her throat and tries again. "I came."

"I've got a little dressing room in back. Your book is there. If you want to go—pretty girl like you might have a date—I can get it now for you to sign. But if you want to hang out a bit . . ."

"I do," Barbara says. "Want to hang out, I mean. I can hardly believe I'm here." What she says next just spills out. "You're so goddam talented!"

"So are you, honey. So are you."

Chapter 5

1

At quarter past nine the next morning, Holly is going over the Corrections Department's daily list of bail jumpers. There are usually four or five; today there's an even dozen. *Spring fever*, she thinks, and as if the thought had summoned her, Barbara Robinson blows in, almost literally. She doesn't knock, just barges into Holly's office and plops down in the client's chair. The look of her—eyes too wide, zero makeup, clothes wrinkled as if she slept in them—is alarming.

Holly pushes her laptop aside. "Barbara? What's wrong?"

Barbara laughs and shakes her head. "Nothing. Nothing's wrong. If I'm dreaming, don't wake me up."

Holly thinks she understands. She's both glad and concerned. "Did you meet someone? Maybe . . . I don't know . . . spend the night?"

"Not the way you mean, although it was late for sure. I got to bed around three, woke up at eight, put on the same clothes. Had to come over and tell you everything. *Jerome* has met somebody, did you know that?"

"Yes. Georgia Nickerson. He introduced us. Nice young woman."

"And you know those tickets I won, calling into the Morning Circus on K-POP?"

"Yes. Sista Bessie's first show at the Mingo."

"I can give them to Jerome. He can take Georgia. *We're* going as Sista Bessie's guests. Only her real name is Betty Brady."

With that, Barbara spills everything, starting with her out-of-the-blue call from Sista Bessie. Her trip out to Sam's Club. The people she met (some names she remembers, most she doesn't). The singing, most of all that.

"It was past one when they finally finished up . . . or tried to. Tones Kelly, her tour manager, pointed at his watch and said, 'Time to call it a night, kids,' so most of the band . . . they call themselves the Bam Band, did I tell you that?"

"Yes, Barbara."

"They started to put their instruments down, but then the keyboard guy started a riff on his organ that was just too good. For the next eight minutes they sang 'What'd I Say,' with the Dixie Crystals doing the backing vocals. They grooved on it. No other word. I don't know if you know that song—"

"I do, actually." Holly knew it long before Barbara Robinson was born.

"It was so great! She was two-stepping with Red Jones, the sax player. And then Betty starts waving to *me*! She's yelling, 'Get on up here, girl!' in that big strong voice of hers. So I went up . . . I felt like I was dreaming it all . . . and the Crystals pulled me in, and *I sang with them!* Do you believe it?"

"Of course I do," Holly says. She's full of happiness for her friend. This is an excellent way to start the day. Certainly better than looking for slow-moving bail jumpers she can scoop up.

"Then we went out to the Waffle House, because they're open twenty-four/seven. Everyone! Holly, you should have seen Sista—Betty, I mean Betty—you should have seen her *eat*! Eggs, bacon, sausage, hash browns scattered and smothered . . . and a *waffle, too*! She's big, but if I ate that much, I'd *explode*! I guess singing must burn a lot of calories. I *sat* with her, Holly! I ate scrambled eggs with Sista Bessie and her agent!"

Holly smiles her widest smile, in large part because it was Holly that Barb chose to tell all this wonderfulness. "But did you sign her book?"

"I did, but that's not the important part. There are two rhymed poems in my book, mostly because of Olivia Kingsbury. As a mentor she could be tough. She insisted that I write some stuff that rhymed. At least two. She said it was good discipline for a young poet.

"Early on, when I was getting to know her, we read a poem by Vachel Lindsay called 'The Congo.' It's racist as hell, but it has a swinging beat." Barbara thumps her feet to demonstrate. "So I wrote a poem called 'Lowtown Jazz' to sort of, I don't know, tell the other side of the story. It's not rap, but almost. It rhymes all over the place."

Holly nods. "I love that one."

"Betty said she did, too. Holly . . . *she wants to set it to music and record it!*"

Holly just stares at her for a moment, mouth open. Then she begins to laugh and clap her hands. "*That's* why she wanted to get together with you!"

Barbara looks a little crestfallen. "You think?"

"No, I mean because you're you, Barbara. Your poems are a part of who you are, and they're so good."

"Anyway, we're going to the show at the Mingo as Betty's guests, and I can go back to rehearsals any time I want. She said my friend could come with me, and that's you."

"Great, I'd love that," Holly says, with no idea that she won't be in Buckeye City for the next little while, or even in the state. "So tell me what you wrote in her book."

Barbara looks astounded. "I can't remember. I was so excited."

And with that, Barbara bursts into tears.

2

The next morning, Izzy is sitting on a bench in the mellow morning sunshine not far from Courthouse Square. She's drinking a latte from the Starbucks half a block down First Street. Beside her on the bench is another latte. The name on the cup is Roxann, which is short an *e*, but you can't expect baristas to know every name, can you?

The sun on her face is wonderful. Izzy feels she could sit here sipping coffee all morning, but here comes her target, a well-padded woman in a gray pants suit. She approaches Izzy's bench with her purse swinging from one shoulder and her eyes firmly fixed on the prize, which happens to be the Starbucks. Izzy has tracked Roxanne's coffee-break routine on two mornings, but hasn't approached. Today, with the lady's bossman safely out of the way in Cincinnati, she pounces.

Well, maybe nothing so predatory. She just holds up the cup and says, "I believe this is yours, Roxanne."

Roxanne Mason stops and looks warily at Izzy. Then at the cup. She says, "That's not mine."

"It is. I bought it for you. My name's Isabelle Jaynes. I'm a detective with the BCPD. I'd like to talk to you."

"About what?"

"About certain beyond-smut magazines. *Toddlers. Uncle Bill's Pride and Joy. Bedtime Story*. Mags like that."

Roxanne's face, cold to begin with, now freezes solid. "That's court business. *Old* business. Drink that extra coffee yourself." She takes a step toward Starbucks.

Izzy says, less pleasantly, "You can talk to me here in the nice sunshine, or in a hot interview room at the station, Ms. Mason. Your choice."

In a way, she already knows what she needs to know; the way Roxanne Mason's face froze up told her most of it.

Roxanne halts in mid-step, as if playing Statues, then slow-steps back to the bench and sits down. Izzy holds out the coffee. Roxanne waves it away as if it might be poisoned, so Izzy sets it down between them.

"How do I know you're not a reporter *pretending* to be a cop?"

Izzy takes her ID folder out of her back pocket and flops it. Roxanne looks at the photo, then looks away with a child's pout on her round face: *If I don't see you, you're not there.*

"You work for Douglas Allen, correct?"

"I work for *all* the ADAs," Roxanne says. Then—still not looking at Izzy—she bursts out: "I don't know why you people have to keep digging at the Duffrey thing. If that man was telling the truth, it was a tragic miscarriage of justice. They happen. It's sad, but they do. If you want to blame somebody, blame the jury, or the judge who *instructed* the jury."

Roxanne—the assistant to the six Buckeye County Assistant DAs—doesn't know that three people have been killed with the names of Duffrey jurors in their hands. To this point the police have been able to keep a lid on that. Sooner or later someone will blab, and when they do, the papers will be on it like white on rice. Or (Izzy's thinking of Buckeye Brandon's blog and pod), like flies on shit.

"Let's just say that some questions have come up."

"Ask Cary Tolliver, why don't you? He's the one who framed Duffrey, and did a good job of it, too."

Or maybe he had a little help from an ambitious ADA, Izzy thinks. *One who'd like to step up to the big chair currently occupied by Albert Tantleff. An ambitious ADA who had a headline-friendly case dumped in his lap and didn't want to see it overturned.*

"Cary Tolliver is in a coma as of this morning and won't be answering any questions." Which is a shame, because he could have told them what Izzy is currently fishing for, but—as Tom Atta pointed out—they didn't know the right questions to ask, and Tolliver, half gorked out on morphine, hadn't thought to tell them. *Or he might have thought we already knew*, Izzy thinks.

"Are you familiar with the name Claire Rademacher, Roxanne? She works at First Lake City Bank, where Alan Duffrey and Cary Tolliver also worked."

Roxanne finally takes the cup of coffee. Removes the lid and sips. "I recall the name. I think she was interviewed. Everybody who worked with Duffrey at the bank was interviewed."

"But she was never called to testify."

"No, I'd remember that."

"My partner and I talked to her. It was an interesting conversation. Did you know that Alan Duffrey collected vintage comic books?"

"Is this going somewhere?" From her face, Roxanne Mason knows *exactly* where it's going.

"Vintage comics come in special Mylar bags. Duffrey was particularly taken with a character named Plastic Man. Sixty-four issues were published between 1943 and 1956. I googled it. But then, about seven years ago, DC Comics did a six-issue run of *Plastic Man* comics—what they call a mini-series. And do you know what? Cary Tolliver gave

Duffrey those six issues as a goodwill gesture when Duffrey got the chief loan officer's job. Now, don't you think that's strange? Considering that Tolliver was also in the running for the job, then went and framed Duffrey as a pedophile?"

"I don't know what you're on about," Roxanne said. "We know what Tolliver did, or at least what he says he did. He spilled his guts on that podcast!"

"He said he spilled his guts even before that. Said he wrote a letter to ADA Allen in February, owning up to everything. Gave him info that wasn't in the press."

"Really? Then where's that letter?"

Probably went through Douglas Allen's shredder, Izzy thinks.

"Let's go back to the *Plastic Man* comic books. Ms. Rademacher said that Duffrey was very pleased with those. Showed them to her. Said he was relieved Cary didn't have any hard feelings. But here's an interesting thing, Roxanne. When he showed Ms. Rademacher the comics, they weren't in the Mylar bags. I have no idea why Tolliver wanted the bags back—or rather, what *story* he told Duffrey about why he wanted those bags back—but he took them."

"So *what?*" Only Roxanne knows what. It's on her face. It's on the way the coffee cup trembles in her hand. "This is a waste of time. I've only got a fifteen-minute coffee break." She starts to get up.

"Sit down," Izzy says, using her best cop voice.

Roxanne sits down.

"Now let's talk about those kiddie porn mags that were found behind Duffrey's furnace. The ones that supposedly had his fingerprints on them. Detective Atta and I assumed they were slicks, like *Playboy* and *Penthouse*, until we looked at the photos of the exhibits entered at the trial. They're actually more like pamphlets, not bound, just stapled together. Done in some sick pedo's basement, most likely, and mailed out in plain brown wrappers from a Mail Boxes Etc. under an assumed name. Cheap paper, pulp stock. Digest-sized."

Roxanne says nothing.

"Pulp stock takes fingerprints, but not very well. They're blurry. The ones ADA Allen submitted as evidence were clear. Every ridge and whorl sharp. There were two on *Uncle Bill's Pride and Joy*, two on

Toddlers, and three on *Bedtime Story*. Now are you ready for the big question, Roxanne?"

Izzy sees that Roxanne is indeed ready. The coffee cup has stopped shaking. She has decided that if someone's ass is going to be grass, it's not going to be hers.

"Were those fingerprints on the *magazines*, or were they on the *bags* the magazines were stored in when they were found behind Alan Duffrey's furnace?"

Roxanne makes one final feeble attempt. "What difference does it make? They *were* Duffrey's fingerprints."

Izzy keeps quiet. Sometimes silence is best.

"They were on the bags," Roxanne says finally. "It wasn't *crooked* or anything, just that when the magazines were photographed in the bags—"

"The fingerprints looked like they were *on* the magazines, didn't they?"

"Yes." Roxanne mutters it into her coffee.

"You and I might have a difference of opinion on what constitutes crooked, Roxanne. Certainly if Allen got a confession letter from Cary Tolliver and trashed it, that would be as crooked as a dog's hind leg. Claire Rademacher—"

"You have no proof of that!"

No, Izzy thinks, *and if it went into the shredder, I never will.*

"Claire Rademacher wasn't on Allen's witness list, so Grinsted, Duffrey's lawyer, never questioned her. She didn't come forward because it never crossed her mind that the comics were important. Basically, your boss concealed evidence, didn't he?"

"They're *all* my bosses," Roxanne says angrily. "Most days I'm like a one-legged woman in an ass-kicking contest."

But Allen said he'd take you with him if he moved up, didn't he?

It's a question Izzy won't ask.

"In fact, it was more than concealment. It was deliberate misdirection, and a contributing factor in Alan Duffrey's murder."

"Some con murdered Duffrey. Stabbed him with a stiletto made from a toothbrush handle." Roxanne pours out her coffee, staining one of her shoes. "We're done here." She gets up and starts back toward the county courthouse.

"Doug Allen won't be moving up to DA," Izzy calls after her. "Never mind the letter from Tolliver he might have trashed, when this comes out, he'll be lucky to get a job in the private sector."

Roxanne doesn't turn, just keeps on trucking. That's all right. Izzy now knows what she (and Tom) had only suspected: Cary Tolliver wasn't the only one responsible for putting Alan Duffrey in the frame. He had help. If "Bill Wilson" knows this, he could consider ADA Allen the guiltiest one.

Izzy raises her face to the day's welcome sunshine, closes her eyes, and sips her latte.

3

Kate and Corrie arrive in Omaha at two in the afternoon, Kate driving most of it with the hammer down. They take half-hour turns playing the Sirius XM, Kate bellowing 80s rock anthems at the top of her lungs, then Corrie singing along with Willie, Waylon, and Shania. Tonight's gig for *A Woman's Testament* is at the Holland Performing Arts Center. Two thousand seats and, as Corrie gleefully reports, "A butt in every one!"

Corrie stands in her accustomed position, behind the house manager with his earphones and little wall-mounted TV screen, as Kate strides onstage to thunderous applause that drowns out the booing section. She hasn't bought a new Borsalino or even ordered one. Tonight she's wearing a red Cornhuskers lid. She sweeps it off in her usual bow, grabs the mic from the podium (at every stop Corrie emphasizes that it *must* be a cordless mic and not a lav; Kate considers lavs unreliable), and walks out to the apron of the stage.

"Woman Power!"

"*Woman Power!*" the audience roars back.

"You can do better! Let me *hear* you, Omaha!"

"*WOMAN POWER!*" the crowd bellows. Most of it, anyway.

"Good, that's good," Kate says. She's moving around. Pacing. Brilliant red pants suit that matches the hat. Corrie found it for her in Fashion Freak. "That's great. Go on and sit down. I need to testify, Omaha. I feel the spirit strong in me tonight, so sit."

stationers' shop, allowing you to put your own message on the outside and also on the inside. What's on the outside of this one is A BASIC CARD FOR BASIC BITCHES.

"Nice," Kate says. "What's on the inside? Best wishes from your crazy-as-fuck friend?"

A fourth photo is passed across the desk. Printed inside, once again in caps: HELL AWAITS THE DECEIVER.

5

On the night of Kate's Omaha gig, Chrissy Stewart is staying at the Sunset Motel on the outskirts of Omaha. It's a pit. Such fly-by-night businesses still take cash, and sometimes rent rooms by the hour. Chrissy will stay the night, but be up bright and early the next day. She wants to beat the baby-killing bitches to their next stop.

Or not, if the anthrax has done its job.

In Room 6, Chrissy takes off the gray pants, white shirt, and blue blazer that served her as an usher's uniform—probably wasted effort, the stupid rent-a-cop hardly looked up from his book. She takes off the wig and the bathing cap she wears beneath it. She goes into the plastic-walled closet that serves as a bathroom, and washes the light makeup from her face. Tomorrow she'll throw the usher clothes, plus the wig and bathing cap, in a rest area dumpster miles from here.

Chrissy can't murder *all* the women who want to regain the right to kill the next generation, but she and her brother can get the one who makes the most noise, who stands so stridently and shamelessly against God's law. Although childless herself, Chrissy knows what the equally childless Kate McKay doesn't: the loss of a child is like the loss of heaven.

"Don't think about it," she mutters. "You know what will happen if you do."

She certainly does. Thinking about the loss of the child will bring memories. A limp hand for instance, fingernails sparkling in the morning sun. It will bring on a headache, one of the bad ones. As if her brain is trying to rip itself in two.

She travels with two suitcases. From one she takes a shorty nightgown, then lies down and turns off the light. Outside, to the west, an endless freight train is thundering by. *Maybe Kate's dead already. Kate and the bitch she runs with. Maybe my work is done.*

So thinking, Chrissy drifts off to sleep.

6

Corrie has asked for all the pictures the sheriff showed them to be forwarded to her email, and the sheriff agreed. The next morning, Kate comes into Corrie's room. Kate looks both younger and more vulnerable in her pajamas.

"Had enough?"

Corrie shakes her head.

Kate flashes a grin. "Screw that bitch if she can't take a joke, right?"

"Right. FIDO."

Kate frowns. "What?"

"FIDO. Marine saying. It stands for 'fuck it, drive on.'"

"Good one," Kate says, "but we've got some time off before we have to FIDO to Des Moines. Thank God. There's a sports bar down the street, we could watch the Yankees play Cleveland. Day game. Split a pitcher of suds. Interested?"

"Sure," Corrie says.

"Hey, wait—are you old enough to drink?"

Corrie gives her a look.

Kate bursts out laughing.

7

Kate and Corrie watch the Yankees play the Guardians at DJ's Dugout Sports Bar in Omaha. In Buckeye City, Dean Miter is watching the game in Happy, the bar where John Ackerly works most days. Dean is an eighteen-year veteran of the Buckeye City police force and has been slated by Lew Warwick to be the starting pitcher for the police team in the Guns and Hoses softball game at the end of the month. Why not? Dean hurled three shutout innings last year before the FD broke through and scored six runs against two relief pitchers.

Dean is off-duty today. He's drinking his second beer-and-a-shot, watching the game, bothering nobody. Someone sits down next to him at the bar, giving his shoulder a hard bump. Beer sloshes on the bar top.

"Oh, pawdon *me*," the newcomer says.

Dean looks around and sees, glory be, the fireman he struck out to end his stint in last year's game. Before that game, this fellow had yelled across the field that he'd never seen such a bunch of blue pussies. After Dean struck him out, Dean had called, "Who's the pussy now, Bush League?"

"Watch yourself," Dean says now.

The fireman, a burly fellow with a big head, gives Dean a look of exaggerated distress. "Didn't I say pawdon me? Why so touchy? Could it be because we're going to light you up again this year?"

"Pipe down, fool. I'm trying to watch the game."

The bartender—not John Ackerly, it's John's day off, but just as adept at seeing when trouble may be brewing—ambles over. "All friends here, right?"

"Right, just yankin his chain," says the fireman, and when Dean raises his shot-glass to his mouth, the fireman doesn't just bump him but shoulder-checks him good and hard. Instead of drinking his whiskey, Dean finds himself wearing it.

"Oh, pawdon *me*," the fireman says. He's grinning. "I seem to have—"

Dean spins on his stool and hauls off, fist wrapped around the shot-glass. The big-headed fireman sees the punch coming—Dean isn't exactly speedy—and ducks. Mr. Big Head's not especially speedy, either, and instead of swishing harmlessly over his head, Dean's fist connects with the broad shelf of the fireman's brow. Mr. Big Head tumbles off his barstool.

"That's it, that's it!" the bartender says. "Take it outside if you want to continue this!"

Dean Miter has no intention of taking it outside or continuing anything. He unrolls his fist with a cry of pain. Three of his fingers are dislocated and one is fractured. The shot-glass has broken in his hand. There are deep lacerations from which fangs of glass protrude. Blood patters down on the bar.

Dean's pitching days are over.

Chapter 6

1

After a string of pleasant May weather, Monday the 19th dawns bleak and drizzly. While Holly is doing more insurance paperwork (and struggling to stay awake; she has a problem with rainy Mondays), she gets a call on her personal. It's Izzy.

"I've got something for you, but I don't want to send it by text or email. Those things can come back to haunt lowly bureaucrats like me. Can you come see me?"

Any excuse to ditch the paperwork is a good excuse. Holly asks if Izzy is at the cop shop.

"Nope. Bell College. Stucky Memorial Gym."

"What are you doing there?"

"Long story. I'll tell you when you get here."

2

Holly finds Izzy in the Bell College fieldhouse, dressed in sweatpants, sneakers, and a Police Department tee. Her hair is tied back and she's wearing a fielder's glove on her left hand. Tom Atta is crouched down about forty feet away. He pounds his fist into a catcher's mitt, then holds it up at chest level. "Throw the dropper. You're warm enough. Bring it, Iz."

Izzy's more than warm enough, Holly judges; there's a tree of sweat down the back of her shirt as she winds up and lets loose. The ball starts out high, probably out of the strike zone, then drops what looks like three inches. It's like a magic trick.

"Nice one," Tom calls, "but you have to start it out lower, or else it's gonna wind up in some fireman's wheelhouse. One more."

He tosses the ball back. This time the pitch she throws starts out at the height of an imaginary batter's upper arms, then does that same crazy three-inch drop.

"Perfect," Tom says, rising from his crouch with a grimace. "If they can hit that, probably they won't, but if they do, they'll beat it into the ground. Save your arm. Your company's here."

"Save your knees, old fella," Izzy says with a grin. She takes a return throw from Tom and walks over to Holly. "We'd be outside on the softball field, if not for the rain." She flaps her shirt against her neck. "This place is too hot."

"What exactly are you doing?" Holly asks.

"My master's bidding."

Tom joins them. "She means Warwick. Captain of this year's PD softball team. Also our boss."

Izzy leads them over to the bleachers and sits down, rubbing her shoulder. "Lew has drafted me to pitch in this year's Guns and Hoses game because Dean Miter—who was *supposed* to pitch—broke his hand in a bar fight downtown."

"The bar's called Happy, but Dean ain't," Tom says.

Holly knows the bar well but doesn't say so. Tom takes off his mitt and shakes his hand in the air. The palm is red. "You can really bring it when you get warmed up, Iz."

"I'll choke once I'm facing real batters," Izzy says glumly. "I haven't pitched since college, and that was a *long* time ago."

"That dropper's still nasty," Tom says. "There's your out pitch."

Holly knew Izzy was in shape, but this side of her—the athletic side—is a surprise.

Izzy gets up, stretches, and plants her fisted hands in the small of her back. "I'm too old for this shit. Come with me, Holly."

Izzy leads her into the women's locker room. Izzy spins the combo on one of the lockers. Her street clothes are hanging inside, along with her Glock. Her purse is on the shelf. She rummages and brings out a folded sheet of paper. "Here. If you get caught with this, you didn't get it from me."

"Of course not."

Izzy sighs. "Of course, who else *would* you have gotten it from? Lew knows we're friends." She brightens. "On the other hand, he can't fire me, at least not until after the Guns and Hoses game."

Holly unfolds the paper and scans it.

Andrew Groves (1), Philip Jacoby (2), Jabari Wentworth (3), Amy Gottschalk (4), Ellis Finkel (5), Turner Kelly (6), Corinna Ashford (7), Letitia Overton (8), Donald Gibson (9), Belinda "Bunny" Jones (10), Steven Furst (11), Brad Lowry (12).

Judge: Irving Witterson

Prosecuting Attorney: Douglas Allen

"For whatever it's worth," Izzy says.

"You didn't add Duffrey's lawyer. I guess I could look it up—"

"No need. His name's Russell Grinsted, and I doubt if he's the guilty one Bill Wilson wrote about. So far as I can tell, Grinsted did everything he could to get Duffrey off, once his client made it clear he wanted to take it to trial."

"Could he have made a deal?"

"According to Grinsted, yes. Evidence was thin, the argument that the shit was planted was fairly strong, if not powerful. He says Al Tantleff, the big boss, would have allowed Duffrey to plead down to one count. Might have gotten a year in prison, might even have gotten supervised release along with community service. But Duffrey claimed he was totally innocent . . . framed . . . set up. He especially didn't want to go on the Registry, which a guilty plea would have entailed. Tantleff handed the case off to Doug Allen, and Allen took it from there. Tom and I need to talk to Grinsted again, just to fill him in, and we *really* need to talk to Allen."

"About?"

"About what I found out from Claire Rademacher. She's—"

"The chief cashier at the bank where Duffrey and Tolliver worked."

"You've been digging, Gibney."

Holly gives an uncomfortable smile. "Not enough to do."

"The DA's office found out something from Rademacher." Izzy explains about the Mylar comic book bags, which Cary Tolliver took back after Alan Duffrey handled them.

"Allen kept the Rademacher woman off his witness list. Why wouldn't he? She couldn't help his case, only hurt it. Which left it up to Grinsted to find out what she knew, and he never did."

"No investigator this Grinsted could call?" Holly herself has only worked for criminal lawyers on a couple of occasions, but she's pretty sure *she* would have located Claire Rademacher and heard her story.

"Nope, Russell Grinsted's a one-man band. He talked to all the witnesses on Allen's list and depo'd some of them—including Tolliver, who wasn't sick yet and hadn't had his come-to-Jesus moment—but he didn't get to Rademacher. Probably didn't see any need to. When he finds out what Allen was hiding from him, he's going to be furious."

"Poopy behavior."

"Poopy but not out of bounds. A prosecutor trashing a confession letter would have been—if Allen actually did it—but playing three-card monte with witnesses is classic prosecution strategy. Defense lawyers do it, too. What *is* out of bounds are the photographs Allen submitted at trial. They purported to be of Duffrey's fingerprints on the kiddie porn magazines. They were actually photos of Duffrey's fingerprints on the *bags*, carefully lit so you can't see the bags themselves."

"He falsified the evidence!" Holly exclaims. This kind of trickery always makes her furious. It's not so different from how some of the insurance companies with whom she does business operate . . . including the one with the talking donkey.

"He'll smile and say he did no such thing when I confront him. He'll say there's a difference between *claiming* something and letting people—in this case the jury—draw their own conclusions. He'll say that all he did was point out the fingerprints were Duffrey's. He never specifically said they were on the porno mags themselves."

Holly is flabbergasted. "Can he do that?"

Izzy gives a sharklike smile. "No. It's an ethical violation. The state Supreme Court won't disbar him, but I think he'll be subject to disciplinary revocation, which is *tantamount* to disbarment. Because, see, Alan Duffrey can't ask for another trial, can he?"

"No."

"Confession letter or no confession letter, Douglas Allen is never going to sit in the County Attorney's chair. But right now that's not the important thing."

"You think Bill Wilson considers *him* the guilty party."

"If he knows about the dirty trick with the bags and the mags, I think it's likely. If he believes Tolliver actually did write a letter confessing to the frame in February, it's almost sure. And Tolliver told that podcaster, Buckeye Brandon, about the letter. Brandon called it the *purported* letter on his pod, but still . . ."

"Still, ADA Allen could be in big trouble," Holly finishes.

Izzy strips off her shirt and wipes sweat from her face with it. "I'm going to take a shower."

"I'll leave you to it."

"And Holly?"

She doesn't need to say it. Holly zips a finger across her lips and turns an invisible key.

"One other thing. You said you knew someone in the local recovery programs. Have you talked to him? Or her?"

"Not lately," Holly says, which is technically not a lie, but once she's out of the gym, she calls John Ackerly. He answers on the first ring.

"Yo, Holly."

"Sorry to bother you while you're working, John."

"No worries. It's slow today."

"Did you get a chance to talk to that guy you mentioned?"

"Big Book Mike. Tell you what, I haven't. I kind of forgot."

"So did I," Holly admits.

"I will, but I probably won't get anything out of him. He never shuts up in meetings, but he takes the anonymity business very seriously."

"Ah. Okay, understood."

"The Rev sometimes hits the Straight Circle meeting on Wednesdays, then goes to The Flame afterward. You know that place? Little coffee shop on Buell Street?"

"Yes." She's had coffee there herself. It's close to her office.

"I'll go to the meeting, and if he's there, I'll ask him afterward. Ask a few others if he's not. You're interested in someone calling himself Bill, or Bill W., right?"

"Right."

"Anything else?"

"Ask this Big Book Mike if he's heard anyone expressing anger about the murder of Alan Duffrey."

3

Tapperville is a pleasant, well-to-do little town, mixed rural and suburban, about twenty miles north of the city. It's where Michael Rafferty—sometimes known as the Rev, sometimes as Big Book Mike—hangs his hat when he's not attending AA and NA meetings all over Upsala County. It's also the home of the Tapperville Rec Center, where there are three Little League fields and one Senior League field. All are lighted, and the Rec is only half a mile from the Rev's house.

Trig has scouted the area carefully but could only hope beforehand that it wouldn't rain on this Tuesday evening. Bad weather would scrub the baseball games, which would in turn scrub his plans. But the day has been cloudless and warm after yesterday's showers. Trig won't say this is God's stamp of approval, but he won't say it's not.

Games are going on at all four fields, and both parking lots are almost full. Trig slips his unremarkable Toyota into one of the few remaining slots, dons a pair of sunglasses and a Cleveland Cavaliers hat, and gets out. He's wearing a gray jacket that's as forgettable as his gray car. In one of the pockets is a .38 Smith & Wesson revolver. He would prefer his .22, but has decided—reluctantly—that the Rev can't be the fourth juror stand-in. The Rev takes the Eleventh Tradition ("We need always maintain personal anonymity") very seriously, but is Trig willing to risk his mission on the belief that Big Book Mike hasn't let slip to anyone that he is coming tonight? No.

Why did I ever say that thing about how the person I was mourning died in lockup?

His thought, but in his long-gone daddy's voice.

"Because I was upset," he mutters as he turns up the collar of his jacket and starts walking down the street to the little one-bedroom house where the Rev lives.

Even if the Rev hasn't told anyone that Trig is coming for a counseling session, they have been in meetings together. Mostly out of the city, but still. If Trig leaves a juror's name in Mike's hand, someone might connect the two of them. It's extremely unlikely, because Trig doesn't ever give his own first name at meetings, but unlikely isn't impossible.

Better to make it look like a robbery. It means killing an extra, but Trig has made his peace with that.

Killing really does get easier, it seems.

4

The Rev meets Trig at the door and asks an unexpected question. "Where's your car?"

Trig fumbles, then recovers. "Oh. Right. I left it at the Rec. Didn't want to clog up your driveway."

"Shouldn't have bothered, mine's in the garage, plenty of room. Come in, come in."

The Rev leads Trig into a cozy little living room. Framed on one wall is "How It Works," from the Big Book. On another there's a photo of AA's founders, Bill W. and Dr. Bob, with their arms around each other.

"Would you like a drink?" the Rev asks.

"Martini, very dry."

The Rev bursts out laughing. It reminds Trig of the way the Talking Donkey laughs in those insurance ads: hee-haw, hee-haw. The Rev even has the Talking Donkey's big teeth.

"I'd take a Coke, if you have one."

Reminding himself to keep track of everything he touches because of fingerprints. So far: nothing.

"No Coke, but I have ginger ale."

"Perfect. Could I use your bathroom?"

"Right down the hall. Is your problem about this friend of yours who died in prison?"

"That's the one," Trig says, thinking that if the nosy son-of-a-buck's fate wasn't already sealed, that would do the job. "Excuse me."

Although the Rev is a lifelong bachelor, the bathroom is a girly pink. Trig couldn't pee if his life depended on it—his bladder is high and tight—but he flushes the toilet, then pulls a hand towel (pink) from the rod and wipes the flush lever. He takes the .38 from his jacket pocket and wraps the towel around it, the way Vito Corleone did in *Godfather 2*, when he shot Don Fanucci. Will that muffle the report in real life? Trig can only hope so, even though the .38 is a bigger gun than his Taurus .22.

At least there's no house next door.

With a prayer to the God of his understanding, Trig steps out of the bathroom and goes down the short hall to the living room. The Rev is coming in from the kitchen with two glasses of ginger ale on a tin tray. He gives Trig a smile and says, "You forgot to leave the tow—"

Trig shoots him. The shot is muffled but still loud. In the movie, the towel caught on fire, but this is real life and it doesn't. The Rev stops, looking comically amazed, and at first Trig thinks he's missed because there's no blood. Thinks it hit the wall or something. Then, very slowly, the tray tilts. The glasses of ginger ale slide off and hit the living room carpet. One of them breaks. The other doesn't. Rev drops the tray. He's still staring at Trig with amazement.

"You shot me!"

Oh God I'll have to shoot him again. Like the woman and the wino.

The Rev turns around, and now Trig can see blood. It's coming from a hole in the middle of the Rev's plaid shirt. "*Shot* me!"

Trig re-wraps the towel (not much of a silencer but better than nothing) and raises the gun again. Before he can fire, the Rev collapses to his knees, then falls on his face in the doorway to the kitchen. One of his feet spasms and kicks the unbroken glass. It rolls a foot or so, still dribbling ginger ale, then stops.

Trig goes to the Rev and feels for a pulse on the big man's neck. He can't find one and thinks the man is dead. Then the one eye Trig can see slips open. "Shot me," the Rev whispers, and blood trickles from his mouth. "Why?"

Trig doesn't want to shoot again and decides he doesn't have to. There are two pillows at either end of the small couch. Embroidered on one is TAKE IT EASY. On the other, LET GO AND LET GOD. Trig takes LET GO AND LET GOD and puts it over the Rev's face. Holds it down for a minute or maybe a little longer. His Daddy-voice says, *This would be a bad time for someone to show up*.

When he takes the pillow away, the Rev's one visible eye is open but glazing. Trig darts a finger at it. There's no reflexive blink. He's gone.

"Sorry, Rev," Trig says.

He rummages in the Rev's rear pocket, extracts the man's wallet, and looks inside. Thirty bucks and a Visa card. He puts the wallet in his own pocket. He strips off the Rev's Shinola wristwatch and pockets that as well. He goes into the Rev's bedroom. He uses the towel to open the closet slider, pulling it hard enough to knock it off its rails. He knocks the clothes—mostly jeans and cheap shirts—to the floor in a jangle of coat hangers. He uses the towel to open the bedside table. Inside it he finds a Bible, a Big Book, *Twelve Steps and Twelve Traditions*, a heap of AA sobriety medallions, forty dollars, a pair of what look like drugstore eyeglasses, and a photograph of the Rev sucking a young man's penis. Trig thinks he's seen the young man at meetings. He's maybe named Troy. Trig takes the money, and after a moment's thought, takes the picture. He wouldn't want the police to find it. The young man could get in trouble.

In the kitchen he finds an appointment book, and printed in capital letters on the square for the 20th is TRIG 7 PM. This presents a vexing dilemma. Would a random thief take something as valueless as an appointment book? No, somebody might notice it's gone. A housekeeper, for instance, if the Rev has one. Would a thief take *one page* of an appointment book? Absolutely not. When Trig goes back through the months, he finds several other appointments carefully printed in the same caps. Probably other counseling sessions. Or trysts.

What to do?

His first impulse is to scribble out a bunch of random names and times—including his own—thinking this is what the Rev might do if people didn't show up for their scheduled "sessions." He picks up the pen beside the appointment book to start scratching, then puts it down again. There may be other appointment books for other years stored somewhere, possibly in the attic or basement or garage. If the cops find those and find no names scratched out, they'll suspect something, won't they? They'll look at today's date with special care, and if they can do some scientific juju to see through the scribble over his name . . . infrared, or something . . .

He barks a laugh. To have committed four murders and then find himself balked by an address book! Absurd!

You're an idiot, the Daddy-voice says, and Trig can almost see him.

"Maybe, and maybe this is all your fault," Trig says.

Hearing his voice settles him and an idea strikes. He picks up the pen and bends toward the square with his name in it. *Be careful*, he tells himself. *Do this as if your life depends on it, because maybe it does. But don't hesitate once you start. Don't flinch. It has to look right.*

5

By the time Trig leaves the house, it's almost dark. He walks back toward the lights surrounding the baseball fields and the sounds of people cheering. No one sees him, which he takes as a sign that his daddy approves of both his mission and the small but crucial alteration he made to the Rev's appointment book. Daddy is dead, but his approval still matters. It shouldn't, but it does.

Trig gets into his car and drives away, pausing only to wipe the .38 and throw it into Crooked Creek. The Rev's wallet and watch also go in. Back at Elm Grove, he fishes an empty tomato soup can out of the trash, puts the photograph in it, and sets it on fire. The trip to Tapperville has been a necessary detour, but now he can get back on track with his main mission.

He finds he's actually looking forward to it. If it's also how he looked forward to the next drink, so what?

6

Izzy has never had anything to do with ADA Doug Allen, but Tom has. "The guy's a dork," he opines as they walk down the hall to Allen's office.

Allen is a tall, slope-shouldered man who is cultivating a goatee that doesn't suit his thin, pale face. There's no secretary or assistant; he shows them in himself. His desk is stringently neat, nothing on it but his desktop computer and a framed picture of his wife and two little girls. On the wall is his diploma and a photo of Allen with JD Vance, their arms around each other's shoulders.

Tom Atta takes the lead, first showing Allen the letter from "Bill Wilson," then outlining the case so far. When he recaps the part about Tolliver claiming he wrote a letter confessing ("Addressed to *you*, Mr. Allen"), a flush rises in Allen's pale cheeks, starting at the jawline and ascending to his temples. Izzy has never seen a man go red in this way and finds it fascinating. He reminds her of someone, but for the moment she can't think who.

"He was lying. There was no letter, as I told that absurd Buckeye Brandon fellow when he asked for a comment." Allen sits forward in his chair, hands so tightly clasped the knuckles are white. "You are just bringing this to me now? After three murders related to the Duffrey case?"

"At first we didn't relate the names in the hands of the murder victims to the Duffrey jurors," Tom says. "Those names were kept quiet, like the names of the jurors in the Trump and Ghislaine Maxwell trials."

"But when you *did*?" Allen shakes his head in disgust. "Jesus, what kind of detectives are you?"

And what kind of a prosecutor are you*?* Izzy thinks.

Tom says, "We didn't come to you immediately for two reasons, Mr. Allen. First and foremost, because this office is kind of a sieve. Information comes in and then flows right out."

"I resent that!"

"Rodney and Emily Harris are a case in point," Tom says. "Once your office had it, everyone had it, starting with your pal Buckeye Brandon."

"That was not my case and he's not my *pal*!"

"What about the porn magazines found in Alan Duffrey's basement? That *was* your case, and pre-trial it was all over the newspapers and the internet."

"I have no idea who leaked that information, and if I did know, that person would be looking for another job."

Izzy suddenly realizes who Allen reminds her of: Alan Rickman, who played the principal bad guy in *Die Hard*. She can't remember that character's name, although she's sure Holly could.

Tom forges ahead. "This isn't a matter for the County Attorney's office as of now, Mr. Allen. Until we make an arrest, it's strictly a police matter. None of the other jurors have been informed, because we don't think they are personally at risk."

Izzy says, "This psycho isn't killing jurors, he's killing people in their names. His victims are—"

"Proxies. I understand that, Detective Jaynes. I'm not stupid."

"According to Wilson's letter," Izzy says, "he plans to kill thirteen innocents plus—or including, the letter's not clear, perhaps intentionally—one guilty. Judge Witterson could be the one he thinks is guilty, but more likely—"

"Tolliver," Allen breaks in. "The man who framed him." He spreads his hands as if to say, *There you go, I solved your case for you.*

"Cary Tolliver died in Kiner Hospital early this morning," Tom says. "When it comes to the one he considers guilty, we think *you're* the likely target."

"Why?" But Allen's eyes say he thinks he knows why. The letter (the *purported* letter).

But Izzy goes in a different direction. "Duffrey's fingerprints weren't on those kiddie porn pamphlets, were they?"

No reply from Allen, but Izzy can read his thought: *Nobody said they were.*

"They were on Mylar comic book bags that Tolliver took back after Duffrey handled them. You led the jury to believe the prints were on the pamphlets themselves."

There's a brief look of panic in ADA Allen's eyes as he considers the ramifications of what they know . . . and who they could tell. Then he gathers himself. "I . . . that is to say, I and my second . . . never lied about the location of those prints. It was incumbent on Russell Grinsted to—"

"Save your justifications for the board that will decide on whether or not to sanction you," Izzy says. "Our concern is whether or not this Bill Wilson knows you railroaded Alan Duffrey and got him killed. The letter Tolliver might have lied about—"

"Of *course* he lied! He wanted his fifteen minutes of fame by getting a guilty man out of Big Stone! Name in the papers! Interviews on TV! Were we going to put him on trial for lying? Of course not, and he knew it! Not when he was dying already!"

"I'm guessing Bill Wilson took that into account," Izzy says. "But the mischief with the fingerprints, Mr. Allen . . . that was all you."

"I resent—"

"Resent all you want," Tom says. "We want to see your files on the case. We need to find Bill Wilson before he kills more innocent people. And, quite likely, *you*."

Doug Allen stares at them. Words are his living, but at the moment he seems to have nothing to say.

Izzy, however, does. "Are you interested in police protection until we catch this guy?"

7

That afternoon John Ackerly attends the Straight Circle meeting on Buell. It's a lively discussion about how to deal with the nearest and dearest who are still drinking and/or using, and John enjoys listening to various points of view. Big Book Mike Rafferty isn't there, however, nor is he at The Flame coffee shop afterward.

Because John's at odds and sods for the rest of the day—also because he likes Holly and is sorry he forgot what she asked him to do—he decides to take a run out to Tapperville. He doesn't know exactly where the Rev lives, but it has to be near the Rec, because the Rev has a barbecue there for a bunch of Program people every year on Bill Wilson's birthday. Which, according to the Rev, should be a national holiday (a sentiment John actually agrees with).

John asks at the nearby Piggly Wiggly. The clerk doesn't know, but a postman outside does. He's sitting on a bench in the shade and drinking an end-of-shift Nehi.

"Go on down that way about a quarter of a mile." The postman points. "Number 649. Little house sitting all by itself. Turdy-brown paintjob."

"Thanks," John says.

"You a friend of his?"

"Kind of."

"Does he ever shut up?"

John smiles. "Rarely."

"Take him his mail, would you? Box is full. I had to really stuff in today's."

John says he will and drives on down to the Rev's house, which is indeed turdy-brown. The mailbox is stuffed full of bills, catalogs, and magazines, including a copy of this month's AA *Grapevine*. John parks in the driveway and gets out, carrying the Rev's latest charge of mail in his hand. He goes to the back door, climbs the steps, and goes to ring the bell. His thumb freezes before it can press the button. His hand opens and he drops the Rev's mail on his shoes. There's a window in the door, and looking across the kitchen, he can see Mike Rafferty's feet. The door is unlocked. He goes in and makes sure the Rev is dead. Then he goes back outside, picks up mail that will never be read, and dials 911.

Chapter 7

1

May 22nd. The day after the Des Moines disaster.

Corrie lets herself into Kate's mini-suite with a key card that works for both rooms. She comes bearing coffee, croissants, and the morning paper. Kate is looking out the window. There's nothing to see out there but the parking lot, Corrie knows because she has the same view, but Kate doesn't look around when the door closes. Her iPad is open on the table next to the window.

"Maybe I should cancel the rest of the tour," Kate says to the window. "Ever since Reno, if it wasn't for bad luck I'd have no luck at all."

Hey, I'm here, too, Corrie thinks. *Been here from the jump. And you weren't the one who got Clorox thrown in her face. Not the one who could have inhaled anthrax. That was me, Kate. That was me.*

As if hearing her thought (and Corrie believes such things are possible), Kate turns from the window and gives her a smile. There's not much wattage in it. "So are you the Jonah, or is that me?"

"Neither of us. You're not seriously thinking of canceling the tour, are you?"

Kate pours a cup of coffee. "Actually, after last night, I am. Have you seen this morning's paper?"

"No, have you? You left it outside your door. I picked it up." A bear for her news, is Kate McKay. Ordinarily.

"Got it on my iPad. Didn't even have to cough up to get past the paywall. First five articles free, such a deal. I'm on the front page. My photo right next to one of a woman screaming in pain."

"If you cancel the tour, your people—*our* people—will call you a coward. *Their* people will gloat. You're a loser either way. The only way you win is if you keep on keeping on."

Kate looks at her fixedly. Corrie, unaccustomed to such close and protracted scrutiny, looks down and starts spreading jam on a croissant.

"What do your parents say, Corrie?"

"I haven't called them. Don't need to." Because she knows what they'd say. At this point, even her father might tell her it was time to cut her losses.

Kate gives a humorless laugh. "Either the last few days have changed you, or you were tougher than I thought all along. When we started out, I thought you wouldn't say boo to a goose."

Corrie thinks, *That's one of the reasons you picked me. Isn't it?* A new insight, and not a particularly welcome one.

"So which is it, Cor?"

"I don't know. Maybe a little of both."

Corrie can feel a blush heating her cheeks, but Kate doesn't see it. She's turned back to the window, hands clasped at the small of her back. She makes Corrie think of a general surveying a battlefield that's been contended for and lost. That might be overblown, but in the current case maybe not. What happened last night after the gig was an authentic horror show.

She glances at Kate's iPad, which shows the front page of *The Des Moines Register*. Looking at the juxtaposition of the two women shown there makes Corrie wince. Kate on the right, smiling brilliantly (not to say sexily), the screaming, disheveled woman on the left, wearing a Woman Power tee.

Looking out the window, Kate says, "Who knew there was so much fucking Iowa?"

"The Iowans," Corrie says. She's still looking at the screaming woman. Disheveled or not, she looks like a librarian. The kind who'd stand up to would-be book-banners politely but firmly.

"It was a good gig, wasn't it, Cor?"

"It was." Nothing but the truth.

"Until it wasn't."

Also nothing but the truth.

2

The usual scrum was waiting for them outside the stage door; women who wanted selfies, women who wanted autographs, speculators with rarities they wanted signed, women who wanted to show off their Woman Power tats, women who just wanted to shout *I love you, Kate!*

Their security guy in Des Moines was no Ham Wilts. Sergeant Elmore Packer was young, strong, alert. And after what happened in Omaha, he was taking no chances. Which turned out to be a problem.

Packer saw what appeared to be the barrel of a gun poking out from the crowd of jostling, excited women, and didn't hesitate. He grabbed the supposed gun barrel, not registering in his amped-up state that it was glass rather than steel. The woman on the other end came with it, either too shocked to let go or afraid someone was trying to steal the rather expensive present she had brought for her idol. Packer grabbed her, whirled her around, and fractured her arm in so doing. The bottle she was carrying fell to the pavement and exploded, spraying a crowd of screaming, horrified women with Dom Pérignon 2015, a very good year. Three dozen cell phones recorded the moment for posterity.

The woman with the broken arm is Cynthia Herron, not a librarian but the assistant superintendent of the Polk County DMV. An authentic Good Person, she does charity work in her church and volunteers at a city animal shelter. She suffers from type-2 diabetes and osteoporosis. The caption beneath her screaming face reads: *I just wanted to bring her something nice.*

"*Breitbart* didn't waste any time," Kate says. "You know what they call me, right?"

Corrie knows: RJ, for ratchet-jaw.

"They say, and I quote, 'RJ is against police brutality except when the brutality in question is employed to protect her precious butt.' Nice, huh?"

Corrie says nothing, so Kate employs her chick telepathy. "Okay, the pity party's over. You're right, the show must go on, so how do we handle this? I have a couple of ideas, but I want yours."

"Start with a statement. There's a ton of press downstairs. Something along the lines of how everyone's on edge after what happened in Reno and Omaha."

"What else? Show me how much you've learned."

Corrie is simultaneously amused and resentful. It crosses her mind that by the end of August, which is how long the tour is supposed to last, she might actually dislike Kate. If they were together until Christmas (*please no*, she thinks reflexively), dislike might become outright loathing. Is it always that way with famous people, or only famous people who are totally fixated on their causes?

"I'm waiting," Kate says.

"We need to go straight to the hospital and visit Ms. Herron. If she'll see us, that is."

"She will," Kate says with utter confidence.

And she does.

3

Kate gives Cynthia Herron a signed Woman Power shirt. ("To make up for the one that got champagne stains on it.") One reporter and an accompanying photographer are present, and in tomorrow's *Register* there will be a photo of Herron not screaming in pain but holding Kate's hand and looking up at her with starry eyes.

Kate answers a few more questions in the hospital lobby. Then they're back in the truck and bound for Iowa City. No bustling metropolis, maybe, but Kate's motto is "when you go small, you get big rewards."

"I think that went all right," she says.

Corrie nods. "It did."

"I want you to get on your iPad, hon. Research the next stops on our tour. We need somebody watching out for us, you were right about that, but no more men. Packer meant well, but the big strong man protecting the damsel in distress . . ." Kate shakes her head. "Wrong look. You agree?"

Corrie does.

"No more men," Kate says, "and no more cops."

"Who does that leave?"

"Fifty per cent of the population. You figure it out."

And before they get to Iowa City, Corrie thinks she has.

4

While Kate and Corrie are on their way to the Athens of the Midwest, Holly, Izzy, and Barbara Robinson are having lunch in Dingley Park. Barbara regales them with stories of Sista Bessie's rehearsals at the Sam's Club and tells them about how she and Betty are actually collaborating on turning Barbara's poem "Lowtown Jazz" into a song.

"Except she just wants to call it 'Jazz,'" Barbara says. "She says that when she plays the Mingo, starting the thirty-first, she'll sing 'Jazz, jazz, that razzmatazz, play that Lowtown jazz.' But when she's in Cleveland—"

"It'll be that Hough jazz," Izzy says. "And in New York, that Harlem jazz. The personal touch. I like it."

"That's not all," Barbara says. "One of Betty's roadies had a heart attack, not too bad but he's got to take it easy for awhile. I talked to Acey Felton, he's in charge of the crew, and asked if I could take Batty's place."

"Batty," Holly says, and chomps into her Chicago dog. "That's quite a handle."

"His real name is Curtis James, but the story is that when he was on a Black Sabbath tour, he . . . never mind, it's just that roadies have the best nicknames and the best stories. I'm writing them down in a notebook. Might do something with them, I don't know what. Anyhow, Acey made me roll one of the monitors and lift it, and when he saw I could, he hired me! I think Betty—you know, Sista—thinks having a poet move trusses and roll amps is sort of funny."

This is all very interesting, but Holly can no longer rein in her curiosity. "What do you know about the man who was murdered out in Tapperville, Izzy? Was he Bill W.'s work?"

Izzy gives a meaningful look at Barbara.

"I think you can trust Barb," Holly says. "She was offered a lot of money to contribute to Buckeye Brandon's *House of Horrors* podcast about the Harrises, and turned it down." Nor is that all. Barbara once saw something in the elevator of Holly's building that was beyond all rationality, and has never said a word about it . . . unless you count the title poem of her book, which is of course about the nightmare who went (in Buckeye City, at least) by the name of Chet Ondowsky.

"I can take a walk over to the softball field, if you want," Barbara offers.

"No need. If Holly says you can keep quiet, that's good enough for me."

"What you hear here, who you see here, when you leave here, let it stay here," Holly murmurs.

"What's that?" Izzy asks.

"It's what they say at the end of Alcoholics Anonymous meetings. I know about it from my friend John Ackerly."

Izzy's eyebrows go up almost all the way to her hairline. "You *know* the guy who found Rafferty's body?"

"In a way, I'm responsible for him finding it. Remember I said I knew someone in the Program? That was John. He told me if anyone knew who might want payback for Duffrey's death, it would be a guy called Big Book Mike, or the Rev. He lost his church because of an opioid habit and John says he pretty much replaced church with AA and NA. Did you find a juror's name in his hand?"

"Holly, you're a spook. Always one step ahead of me."

Barbara says, "She's got mad skills, all right."

"No name in the dead guy's hand. A Tapperville cop and a detective from the County Sheriff's office responded to your friend's call. They vibed it as a robbery. Wallet gone, wristwatch gone, clothes knocked off their hangers in the closet, bedside drawers open. They filed a report with us, and I thought of Bill Wilson right away."

Barbara: "That's the bad guy?"

"It's the alias he's using," Holly says. And to Izzy: "This Rafferty must have known something, or Bill Wilson thought he did. He was killed to shut him up." An uncomfortable thought comes to her: If John Ackerly had gone out to Tapperville earlier, he might also have been killed. *And I'd be responsible.*

Holly leans toward Izzy. She's not good at invading the space of others (or having hers invaded), but this is important. "Can you make it your case? I know Tapperville is county jurisdiction, but—"

"We get along pretty well with the state cops and the Sheriff's Department. They're actually covering for us the night of the Guns and Hoses game because so many of our guys are playing or want to watch. They won't give us the case, but they'd share, no doubt."

"Someone needs to go through his house. Bill Wilson killed him for a reason. Maybe the reason is still there."

"Tom and I will take a run out there this afternoon." She pauses. "No, make it this evening. I've got court this afternoon."

"And I've got a bail jumper to locate. Plus a stolen truck. One of those Cyber thingies. A Musk-mobile."

"Since we're sharing secrets, can I tell you one?" Barbara asks.

"Of course," Holly says.

"The mayor asked Sista—Betty, I mean—to sing the National Anthem at the Guns and Hoses game. And she said yes!"

"Finally some good news about that fucking game," Izzy says. "Anyone want another hotdog?"

5

Christine's twin brother, Christopher, is staying in another fleapit motel, this one in Iowa City. The murdering women are of course in a much better place, probably enjoying room service breakfasts and possibly mani-pedis in the spa. There won't be room service in hell, only doom service.

This makes him laugh.

His room is hot, almost stifling. He turns the air conditioner up to high. It rattles madly but doesn't cool the room very much. He picked up a manila envelope at Mail Now on Kirkwood Avenue. It helps that the entire tour is on Kate McKay's website; he and Chrissy can get mail anywhere. The only mail he expects is from Andrew Fallowes, the treasurer of Real Christ Holy in Baraboo Junction, Wisconsin. Do the Real Christ Holy congregants know where a portion of their considerable tithes are going? Chris doesn't think so, but he thinks most—not all, but most—would approve if they did. Still, Andy Fallowes is right: compartmentalization is the only way this mission can work; if they are caught or killed, the church must not find itself caught in the blowback. Real Christ Holy is already on the FBI and ATF radar.

He opens the envelope. There's no note, only sixty twenty-dollar bills in Saran Wrap. There will be more, probably in Madison or Toledo. He puts a few of the twenties in his wallet, the rest in his shaving bag. He's traveling with two good-sized suitcases, one pink and one blue.

Chris goes into the bathroom and examines his face in the mirror. *Looking haggard, Christopher*. Yes. He is. Chrissy can wear makeup and is quite good-looking. Not a stunner, but she won't crack any mirrors, either.

He thinks, *They have been warned. We gave them a chance to back off.*

But did he think they would? Chrissy might have—she's very much her mother's daughter—but not him. The McKay bitch is as much of a crusader as those knights who wanted to liberate Jerusalem in the eleventh century. He can admire that; he is also a crusader. So, in her slightly gentler way, is Chrissy. Zealots, some would say. And really, wasn't Reno a chance to end it without bloodshed?

He's not stupid, knows perfectly well that Andy Fallowes has sent them on what's probably a suicide mission, but that's okay. He means to follow through. Chrissy will, too. Perhaps once the job is done and the leader of the abortion murder cult is no more, they can make an end to this miserable divided life he and his sister have been leading.

He undresses slowly. Shirt, shoes, pants, socks. In the other room, the air conditioner rattles and rattles. He thinks about the bunk bed, of course he does. The hand hanging down in a beam of morning sun dancing with motes of golden dust. That dead hand. He tells himself to stop, that she's not dead—*never died, never died*—but that memory torments him. He can erase the rest, but never the hand in the sunlight, hanging down from the upper bunk.

Our secret, Mama said. *Our secret.*

"This is God's work, God's will, and God's will be done," he says to his reflection in the mirror. "Thou shalt not suffer a witch to live. Exodus 22, verse 18."

Our secret, our secret.

Will he go to hell after killing McKay, or will God welcome him in with a *Well done, thou good and faithful servant?* He doesn't know, but he knows it will make an end to his torment.

Our secret.

In the other room, the air conditioner rattles and rattles.

6

At three-thirty that afternoon, Holly is on the phone with her ex-partner, Pete Huntley. Pete is extolling the virtues of retirement in Boca Raton, and each time she thinks he's reached the end of his encomiums, he comes up with another one. It's a relief when the office line rings.

"Pete, I have to get that."

"Sure, duty calls. But if it stops calling, you should get your skinny butt down here for a visit. Boca's fantastic!"

"I will," Holly says, although she probably won't. She's afraid of hurricanes. "You take care, now."

She ends the call and goes to the office phone. "Finders Keepers, Holly Gibney speaking. How can I help?"

"Hello, Ms. Gibney. My name is Corrie Anderson. I work for Kate McKay. Do you happen to know who she is?"

"I certainly do," Holly says. "I was hoping to attend her lecture at the Mingo Auditorium here, but I understand it's been postponed."

"It has, but we're still coming. Actually hoping to attend one of the Sista Bessie concerts." A pause. "We've had some trouble along the way, Ms. Gibney."

"So I understand." In her spare time Holly has mostly been fixated on Izzy's case (and wishing it was hers), but she's been following the Kate McKay news as well. She's curious about where this is going. Also excited. If McKay's PA is calling, meeting the woman, up close and personal, isn't out of the question. "There was a bleach-throwing incident in Las Vegas, I understand. Were you the one that got it in the face?"

"It was Reno, not Vegas, but yes, it was me. Kate was the actual target. It was raining, and I happened to be wearing her hat."

Corrie goes on to tell Holly about the anthrax in Omaha. That one Holly knew about, but not about the champagne fiasco in Des Moines. Then Corrie cuts to the chase, asking Holly if she does bodyguard work.

"I never have. I'm sure you could get an off-duty police person to do that, and for a fee considerably less than I would—"

"That's just what we . . . Kate, I mean . . . *doesn't* want. She wants a woman who's not associated with the police."

"I see."

She does. Those who oppose the things Kate McKay stands for will be having a field day with a big male cop breaking a woman's arm or shoulder or whatever it was, although some of those same people cheer when a cop shoots an obstreperous suspect.

"Can you hold on? I need to look at my schedule."

"Fine. This is a big deal for Kate. And, you know, for me."

Of course it is, Holly thinks. *You're the one who got the bleach shower.* "Hold on."

Holly checks her appointment book, knowing she's going to find a lot of white space. There's that female bail jumper she needs to locate (probably with her family, that's where the gals usually go), and there's the stolen Tesla Cybertruck she's been hired to find, but maybe Barbara's brother, Jerome, could be persuaded to look for it. Otherwise, she's free. And new things can be good things. New things are almost always a chance to learn.

"Ms. Anderson? Are you still—"

"Yes," Corrie says.

"If I take this on, my rates are six hundred dollars a day, three-day minimum. Plus expenses, which I track by Microsoft Excel. I take Visa, Master, or a personal—"

"Could you join us in Iowa City? Tomorrow? I know that's short notice, but I've had problems finding someone who meets Kate's needs. I know you can't get here in time for her lecture tonight, but we'll have a police escort both to and from. Kate kicked about that, but I insisted."

Good for you, Holly thinks.

Corrie continues, clearly worried. "No one at the venue, though—*she* insisted on *that*. You'd be with us for quite awhile. Before we get to your city, we've got Davenport, Madison, Chicago—that's a big one—and Toledo. We have a break in your town because of the Sista Bessie concert."

Holly says, "I'm supposed to go to that with a friend. She actually knows Ms. Brady."

"Kate has half a dozen front-row seats, if that's any inducement. The venue's manager comped us. I think it was a make-up call for us not making a big fuss about getting bumped from our original date."

Holly is doing the math in her head and realizing this could be a good payday. Check that, an *excellent* payday. Thanks to an inheritance from her mother, the agency is in good financial shape, but Holly believes the only real money that matters is earned money. Payday aside, joining one of the most influential feminists now working and writing in America is a big inducement. Her curiosity has always been strong, and this would be a chance to see what the woman is really like. With her shoes off and her hair down, so to speak. She's also curious about McKay's assistant, this Corrie Anderson. She sounds very young for such a responsible position. So, all in all . . .

Then the Holly who lives inside her even now—the young one, the scared one, the girl who always got cold sores and acne outbreaks before a big test—holds up a big red stop sign.

What if this person who threw the bleach and sent the anthrax gets McKay anyway? You know anybody can kill anybody, as long as they're willing to give themselves up to do it. Then you'd have your own publicity problem, wouldn't you? You'd be the woman who let Kate McKay get maimed or killed on your watch. It would destroy the agency.

Never mind the agency, Holly thinks. *It would destroy* me. *With guilt. And what do I know about being a bodyguard, anyway?*

Not much, that's true, but she knows how to keep her eyes and ears open. Her nose, too—she's gotten quite good at smelling danger. Plus, *somebody* has to watch out for those women, and since McKay insists on a female who's not police, she might be a good choice.

"Ms. Gibney?"

"My schedule is fairly clear, and I'm inclined to do this, but I'd like to speak to Ms. McKay before coming to a final decision. Can you put her on the phone?"

"I'll get with her and call you back in ten minutes. No, five!"

"That will be fine."

Holly ends the call. Inclined to do this? Nonsense. She's *going* to do it, assuming Kate McKay doesn't come across as an arrogant poophead. That's always possible, but the woman didn't get to where she is without putting on the charm.

It will be something new and out of the ordinary, she thinks.

To which the mother who, dead or not, will always live on in Holly's head responds, *Oh, Holly. Only you could think of a trip to Iowa City as something out of the ordinary.*

Holly leans back in her office chair, hands clasped above her small bosom, and laughs.

7

Izzy and Tom are escorted into Reverend Michael Rafferty's Tapperville house by a County Sheriff's detective named Mo Elderson. He says, "Have a look around, then I'll show you something interesting."

They skirt the chalked outline of the body, mostly out of superstition, and pass through the living room. The door of the bedroom closet has been pulled free of its tracks and hangs agape. The clothes are scattered on the floor.

"Guy might have been looking for a safe," Tom says.

Izzy goes to the half-open drawer on the nightstand, using a handkerchief to pull it open all the way. She doesn't want fingerprint powder on her hands. It's nasty stuff, hard to get out from under the fingernails.

She sees a Bible, some recovery-type books, and a bunch of medallions. These have also been dusted for prints. She picks one up, handling it by the edges. On the front are the co-founders of AA. Below them is the Roman numeral IX. On the back is an AA motto: *Rarely have we seen a person fail who has thoroughly followed our path.*

"Tom." He comes over. Izzy shows him the medallions. "A regular thief might have taken these, thinking they could be worth something. A person in AA or NA would know better."

"And this Rafferty guy was AAed up the ying-yang," Tom says. "Did you see the pictures in the living room? And those sofa pillows?"

From the doorway, Mo Elderson says, "One of those pillows was used to smother him when the bullet didn't do the job. You could say that he got AA literally crammed down his throat."

Tom laughs. Izzy doesn't. She asks, "What did you want to show us?"

"Maybe the killer's name. Can't say for sure, but confidence is high."

Elderson leads them into the kitchen and shows them the appointment book. Neatly printed in caps on May 20th is BRIGGS 7 PM. "Can't be sure, but we think most of these names are for counseling sessions." He thumbs back to April, where there are three other names and times—BILLY F., JAMIE, and TELESCOPE. None in March, but four in February and two in January. Izzy takes some pictures with her phone.

"Somebody named Telescope?" Tom asks. "Really?"

"Probably a nickname," Izzy says. "And Billy F. to differentiate him from some other Billy."

Elderson: "We feel like if we find this guy Briggs, we find the killer. The problem is the goddam anonymity shit."

"I might be able to do something about that," Izzy says. *Or Holly can.*

8

Kate McKay was—on the phone, at least—every bit as charming as Holly thought she might be, and that night Holly is packing for Iowa City and points east. She's quite excited and has downloaded a book called *Essentials for Bodyguards* to her Kindle. Flipping through the chapters, she thinks it could have been called *Bodyguarding for Dummies*.

She's debating on whether to pack another pants suit or a pair of jeans when her phone rings. It's Izzy. She tells Holly about the visit she and Tom made to the Rafferty house. "I don't want you to go breaking anyone's anonymity, Hols, but can you meet with this John Ackerly? Ask him if he knows someone in the Program named Briggs?"

"Can't. I'm leaving town tomorrow. It's nuts, but it looks like I'm going to be doing bodyguarding duty. For Kate McKay."

"Shut *up*!"

Holly doesn't. She tells Izzy how it happened and *why* it happened, which is basically political.

"Her PA, Corrie Anderson, read up on me a little, and decided I might be the right woman for the job. *Woman* being the main requirement. I talked to Ms. McKay—Kate—and she seems pleasant enough."

"Ordinarily you don't get to be famous by being pleasant, Holly."

"I know that," Holly says. "I can put up with a little attitude, because the payday is a good one."

"As if you need it."

"It's also a change," Holly says defensively. "It will be interesting."

"Yes, especially if the woman stalking her shoots her."

"That *would* be a drawback," Holly says.

"Maybe you could at least give John Ackerly a call?"

Holly is better at saying no than she used to be. Not much, but a little. And she doesn't want to get dragged any deeper into police business. "I'm kind of out straight, Izzy. Can't you—"

"Interview him? The County Mounties already have, because he found the body. Tom and I could re-interview, but it's technically a county case. And then there's the anonymity issue. I thought he might be more willing to talk to you."

"I have an idea. Jerome knows him. I introduced them. They hit it off. John went to Jerome's book launch party. He gave Jerome a fake tommy gun he got on eBay. You just want to know if John's been to meetings with somebody calling himself Bill W., or somebody named Briggs, correct?"

"We believe Briggs *is* Bill W. The county detective in charge of the case asked Ackerly about the name, but he said it didn't ring any bells."

"You think if Jerome asked John, he might be more willing to share?"

"Unlikely, I'd rather it was you, but possible. The problem is this thing about first names only in recovery meetings. Or nicknames, in some cases."

"Briggs is more commonly a *last* name," Holly muses. "Of course, there was Briggs Cunningham. He was a captain in the America's Cup race. Also a race car driver."

"Only you would know that, Gibney."

"I'm a crossword puzzle junkie. Would you like Jerome to drop by the bar where John works? I could call Jerome tomorrow on my way to the airport."

"Ackerly works in a *bar*?"

"I told you. He says it doesn't bother him."

"Okay, ask Jerome to talk to me, then Ackerly. Now both Robinson sibs know about my case. Oy vey."

"They'll keep it quiet."

"I hope so. Good luck with Kate McKay, Hols. Send me a picture of you and her. I've read all her books. She rocks. And don't let her get killed."

"That's the plan," Holly says.

9

That night, Trig goes to a meeting in Treemore Village. This is far afield for him, but he doesn't question why. Not on the surface part of his mind, anyway. A deeper part is aware of the Taurus .22 in the Toyota's center console. It makes him think of an old AA joke about a magic trick only drunks can do: Recovery Guy is cruising along, headed for a meeting and thinking of nothing in particular, and presto, his car turns into a tavern.

The meeting is in the basement of St. Luke's and the group is called New Horizons. There are twenty or so in attendance. The subject is "honesty in all our affairs," and everyone has a chance to share. When it's Trig's turn, he says he just wants to listen tonight. There are murmurs of *right on* and *keep coming back, Trig*.

After the meeting, most of the alkies stand around the urn in the kitchen, drinking coffee, eating cookies, telling war stories. Trig sees a couple of people he knows from other meetings closer to the city, but doesn't speak to them, just slips out. A mile down Route 29-B is John Glenn State Park. A young man in a duffle coat is standing under the single streetlight by the side of the road, holding a sign that says WASHINGTON D.C. When he sees Trig slowing down, he grins and flips the sign over to show OR WHEREVER. Trig pulls over and shifts into park so the young man can open the passenger door and get in.

"Thanks, man—where you going?"

Trig holds up a finger in a casual *wait a sec* gesture and opens the center console. He takes out the gun. The young man sees it. His eyes widen, but he freezes for a lethal two seconds before scrabbling at the doorhandle. Trig shoots him three times. The young man jumps as every bullet enters his body. His back arches, then he slumps forward. As he did with Annette McElroy, Trig places the muzzle of the Taurus against the young man's temple and fires a fourth time. Smoke drifts up. He can smell burning hair.

What are you doing? he asks himself, and this time it's not Daddy's voice but his own. If thoughts could scream, that's what this one would be doing. *You'll never get all of them if you kill on impulse! Your luck will run out!*

Probably true, but it won't run out tonight. The road is deserted, and although the swing-gate is down across the park's entrance—it closed at seven PM—he's able to drive around it. He douses his lights and pulls into a picnic area from which several trails begin, each marked EASY or DIFFICULT or EXPERT.

Trig goes around the hood of his car and opens the passenger door. The young man in the duffle coat spills out onto the gravel. There is no blood in the car, at least that Trig can see. The young man's heavy coat has caught it all. Trig gets him under the arms and drags him toward the line of Porta-Johns beyond the picnic area. A car comes down the highway. Trig crouches, aware of the dead man's head lolling between his feet. The car passes without slowing. Red taillights . . . and gone. Trig resumes dragging.

In the Porta-John he picks, the pink disinfectant disc in the plastic urinal is no match for the smell of shit. The walls are covered with graffiti. It's a poor tomb for a man who did nothing but try to hitch a ride. Trig feels a moment of regret, then reminds himself that the man's innocence is exactly the point: he did nothing, just as Alan Duffrey did nothing. Also, Trig has to admit to himself that regret isn't the same as guilt, of which he feels none. Didn't he know this might be the way his evening ended, with his car—abracadabra!—turning into a murder scene? Isn't it why he came to Treemore in the first place? Telling himself to take some time off from killing these innocents was rational. The need to get on with his mission is the exact opposite. It's so much like the bad old days, telling himself he could stop anytime . . . just not tonight. The idea that murder might indeed be an addiction freezes him for a moment with the young man partially lifted onto the toilet seat.

If it is, what does it matter? There's a cure for addiction that's even better than AA or NA.

When the young man is seated, Trig takes one of his cooling hands and folds it over a slip of paper with the name STEVEN FURST on it. He goes back to the car and inspects the passenger side for bullet holes. He finds none, so all the slugs stayed in the young man's body. Even the head shot, which could have resulted in a cracked window. Which was good. Lucky. There are a few spots of blood on the seat, but there are tissues in the center console. He wipes up the spots and puts the tissues in his pocket for later disposal.

You only need good luck if you do this impulsively. And sooner or later, luck always turns.

He resolves not to do any more of them according to impulse and knows he may be powerless to stop himself. As when, in the bad days, he would tell himself he would have a sober weekend, that just once he would wake up on Monday morning without a hangover. Only what was a Sunday afternoon football doubleheader without a drink or two? Or five or six?

"Never mind," he says. "Four down, nine to go. Then the guilty one."

He drives back to the city. He's got a call to make.

Chapter 8

1

Holly's flight to Iowa City on May 23rd is scheduled early and leaves late. It's not the way she would run the world if she were in charge, but pretty much SOP for a puddle-jumper like Midwest Air Service. She doesn't mind; it gives her time to speak to Jerome before the flight leaves.

He doesn't pick up until the fifth ring, and sounds muzzy. "Hey, Holly. What time is it?"

"Quarter past seven."

"Are you kidding? That isn't even a real hour."

"I've been up since four-thirty."

"Good for you, but most of the world doesn't run on Holly Time. Where are you? I hear planes."

"The airport. I'm going to Iowa City."

"Are you kidding?" Jerome sounds a little more awake now. "*Nobody* goes to Iowa City. At least not of their own free will."

Holly explains why she's traveling. Jerome is impressed.

"Bodyguard duty for a woman who was on the cover of *Time*! A new page in your résumé. Very nice, big props to my homegirl, but why are you calling me?"

"It has to stay confidential. You can talk to your sister if you want to, but otherwise, keep it totally quiet. There may be a serial killer at work in the city."

"Let me stop you right there," Jerome says. "Might your serial killer be responsible for a woman killed on the Buckeye Trail and a couple of homeless dudes whacked behind a washateria? Names in their hands? Possibly the names of jurors in the Duffrey trial?"

Holly's heart sinks. Not on her account, but on Izzy's. "Where did you get it? Not the paper, I already looked."

"Three guesses and the first two don't count."

"Buckeye Brandon."

"Correctamundo," Jerome says.

"Where did *he* get it?"

"No clue."

"Izzy was afraid this might happen. What about a man found murdered in Tapperville?"

"That is in the paper, victim unnamed pending notification of next of kin, but if it's related to the three others, no one has made the connection yet. Including Brandon. What's your part in this, Holly?"

It's been months, maybe even a year, since he called her Hollyberry, and she kind of misses it.

She tells Jerome about Izzy showing her the original note from the man calling himself Bill Wilson, and how she, Holly, spoke to John Ackerly. How it was John who found the body of Michael Rafferty, aka Big Book Mike.

"John found him and now you're consulting with the police!" Jerome says gleefully. "Holly's Sherlock Holmes and Izzy's Inspector Lestrade! Totally cool!"

"I wouldn't put it that way," Holly says . . . although really, what other way is there to put it? "The night Rafferty was murdered, he was supposed to meet someone named Briggs. Izzy took a picture of Rafferty's appointment book calendar. If I sent you the picture, would you show it to John? Ask him if he knows the name? He might; if it's a first name, it's a little on the odd side."

"Happy to."

"I'm sorry to interrupt your work—"

"No interruption about it. I have done hit a wall on the new book."

"When you hit a wall, break through it. Old Chinese saying."

"Bullshit. I know an old Holly Gibney saying when I hear one."

"Good advice, either way," she says, putting on her prim voice.

"No problem. I've been wanting a distraction. I think maybe I was cut out to be a one-book author."

"Now *that's* bullpoop," Holly says.

"Maybe yes, maybe no. Either way, a break will do me good. Izzy's Lestrade, you're Sherlock, I'm just a lowly Baker Street Irregular."

Still in her prim voice, Holly says, "I think you're *very* regular, Jerome."

"Thanks. Hollyberry." And he ends the call before she can make a token protest.

2

There's no Wi-Fi on the plane (of course not), but her phone bings with a text while she's going down the air-stairs to a hot spring Iowa morning. It's from Izzy.

Our pal Bill W. got another one. Call me.

Once she's inside the terminal, Holly calls Isabelle, who tells her the latest victim was a young man named Fred Sinclair, a native of New Haven, Connecticut, his reason for being in the rural town of Treemore, outside Treemore Village, on Route 29-B so far undetermined. Shot four times. A troop of Boy Scouts were camping a little way into John Glenn State Park. One of them walked down the trail just after dawn to use a Porta-John, and got an unpleasant surprise when he opened the door. One he'll probably be telling a psychiatrist about in another fifteen or twenty years. "Primal scene, honeychild," Izzy says. "I read about those in Intro to Psychology."

"Did any of the Scouts hear the shots?"

"Their campsite was a mile deeper into the park. The kids were all singing around the campfire or asleep, I assume. One of the adults with them—I guess the Scoutmaster—said he thought he heard a car backfiring. That could have been gunshots. Probably was."

"You found a name in Mr. Sinclair's hand, I take it."

"Well, not me personally. The State Police who responded to the Scoutmaster's 911 call found it on the floor of the Porta-John. Fell out of his hand. Steven Furst. Another juror."

"Same gun used?"

"Too early for the forensics, but based on the pictures the Staties sent me, Sinclair got it with a small-caliber weapon, almost certainly the same .22 he used on the others. The guy in Tapperville, Rafferty, was shot with a different gun, larger caliber, probably a .38. The county cops are still investigating it as a robbery-murder. In which case, their Briggs and our Bill W. aren't the same man."

"It is, though," Holly says, almost absently. "Briggs brought a different gun to use on Rafferty, that's all. Tried to make it look like a robbery. Total premeditation. This guy is smart, Iz. The question is why, since he didn't leave a juror's name."

"I know." Izzy sighs. "Then there's Buckeye Brandon."

"Jerome told me."

Buckeye Brandon, who sometimes refers to himself as the Great BB, or the Outlaw Podcaster, mostly specializes in gossip, political dirt, and whoop-de-do scandals on his blog and podcast. He favors the moneyed class living in Sugar Heights or The Oaks. He also dishes on crime.

"He's calling it the Surrogate Juror Murders, and I'm afraid it's going to catch on."

"Does he know about Fred Sinclair?"

"Oh yes. Bad news travels fast. Not about the note with Furst's name on it, at least not yet, but he's already speculating it may be related to the others. If I could find the person leaking this stuff, I'd happily tear him a new asshole."

"He could have done it himself," Holly says.

"What? Who?"

"Bill W. Or Briggs, if that's his real name. He wants people to know. He wants the *jurors* to know. And the judge. And ADA Allen. He wants them eaten up with guilt. He wrote to your Chief and your lieutenant, announcing what he meant to do beforehand."

"True enough," Izzy says, and sighs.

"He could have called BB. I bet he did. The more legitimate news outlets would have a problem giving publicity to a killer."

"Then why didn't Brandon *say* he called him? I'd think that was right up his alley—telling his audience he has a direct line to the killer."

"Briggs might have told him not to, if he wants him to continue staying in contact."

"I have to split, Holly. Tom and I are going out to Glenn Park. It's technically out of our jurisdiction, but the Staties want to make sure we're holding this baby, too. Let me know if Jerome and Ackerly come up with anything."

"Absolutely."

"Are you in Iowa City?"

"Yes."

"Go, you," Izzy says.

"Thank you."

"I was being sarcastic."

"I know," Holly says. "Would I be belaboring the obvious to say that Bill W. is speeding up?"

"You would indeed be belaboring it."

"Catch him as fast as you can, Izzy, because he really means to carry through with his plan. Which he probably thinks of as his *mission*. He's dangerous because he thinks he's sane." She pauses. "To belabor something else that's obvious, he's not."

3

Holly totes her carry-on bag to the luggage carousel and sits down to wait. Her phone rings again. This time it's Barbara. She also wants to know if Holly is in Iowa City. It seems to be the question of the day.

"I am. Go, me."

"Jerome is going to talk to your bartender friend on his lunch break," Barbara says. "I would have gone along, but we're moving a bunch of band gear from the old Sam's Club to the Mingo."

"Don't strain your back," Holly says. "Lift with your legs, not your—"

Barbara laughs. "I love you, Holly. How do you get involved in these things? Hartsfield, Morris Bellamy, the Harrises . . ." She pauses, then adds, "Ondowsky."

There's someone else as well, one that Holly tries not to think of . . . but of course Ondowsky makes her think of the outsider who looked like Terry Maitland. Both were vampires who drank pain instead of blood.

"This isn't my case, Barb. It's Izzy's."

"Keep telling yourself that. You attract weirdos the way a magnet attracts iron filings." She pauses, then says, "That might have come out wrong."

"I think it did." In Holly's opinion, Barb doesn't need to know that Holly has already been on the phone with Izzy about the Surrogate Juror Murders . . . which, give the Outlaw Podcaster his due, is actually a pretty good name. "But I forgive you, because it's possibly true. No weirdos on this job, though."

"You hope."

"Yes. I hope."

Barbara says, "In a mystery novel, McKay would have ordered one of her dastardly minions to kill those people in order to get her precious lecture date back."

"That makes no logical sense," Holly says, "and in any case, life isn't a mystery novel." Although sometimes it seems that way. Her life, at least.

The luggage carousel begins to turn, and the first bags appear.

"I have to go, Barb. And remember, lift with the *legs*, never with the back."

"Will do. You take good care of yourself, Hol. Guard that woman's body."

"True, Boo." She has picked this expression up from Jerome and uses it when it seems appropriate. She believes it makes her sound hip.

4

Her little gray suitcase—slightly scuffed, the veteran of many trips—appears on the carousel. It's followed by a piece of luggage she's never had occasion to use before: a yellow box made of high-impact plastic. Unlocking it requires a four-digit code. Hanging from the handle is a red tag that reads **FIREARM UNLOADED**. The handgun carry-case was a Christmas present two years ago from Pete, her ex-partner.

Before Holly can put her personal phone back in the jacket pocket of her sensible pants suit, her Finders Keepers phone begins to ring in the jacket's other pocket. Holly takes it out, aware that she now has a phone in each hand. *I am the perfect twenty-first-century woman*, she thinks. The screen says BLOCKED NUMBER, but she's pretty sure she knows who it is.

"Finders Keepers, Holly Gibney speaking. How can I help?"

"It's Corrie, Ms. Gibney. Corrie Anderson, Kate's assistant? How was your flight?"

"Fine." It was actually quite bumpy, as puddle-jumper flights tend to be.

"Kate wants to know if you'd like the hotel to send a car to pick you up."

"I've reserved a rental." Holly knows from her conversation with McKay that they are driving from city to city, so Holly will drive, too . . . but not exactly with them. She'll post up and back, looking for any followers. "I hope to be there in an hour, maybe sooner."

"We—that is, Kate—wants you onboard as soon as possible. Our secret admirer has been in touch again. Sent a picture of Kate and me with our arms around each other after the Reno gig. One word scrawled across it in red lipstick. Any idea what it was?"

"I'm going to take a wild guess and say it was probably *lesbians*."

"Wow, you really are a detective."

Holly considers saying *true, Boo*, and doesn't. Instead she says that one wasn't particularly tough and tells Corrie she'll be there as soon as possible . . . but first she needs a moment to think. To *clarify*.

Holly sits in the deserted baggage claim area, a small neatly dressed woman wearing sensible shoes. Her hair is stylishly but sensibly cut. Her hands are clasped in her lap. She's ignored by the remaining passengers, which she also considers her superpower. An unobtrusive investigator who is good at her job can be a great detective, and on several occasions Holly has risen to greatness. She herself would protest that, but Izzy knows. So do Jerome and Barbara Robinson.

Her other superpowers are clarity of thought and the ability to take the time necessary to work out difficult problems. She is sitting quietly, seeming to have no interest in anything but the gray suitcase and yellow box circling on the luggage carousel, but beneath that sensible short haircut, her thoughts are running on two tracks.

One of those tracks has to do with Izzy's case—the elusive Bill Wilson, who has killed four people at least, and probably five. A huge number in a short time. Using the Wilson name as an alias suggests (to Holly, at least) a certain arrogance. Either that, or a desire—possibly subconscious—to be caught. And *Briggs*. Because surnames are frowned on in AA and NA, it's almost certainly a given name or a nickname. If Briggs is in the Program, John really might be able to ID him.

She wishes, not for the first time, that this was her case.

The other track has to do with Kate McKay. Her stalker has proved in Reno that she's not harmless, but the bleach was only a warning. The anthrax was a serious attempt to kill, and to hell with any bystanders who happened to inhale the poison fairy dust. What would come next? A gun seems most likely, which is one reason why Holly has—very reluctantly—brought her own.

Essentials for Bodyguards contains a list of precautions for keeping controversial people like Kate McKay as safe as possible, although the author, Richard J. Scanlon, warns that no one can be kept entirely safe, not even the President of the United States . . . as Lee Harvey Oswald, John Hinckley, and Thomas Crooks proved.

Holly wonders how many precautions McKay will be willing to take. She's guessing the woman won't like the idea, and wonders if she'll be able to convince her. Convincing isn't Holly's strong point, but she thinks she'll have to try. Corrie Anderson may help.

She gets her bags and heads for the rental counter. Ordinarily Holly would rent a small car like her Prius. Today she's asked for something with a lot more oomph. After mulling the options, which aren't that great in Iowa City, she decides on a Chrysler 300. If she needs extra horses—unlikely but possible—the Chrysler will deliver them. Holly picks up the folder for her car and takes the insurance. *Always safe, never sorry* was another of Charlotte's sayings. Once she's seated in it—plushy!—she sets her phone's GPS for the fastest route to the Iowa City Radisson in the suburb of Coralville. The Chrysler has a nav system, but Holly trusts her own gear.

Always.

5

Trig gets to work on time, says hello to Maisie in his outer office, and spends the first hour of his workday making phone calls and putting out small fires. In his business, there are always fires to put out. You just can't let them grow into big ones.

Like Holly's, his mind is running on two tracks. On one he's a professional man doing his professional best—never arguing, always being reasonable, trying to convince, sometimes resorting to base flattery. *You catch more flies with honey than with vinegar*, his mother used to say. Before she was *gone*.

On the other track, he's waiting to be arrested. He doesn't know if other serial killers (and that's what he is now, call it what it is) have a sense of invulnerability, but Trig doesn't. How far is it from St. Luke's, where the Thursday evening New Horizons group meets, to John Glenn State Park? Not far. What if someone makes the connection? What if there are security cams in the park? He never even checked, but in retrospect it seems logical, especially around those Porta-Johns, where all sorts of drug deals might be going on. And then there's the Rev's appointment book. Leaving it seemed so clever at the time, but if he had it to do over again, he would have just taken the fucking thing. Who would have known? The housekeeper? Why would the Rev have had a housekeeper anyway, a little house like that? And how would he have paid her? So far as Trig knows, the Rev's only job these last few years has been going to meetings and quoting the Big Book from memory.

Trig is fucking up all over the place.

He keeps expecting the cops to come through the door, ignoring Maisie's protests, one of them reciting his rights in a speed-rap, the other holding up a pair of handcuffs. He's visualizing Fin Tutuola and Olivia Benson from *Law & Order*, which is crazy. It will be the two that were announced in the *Register* as lead investigators: Atta and the woman, he can't quite remember her name.

That they will get him eventually seems inevitable, but now that he's begun down this path, he'd like to finish before they do. If not all of it, as many as possible. *Thirteen innocent and one guilty*, he thinks.

Murder, it seems, is addictive. He never would have believed it. Oh, maybe for sex-killers like Bundy and Dennis Rader, but he wasn't like them. There was no *joy* in the killing . . .

Or maybe there was.

If you're in it too deep to turn around, it's no good fooling yourself, he thinks. Is that the Daddy-voice? He can't tell. *There's nothing sexual about it, at least. They just need to know the blood of innocents is on their hands. And if I want to speed up, is that wrong? There's an end in sight, after all, a day when the guilty one will die and this will be over.*

He uses his tablet to go to Buckeye Brandon's blog. Under the flashing red banner that reads BREAKING NEWS, he finds this:

> *John Glenn State Park is now the site of another MURDER MOST FOUL! The body of Fred Sinclair, age unknown, was discovered by 12-year-old Matt Fleischer, who will never forget the TRAUMA of opening a porta-potty and discovering a DEAD MAN sitting inside! Is this CRIMSON CRIME related to the Surrogate Juror Murders? Buckeye Brandon's Magic 8-Ball says YES, but stay tuned. And remember: LISTEN TO MY PODCAST & SUBSCRIBE TO MY PATREON!!*

Trig called the Buckeye Brandon tipline, but he didn't give the recording the young man's name—how could he? The Great BB got that some other way. And a twelve-year-old boy found the body? What was a kid doing in a state park, anyway? This is followed by the unlikely yet weirdly persuasive idea that the kid actually *witnessed* the murder, and when Trig is caught, the kid will point to him and say, *That's him, that's the guy who dragged the body into—*

The intercom buzzes, and Trig almost screams. He has to force himself to answer, imagining Maisie's puzzled voice saying, *There are police here, and they say they need to talk to you.*

Instead, Maisie reminds him of his two o'clock dentist's appointment. Trig thanks her and clicks off. He's in a cold sweat, and not at the prospect of having three cavities filled. There are so many ways he could be caught!

I need to hurry up, he thinks, and finds that he's actually looking forward to it.

6

John Ackerly meets Jerome for lunch at the Rocket Diner. They both order the lobster mac (it's on special), and Arnold Palmers. John tilts a thumb out the window at the Garden City Plaza Hotel across the street. "Royalty staying there, man."

"Really?"

"Sista Bessie, the seventies and eighties rock-and-soul queen. I can't wait to see her. Tix for the show on the thirty-first were sold out, but I scored two for the next night."

"Good for you." Jerome waits until their drinks have been served, then shows John a photo—courtesy of Izzy and Holly—of Michael Rafferty's appointment calendar. He taps BRIGGS 7 PM on the square for the 20th of May. "Do you happen to know this guy? Don't worry about breaking your anonymity vow, or whatever you call it. I'll tell Holly and she can pass it on to the cops, your name not needed."

"The cops already know my name," John says. "I found the body."

"Oh. Yeah. Holly told me that." Jerome feels like a doofus. "What do you think? Ring a bell?"

John's reply comes with disheartening speed. "Nope." He taps the square for May 4th. Printed in the Rev's neat block letters is CATHY 2-T. "I know her. Seen her at meetings off and on for a couple of years now. Had one side of her hair dyed red, the other side green. People started calling her Cathy 2-Tone, and eventually she started IDing herself that way at meetings. These other names could be almost anybody. Do you know how many AA and NA meetings there are in the metro area?"

Jerome shakes his head.

"Three dozen is what I told your boss, but when I checked the meeting book, I found out it's almost triple that, if you put in Overeaters Anonymous and DDA, which is Dual Diagnosis Anonymous. Once you add the burbs, you're over four hundred groups."

"Holly's not my boss," Jerome says. "She's my friend."

"Mine, too. Holly's a skate."

"What does that mean?"

John grins and slides his hand palm down above the table. "She's *smooth*, man."

"Got that right. How long have you known her?"

John calculates while the waitress brings them lunch. "Long time, man. It was around the time her friend died, the ex-cop—"

"Bill Hodges."

"If you say so. I guess they were tight."

"They were."

"She was struggling to keep the agency open, too," John says, "but she managed to keep it afloat, and good for her."

Jerome doesn't tell him about the inheritance she got from her late mother. That's not his information to share, and besides, by the time Charlotte Gibney died, Finders Keepers was in the black.

"How did you meet her?" Jerome asks. He's never thought of Holly as a drinking-establishment habitué, let alone a barfly.

John laughs. "That's a good story, man. You want to hear?"

"Sure."

"She was skip-tracing a guy wanted for all sorts of debt-related shit, including taking a pickup truck on a test drive and 'forgetting' to bring it back. I was newly sober. Holly talked to the guy's mom, who said he was going to look for a guitar at Dusty's Pawn & Loan, which is just three doors down the street from my bar. So Holly's pulling into a parking space across from Dusty's and sees this guy, his name was Benny something, walking from Dusty's down to Happy with a guitar case in his hand. She follows him in. By then my man Benny's at the bar, asking for a bourbon-rocks, which I didn't want to sell him."

"Why?"

"I'd seen him at meetings. I'm like, 'Do you really want to do that? Sobriety's a gift, man.'"

Jerome can't wait to hear the punchline.

"This Benny was a big guy, well over six feet and had to go two-seventy. Holly, on the other hand, is five-three and change. She's put on some weight since then, but back in the day she couldn't have gone much more than one-oh-five soaking wet, as they say. Benny sees her, okay? Knows who she is because Holly has talked to some of his friends, and the friends have reported back to Benny. So he hauls ass for the door, which she's standing in front of. I think, holy shit, he's gonna run her down like a Mack truck. But she never moved a step. She says, 'If you don't go to Provident Loan to make a plan, Benny, and bring back that truck, I'll tell your mother you're in a bar.'"

Jerome is too gobsmacked to even laugh. It's the perfect Holly Gibney story.

"Benny stops two feet in front of her. Towers over her. She has to look up at him, but she still never budged. She says, 'I'll trust you on your own, at least this once, because it'll look better.' Benny says okay and kind of shuffles out. Holly comes to the bar and orders what she always orders in here, a Diet Coke with two cherries. I tell her I know Benny from the meetings I go to, and I was trying to persuade him not to buy a drink. Or at least not an alcoholic drink. I asked her if she thought Benny would really go to Provident to make a restitution plan, and Holly says probably, because he's scared to death of his mom. She got that from his friends. She also says, 'I always like to give a fellow one chance, if I can.' Then she picks up the guitar case, which Benny left behind on account of he was so foozled, and lifts it over the bar to me and says, 'Hold my drink.' I do, and she goes out."

"To Dusty's."

"I guess you know her, all right. Yeah. She comes back five minutes later and tells me Benny actually paid for the axe. With cash. Says when he comes back in, I can give it to him."

Jerome nods. "That's Holly."

"So anyway, we get talking. She gives me her card and the names of four skipjacks and jills she's looking for. Says if any of them come into the bar, will I give her a call. It was a cash-for-info thing at first, but I got to like her. She's got a lot of bells and whistles, but like I say, she's *smooth*."

Jerome nods. "Also got a yard of guts."

"She does."

"Have you ever seen one of her runners at your meetings?"

"From time to time," John admits, "but I only tell her if someone she's hunting comes into Happy. I'm not a bleeding deacon like the Rev—Mike R., I mean—but I support the anonymity rule. Meetings are off-limits. I made an exception this time because if she's right, that son of a bitch Briggs is a murderer as well as an alcoholic." He pauses, takes a bite of his lobster mac. Then he says, "Also because it's her. Holly."

Jerome nods. "Got that right." He smiles and holds a fist out over the table. "Always Holly."

John bumps knuckles with him and repeats it. "Always Holly."

7

The subject of their discussion pulls her Chrysler—which seems the size of a yacht after her Prius—into the lot of the Radisson. She sees a woman standing in the shade beneath the lobby overhang. She's tall and looks young. Short sandy hair, jeans and a sleeveless blouse. Tennies on her feet. Holly guesses this is Kate McKay's assistant. Anxious to meet the new security person and get things rolling. The girl—she looks young enough to still be called a girl—gives a tentative wave, and Holly raises her own hand in return.

In a rented Kia a few slots down, Chrissy Stewart watches this newcomer walk to the hotel's overhang and shake hands with the Anderson bitch. Wondering, *Who is this, now?* Not that it matters. Nothing changes. The job is the job. The slaughter of the innocents, on account of politics and by abortion, must be stopped.

At all costs.

Chapter 9

1

Corrie has seen Holly's picture on the Finders Keepers website, but she's surprised at how petite the woman is. And her hair is grayer than in the website photo. Her thought, as Holly gives her outstretched hand a short but firm shake, is how different she is from the male security people they've had, especially Elmore Packer, he of the unfortunate champagne incident.

That's probably good, Corrie thinks. *Another beefcake is the last thing we need. Nobody will even notice she's around. I just wish she wasn't so small. She looks almost . . . frail.*

For her part, Holly is thinking Corrie Anderson looks like a high school senior. But of course the older she herself gets, the younger the rest of the world becomes.

"We're getting packed up," Corrie says as they cross the Radisson's lobby. "Actually, we *are* packed up. It's only a short run to Davenport, our next stop, but Kate likes to swim if she can before her . . . her lectures, and I'll have a bunch of things to do." They get in the elevator. "The . . ." Again, that slight hesitation. ". . . Iowa City lecture is tonight, of course, and Sunday's off. Well, most of it. We'll be driving to Madison. The dates are speeding up a little now. I did tell you we're driving, right?"

"You did," Holly says. "And you don't really think of them as lectures, do you?"

Corrie blushes a little. "Well . . . Kate's colorful. Put it that way."

"I was looking forward to her talk in Buckeye City," Holly says. "Now I guess I'll get to hear her, after all." Although she won't be able to give Kate her full attention. Holly's not here to be entertained.

Corrie uses a key card to let them into a small suite on the fourth floor. Kate McKay is sitting in a shaft of sunlight by the window, one foot curled beneath her, making notes on a yellow legal pad. There are two suitcases by the door. Small ones. *She travels light*, Holly thinks approvingly.

Kate shoots to her feet, gives Holly a quick up-and-down, then busts out the radiant smile that has graced magazine covers, newspapers, and blog posts without number.

"Holly Gibney!" She hijacks both of Holly's hands in both of hers. "Welcome to Kate and Corrie's Excellent Adventure!"

"It's a pleasure to be here. As I was telling Corrie, I was planning to come and see you at the Mingo."

"We wuz robbed!" Kate cries. She spreads her hands, as if making headlines. "Soul Singer Defeats Sisterhood! 'Get Down Tonight' Defeats 'We Shall Overcome!' Stop the presses!"

Kate laughs, her green eyes alight. Holly thinks there's an aura about her, a crackle of psychic static electricity. Holly could tell herself that's nonsense, she's just feeling the awe ordinary folks feel when in the same room as a very famous person, but she suspects that persons who've attained a certain renown really do have that electricity about them. Not because they're famous; it's how they *became* famous.

"Do you think I should lodge a protest, Holly?"

"It would probably be good public relations to give in graciously."

Kate smiles at Corrie. "See? We have the right woman! Would you like something to drink, Holly?"

"Maybe a Coca-Cola, if there's one in your minibar."

"If there isn't, I'll complain to the management," Kate declares. "Corrie, find this woman a Coke."

Corrie goes to the minibar. Kate focuses her full attention on Holly. It's a little like being hit with a spotlight.

"I have a show tonight." She isn't as hesitant about using the word as Corrie was. "I'll want you with us. Macbride Hall, North Clinton Street, seven PM."

Holly has a notebook in her bag. She writes down this information.

"May I ask if you're armed, Holly?"

"I will be for your events," she says . . . and little does she like it.

"Please God, don't shoot anyone," Kate says. "After Des Moines, that's the last thing I need. Unless they deserve it, of course."

"Glass, Holly?" Corrie asks.

"No, thanks." She takes a can of Coke from Corrie and sips. It's cold and good. To Kate, Holly says, "If we exercise reasonable caution, everything will be fine. Here and elsewhere. No one is going to get shot. No confrontations of any kind. We'll avoid them."

"Confrontation is part of what Kate *does*," Corrie says.

Kate wheels on her, eyebrows raised. Corrie looks like she wishes she could take that particular observation back. Then Kate lets loose with that hooting laugh again. "She's right, but I'd like to stick to verbal fireworks from here on out. Everybody has a good time and nobody gets hurt."

"That sounds fine to me, Ms. McKay."

"Make it Kate. We're going to be friends."

No, Holly thinks, *I don't believe we will. What I'm going to be is an employee, just like young Ms. Anderson*. Only Kate McKay might be the sort of person who wants *everyone* to be her friend. To fall under her spell. With some people, Holly knows, it's a compulsion. She could be wrong, snap judgements are never to be trusted, but she doesn't think she is.

"Kate, then. My number one job is to make sure you can go about your business without being harmed. It would be easier to do that if the woman who's menacing you can be found and arrested. For that reason, I'd like to go over her communications with you. And I want to find out about your—"

"My enemies?" Kate laughs. "That would be a long list, but most of them limit their aggression to cable news panels and mean tweets. I can't think of anyone who'd put anthrax in a greeting card."

"If we put our heads together, we might come up with someone who would. Maybe more than one."

"Okay," Kate says, "but later. I have a Zoom call coming up, I want to take a swim, then the presser, the Macbride tonight, and the

RiverCenter in Davenport tomorrow. What about Sunday? That's a day off, thank God. Except for the drive to Madison. Did Corrie tell you—"

"That you'll be driving? Yes. I have my own car. Corrie can fill me in on your route. Some of the time I'll be behind you, and you'll see me—it's a blue Chrysler 300, hard to miss. Some of the time I'll be ahead of you, and you won't."

Kate points a finger at Holly and gives her a wink. "Trying to spot our stalker. Smart. And we'll bring you up to speed as soon as possible."

Holly doesn't like it. This is only Friday; surely they could find time to go over the stalker's communications before Sunday. Kate could skip her swim in the hotel pool, for instance. (*Hotel pools and yeast infections go together*, Holly thinks. *Oough.*) She thinks Kate isn't taking this as seriously as it deserves to be taken.

For that matter, Holly thinks, *it's hard to tell how seriously she's taking me*. No surprise there. She's used to being underestimated. Sometimes it comes in handy. In this case, it might not.

"I also have a GPS tracker I'd like to put on your car, if you don't mind."

"It's not a car, it's a truck, and I have no problem with that."

"Where are you supposed to be staying in Davenport?"

Kate shrugs, but Corrie knows. "The Axis. It's actually across the state line in Illinois."

"Keep that reservation but book a different hotel," Holly says. "Three rooms, in my name. Your stalker knows your names, but she won't know mine."

"I'll want a suite," Kate says. "Connecting with Corrie's room. And with yours, if possible."

Yes, I'm an employee, all right, Holly thinks.

"What about the press conference?" Corrie asks Holly. She's clearly not happy about this change. Maybe also not happy about Holly taking charge. "There's *always* a press conference."

"That can still be at the Axis. Corrie, I understand this is annoying. As a person who's a scheduling nut myself, I understand that. But your stalker knows your schedule, it's on Kate's website for anyone to see, and this crazy person has shown she's interested in inflicting mortal harm. If you're serious about protection, we *need* to make these changes."

Holly hopes that throwing the stalker off her schedule will make the woman easier to catch. If Holly had Pete Huntley with her—or Jerome—she would have one of them stake out the Axis, looking for someone who's looking for Kate and Corrie. But Pete's retired and Jerome is keeping an eye on Izzy's case. She hopes he's also gone back to work on his new book.

"Got it," Corrie says. "Give me your credit card, Holly. We're going to switch hotels all the way down the line, I suppose? The whole tour?"

"I'm afraid so."

Corrie sighs but makes no further objection. Holly guesses she's already calibrating the changes that will have to be made. And Kate? It's nothing to her, either way; for her it's on with the show. Holly knows, even on brief acquaintance, that if she suggested a change that directly impacted Kate—canceling one of her dates, for instance—her response would be more than a sigh. It makes her like the younger woman more, and it takes only a moment to realize why.

She's like me.

2

Chrissy is wearing the plain brown dress of a chambermaid, purchased yesterday at A-1 Uniforms in Coralville, and paid for with cash—love offerings from Real Christ Holy, by way of Andy Fallowes.

She gets out of her Kia, circles the hotel on foot, and goes in through the service entrance, which has been propped open by a brick. For smokers, no doubt. Swinging from one hand is a plastic bag that might contain trash. It doesn't, but it *does* contain offal. Chrissy has reached Iowa City by secondary roads and found plenty of usable stuff along the way: squirrels, squashed birds, a woodchuck, an exploded cat. Kate McKay is a fan of blood and destruction?

Fine.

Here's a whole bag of it.

3

Holly doesn't want to wait for Sunday to get after the stalker. She asks Corrie if she has communications from the woman on her phone or tablet.

"I have a computer file with everything in it, including police reports."

"That's great. Send me the file. Maybe I can go over it after your lecture tonight, Kate."

"There's really not that much," Kate says. "The card with the anthrax in it was—"

That's when the hotel's fire alarm goes off in a series of almost deafening whoops. A moment later an overhead speaker comes to life. "There is an alarm," says an automated voice. "Please leave the building. Do not use the elevators. Wait outside for the all-clear. There is an alarm. Please leave—"

"No shit there's an alarm." Kate sounds annoyed. "It's going to blow my freakin eardrums out."

"What do we do?" Corrie asks Holly.

"Nothing," Kate says before Holly can answer. "Somebody probably sparked up a joint in their bathroom, and—"

"We're going to leave," Holly says. She wishes her gun—Bill Hodges's .38—wasn't still in the trunk of her car, locked in its airline box.

"I hardly think—" Kate begins.

"I'm sorry, Kate, but this is exactly what you're paying me for. Follow me down the hall. Wait outside the stairwell door until you hear me say *clear*. Same thing at each floor—wait for my clear. Do you understand?"

Kate decides to play this as something that's amusing rather than annoying. She's not scared, but Corrie is. *Because she's the one who got the bleach bath*, Holly thinks. *Nothing at all has happened to Kate, at least so far*.

Holly goes to the door of Kate's sitting room and looks out into the hall. At this time of day there are few guests on the floor, and only four or five are heading for the stairs. Two others are looking out their doors, wearing the same exasperated expression Holly saw on Kate's face when the alarm started to blare. *False alarm, of course it is*, those faces say. *Nothing happens to me, it's always someone else. I'm exempt*. Those doors shut even as Holly beckons Kate and Corrie out.

They go down the hall, now empty, in single file. Holly peers into the stairwell, keeping low. There's no one there; the few guests who elected to heed the alarm are already most of the way down. She calls, "Clear!"

Kate and Corrie follow her down, stopping on the stairs until Holly can check the landing and then the third-floor hallway, where a head-down chambermaid in a brown dress is pushing a trolley, seemingly oblivious of the alarm. They reach the lobby in this fashion. Here the reception clerks and a man in a suit—probably the manager—are ushering people out.

"I'm sorry, Ms. McKay," he says as they pass. "Probably a false alarm."

"Women are very familiar with falsies," Kate says. The man in the suit laughs as if it's the funniest thing he's ever heard.

Outside, two or three dozen guests mill around beneath the lobby overhang where Holly first glimpsed Corrie waiting for her. Kate looks at her watch. "I had hoped to be on my next call by now," she says. "First you were late, Holly, now this. It's obviously a false alarm."

"I think—" Holly begins, but Kate has reached a decision.

"Fuck this, I'm going back."

Holly is dismayed. Should she go with? Try to restrain her? She has an idea that trying to restrain might get her fired. As it happens, there's no need to decide. The alarm quits, and the man in the suit comes out.

"Folks, you can go back to your rooms. We're very sorry for the inconvenience."

"You should be," Kate says.

"It looks as if some prankster—" the manager says, but Kate is already power-walking past him.

"Where was the alarm triggered?" Holly asks. "Which floor?"

"I'm not sure," the manager says.

Holly wonders if that's the truth, but this is not the time to probe. Her client is already approaching the elevators, a Type A who is well ahead of the other guests, meaning to get the first available car. Corrie is close behind, but looking back at Holly, who catches up to them and steps in just as the doors begin to close.

"False alarm, as I told you," Kate says.

"Seems so." Holly isn't entirely convinced. It feels wrong.

"I appreciate your dedication to the job, Holly, but you might be a little too eager to show off your skills." Kate is watching the digital floor indicator count up, giving Corrie the chance to shoot Holly a quick sidelong look that says *sorry, sorry*.

Holly makes no reply to Kate, but when the elevator doors open, she makes sure she's out first. She takes four steps down the hallway toward Kate's suite, then spreads out her arms. "Stop, stop."

"For God's sake, *what?*" Kate's not exasperated now; this is annoyance edging into anger.

Holly hardly notices. Her sensors, which have been in the yellow, now turn bright red. "Stay where you are."

"I don't need you to—" Kate pushes past Holly, then stops. "Which of you left the door open?"

"Neither of us," Corrie says.

The door to Kate's junior suite opens inward. Holly can see part of the living room rug and a slice of the window where Kate was sitting in the sunshine with her pad of paper. She can also see splinters on the hallway carpet.

"It's not open, it's been forced. Probably kicked in."

Her first impulse is to herd them back into the elevator, get them down to the lobby, and tell the manager to inform hotel security. Only the manager himself may be the only security the day shift has, and she doesn't trust Kate not to bull ahead into the room.

"Wait here, both of you. Please."

"I want to—" Kate begins.

Corrie says, "Let her do her job, Kate. It's what you hired her for."

Holly goes to the door in gliding slide-steps, back pressed to the wall and the room doors she passes. She thinks again of the revolver locked in her trunk and promises herself she won't be without it again—isn't it why she brought her big purse, even though it's ugly? As she closes the distance, she sees something has been written on the door. And even though it looks like it's been written in blood, she relaxes a little. If there's a message, it means the messenger is gone. *Probably g—*

A hand falls on her arm. Holly jumps and gives a small squeak. It's Kate, who obviously has a problem with following instructions. She's looking over Holly's shoulder. "What the hell does that mean?" Scrawled on the door is EX 21 22 23. "Is it *blood*?"

Holly doesn't answer. She shakes off Kate's hand and moves closer to the open door. This time Kate stays where she is. Holly peers around the splintered jamb. What she sees isn't nice—far from it—but it makes her even more sure that the person who did this is gone.

Kate McKay's neat little suitcases have been drenched in blood and the mangled corpses of birds and small animals. *Roadkill*, Holly thinks. *Oough.* Lying on the carpet is the white plastic bag the dead things came in.

"We need to go back down to the front desk," Holly says, but Kate darts past her and stares, disbelieving, at the blood and guts on her previously pristine luggage. She utters a scream that causes the guests who have stayed in their rooms to open their doors and stare out. Several returnees from the false alarm stop in their tracks. Holly has heard screams like that before, on at least one occasion coming from her own throat. Not fear. It's partly horror, mostly fury.

Kate is no longer exempt.

4

Izzy and Tom are looking at the Porta-John where the Boy Scout found the body. With them is a State Police detective lieutenant named Ralph Ganzinger. The toilet has been blocked off with a square of DO NOT CROSS tape, but the door has been propped open. The bench seat, urinal, and plastic walls are black with fingerprint powder. The State Police forensic unit has been and gone.

"They got plenty of prints," Ganzinger says, "all probably useless. Most of them in one place. Men who use the urinal have a tendency to prop their fingers on the wall while they do their business."

Izzy thinks of what Holly would say about that: *Oough*. Even with the Porta-John's door open, the smell of human waste wafts out.

"Security cams?" Tom asks.

"Six." Ganzinger cocks a thumb toward the woods. "Five of them point at the trailheads. The sixth is up there on that pole, looking at the toilets. That one's been broken since last year. The Park Service guy who came out says it gets vandalized regularly. What happens is people who don't want to be seen sometimes use those toilets for what you might call nefarious purposes. This last time it was too broke to be fixed, and there's no money for a replacement."

"Pretty high up there," Izzy says. "Someone with good aim must have hucked a rock at it."

"I bet you could hit it," Tom tells her. And to Ganzinger, "She's our starting pitcher in next week's Guns and Hoses game."

"Don't remind me," Izzy says.

Lew Warwick has requested—no, *mandated*—her appearance at a City Center press conference later this afternoon, the purpose being to build interest in the game and thus drive up charitable contributions. He's promised that she won't have to say much, but she doesn't entirely trust him on that, and although Lew is her boss, she couldn't resist pointing out that with Sista Bessie onboard to sing the National Anthem, "building interest" is really unnecessary; the game will be SRO. She knows the presser is actually an opportunity for PD Chief Alice Patmore and Fire Commissioner Darby Dingley (the stupidest name in the universe, as far as Izzy is concerned) to get their faces on the evening news. And all that's for later. Now she asks Ganzinger if there were tire tracks.

"Yes. Good ones." He holds up his pad, shielding it from the sun with his hand so she and Tom can get a good look at the photos. "Confidence is high that these were made by the perp's car. This was a spur-of-the-moment deal."

"Impulse murder," Tom says.

Ganzinger nods. "Sinclair was hitching his way to D.C., then maybe on to New York. Perp didn't take his wallet, so we were able to talk to his parents."

"I hate making those calls," Tom says.

"Don't we all," Ganzinger says. "We've got a gal at the post who's pretty good with breaking news like that."

No one is good at those calls, Izzy thinks.

"Anyway, perp picks Sinclair up. Pulls into the park, just drove around the gate, which is where we got these tire impressions. Shoots him multiple times in the car—less noise that way, but the Scoutmaster still heard it—then drags him to the toilet. The drag marks start near the tire tracks."

"Are the tracks useful?" Tom asks. "Please say they are."

Ganzinger shakes his head. "We got a computer match right away, because they're nice and sharp. Toyo Celsius II. They come on Toyotas, Highlanders, RAV4s. Other models, too, like Priuses, but the vehicle that made these is bigger. I think it was a Toyota sedan."

"Of which there are roughly a gazillion in this state," Izzy says. "Did the guy have a sign?"

"Sign?" Ganzinger looks blank.

"Hitchhikers sometimes hold up signs with their destinations on them."

"We didn't find anything like that," Ganzinger says. "Do you want to poke around a little?"

Izzy and Tom look at each other. Tom shrugs. Izzy says, "We should get back to the city. I've got a dog-and-pony show to attend. If you get any interesting hits on those fingerprints, let us know."

"Will do. You guys have a nice day."

On their way back to their car, Tom says, "It would be a nice day if the guy stopped to take a piss after propping the guy on the bench seat."

"And braced himself against the wall with his fingertips," Izzy adds. "Wouldn't that be a world. You want to drive?"

5

In Iowa City, Kate and Holly are consulting with Detective Daniel Speck in the office of the Radisson's manager. Corrie has gone in search of new luggage for her boss. Holly doesn't love the girl going out on her own, but Corrie has her marching orders, and at least she can't be mistaken again for the woman the stalker is really after. At least Holly hopes not.

Kate is furious about the ruination of her L.L.Bean suitcases, but glad the bitch who did the deed didn't have time enough to rip them open and trash her clothes.

Holly is also interested in clothes, but not Kate's. She asks the manager what sort of outfits the Radisson chambermaids wear. He tells her blue dresses with scalloped collars. Holly turns to Detective Speck. "I'm pretty sure I saw the woman who did it. She was on the third floor, pretending to push a trolley. Wearing a brown dress that looked very . . . very housekeeperly."

"I'll check the security footage," Speck says, "but if she knew enough to keep her head down . . ."

"She did when she brought the card with the anthrax in it," Kate says. "And in Reno she was wearing a wig."

Detective Speck says, "She'll be in the wind by now."

If so, it will be blowing her on her way to Davenport, Holly thinks. *If not, she'll be at the Macbride tonight. Maybe with a gun.*

"Are you going to talk about this tonight, Kate?" Holly asks. "Or at your press conference?"

"Damned right I am."

Keeping her voice mild and (she hopes) nonconfrontational, Holly says, "This woman will love that."

Kate gives her a startled look that turns thoughtful. "How can I not? I can't look like I'm covering it up. That would make me seem ashamed."

Holly sighs. "I see that, but can I make a suggestion?"

"Go on."

"Keep it brief. Make it seem almost like a joke. And maybe . . . call her a coward?"

"Wouldn't that be egging her on?" But Kate is smiling. She likes it.

"Yes," Holly says. Sometimes the best thing you can do is force the issue. And from now on she'll be carrying her gun. "Because the sooner this person is caught, the sooner my job will be easier."

Speck says, "The writing on the door, now."

"Exodus, chapter 22," Holly says. She opens her iPad and reads. "'If men strive, and hurt a woman with child, so that her fruit depart from her, and yet no mischief follow: he shall be surely punished, according as the woman's husband will lay upon him; and he shall pay as the judges determine.'"

Kate gives a short laugh with no humor in it. "Heard it before, just without the attribution. The God-botherers love it. That verse is actually about assault—guys brawling and knocking over a pregnant woman and causing her to miscarry. Do you know what the Bible actually says about abortion? Nothing. Zilch. So they twist this."

"That's the first verse," Holly says. "The next one goes, 'And if any mischief follow, then thou shalt give life for life.'" She closes her pad. "To this woman, Kate, *you're* the mischief-maker."

"Have you thought about canceling tonight?" Speck asks.

Kate gives him a frostbite smile. "Not a chance."

6

Maisie buzzes Trig at quarter past one and reminds him it's D-Day, as in dentist. "You better get going now if you want to be on time, because the crosstown traffic builds up early on Friday."

Trig thanks her and wishes her a pleasant weekend. His Toyota is parked next to Maisie's Nissan Rogue on the side of the building. He seatbelts up and starts to back out, looking to his right because he doesn't want to scrape Maisie's car. He sees something alarming and jams on the brakes. Lying in the passenger footwell of his car is the hitchhiker's sign, the side reading OR WHEREVER facing up.

There are a few droplets of dried blood on it.

How could you be so stupid? he asks himself. No, it's not an ask, it's a yell, and it isn't him. It's his father. Trig can almost see Daddy in the passenger seat, Daddy in his brown workpants with the chain holding his wallet. *Do you want to be caught? Is that what this is?*

"No, Daddy," he mutters. That "wanting to be caught" stuff is so much psychobabble. He was just upset, anxious to get out of the state park.

But Maisie parked right next to him. What if she glanced in his car window and saw the sign? Saw the droplets of blood?

She didn't. She would have said something.

Would she?

Really?

Trig gets out, goes around to the passenger side, and after a quick look to make sure he's alone, grabs the sign and tosses it in the trunk. There's an incinerator barrel behind the office at Elm Grove, where he now lives, and he can dispose of the cardboard sign in it this evening. The residents aren't supposed to use it—air pollution—but most of them do, anyway, and the management winks at it.

He gets back into the car and arms sweat from his forehead. *She didn't see it. I'm sure of it.*

Almost *sure of it.*

Maybe I should think about—

But he cuts that off. Amputates it. Think about shooting Maisie? Well-meaning, slightly overweight, always-thinking-about-Ozempic Maisie? Never!

Never? Really?

Is that a thought . . . or a voice?

He looks in the rearview mirror and for a moment sees Daddy, now back there instead of in the passenger seat, grinning. Then he's gone.

7

Rothman, Trig's dentist, points to the wall-mounted TV screen, where an X-ray of Trig's teeth is currently on view.

"Number eighteen, your second molar." He sounds like a funeral director. "It has to come out. No way to save it. Infection underneath." Then he brightens. "Good news, your insurance will cover eighty per cent of the expense. May I go ahead?"

"Do I have a choice?"

"Not if you don't want to keep taking an antibiotic for a low-grade gum infection. And you might consider wearing a night guard. You grind your teeth, and that poor molar has taken the worst of the abuse."

Trig sighs. *I thought the possibility of getting arrested was my only problem today.* "Go ahead."

"I'll localize the area, but I recommend nitrous oxide to make the experience as pleasant as possible." Rothman considers. "Well . . . extraction is never pleasant, but more comfortable."

Trig considers. He doesn't have a drug problem, alcohol was his downfall (not to mention a certain bullheaded certainty, a dubious gift from his father), but he's heard that people under nitrous can be . . . what's the word? Indiscreet? But with a rubber bite block holding his mouth open, he'll be incapable of saying anything but *oooo* and *aaaa*.

"Nitrous, by all means," he says.

After several pain-killing injections, Rothman's second-in-command puts on the nasal hood and instructs Trig to breathe through his nose only. "And relax."

Trig does. For the first time since Annette McElroy, he relaxes completely. He's barely aware of Rothman's poking, prodding, drilling, and—finally—wiggling the bad tooth back and forth in its socket, cajoling the roots to let go.

Must finish up as rapidly as possible, he thinks, *so I can also let go*. This isn't an entirely new thought, but his mind has been set free and the one that follows it is. *Suppose I could be like the tailor who got seven at a blow?*

Seven would be too many, but suppose he could finish with *several* at a blow? Including the one who's most guilty? Is there a way that could be done?

With his mind floating free of anxieties, Trig sees that it could happen. And if it did, it would turn his crusade into a worldwide sensation; Trump getting shot in the ear would pale beside it. He's not interested in being famous (so he tells himself), but suppose his actions could start a useful conversation about how often the innocent are branded as the guilty? There's going to be one—possibly two—famous women in town the following week, and if there was a way to make *them* part of the atonement for Alan Duffrey's death . . .

"Just finishing up," Rothman says.

"*Iiii uhhh ayyy*," Trig replies.

"What was that?"

But Trig only smiles as well as he can around the block in his mouth. *Innocents must pay.*

Chapter 10

1

The Sista Bessie crew's move from the old Sam's Club to the Mingo Auditorium is a work in progress. Jerome gets in by mentioning his sister's name to Tones Kelly, the tour boss. He wasn't sure it would work, but it does. Tones has been sitting in the lobby, idly plunking away on a Fender bass guitar, but he jumps to his feet as if Jerome had said *open sesame* instead of *Barbara Robinson*.

"Barb is Betty's new best friend," Tones says, "and a bear for work, which makes her a friend to everyone on the crew. Who knew a poet could move a Marshall stack all by herself?"

"We were taught hard work is the way you get on in the world," Jerome says.

"I hear that. Until the lights go down and the music starts, it's all grunt work. Movie crews, carny crews, the rock and roll army . . . all basically the same. Sweat equity."

The auditorium is half-lit. Jerome spots a stout lady sitting at a piano stage left, playing what has to be "Bring It On Home to Me." Barbara is halfway up the main seating area (with recently added balconies, the Mingo seats 7,500), carrying a boxy Yamaha gadget to the sound engineer, whose mixing board looks like it's only partially assembled. Barb's wearing high-waisted jeans held up with suspenders, a Rolling Stones *Steel Wheels* tee (which Jerome is pretty sure was filched from their parents' attic), and a red bandanna around her smooth brown forehead. Jerome thinks she looks like a roadie if ever a roadie there was, which isn't surprising. Barbara has a chameleon-like quality. At a country club party, she could wear an evening dress and a sparkly faux-diamond headband with similar ease.

"Barb!" he says. "I brought your car back." He hands her the keys.

"No dents or dings?"

"Not a single one."

"Ross, this is my brother Jerome. Jerome, this is Ross MacFarland, our FOH."

"Don't know what that is, but pleased to meet you," Jerome says, shaking MacFarland's hand.

"Front of the house," MacFarland says. "Although for our show, I'll be mixing right here. The Program Director doesn't like it because those are prime seats he can't sell—"

"Program directors never like *anything* we do," Tones says. "It's part of their dubious charm. Gibson ain't as bad as some I've worked with."

Someone yells, "*Three o'clocks, everybody! Threes!*"

Barbara shouts, "I'll be right there, Acey!"

A woman says, "Who might this handsome young man be?"

Jerome turns and sees the stout piano lady making her way up the aisle. He realizes belatedly that this woman, dressed in a frumpy jumper and bulging moccasins, is Rock & Roll Hall of Fame inductee Sista Bessie.

"Betty, this is my brother Jerome. The other writer in the family."

Betty shakes like a man. "You got a talented sister, Jerome. And you not bad yourself. She gave me your book and I'm partway through it already."

"*Barbara!*" someone bawls. "*Spikes and stands after three o'clocks!*"

Barbara turns to Jerome. "We're non-union, but we follow most of the union rules. Three o'clock break is mandatory." Then, raising her voice: "*I heard you, Bull, was you born in a barn?*"

General laughter greets this, and Betty Brady gives Barbara a quick sideways hug. "Go on now, and save me a bagel if they got such a thing in this primitive town. I want to speak to this young man."

Barbara gives a slight frown at this, then joins Tones Kelly and Ross MacFarland, presumably heading for their three o'clock break. She looks back once, and for just a moment he sees her as she was at eight, worried that the girls at her new school wouldn't like her.

Betty puts an arm around Jerome's shoulders. "Does that girl listen to you?"

"Sometimes," Jerome says, bemused.

"Did she tell you we're collaborating on a song? Her words, my music?"

"Yes. She's totally stoked."

Betty begins leading Jerome down the aisle toward the stairs, her arm still around his shoulders, one extremely large breast prodding his side.

"Would she listen to you about going on the rest of the tour? Do some singin?"

Jerome stops. "She said *no?*"

Betty laughs. "It's complicated, and not just because I want her to sing some backup with the Dixie Crystals. She got a real good voice. Tess, Laverne, and Jem, they all like her, say she fits right in. The four of em were doing 'Lollipop' the other night, *a capella.* You know, that old Chordettes thing?"

Jerome doesn't know "Lollipop," but he knows Barbara has a good voice, and ordinarily she isn't shy about belting it out for an audience. She played the only Black Calamity Jane in history as a high school senior and has done a couple of community theater things since then . . . at least before poetry became her life.

"She said no to *that*?"

"Not . . . exactly. But when I asked her to duet with me on 'Lowtown,' she's all no-no-no."

"You're important to her," Jerome says. "She's not as shy as she once was, but she still can't even believe she's here, let alone all the other stuff."

"I get that, but she *fits*." She gives him an intense look. For the first time Jerome sees not a stout lady in a frumpy jumper but a diva who is used to getting her way. "I got as far as her saying she *might* sing 'Lowtown' with me here and go along with the tour as far as Boston, but as a roadie. She's *wasted* as a roadie!"

"I got *that*," Jerome says, and when Betty gives him a hearty slap on the back, he almost falls into the orchestra pit.

"She listens to you?"

"Sometimes."

"Maybe she'll listen to you about this." She pulls him close and whispers in his ear. *"Because she wants to do it."*

The crew and musicians are gathered backstage, eating White Castle sliders, fruit, crackers and cheese. Betty breaks away from Jerome to talk to an elderly Black man. Barbara seizes Jerome's hand. "What did she want?"

"Tell you later."

"She wants me to sing with her."

"I know. And not just here."

"I'm a *poet*, Jerome! Not a . . . a rock and roll girl!"

Jerome kisses her below the red bandanna, which is damp with sweat. He's not thinking about John Ackerly, or the Briggs name in Mike "the Rev" Rafferty's appointment book. Right then he's just thinking about how much he loves his pretty, multi-talented sister.

"Who says you can't be both?"

2

Holly stands in the back of the Radisson's Conference Center during Kate's press conference. Her purse is slung over her shoulder, unzipped. Her revolver (she still thinks of it as Bill's revolver) is inside, with the first chamber—the one the cylinder will rotate to when the trigger is pulled—unloaded, just as her mentor taught her. There's also a can of pepper spray and an Original Defense anti-rape siren. She reminds herself to get two more of each, for Kate and Corrie. The spray or the siren would be her own first choices, the pistol only a last resort.

Turnout for the press conference is good; after Reno and Des Moines, Kate is hot news. In what Holly considers to be the unpleasant parlance of the Social Media Age, Kate is "trending," if not yet "viral." There are cams and reporters from KWWL and KCRG. A grizzled old guy from the *Press-Citizen*. Stringers from various internet sites, most leaning left on the political spectrum. Kate is looking good in a plain white tee that emphasizes her full breasts, and tight jeans that speak to her slim hips. Tilted back on her head is a blue Iowa Cubs cap.

Kate gives a brief statement, not mentioning the fact that her luggage was drenched in blood and guts. She does, however, share that her room was childishly vandalized and brings up those verses from Exodus, saying that pro-life religious zealots have twisted them out of context—*tortured* them out of context—to give them a meaning they don't have. Holly is pretty sure the stalker will get the message and be pissed.

One of the reporters asks, "Isn't there a big difference between God ending fetal life and doctors destroying it?"

"Depends on whether or not you believe in God, or which God you believe in. Either way, this country is a democracy, not a theocracy. Read the Constitution, son."

Holly is barely listening. She's scanning the attendees for anyone who doesn't have a press credential. A few lookie-loos wander in, but no one makes a move Holly considers suspicious. She wishes she'd gotten a better look at that woman in the housekeeperly brown dress on the third floor, but most of her attention was fixed on Kate and Corrie. Was the woman blond? She thinks so but isn't sure.

Kate buttons up the presser by saying she's happy to be in Iowa City, she'll be speaking at Macbride Hall at seven PM, and some seats are still available. The woman with the credential saying she's from *Raw Story* patters a little applause, but no one else joins in; they just file out. Kate goes to a new suite. Hers has been taped off by the police, and after the gig tonight, the three of them will be going to a different hotel.

"That went pretty well, didn't it?" Kate asks Corrie. Always the same question.

"Dynamite," Corrie says. Always the same (correct) answer.

3

At roughly the same time, another press conference is going on in another city. Alice Patmore, the Buckeye City Chief of Police, is standing at the microphones with Darby Dingley, the city's Fire Commissioner. Behind them are two designated members of the opposing teams in the upcoming Guns and Hoses tilt. One is a tall young man named George Pill, looking overdressed in his ceremonial FD whites and hat. The other is Isabelle Jaynes, looking more comfortable in her summerweight blues.

Lew Warwick told Izzy before meeting the press that a little trash talk wouldn't be out of place. "All in good fun, you know."

Izzy *doesn't* know. She feels like a horse's ass in her short-sleeved uni. She has a serial murderer to catch, and instead she's up here playing fiddly-fuck at what is essentially a photo op. She looks at Pill to see if he feels the same, but he's staring out at the assembled reporters with a severe and heroic can-do look on his face. If the brain under that stupid white shovel hat is uncomfortable, he's not showing it.

Meanwhile, the big dogs drone on about the wonderful charities this year's competition will benefit. Chief Patmore speaks first, then Commissioner Dingley gets his turn. Izzy hopes that's enough from them and she can get back into her street clothes (and back to work), but no joy; each takes another turn. The assembled press looks as bored as Izzy feels, until Chief Patmore announces that Sista Bessie has agreed to sing the National Anthem; wishful thinking has become a firm commitment. This causes a murmur of interest in the reporters, and brief applause.

"Before we send you to the refreshment table," Commissioner Dingley says, "I'd like to introduce two of this year's star players. For the Hoses team, Fireman First Class George Pill, who will be playing center field."

Patmore takes her turn. "And for the Guns team, Detective Sergeant Isabelle Jaynes, our starting pitcher."

The big dogs step back. Izzy doesn't know what to do at first, but Pill does. He flashes a movie star grin, grabs her by the arm, and pulls her forward. She stumbles a little. Cameras flash. Some of the reporters chuckle.

"Looking forward to the game, and looking forward to lighting this little lady up," Pill says, still grinning and holding her arm, as if she were a child who might run away.

Genuinely nettled, Izzy looks up at him—Pill has at least six inches on her—and says, "The little lady might have something to say about that."

Pill's grin widens. "Ooh, this one's *feisty*."

Laughter from the reporters.

Izzy says, "What's that on your head? Will you be wearing it in the game, when I strike you out?"

Pill's grin freezes in place. *Maybe too much*, Izzy thinks. Or maybe fuck it. She doesn't like being dragged.

Before Pill can reply, a woman in the front row stands up. Izzy recognizes her as Carrie Winton, who covers the crime beat for the local paper. She's out of place covering fluff like this. Izzy already knows what's coming.

"Detective Jaynes, can you update us concerning the so-called Surrogate Juror Murders? Is the murder of Fred Sinclair related?"

Chief Patmore steps between Izzy and George Pill. "That investigation is ongoing," she says smoothly, "and you'll be updated at the proper time. Just for one afternoon, let's concentrate on something positive, shall we? Police and firemen, taking the field for charity! And let me tell you, these guys are ready to rumble."

Winton is still on her feet, ignoring Patmore. "Do you have any leads, Detective Jaynes?"

She's about to say she can't comment, but then Buckeye Brandon sticks his oar in. "Should you be concentrating on a charity softball game while a killer is on the loose?"

Pill inserts himself. "I believe it's time I led Officer Jaynes away. It's her naptime."

Lots of chuckles, and that ends it. The press corps head for the back table, where rookie cops and firemen are waiting to dispense rubbery supermarket shrimp and wine coolers (a two-drink limit). Izzy shakes off Pill's grip and leaves by the door at the back of the podium, wanting to get back to 19 Court and change before her blue uniform shirt gets sweaty. Pill follows her, his movie-star grin gone.

"Hey. You. Girlfriend. I didn't appreciate that crack about my hat. I was told to wear it."

As I was told to wear my uniform, Izzy thinks. *We all serve the big dogs*. "I didn't appreciate your last crack, either. About naptime."

"Put it on your T.S. list and give it to the chaplain." He takes the hat off and stares at it as if something important is written inside. "This hat was my father's."

"Good for him. As for you, put it on your T.S. list."

"I heard your starting pitcher broke his hand in a stupid bar fight. You're the sub."

"So what? It's a *game*. Don't be a bonehead."

He bends down to her, once again making her feel like a child. "We're going to beat you like a drum. *Little lady*."

She can't believe this. "We were supposed to put on a show, and the show is over. It's a charity game, not the World Fucking Series."

"We'll see." With that, Pill walks away. Except it's more like a strut.

Unbelievable, Izzy thinks, but by the time she's changing in the locker room, she's forgotten all about it.

Pill, it turns out, has not.

4

Holly and Corrie take a Lyft to Macbride Hall. Corrie chats with the book people from Prairie Lights and with the stage manager, specifying a handheld mic for Kate instead of a lav. She's testing the sound—"*Check one, check two*"—while Holly examines the stage door, where they will enter and leave, and notes the other entry points.

She identifies herself to the Macbride's Program Director, Liz Horgan, and asks if the audience will have to pass through security detectors. Horgan says no, but if people carrying bags refuse inspection, they will be denied entry. Holly isn't delighted with that, but recognizes the limits of what she—and the venue—can do. She reminds herself again that if someone really wants to attack a visiting celebrity, nothing but luck, a hair-trigger response, or a combination of the two will keep it from happening.

Corrie remains at the venue. Holly takes another Lyft back to the hotel. Kate's new suite is on the third floor. "It's a comp," she tells Holly. "What they call a holding room. At least it's not a holding *cell*. Where are we going after the show? Corrie must have that arranged. She's terrific."

"A Holiday Inn," Holly says.

Kate wrinkles her nose. "Needs must when the devil drives, I suppose. Shakespeare."

"All's Well That Ends Well."

Kate laughs. "Not just a bodyguard, an English major."

"No, I just read a lot of Shakespeare as a teenager." *Romeo and Juliet*, for instance. Over and over.

"Let's get some dinner," Kate says. "That's also on the house, so order something expensive. I'll have fish. Anything else, I'm apt to burp and fart onstage."

"Do you get nervous before your . . . before you go on?"

"It's a *show*, Holly. You don't have to be afraid to say it. No. Excited. Call me a partisan, I don't mind. I try to hide zeal with humor. It's stand-up, funny as I can make it, but deadly serious underneath. This isn't the country I grew up in, it's Funhouse America now. Don't get me started on that shit. What about you? Are *you* nervous?"

"A little," Holly admits. "Bodyguard work is new to me."

"Well, you were fine when that alarm went off. I was something of a pisshead about it, wasn't I?"

Holly doesn't want to say yes or no, so she just seesaws her hand in the air.

Kate smiles. "Good in a crisis situation, knows Shakespeare, also diplomatic. A triple threat." She hands over the room service menu. "Now what do you want?"

Holly orders a chicken club, knowing she won't eat much of it. It's almost time to start earning her keep.

5

By the time Trig gets back to work, the numbing agent Rothman used—Novocain or whatever has replaced it these days—is wearing off, and the socket where his molar used to be is throbbing. Rothman gave him a scrip for painkillers, and he stopped on the way back to pick them up. Only six tablets; they've gotten so *stingy* about that stuff.

Maisie asks how he feels. Trig tells her not so hot and she says, "Poor *you*." Trig asks if there's any biz he should attend to or calls he should return. She tells him there's nothing she can't deal with, just the current agenda he already knows about. She suggests he go home. Lie down. Maybe put an icepack on his cheek.

"I think I will," he says. "Have a good night, Maisie."

He doesn't go home; he goes to Dingley Park.

There's a small lot for park personnel near the rickety silo shape of the old Holman Hockey Rink. He parks there, starts to get out of his car, then rethinks and takes the .22 from the center console. He puts it in the pocket of his sportcoat.

I'm not going to do anything with it, he thinks. Which reminds him, perhaps inevitably, of his drinking days. Going into the Three-Ring on the way home from the office and telling himself he'll only have a Coke. *But this time I mean it.*

Which makes the ghost of his father laugh.

The old rink is surrounded by pines and spruces. There are picnic benches and food wagons off to the right—Frankie's Fabulous Fish, Taco Joe's, Chicago Dogs & Pizza—now closed and shuttered for the afternoon. Further off, Trig can hear men shouting as they practice for the big cops vs. firemen charity game. He hears the clink of aluminum bats and laughter.

The rink's sagging double doors are flanked by paintings of ghostly, barely-there hockey players. A sign reads HOLMAN RINK CONDEMNED BY ORDER OF CITY COUNCIL. Below this, someone has chalked BECAUSE JESUS DON'T SKATE! Which makes no sense to Trig.

He tries the doors. Locked, as he expected, but there's a keypad, and the red light at the top tells him the batteries are still putting out juice. He has no idea what the passcode might be, but that doesn't mean he can't get in. His father was an electrician, and when he wasn't yelling at Trig, or beating the shit out of him, or taking him to this very place, he sometimes talked about his work, including certain tricks of the trade. *Always take a picture of the breaker panel before starting work. Keep zip ties handy; they have all sorts of uses. Don't stick your finger where you wouldn't stick your dick.* As a boy, Trig had encouraged these sermons, partly because they were interesting and mostly because when Daddy was talking, Daddy was happy. *Hockey* made him happy, especially when the players would drop their gloves on the ice and go at it—*whap-whap-whap*. Sometimes he would even put his arm around Trig and give him a careless hug. *Trig*, he'd say. *My good old Trigger*.

Sermons and instructional talks at the Holman Rink usually lasted eighteen minutes, no more, no less. That was the length of the breaks between periods.

Trig looks around, sees no one, and plants his fingernails beneath the keypad's cover. He levers it up, pulls it off, and looks inside. Printed there is PC 9721. The PC stands for Plumber's Code, but his father told him that was just a holdover from the old days. All kinds of service people—rink maintenance guys, electricians, the Zamboni operator—used the PC.

Trig puts the cover back on the keypad and pushes 9721. The yellow light turns green. He hears the locking bar clunk as it withdraws, and then he's inside. Easy as pie. He crosses the lobby, where an abandoned popcorn machine stands guard over an empty snackbar. Yellowing paper posters of long-gone Buckeye Bullets hockey players hang on the walls.

He walks into the rink itself. The slowly disintegrating roof is split with blinding lines of light. Pigeons (Trig guesses they're pigeons) flutter and swoop. Unlike the sturdy metal bleachers at the soccer and softball fields, the ones in here are wooden, sagging, splintery. Fit for ghosts like Trig's daddy instead of people. The ice is long gone, of course. Creosoted boards, twenty-footers, crisscross cracked concrete, making tic-tac-toe patterns. Hardy weeds sprout from between many of them. There's surprisingly little trash—no snack bags or busted crack vials, no discarded rubbers. The druggies have been kept out in the surrounding trees, at least so far.

Trig walks to what was once center ice. He drops to one knee and runs his hand over one of the boards—lightly, so he won't pick up a splinter and add a throbbing palm to his throbbing mouth. He has no idea what these boards are doing in here. Maybe they're supposed to discourage skateboarders, or somebody just wanted to get them out of the sun and rain, but he knows one thing: they'd burn fast and hot. The whole place would go up like a torch. And if certain innocent people were in here—some perhaps famous—they would also go up like torches.

I wouldn't be able to put the names of the guilty ones in their hands, he thinks, *because they'd be burned to cinders*.

But then an idea strikes him, one so brilliant that he actually rocks back a little on his knee, as if from a sudden blow. Putting the names of the guilty in the hands of the innocent might not be necessary. There could be a better way. He could put their names in a place where everyone in the city would see them. All over the *world*, once the TV news crews descended.

I won't be able to get all of them, anyway, he thinks, rising to his feet. *That was too ambitious. A foolish dream. I can't keep getting lucky. But I might be able to get most of them, including the guilty party. The one who most deserves to die.*

"I have to make a plan," Trig murmurs as he walks back along the crisscrossing boards. "Have to find a way to get them here. As many as possible."

Why does it have to be here?

It just does, that's all. He thinks about the eighteen-minute sermons, and the occasional rough hug from his dad. Beyond that

(*Trig, my good old Trigger*)

he won't let himself go. Certainly not to his mother, who was *gone*.

"Shut up," he says, loud enough to startle some of the pigeons into flight. "Just shut up."

He crosses the abandoned snackbar and passes the ticket booth. Cracks the door and sees no one. A breeze rattles the posters in the lobby. Steps out and taps the Plumber's Code, relocking the door. He starts down the weedy cement walk to his car, then changes his mind and decides to take a look at the practice happening at the softball field.

He's halfway through the trees when a girl—dirty hair, hollow eyes, scrawny body, maybe twenty—approaches him.

"Hey, guy."

"Hey."

"You wouldn't be holding, would you?"

Although he's attended NA meetings as well as the AA ones—they all treat the same disease, that of addiction—the tidal pull of the jonesing addict never ceases to amaze him. This girl sees a man who, in his sportcoat and Farah slacks, looks more like a business guy (or a narc) than a user/pusher, but her need is so great that she still comes on to him. He thinks she'd probably ask an old geezer pushing a walker if he was holding.

Trig is about to say no, then changes his mind. She's serving herself up on a platter, and if she dies, the only loser will be the rehab she's undoubtedly heading for. He touches the gun in his pocket and says, "What are you looking for, sweetheart?"

Her previously dead eyes take on a spark. "What have you got? I got these." She cups her breasts.

He thinks of the Baggies he's seen in various gutters and alleyways just lately. "Would you possibly be interested in Queen's Best?"

The spark kindles into a flame. "Good. Great. Yes. What do you want? Handjob? Blowjob? Maybe a little of both?"

"For the Queen," Trig says, "I want to get with you. All the way."

"Oh, man, I don't know. How much do you have?"

"A cueball." He knows the lingo; a cue is an eightball times two.

"Where?" She looks around dubiously. "Here?"

"In there." He gestures at the Holman. "Privacy."

"It's locked, man."

He lowers his voice, hoping he doesn't look like a man contemplating a chick who is probably incubating half a dozen different diseases. "I have a secret code."

After another look around to make sure they're alone, he takes her by the hand and leads her back to the abandoned rink.

No flinching. Never flinch.

Later, the name he puts in her hand is Corinna Ashford.

6

When Kate walks onstage—no, *struts*—most of the audience rises to its feet, cheering and applauding. Standing in the shadows at stage left with Corrie, Holly gets goosebumps. She has learned courage and bravery because those things were required. They made her a better person, too, but at heart she'll always be a fundamentally shy woman who often feels inadequate, unable to put any foot forward that isn't the wrong foot, and she can't comprehend how anyone can stride so confidently into the view of all those people. And not all of them are applauding. A contingent toward the back, wearing blue shirts that say LIFE AT CONCEPTION, are booing heartily.

Kate stands at center stage, sweeps off her ball cap, and makes a deep bow. Then she grabs the mic and gives it a baton-twirl.

"Woman Power!"

"Woman Power!"

"Woman Power, let me hear you, Iowa City!"

They shout it back at her, ecstatic. The Life at Conception folks are sitting with their arms crossed like sulky children.

A hand grasps Holly's elbow.

"She's something, isn't she?" Corrie asks quietly.

"Yes," Holly says. "She is."

Especially because the woman who threw bleach at Corrie and dumped blood and guts all over her luggage could be in that audience right now. Armed. Not one of those in the blue shirts, either. Nor in a brown housekeeper's dress. Someone who probably looks mild-mannered and interested. Applauding and cheering.

A woman, in other words, who might look like Holly herself.

Most of the crowd quiets. Not the Life at Conception cadre, however. As soon as the rest of the audience sits down, they leap to their feet and begin chanting, "*Abortion is murder! Abortion is murder! Abortion is murder!*"

Holly tenses and slides her hand into her purse. The majority of the crowd boos. There are cries of "Sit down and shut up!" A ragged chant of "Our bodies, our choice" gets going. Ushers are moving toward the blue shirts.

Kate raises her hands. She's smiling. "Quiet, you libtards, you snowflakes. Rest easy. Ushers, stand down. Let them get it out of their systems."

The Life at Conception people at first continue to chant, then realize they are being watched by the majority of the crowd the way monkeys in a zoo are watched when exhibiting some peculiar kind of activity—throwing feces at each other, perhaps. The chanting loses force, becomes ragged, fades . . . stops.

"There," Kate says kindly. It's the voice a parent uses when speaking to a child exhausted by their own tantrum. "You've said what you wanted to say. Stood up for what you believe in. That's how we do it in this country. Now it's my turn, all right? The turn of a woman who believes *a raped child who turns up pregnant should have an option*!"

A roar of applause. Corrie turns to Holly, and if Holly never saw a person with actual stars in her eyes, she's seeing one now.

"It always gets me," Corrie says. "*She* always gets me. Sometimes she's a pain in the ass, but when she gets onstage . . . you feel it, don't you?"

"Yes."

"She means it. Every word. Top to heels. She means it."

"Yes."

"Okay, I've got my fix." Corrie laughs and wipes away a few tears. "I'll be in the greenroom, making calls and getting ready for Davenport. You can find your way back to the green, can't you?"

"Yes. Remember we're not going out the stage door."

Corrie flashes a thumbs-up. "From the South Hall, right. Luggage and vehicles stay at the Radisson. We'll get them tomorrow."

Another wave of applause from the auditorium as Kate makes her patented *c'mon c'mon c'mon* gesture, wiggling the fingers of both hands.

7

Chris is sitting in the third row, short blond hair neatly combed, dressed in a blue Oxford shirt and new bluejeans. He has no weapon. He thought there might be metal detectors, but that's only one reason. He will die if necessary, but is hoping he and his sister can end the bitch and get away clean. There are plenty of stops left on McKay's Tour of Death. Martyrdom is a last resort.

She's magnetic, he has to admit that. No wonder the women around him are enthralled. No wonder that Pastor Jim of the Real Christ Holy Church calls her "the handmaiden of the antichrist." But it was Andy Fallowes, Pastor Jim's First Deacon and the church's finance officer, who set Chris on his current course. Because, he said, Pastor Jim could only be seen talking the talk.

"It's up to Christian patriots like us, Christopher, to walk the walk. Do you agree?"

He did, most heartily. So did Chrissy.

Onstage, Kate is telling them to pretend they're in school. "Can you do that? Good! I want all the men in the audience to raise a hand. Come on, guys, pretend I'm the teacher you crushed on in the sixth grade."

There's a murmur of laughter. Men raise their hands, Chris among them.

"Now those men who've had an abortion, keep your hands up. Those who haven't, put your hands down."

Chris can hardly believe what he's hearing. It's as if she's speaking directly to him.

"Do I see one amazing man out there?" Kate asks, shading her eyes. "The XY chromosome version of the Virgin Mary?"

Chris realizes his hand is still up. He lowers it to good-natured laughter, which sounds to him like jeers. He joins in because it's protective coloration, but his mind is yammering and hammering, as he sometimes hammers his fists against the walls of the cheap motel rooms where he stays, which are all he deserves, hammering until someone shouts, "Shut up, goddammit, we're trying to sleep here!"

Go ahead, he thinks now. *Laugh at me. Laugh your fool heads off. Let's see how much you laugh when I send your queen bitch to hell.*

"Enough kidding around," Kate's saying. "Men don't have abortions, we all know that, but who makes the *laws* in Iowa?"

And with that, she's off.

8

Izzy works late that night, catching up on her other cases. At times like this, when most of the other carrels are empty and even Lew Warwick's office is dark, she thinks that maybe she should take Holly up on her offer to join Finders Keepers. There would still be paperwork, but she might not have to endure dog-and-pony shows like this afternoon's press conference and the odious George Pill.

Her cell phone rings. The screen says 911.

"Jaynes."

"Izzy, this is Patti downstairs. I just got a call from someone who says he's your serial. He wanted your extension if you were here. I gave—"

Izzy's desk phone lights up.

"Trace it, trace it," she tells Patti, and ends the call. She picks up her landline. "Hello, this is Detective Jaynes. To whom am I speaking?"

When Izzy was in her first year as a detective, Bill Hodges told her she'd be amazed how often that question can surprise a name out of someone.

Not this time.

"Bill Wilson." The name has been withheld from the press. "Give me your cell number, Detective Jaynes. I want to send you a picture."

"What kind of a—"

"I know how you people play for time. If you want the picture, give me your number. If you don't, I'll hang up and send it to Buckeye Brandon."

Her caller is an adult male with no accent, at least that she can pick up. A linguistic expert who listens to the tape may be able to hear one. Izzy gives him her number. Next time he calls—if there is a next time—she'll record it.

"Thank you. I'm sending the picture because I want you to see the name of another person who aided and abetted in the killing of Alan Duffrey. Goodbye."

And just like that, he's gone, but seconds later her phone bings with a text. She opens it and sees a woman's hand in extreme close-up. Everything in the background is gray. Possibly concrete. A sidewalk, maybe?

In the woman's hand, printed in block letters, is the name Corinna Ashford. In the Alan Duffrey trial, she was Juror 7.

9

Trig ends the call on the burner he's used (there are three more in the tool-and-spare compartment of his Toyota). He doesn't bother to pull the SIM card. Let them trace the location if they can. He's in the parking lot of the Mingo Auditorium, where this Friday night's event is a custom car show with a country group called the Ruff Ryders as an added attraction. The main lot is full of cars, many bearing stickers like THINK TWICE BECAUSE I WON'T and GIRLS LIKE GUNS TOO.

Trig takes the phone to a nearby trash barrel, wipes it down, drops it in, goes back to his car, drives away. They might or might not find the phone (the Saturday morning trash haulers may take it away). Even if they don't, they can use the International Mobile Equipment Identity—the phone's fingerprint—to trace the text he sent Jaynes to the phone's point of purchase, which happened to be a convenience store in Wheeling, West Virginia. Bought for cash over two months ago. If security footage from that long ago still exists—doubtful—it will show a Caucasian male of medium height wearing a Denver Broncos gimme cap and Foster Grant sunglasses.

Trig thinks he's got the situation covered but knows he may have forgotten something. The way he forgot the hitchhiker's sign, for instance. Which is still in the trunk. He may be a serial killer (he has come a long way toward accepting the appellation, if not welcoming it), but he does *not* have a God complex. If he keeps going—and he intends to—they will catch him eventually.

Talking to the 911 operator, then to Jaynes, was risky. Sending the picture to Jaynes was even riskier, but he can't bear to let the druggie girl go to waste. That would be murder for the sake of murder, and he hopes he hasn't sunk to that level. They must know she was murdered in the name of Corinna Ashford. *Ashford* must know.

He could have told Jaynes the location, but then the Holman would become a crime scene, and he wants to save it for what he's now thinking of as the grand finale. Of course the druggie girl's body may be found anyway, he knows that. It depends partly on whether any maintenance people have reason to visit the Holman Rink over the next week or so. He doesn't think they will. The building is condemned, after all. But city workers aren't the only reason the body might be found. Just because few if any drug users have gained access to the building so far doesn't mean they won't get in at some future point. Surely Trig isn't the only person who's wise to the Plumber's Code trick. For all he knows, users have already been in the rink, and just picked up after themselves—who says all druggies are slobs? It's possible a fiend might not report the body, but it's more likely he or she would make an anonymous call (probably after searching the corpse for drugs or money).

Another possibility: Depending on how hot the following week is, someone may smell decomp and send one of the park workers to investigate. That would be a shame because he wants to use the rink again. If the body is discovered, he'll have to revise his thinking. As the wise men of the ages have all agreed, shit happens.

10

Holly gets them out the South Hall of the Macbride as soon as Kate's gig ends, leaving the autograph seekers empty-handed at the stage door. (She discovers later it won't always be that easy.) The bookstore has provided a sedan. Kate, floating on a post-performance high, doesn't even complain about going to a Holiday Inn.

"It was good tonight, wasn't it?" she asks.

Corrie says it was very good and Holly says the same, but once Kate really got rolling, Holly didn't have a chance to appreciate the woman's wit and outrage. Her clarity. She would have relished those things as a member of the audience. But she's not here to relish and appreciate.

She gives Corrie several photographs, screengrabs she asked the stage manager to provide her. They are from the audience cams and show the first three rows of the center section. Due to the stage lights, the faces are quite clear and turned up to look at Kate. "Do you see anyone who looks like the woman who attacked you in Reno?"

Corrie goes through them and shakes her head. "It all happened so fast. And it was raining. I can't say she's not in one of these and can't say she is."

Holly takes the pictures back. "It was a long shot."

Kate is paying no attention. "You thought it was good, right? Tell the truth."

Corrie assures her again that it was good. Holly checks behind them—it's the fourth or fifth time—for follow cars, but now that it's dark, who can tell? They're just shapes behind headlights. She's got a headache, small but nagging, and needs to pee. She reminds herself—also for the fourth or fifth time—that if another potential bodyguarding job comes along, to think twice.

Her dead mother sometimes speaks up in Holly's head, usually at the most inopportune times. Like now.

If Kate McKay is killed on your watch, you won't have to worry about any of that, will you? And then, with her old longsuffering sigh: *Oh, Holly.*

Chapter 11

1

Holly is in and out of sleep, and what she gets isn't particularly restful. Their Holiday Inn is in the Coral Ridge Mall, which is fairly quiet after ten PM, the only party at the far end and by midnight it was winding down, but the motel is between I-80 and the Grand Army of the Republic Highway, and the long-haul trucks—eastbound, westbound—drone 24/7. That sound usually soothes her, but not tonight. She'd specified three rooms, Kate's on one side of her and Corrie on the other. She keeps waiting for the sound of a door breaking in or one of their anti-rape alarms blasting off. She knows she'll be having thin sleep for the next week. Longer, if she continues with the tour. Catching the woman who threw the bleach and delivered the anthrax would help, but even then . . .

Holly keeps thinking of the booing section last night, those men and women wearing blue shirts saying LIFE AT CONCEPTION. How righteously angry they looked. These are the people who protest at abortion clinics. Sometimes they throw bags of animal blood at the women and girls who come to have the procedure. And in several cases they have attacked doctors and nurses. At least one doctor Holly knows of, David Gunn, was shot and killed. She finally drifts off into a deeper sleep and dreams of her mother.

The idea that you can protect those women is ridiculous, Charlotte Gibney says in this dream. *You couldn't even remember your library book when you got off the bus*.

While she's brushing her teeth at quarter past six, her phone rings. It's Jerome, asking if he can treat John Ackerly to breakfast on the company dime. "I want to ask him something about that AA guy. The one he found dead? I tried to call you yesterday, but your phone was off."

Holly sighs. "This job doesn't allow for outside distractions. What do you want to ask him? Keeping in mind it's police business, not ours."

"It's about the appointment book. Never mind, I'll go ahead and pay for breakfast. We're talking twenty bucks, thirty tops."

With the success of your book, you could certainly afford it, Holly thinks. "No, put it on the Finders Keepers card. Just tell me if there's anything to tell."

"I will. It's probably nothing."

"Then why did you call? Not just to ask if the company would buy breakfast for a possible source. I don't believe that for a second."

"I'll tell you if anything comes of it. Even if it doesn't. How's it going out there in flyover country?"

She thinks about pushing Jerome for what's on his mind—he'd tell her, she thinks it's why he called—then decides not to. "It's all A-OK so far, but I'm a little on edge. The woman stalking Kate means business." She fills Jerome in, finishing with the forced door and the bloody mess poured over Kate's luggage.

"Has she thought about packing it in?"

"She won't. She's . . . dedicated."

"Do you mean stubborn?" Jerome suggests.

A moment of silence from Iowa City. Then Holly says, "Both."

"I'm a little surprised her publisher didn't pull the plug. Those people tend to be timid." He's thinking of the run-up to the publication of his own book, and how the editor brought a sensitivity reader onboard to go over his manuscript. She suggested a few minor changes. Which Jerome made, guessing there would have been more if he were white.

"The publisher's not in charge," Holly says. "Kate's doing this tour on her own. It's politics more than publicity for her new book. She does have an assistant that's coordinating with bookstores along the way. Her name is Corrie Anderson. I like her. She's very capable. Which is good because Kate can be demanding."

"The assistant's the one who got the bleach shower? And the card with the anthrax in it?"

"Yes."

"But she's also continuing?"

"Yes."

"Looks like you've got your work cut out for you."

"Yes."

"Sorry you took the job?"

"It's stressful, but I look at it as a growth opportunity."

"Take care of them, Hollyberry. And yourself."

"That's the plan. And don't call me that."

"Just kind of slipped out." She hears a grin in his voice.

"I call poop on that. Talk to John by all means and give him my best."

"I will."

"Now go on and tell me what's on your mind. I know you want to."

He thinks about it, then says, "Later, Gator." And ends the call.

Holly gets dressed, folds her pajamas neatly into her suitcase, and goes to the door to look at a whole lot of Iowa. It's at times like this, early in the morning on a beautiful spring day, that she really wants a cigarette.

Her phone rings. It's Corrie, asking her if she's ready to go to Davenport.

"Ready as I'll ever be," Holly says.

2

Chris wakes from a terrible nightmare. In it he's back in the third row of the Macbride. The woman onstage—magnetic, beautiful, and dangerous—is asking all the men in the audience to put their hands up. *Pretend I'm the teacher you crushed on in the sixth grade*, she tells them, and for Chris that was Miss Yarborough. He was homeschooled, of course; all the kids from Real Christ Holy were homeschooled (the public schools being tools of the deep state), but Miss Yarborough came to give lessons in math and geography. Golden hair, blue eyes, long smooth legs.

In the dream, McKay tells those men who've had an abortion to keep their hands up. There's laughter at this absurd idea and all the men put their hands down. All but Chris. His hand won't come down. It's frozen, sticking straight up. Straight up and thousands of people are looking at him. Someone shouts, *Where's your sister?* Someone else murmurs, *Our secret.* He knows that voice. He turns, hand still upraised and frozen, and sees Mama as she was near the end, so pale and thin. She shouts for everyone in the Macbride to hear: *You are you and she is she!*

That's when he pulls himself out of the dream and finds himself sprawled on the filthy squashed-flat rug of his motel room. The sheet and the threadbare blanket are tangled around him, and he can barely unfist his fingers enough to let them go.

You are you and she is she.

He gets up, staggers into the bathroom, and splashes cold water on his face. He thinks that makes it better, fixes it, but then his stomach clenches and he doesn't even have time to make a half-turn to the toilet, just vomits last night's Taco Bell steak quesadilla into the basin.

Our secret.

For awhile it was.

He stands where he is, sure he's going to retch a second time, but his diaphragm loosens. He runs water into the basin, then mops up the chunky residue with a washcloth, which he throws into the tub—*splat*.

At times like this, in the aftermath of his frequent nightmares, he's *both*. He thinks of the hand hanging down from the upper bunk and he's both. *Never died, never died* usually works, but after the nightmares, in the socket of the night, such words have no power. At times like this he can't deny the fact that Christine will forever be seven, hair growing brittle in her narrow underground home, and the best he can do is to inhabit his sister's ghost.

He can hear Daddy talking to Mama. *I forbid it. Would you be Eve? Would you listen to the serpent instead of your husband and eat from the Tree of Knowledge?*

That day his mother was where she almost never went, in Daddy's barn. Where he invented the things that had made them . . . well, not rich, not when they gave most of the money from Daddy's patents to the church, but well-to-do. *Never brag*, their mother had told the twins. *All we have comes from God. Your father is just a conduit. That means he just passes it along.*

Chris was at the side of the barn, standing in knee-high weeds, grasshoppers leaping around his shins, listening through a crack between two boards. A crack Chrissy had found.

Mama rarely spoke back to Daddy, but that day, after the funeral hack had come and gone, she did. *You're hiding out here, Harold. Can you call yourself a scientist and not want to know what killed your daughter?*

I'm not a scientist. I deny science. I'm an inventor*! They will cut her up, you stupid woman!*

Chris had never heard his father call his mother stupid. Had never even heard him raise his voice to her.

I DON'T CARE!

Screaming! His mother, screaming!

I DON'T CARE! I HAVE TO KNOW!

She got her way. Contrary to the church's teachings, there was an autopsy on Christine Evangeline Stewart. And it turned out to be something called Brugada Syndrome. His seven-year-old sister had died of a heart attack.

You had to know, Daddy told her later. *You had to know, didn't you? And now you know the boy could have it as well, because it's hereditary. There's your knowledge, woman. Your useless and pointless knowledge.*

That time they were in the house, but Chris had become quite the accomplished eavesdropper. He didn't understand *hereditary*, so he looked it up in the big Webster's in the lesson room. He understood that what had killed Chrissy could kill him, as well. Of course it could, it made perfect sense, weren't they twins? Chrissy with her father's dark hair, Chris with his mother's blond hair, faces not identical but similar enough so that anyone who saw them knew they were brother and sister. They loved Mama, they loved Daddy, they loved Pastor Jim and Deacon Andy, they loved God and Jesus. But most of all they loved each other and lived in the secret world of Two.

Brugada Syndrome.

Hereditary.

But if Chrissy were alive, if there had been no hand dangling down from the upper bunk in a beam of dusty morning sunlight, then he could stop worrying that some night his own heart might stop. If Chrissy were still alive, his mother's pain would be gone. *His* pain would be gone as well. The emptiness. The darkness where a monster lurked with its claws outstretched, a monster named BRUGADA. Waiting to pounce.

His father was consoled by the church. It was Chris who consoled his mother. There was no horror the first time he went to Mama wearing one of Chrissy's dresses. No disgust. She simply opened her arms to him.

"I'll be your little girl," he said against her bosom. "I'll be your little boy, too. I can be both."

"Our secret," she said, stroking his hair, as fine as Chrissy's had been. "Our secret."

They kept her alive. When Daddy found out and called him a transvestite, Chris had no idea what that meant until he once again went to the Webster's. Then he had to laugh. He was no such thing, because he *was* Chrissy. Not all the time, but when he was, *she* was.

They had been close; they were close again.

"Leave him alone, Harold." Not screaming that time, just firm. It was a week after Daddy found out. Harold had taken counseling with the church elders. "All of you, leave him alone. And leave *her* alone."

"Woman," Harold Stewart said, "you're crazy."

"He loves her," she said (Chris once more listening at the crack in the wall of the Invention Barn). "And I love them both. I've given you everything, Harold. I gave up my life for your life and your church. You will not take my daughter away from me, nor his sister from Christopher."

"*He's* crazy!"

"No more crazy than you are, using the tools of science and calling it the will of God."

"Do you dispute my understanding?" A warning rumble in his voice, like far-off thunder.

"No, Harold. I never have. I'm only saying that, like him, you have two ways of thinking. No . . . two ways of *being*. Chris is the same." A pause. "And *she* is."

"Will you at least agree to counseling?"

"Yes. If it stays in the church."

So Chris and Chrissy started going to Andy Fallowes. Andy hadn't laughed. He tried to understand. The twins would always love him for that.

Does God make mistakes? Deacon Andy asked.

No, course not.

And do you still have male urges, Christopher? Eyes averted, Deacon Andy pointed vaguely in the direction of Chris's crotch.

Thinking of Deanna Lane, his spelling and math partner—he said he did, at least when he was Chris. And with Deanna, and later with Miss Yarborough, he was always Chris; he was only Chrissy with his mother, because the one time his father had seen him in a dress and in the wig his mother had bought for him . . . that one time was enough.

Our secret, our secret.

"When you are Christine, it comforts your mother, doesn't it?"

"Yes."

"And it comforts *you*."

"Yes."

"You're not afraid you'll die like she did."

"No, because she's alive."

"When you're Christine—"

"Chrissy."

"When you're Chrissy, you *are* Chrissy."

"Yes."

"When you're Chris, you *are* Chris."

"Yes."

"Do you believe in God, Chris?"

"Yes."

"Have you taken Jesus Christ as your personal savior?"

"Yes."

"Very well. You may continue to be Christine—*Chrissy*—but only with your mother. Can you do that?"

"Yes." And oh, the relief.

Later, much later, he would come to understand the concept. Which did not, in the view of Real Christ Holy, exist. Nor in his own view. To Chris (and to Chrissy), they were perfectly sane. There was, however, *possession*, which could be demonic but also benign. Although Fallowes never said so, Chris came to believe that Deacon Andy had decided Chris might have been possessed by the spirit of his dead sister. How old was he then? Nine? Ten?

It was five or six years later when Deacon Andy—after consulting with the church elders, Pastor Jim, and his father—began talking to Chris about Katherine "Kate" McKay.

Never did Fallowes mention to any of them that he was discussing the baby-killing woman with Chris's sister as well as Chris himself.

3

Chris leaves the bathroom and regards the two suitcases at the foot of the bed, one pink and one blue. He opens the pink one. On top are two wigs, one black and one blond (the red one was discarded in Reno). She dresses in skinny jeans and a boatneck shirt. She puts on the blond wig. Today it will be Chrissy who travels to McKay's next stop.

Chris is a doer tortured by jumbled thoughts and nightmares. Chrissy is a thinker who has more clarity. She is perfectly aware that Andy Fallowes, possibly along with Pastor Jim, see this divided person as a God-given tool to put an end to the Murder Queen. Both personae, Chris and Chrissy, will claim they acted on their own, that the church had nothing to do with it. They will, in the vulgar but applicable phrase, dummy up.

Fallowes and Pastor Jim see Kate McKay as a terrible influence working against God's law, not only when it comes to abortion but about the acceptance of homosexuality and her insistence on limiting the Second Amendment (*strangling* the Second Amendment). Most of all, they worry about McKay's influence on various state legislatures. McKay understands that all real change is local, and that makes her a poison seeping into the body politic.

Unlike Chris, Chrissy knows how Fallowes sees them: as pawns.

Does it matter? No. What matters is that the McKay woman wants to arrogate the power of God to earthly creatures who have no understanding of God's plan.

4

Jerome Robinson and John Ackerly have scrambled eggs and about a gallon of coffee at a café down the street from Happy, which John will open at eight AM, ready to serve early birds wanting that all-important wake-up shot of vodka and orange.

"So what's up, buttercup?" John asks. "Not that I don't appreciate a free meal."

"Probably nothing." It's what he told Holly, but it gnaws at him. "Did you get the picture I sent you?"

"Yup." John shovels in scrambled eggs. "Close-up of the May page of the Rev's appointment book. You find the guy yet? Briggs? Because I've checked with a lot of Program people, and no one's heard of anyone calling themselves that."

"It's a police case. I'm just an interested bystander."

John points at him. "Caught the detecting bug from Holly, didn't you? It's more contagious than Covid."

Jerome doesn't deny it, although in his mind it's more like poison oak—a persistent itch. "Look at it again. You can see it better on my iPad than you can on your phone." He shows him the photo of the calendar square.

John takes a good close look, even spreading the image with his fingers to make it bigger. "Okay. Briggs, seven PM, May twentieth. What about it?"

"I don't fucking *know*," Jerome says, "and it's driving me crazy. Briggs in capital letters."

"The Rev put all the names of all the people he was counseling in capital letters." John taps CATHY 2-T, then KENNY D. "So what? His cursive handwriting is probably shit. I know mine is. Half the time even I can't make out what I wrote."

"Makes perfect sense, but still." Jerome takes his iPad back and frowns at the photo of the calendar page. "When I was a kid, I saw this optical illusion in a comic book. At first glance you only saw a bunch of black blobs, but if you looked at it long enough, you saw the face of Abe Lincoln. Blobs at one second, a face at the next. To me, this is like that. There's something weird about it, but I don't know what the fuck it is."

"Then it's nothing," John says. "You want to break the case yourself, that's all."

"Bullshit," Jerome says, but thinks John might be right. Or partly right.

John checks his watch. "Got to get going. The regulars will be lining up."

"Seriously?"

"Seriously."

Jerome asks Holly's question: "Who wants a screwdriver at eight AM?"

And John gives him the same answer: "You'd be surprised. So are we on for Friday night?"

"Guns and Hoses? Sure. You can be my date, or I can be yours. Only if it's a blow-out, I'm leaving."

"We can take off any time after the first inning," John says. "I just have to be there for Sista Bessie singing the National Anthem. That's a gotta-see."

5

The band load-in crew only works half a day on Saturday unless there's a show, and Sista Bessie's first show at the Mingo is still a week away. This is still about rehearsing the music, the tech, and finalizing the set list. Barbara is backstage, watching Batty and Pogo show her how the breakers work with the amps and lights, when Tones Kelly finds her and says Betty wants to see her.

The Mingo's dressing rooms are a floor up, and they're first-class; Betty's is actually a suite. There's already a star on her door, and a photo of her in her sparkly Sista Bessie show clothes. Inside, Betty is sitting on a wine-red couch with Hennie Ramer, her agent. Hennie puts away her word search book when Barbara comes in, and Barbara sees Tones Kelly is also here. All at once she's frightened.

"Am I being fired?" she blurts out.

Betty laughs, then says, "In a way, you are. No more work with the roadies, Barbara."

"Insurance issue," Hennie says. "Also a union issue."

"I thought we *weren't* union," Barbara objects.

Hennie looks uncomfortable. "Yes and no. We abide by most of the AFM rules."

"I don't care about that Federation shit," Betty says, "but you're talent now. If you sprain your back, you won't be able to keep step with the Crystals."

"The Crystals are fine, but I also like the roadies," Barbara protests, "and they seem to like me."

"They do like you, Acey says you pull your weight, but I need you to concentrate on harmony with the girls."

The girls—Tess, Laverne, and Jem—are now in their seventies.

"And our duet on 'Jazz.' That's what I'm all about these days. Girl, we're going to whale the shit out of that thing. By the time we get to New York, it'll be a show closer. The band is going to drop out except for the drums, and we're going to go . . ." She bursts into full-throated song, pumping her moccasined feet. "Jazz, jazz, that Lowtown jazz, give it, take it, move it, shake it, roll it, stroll it . . ." Back to her speaking voice. "Like that, and for as long as it will play. It's gonna be like that J. Geils joint, '(Ain't Nothin' But a) House Party,' but we're gonna soul it instead of rock and roll it. Don't mind me making some changes? Because, girl, we can tear that sumbitch up."

Barbara *does* dig it. The rhythm Betty's putting down is exactly what she heard in her head the first time she read Vachel Lindsay's racist (but crazily addictive) poem "The Congo." Yet at the same time . . .

"Betty, I'm a *poet*, not a singer. I told my brother the same thing. Trying to be a poet, anyway. This is . . . it's *crazy*."

"Legal issues aside, there's a practical side," Hennie says. "Fact is, you're a better singer than you are a roadie. Good pipes. You're not Merry Clayton—"

"Or Aretha," Tones says. "Or Tina."

"But who is?" Hennie says. "You're good at this, and what's a poet without song? Or life experience?"

"But—"

"But nothing," Betty says from the couch. "Patti Smith. Hell of a singer, hell of a writer. Nick Cave. Gil Scott-Heron. Josh Ritter. Leonard Cohen. I've read them all, and I've read *you*. Also your brother now, and I have to wonder if he can also sing."

Barbara laughs. "He's *horrible*. You don't want to hear him on Karaoke Night."

"Ne'mine then, but I've got you," Betty says, "and I *want* this for you. From now on, it's like Mavis says: You belong to the band, hallelu'. All right?"

Barbara gives in, and when she does, discovers it's a pleasure.

Betty holds out her arms. "Now come on, girl, and give this fat old lady a hug."

Barbara steps forward and allows herself to be enfolded. Does some enfolding of her own, too. Betty kisses her on both cheeks and says, "I care for you, girl. Do this for me, yeah?"

"Yeah," Barbara says. She's scared, but she's also young and still willing to spread her wings. Also, she likes the idea of being in the same company as Patti Smith and Leonard Cohen.

Gibson, the Mingo's Program Director, pokes his head in. "Your sound man says you're wanted onstage, Ms. Brady."

Betty stands up, still with an arm around Barbara. "Come on, girl. We are going to sing our fucking hearts out. And you *will* bang the tambourine on 'Saved.'"

6

Kate carries her own new brand-new bags to the truck, which Holly appreciates. The boss is in a fine mood, and so is the boss's assistant.

"We're back at the Mingo Auditorium," Corrie says. "I just spent an hour on the phone with Gibson, the Program Director, and the bookstore people. It's just a day earlier—Friday instead of Saturday. Most of the venues were willing to help out."

"Because I'm *hot*," Kate says, and strikes a pose, hand behind her head, chest thrust out. She laughs at herself, then sobers. Her eyes are bright with curiosity. "Tell me something, Holly. What's it like, working in a male-dominated field like private investigation? Do you find it difficult? And I can't help noticing that you're rather slightly built. Hard to imagine you going toe-to-toe with an escaping miscreant."

Holly, a private person by nature, considers this question a tiny bit invasive. Possibly even rude. But she smiles, because a smile isn't just an umbrella on a rainy day; it's also a shield. And she has gone toe-to-toe with a few bad people, and—through luck and pluck—has come out fairly well. "Subjects for another time, maybe."

Corrie, perhaps more sensitive to emotional nuances than her boss—the *vibe*—chimes in immediately. "We ought to get on the road, Kate. I have a lot to arrange when we get there."

"Right," Kate says, and gives Holly her most winning smile. "To be continued."

Holly says, "Remember that you two are registered at the Axis, but we're actually staying at—"

"The Country Inn and Suites," Corrie finishes. "Registered under *your* name." And, to Kate: "They have a pool, if you want to swim."

"I'd prefer you to stay in your—" Holly begins.

"*I'd* prefer to swim," Kate says. "It relaxes me. Touring is hard enough without being cooped up like a prisoner."

Being dead is even harder than being on tour, Holly thinks . . . but of course doesn't say. She has discovered that the most difficult thing about being a bodyguard is that the bodyguard's subject considers herself, at bottom, to be invulnerable. Even blood and guts on her luggage only gave her a day's pause.

"I still need to look at the communications from your stalker." She also wants to catch up with Jerome. Briggs isn't her case, but Jerome's call this morning was moderately weird.

"Tomorrow," Kate says. "Tomorrow is a day off, oh gloriosity."

And with that, Holly must be content.

7

Late Saturday afternoon, Trig sets sail in his Toyota for the bucolic town of Crooked Creek, about thirty-five miles northwest of the city. As usual, his radio is tuned to WBOB, Buckeye City's "All News, All the Time" station . . . although what the Big Bob mostly broadcasts isn't news but right-wing shouters like Sean Hannity and Mark Levin. With the volume turned low, it's not political, just the company of human voices.

Trig tells himself his current goal is nothing more than dinner at Norm's Shack, which is considered by culinary experts (including Trig himself) to serve the finest ribs in the state, always accompanied by spicy beans and tangy coleslaw. He tells himself it's just a coincidence that the Creek, a facility for teens dealing with substance abuse, is just a block or two from Norm's. Why would he even care if there are runaways and dealers there?

Daddy disagrees. *I got a good idea of where the bear shit in the buckwheat*, as good old Dad used to say.

Trig shouldn't take another one so soon, shouldn't press his luck, and so what if a lot of young road warriors—like the nameless girl now decomposing in the Holman Rink—hang out at the Creek for awhile, before moving on to the next wherever? No-names who are already missing and in many cases presumed dead?

Just outside the town limits, he comes upon one of those no-names, this one a girl in a baggy duffle coat that is too warm for the day. She's got a pack on her back, a barbwire tattoo around her skinny neck, and her thumb out.

Trig opens the console between the front seats, touches the Taurus, and closes it again. Who is he to say no when opportunity knocks? He pulls over.

The girl opens the door and peers in at him. "You dangerous, man?"

"No," Trig says, thinking, *What else would someone like me say, you idiot?* "Where are you headed? The Creek?"

"How'd you know?" She's still peering in. Trying to decide if he's safe. And what does she see? A middle-aged man with a Mr. Businessman haircut, wearing a Mr. Businessman sportcoat over his small Mr. Businessman paunch. Looks like a salesman or something.

"Been there a few times. Once this spring. Chaired the meeting."

"You're Program?"

"A few years downriver from my last drink. And you're a runaway."

She freezes in the act of getting in, eyes wide.

"Relax, kid, I'm not going to out you. Or try to make a move on you. Ran away six times myself. Finally made it."

She gets in and closes the door. "They let you sleep overnight there?"

Trig holds up a finger. "One night only."

"Hot meal?"

"Yes, but not great. If you like ribs, I'll buy you half a rack. Don't like to eat alone."

He pulls back onto the highway. Three miles down is the Crooked Creek Rest Area. He'll pull in there, tell her he wants to stretch his bad back. If there's no one there, he'll shoot her before she knows what's happening. Risky? Yes, of course. Killing isn't the thrill. Risk is becoming the thrill. Might as well admit it. Like driving home with an open bottle of vodka.

"If it's the kindness of your heart, okay. If it's something else, just drop me at the halfway house. That's what it is, right? A halfway?"

"Yup." Trig checks his rearview mirror. Nobody behind him to see his license plate, and so what if there was? Just another dirty Toyota on a country road.

Two miles from the rest area—his heart beating hard and slow as he rehearses the moves he'll make—the hemorrhoid cream ad on the radio cuts off and a horn blares the WBOB Breaking News intro. He doesn't have to turn the radio up; the girl does it.

"This just in," the announcer says. "Two of the jurors in the now infamous Alan Duffrey case have apparently committed suicide. I want to repeat, two of the jurors have apparently committed suicide. Sources close to the Buckeye City Police Department have confirmed it, although the names of the deceased haven't been divulged, pending notification of next of kin. Several recent murders have been linked to the Duffrey jurors. Stay tuned to WBOB, your All News, All the Time station, for updates."

The hemorrhoid commercial picks up where it left off. Trig barely hears, so overcome with joy he can barely keep a poker face. He never believed the surrogate killings would work, but they have, and to what an extent! If only the rest of the jurors would follow suit! But of course they won't. Some probably feel no guilt at all. Especially the shit ADA who sent Duffrey to prison . . . and consequently to his death.

"Fucking incredible," the girl says. "Pardon my mouth."

"No need. I was thinking the same thing myself."

"Like they thought offing themselves would bring that guy Duffrey back."

"Have you been following the case?"

"I'm from Cincy, man. It's on the news all the time."

"Maybe those two were trying to . . . I don't know . . . make amends."

"Like in AA?"

"Yes. Like that."

Here is the rest area. It's empty, but Trig passes by without slowing. Why would he murder this poor girl when he's been given this incredible, unexpected gift?

"Suicide is a pretty radical way of making amends."

"I don't know," Trig says. "Guilt can be powerful." He enters the town of Crooked Creek and pulls into a slant parking space in front of Norm's Shack. "What about those ribs?"

"Lead me to em," she says, and holds up a hand. Trig laughs and slaps her five, thinking, *You'll never know how close you came.*

They get a booth by the window and chow down on ribs and coleslaw and beans. The girl—her name is Norma Willette—eats like a starving wolf. They split a strawberry shortcake for afters, and then Trig drops her at the Creek, where the sign out front suggests that teens TAKE OFF YOUR WEARY BOOTS AND REST FOR AWHILE.

Norma starts to get out, then looks at him dead in the eye. "I been tryin, man. Honest to God. It's just so fuckin hard."

Trig doesn't have to ask her what she means. He's been there, done that. "Don't give up. It gets better."

She leans in and kisses his cheek. Her eyes shine with tears. "Thank you, man. Maybe God sent you to give me a ride. And a meal. Those ribs were some good."

Trig watches until she's safely in the door, then drives away.

8

The two weeping willows in front of the Willow Apartments are dying. The two men on the eighth floor are already dead, having ingested monster doses of a drug that will turn out, upon autopsy, to be synthetic Oxy—what's known among users as the Queen, or the Big Dipper. No one will ever discover which of the dead men purchased it.

Jabari Wentworth was Juror 3 in the Alan Duffrey trial. Ellis Finkel was Juror 5. The apartment where they died was Finkel's. The two men are in bed together, wearing nothing but underpants. Outside, the sun is sinking toward the horizon. Soon the coroner's van will take the bodies away. They would have been gone hours ago, if not for the possible link to the Surrogate Juror serial killer case. The investigation is moving with careful deliberation. Lieutenant Warwick and Chief Patmore were both here; so was Ralph Ganzinger of the State Police. All the brass have since departed.

Watching the three-man forensics team (two investigators and a videographer), Izzy Jaynes takes a moment to consider the difference between fact and fiction. In fiction, suicide by overdose is considered the easy way out, often favored by women. Men are more likely to shoot themselves in the head, jump, or use carbon monoxide in a closed garage. In fact, suicide by overdose can be horribly messy as the body fights to stay alive. Ellis Finkel's lower face, neck, and chest are plated with dried vomit. Jabari Wentworth has shit himself. Both stare at the ceiling with half-lidded eyes, as if considering a purchase of dubious merit.

The sight of them—and the smell of them—aren't the things that will haunt Izzy as she lies awake in her own apartment that night. What *will* haunt her is the waste of them. The note they left behind, signed by both, was simplicity itself: *We will be together in the next world.*

Bullshit, Izzy thinks. *You're going into the dark, and unaccompanied.*

One of them needs to talk some more with Ms. Alicia Carstairs, in 8-B. She found the bodies, was friendly with both men, and understood their "special situation."

"You do it, Iz," Tom says. "Woman to woman. I want to go through this place one more time. Especially Finkel's little studio. But I think it is what it looks like."

"Not guilt about Duffrey, you mean."

"Guilt, maybe, but not about him. Go on and talk to the lady. I think she'll tell you."

Izzy finds Alicia Carstairs standing outside her apartment door, wringing her hands and looking at the pair of uniformed cops guarding the door to 8-A. Her eyes are red, her cheeks wet with tears. At the sight of Izzy with her badge hung around her neck, she starts crying again.

"He asked me last night if I'd check in on him," she says. Izzy already has this in her notebook but doesn't interrupt. "I thought it was work." She raises her hands. The nails, Izzy notices, are beautiful. Otherwise, she has no idea what Ms. Carstairs is talking about.

"Let's go into your place," Izzy says. "Maybe you have coffee? I could use a cup."

"Yes. Yes! Strong coffee for both of us, what a good idea. I'll never forget the sight of them. Not if I live to a hundred."

"If it's any consolation, Ms. Carstairs—"

"Alicia."

"Okay, and I'm Isabelle. If it's any consolation, I don't think they knew it would be so . . ." Izzy thinks of the two men sprawled in the bed. Their bulging, half-lidded eyes. ". . . so rough. I'm not sure what you mean about it being work."

"You know Ellis was a photographer, don't you?"

"Yes." Because of Bill Wilson (or Briggs, or whatever his real name is), Izzy and Tom have gotten thumbnails on all the jurors in the Duffrey case. Finkel's main studio was downtown, but he also worked in his apartment, where he had turned the spare bedroom into a mini-studio.

"I was his hand model," Carstairs says, and holds them up again. "Ellis said I had great hands. The pay was good—he always told me what he was being paid for an assignment, and he'd give me twenty or twenty-five per cent depending on the amount he was being paid for the job."

"For things like nail polish?" Izzy is intrigued. "Hand lotion?"

"Those, but all sorts of other things, too. Scrubbies, dish detergent, Razr phones—that was a good one. Once he photographed me holding a Nook, which is like a Kindle, only—"

"Yes, I know what a Nook is."

"And sometimes Jabari would model clothes. Sports jackets, topcoats, jeans. He's very handsome." She rethinks that, considering what she saw in Finkel's bedroom. "Was."

"You had a key to 8-A?"

"Uh-huh. I watered El's plants when he was out of town. He used to go to New York a lot to talk with ad agencies. Sometimes Jabari would go with him. They were gay, you know."

"Yes."

"They met at that trial. The Alan Duffrey trial. Fell head-over-heels for each other. Love-at-first-sight type of thing."

"Mr. Finkel specifically asked you to check in on him this morning?"

"Yes. I thought he had a hand job for me." She colors. "That sounds dirty, but you know what I mean."

"You thought he had a product he wanted you to hold."

"To display. Yes. I let myself in and said something like, 'Yoo-hoo, El, are you decent?' And then I smelled . . . I didn't know . . . thought something spilled . . . or overflowed . . . I went into the bedroom . . ." She's crying again. She tries lifting her coffee cup and spills some in the saucer and on the arm of her chair.

"Just sit quiet a minute," Izzy says. She goes into the narrow galley kitchen, gets a sponge, and mops up the mess. She can imagine Alicia Carstairs holding the blue sponge for a photograph, perhaps with soap foaming over her perfectly maintained fingers and nails.

"It's the shock," Carstairs says. "Finding them like that. I'll never get over it. Did I say that already?"

"It doesn't matter."

"I'll be better," Carstairs says. "I have two Xanax left over from when I went through the change. I'll take one of them and I'll be better."

"Do you have any idea of why they took their lives, Alicia?"

"I think . . . maybe . . . just guessing . . . that El didn't want Jabari to go alone. Jay's wife threw him out, you know, and his family wouldn't have anything to do with him. This was after they'd been . . . I don't want to say sneaking around, but you know, keeping it quiet . . . for the best part of a year, maybe more. Jay's wife sent pictures she found on Jay's phone to all his Facebook friends. I'm assuming some were . . . you know . . . graphic. I'm no snoop, don't get that idea, *he* told me that. Stay out of other people's business unless invited in, that's my motto. Jay was Muslim. I don't know if that was part of why everyone shunned him or not. Do you?"

"No," Izzy says.

"Someone from Jabari's office saw him and El together, maybe holding hands, maybe kissing, and squealed to his wife. That's how it started. Why would a person tattle like that, Isabelle?"

Izzy shakes her head. All she knows is that sometimes people can be shitty.

"Ellis was having problems with his own family. Also, he had HIV or AIDS, whichever one is worse. He was managing it, but the medicine he was taking made him feel sick a lot of the time. They must have decided . . ." Carstairs shrugs, and her mouth turns down in a moue of grief.

"Did they talk about the trial?"

"Sometimes El did. Jabari, almost never."

"What about after Duffrey was murdered in prison?"

"El said something like, 'Kiddie fiddlers deserve what they get.' He said he hated pedophiles, because so many people assume that gay men are child molesters or groomers or whatever the current buzzword is."

"What about when Cary Tolliver came forward?"

Carstairs sips her coffee. "I don't want to speak ill of the dead . . ."

"Ellis won't mind, and it could help our investigation."

Although for the life of her, Izzy doesn't know how. This wasn't Act 5 of *Romeo and Juliet*, but Act 5 of *Romeo and Romeo*. Their problems might have looked solvable by the light of another day, the idea of suicide an absurdity, but at the time the idea of dying together in bed, holding hands, must have seemed the ultimate in romance . . . not to mention revenge. *They'll all be sorry then*, they might have thought.

"El said, 'We did what we promised to do, that's all. Those awful magazines had his fingerprints on them, and besides, if he didn't do this, he probably did something else.'"

"So you wouldn't say he was guilt-ridden?"

"He felt guilty about Jay's family not having anything to do with him, but about the trial? I don't think so."

"And Jabari? How did he feel?"

"I only brought it up once. He kind of shrugged and spread his hands and said the jury found him guilty on the evidence that was presented. He said there were a couple of holdouts, but they came around on the second day. The others convinced them. He was sorry about what happened."

"Sorry but not guilty?"

"I don't think so, no."

9

When Izzy returns to 8-A, the bodies have been removed. The smells of shit and puke, however, remain. *It was never thus in Shakespeare*, Izzy muses, then has to smile. It's such a Holly thought.

"What's funny, Easter bunny?" Tom is standing by the slider giving on the late Ellis Finkel's balcony. There's a good view of the lake from here.

"Nothing. Can we rule out murder?"

"Sure," Tom says. "Our boy Bill doesn't murder jurors, only people in the *names* of jurors."

"Can we assume he won't be killing two men as surrogates for Finkel and Wentworth?"

"We can't assume *anything* about the guy, because he's crazy. But he can't guilt-trip them if they're dead, can he?"

"No. And the bastard probably assumes he drove them to it, when the Duffrey trial had nothing to do with it."

"*Au contraire*, my little chickadee. That's where they met."

"True. That's where they met." She thinks about it and says, "I would love for the press to find out the real reason, just to take away this psycho nutball's satisfaction. But we can't let that out, can we?"

"*We* can't," Tom says, "but somebody will. If Buckeye Brandon doesn't have it on his shitpod and shitblog tomorrow, it'll be the next day. This department leaks like a defective Pamper."

"Just as long as *you* don't leak it, Tom."

He gives her a smile and a Boy Scout salute. "Never would I ever."

"Did you find anything in his studio?"

"You mean like Bill Wilson's real name written on a piece of paper?"

"That would be good."

"I found nothing but a bunch of photo albums. The raciest thing in them was Jabari Wentworth in swim trunks. There might be other stuff on his computer or up in the Cloud, but that's not our biz. And even if you decide Mr. Bill Wilson won't have to murder two random strangers in the names of Finkel and Wentworth, he's still got plenty of jurors, plus maybe the judge and the prosecutor. Partner, we got nothing. Do we?"

"Pretty much," Izzy admits.

Tom lowers his voice, as if afraid the room might be bugged. "Talk to your friend."

"Who? Holly?"

"Who else? She's not police, but she thinks around corners sometimes. Fill her in, then ask if she has any ideas."

"You're serious?"

He sighs and says, "As a heart attack."

10

In the Garden City Plaza Hotel, Barbara is watching with fascination as Betty Brady and Red Jones have a whisper rehearsal for next Friday night, when they will perform the National Anthem at Dingley Park. Betty says she's done it twice at Sacramento Kings basketball games, but with a Korg accompanying her.

"Don't know what that is," Barbara says.

"Synth," Red says. "That'd be better than this." He holds up his sax. "Who wants to hear 'O say can you see' honked out?"

"Bullshit," Betty says. "It's going to be . . ." She points at Barbara. "Something spooky but in a good way. What's the word?"

"Haunting, maybe?"

"Haunting! That's it! Perfect! Let's do it again, Red. Mostly to make sure I'm on key. Been a long time since I had to go high and low in the same song."

Red has got three pairs of Betty's socks stuffed into the bell of his sax, and Betty sings the National Anthem in a low, melodious voice. They try it first in the "official" key of B-flat major, but Betty doesn't like it, says it sounds like a dirge. They switch to G major. Red, blowing his muted horn, gives her a nod. She nods back. The first time through in G is ragged, the second time better, the third smooth as silk.

"After 'O say does that star-spangled banner yet wave,' I want to go dead-stop," she says, and counts off. "One-two-three-four. Then the last line. Really punch it."

"Cool. It's a groove."

"Let's try it."

They do.

When they finish, Betty looks at Barbara. "What do you think?"

"I think the people lucky enough to go to that game are going to remember it forever."

She's right about that, but not the way she thinks.

Chapter 12

1

The drive from Iowa City to Davenport is a short trip on I-80. Holly, Kate, and Corrie are at the Country Inn & Suites well before noon on Saturday morning. Holly spends the first half of the trip a mile or two ahead of Kate's truck, glancing every now and then at her phone, where the GPS tracker on the F-150 is a pulsing green dot. Then she drops back, hoping to spot a follow car. She sees one that looks likely. It's a little Mustang convertible. It speeds up, swapping lanes to pull even with Kate's truck on the left. Holly's stomach tightens. She also swaps lanes to get behind the Mustang, cutting someone off and ignoring the blare of their horn. Then the Mustang's passenger stands up, her long hair whipping in the wind, and shouts, "*We love you, Kate!*"

The convertible scoots away. Holly lets out a breath and drops back.

They have lunch in the restaurant next door to the hotel and then Kate has her swim. Back and forth she goes, lap after lap, sleek as a fish in her red tank suit. Holly, sitting poolside with a towel in her lap, gets tired just watching her. Kate finally gets out, takes the towel with a muttered thanks, and knots it around her waist. Holly expected some sort of endorphin rush after so much exercise, but Kate seems inward, almost sullen. She picks her phone up from the table where she's left it along with a paperback novel, speaks briefly to Corrie, who's at the venue, and ends the call.

"Going to take a forty-five-minute nap," she says without looking at Holly. "Then the press conference at the Axis. Where we were *booked*."

Holly says nothing.

"These itinerary changes are a pain in the ass, Gibney."

Holly doesn't engage, just picks up Kate's book. "Do you want this?"

Kate's cheeks are flushed and radiant with exercise, but her mouth is turned down at the corners. She's still pissed about having to travel several miles to do her presser instead of just going downstairs. "Keep it or throw it away. It's a piece of shit."

2

In her room during Kate's nap, Holly turns on CNN and is stunned to see a reporter doing her stand-up in front of the Willow Apartments, where Holly herself once looked at a demo apartment before finding her current place downtown. Behind the reporter are police cars with their jackpot lights flashing and two forensics trucks, one from the city PD and one from the State Police. There's also a van marked CORONER. The Surrogate Juror Murders have become a cable news staple, and the possible death of someone who served on the Duffrey jury has warranted the network to break, however briefly, into its usual suds-and-rinse of political news.

The reporter says, "All we know now is that one of the jurors in the Duffrey trial, Ellis Finkel, lives in this apartment complex. While police are tight-lipped, it seems possible to assume from the amount of police activity, that something might have happened to Mr. Finkel. It may be that this strange and unique serial killer, hoping to inculcate a sense of guilt in the Duffrey jurors, has, in this case, possibly succeeded."

A lot of may be and possibly be, Holly thinks.

She considers calling Izzy, but reaches out to Jerome instead. He hasn't been following the news at all, didn't even realize that Ellis Finkel might be dead. Assuming it *is* Finkel that has caused the big police response.

"Have you tried Izzy?" Jerome asks, then before Holly can answer: "Of course not. *Izzy* will be *busy*."

"Very poetic, Jerome."

"True, Boo. And it's not our case, anyway."

"No. It's not."

"But you can't help being curious. That's my Holly. Hey, guess what? I'm going to the Guns and Hoses game with John Ackerly. He really likes you."

"I like him, too. I've got to see my clients to their press conference soon, Jerome. See if you can find anything out. As you say, I can't help being curious."

"Maybe I'll call Tom Atta. He and I go running sometimes."

"Really?"

"Up at Bell College. Every now and then Izzy joins us. We puff and pant all around the track."

"Interesting. Possibly helpful. Are you ready to tell me what's been on your mind yet?"

Jerome sighs. "I wanted to figure it out myself, but I give up. All I know is there's something wonky about the May calendar page in Reverend Rafferty's appointment book. Something about Briggs, the guy who probably killed him. It might have something to do with the other names on that page, too, but I can't tell what it is for the life of me. Can I send you a screen shot?"

"I think I have it," Holly says, "but send it to me anyway. When I have time, I'll take a look. And if you talk to Detective Atta . . . or Izzy . . . let me know."

"I will."

3

The press conference features a brighter, livelier Kate, and that night at the RiverCenter she dials the wattage up all the way. Holly and Corrie watch her opening ten minutes from the wings—the strut to stage center, the deep bow, the mic grab, the chants of "Woman Power." When the boo-birds start to counter-chant ("*Go back to the kitchen! Go back to the kitchen!*"), she makes her trademark *Come on come on come on* gesture, and most of the crowd goes nuts, whooping and cheering. When they settle, she asks all the men in the audience to raise their hands.

Holly whispers to Corrie, "She seemed really flat this afternoon, even after a long swim. Her little nap must have pepped her up."

Corrie smiles and shakes her head. "She's almost always that way before she goes on. Either quiet and sort of glum, or pissed off about something. Then . . . when she's on . . . she lives for this." She adds hastily: "And the cause, of course. Woman Power."

"I know," Holly says. "I know she does. I just wish she really understood that doing this is risking her life."

Corrie gives her a smile. "I think she does."

Maybe, Holly thinks, *but it's academic knowledge. Most in the head, some in the heart, none in the gut.*

Corrie goes back to the greenroom to prepare for a women's club breakfast the next day (also to be held at the DoubleTree) before the three-hour drive to Madison. Holly prowls the hallways, looking for intruders and finding none. Prowls backstage and finds nothing but a trio of stagehands playing Scat with a greasy deck of cards. They have no interest in Woman Power.

She ends up at stage right, watching with fascination as Kate wraps up the evening's festivities with another call-and-response. She takes a moment to peek at the screen shot Jerome has sent her and understands at once what was nagging at him. What he couldn't quite get. Holly understands something else, as well: if she had stared at it for a long time (as Jerome must have), she *wouldn't* have seen it. The quick glance was enough because her mind was mostly elsewhere.

Then her mind makes a second leap, and she staggers a little bit on her feet. *Oh my God. What if it's him?*

The stage manager looks at her and asks in a whisper if she's all right.

"Yes," Holly whispers back.

Onstage Kate asks, "Who you gonna believe?"

"*Believe the woman!*" they yell back.

She makes that waggling gesture with both hands. *"Come on, Davenport, don't pussy out on me, who you gonna believe?"*

"BELIEVE THE WOMAN!"

"When the man says she wanted it?"

"BELIEVE THE WOMAN!"

"When the man swears she said okay?"

"BELIEVE THE WOMAN!"

"You guys! Who you gonna believe?"

"BELIEVE THE WOMAN!" the men yell . . . although if push should come right down to shove, Holly isn't sure what any man will do. She's heard women say men are simple creatures. Holly doesn't argue the idea—such arguments are pointless—but doesn't really believe it. Women have basements; men have sub-basements.

"That's right. Believe the woman, respect the woman, and don't take any shit from people who don't. Thank you, Davenport, you've been so great! Goodnight!"

But they won't let her go until she's come out for three bows. Standing O time. Only the boo-birds refuse to get on their feet. Not so many as in Iowa City, Holly observes, and sitting there in their blue shirts, they look like sulky children. She reminds herself that even children can be dangerous, and that leads her back to what she was thinking when she glanced at that screen shot, expecting nothing and getting a lot. Maybe everything. She needs to talk to Izzy, but first she has to take care of her women.

Later on she will think, *Thank God for the chair. If not for that, Kate could have ended up in Ira Davenport Hospital. Or dead.*

4

The RiverCenter stage door is on Third Street, and so Holly has arranged for them to go out a different way, onto Pershing Avenue, where a car and driver provided by Next Page Books will be waiting to whisk them back to the hotel. After Iowa City, Holly expects no problem with their exit (what's called "exfiltration" in *Essentials for Bodyguards*), but that turns out to be far too optimistic.

Later, in Madison, Corrie Anderson will fill Holly in on what she's learned about Kate's audiences on this tour, much of it from Kate herself. "There are three main after-show groups," she'll say. "There are Woman Power fans who just want to wave and maybe get a picture of Kate leaving the building. There are autograph seekers, who can be a little pushier. Then there are the eBayers."

"The what?"

"Collectors. Brokers. Buy-sell-and-trade guys. They're rabid and they're pushy. It's only partly about money. It's also about the thrill of the hunt. They want first editions signed, or limited editions—Kate did a couple of those. They want posters, eight-by-ten glossies, even one-sheets from the Showtime *Women Now* doc she participated in. They have stuff you wouldn't believe. One woman wanted Kate to sign a pair of *panties*. They sell their goods on eBay or dedicated collectors' sites like Kate 4Eva. The true fanatics are as persistent as cockroaches and just as hard to get rid of."

Holly finds out for herself when they emerge on Pershing. This exfiltration point was supposed to be a dead secret, but there's a crowd of seventy-five or a hundred people waiting for them. They aren't taking pix with their phones; they're waving books, magazines, posters, and other paraphernalia—one has a gay pride rainbow flag—all of them calling things like *Kate! For my mother, Kate, she couldn't come! Kate, I came all the way from Fort Collins! Kate, please! Please! I've been a fan since 2004!* How they knew about Holly's exit strategy is a thing she never finds out, but after being fooled the first time—possibly just by dumb luck—they somehow do.

A RiverCenter usher is sitting in a folding chair and waiting for Kate to come out. When the crowd surges forward, he gets up, spreads his arms, and does his best to hold them back . . . which is like King Canute trying to hold back the tide. Beyond the waving, yelling eBayers, their driver—a young woman who looks like a college student—watches with a face that says, *I have no fucking idea what I'm supposed to do now.*

Holly's phone is on her belt, still set to mute. She feels it vibrate, looks down, sees JEROME in the window. She has no time to consider this, let alone answer, because just then a howl of rage cuts through the persistent babble.

"YOUUUU BIIIIITCH!"

A very large man who looks like a gone-to-seed WWE wrestler bulls his way through the crowd. He's wearing khaki pants and a dirty white tee-shirt. His hair is shaved down to a shadow. His arms are inked and his face is red with fury. He's swinging a baseball bat. The usher steps in front of him and the man (*the Hulk*, Holly thinks, *the Incredible Hulk*) sends him flying into the street with one push.

"YOUUUUU FUUUUCKING BIIITCH!"

Kate freezes, staring with wide, amazed eyes as the Incredible Hulk raises his bat. Corrie lifts one hand in a *stop* gesture that will work on this man no more than a pitcher of water would work on a forest fire.

Holly doesn't think, simply kicks the usher's chair. It skitters across the sidewalk. The Incredible Hulk trips over it and faceplants on the concrete. Blood leaps from his nose and lips. The eBayers are screaming and backing away, some dropping their precious mementos, phones, and Sharpies.

The Hulk rolls over. His lower face is painted with blood. He points at Kate like an explorer pointing out an extraordinary landmark. *"YOUUU! MY WIFE LEFT ME BECAUSE OF YOUUUU!"*

He's struggling to get up. Somewhere a police siren has begun to whoop. Holly says to Kate, "Get in the car."

Kate goes without question or hesitation, hauling her stunned assistant by one arm. The Hulk has made it to his knees, looking after them. Holly dips into her bag, and when the Hulk turns back to her, she hits him with a faceful of pepper spray.

The crowd draws even further back, as if Holly were radioactive, and she realizes she's still holding the spray can out in front of her. To the stunned bookstore girl, she says, "Take the women to the hotel. Don't wait for me. I'll have to talk to the police."

5

Her conversation with the cops doesn't take long. The Incredible Hulk (quite drunk and now more like a sobbing, three-hundred-pound child) is taken away to be booked on an assault charge, and Holly is back at the Country Inn & Suites before the hotel bar closes. She's okay until the glass of white wine she's ordered is placed in front of her, and then she gets the shakes.

So close, she thinks. And: *I hate this job.*

Her phone, still on mute, vibrates. It's Corrie, wondering where she is. Five minutes later the women join her. Kate throws an arm around Holly's neck and plants a kiss on her cheek, uncomfortably close to her mouth.

"From now on I do everything you say, Holly Gibney. I don't know if you saved my life tonight, but you sure to God saved about twelve thousand dollars' worth of dental work."

Corrie slides onto a stool on Holly's left. "Thank you," she says quietly. "Thank you so much. My God, did you see the *size* of him?"

"The Incredible Hulk," Holly says.

Kate throws back her head and shouts laughter. The bartender asks what Kate wants to drink, and she says Jack, no ice. Corrie says she'll have what Holly is having. Holly isn't surprised when the bartender asks her if he can see some ID.

Holly sips her wine. Her phone buzzes. It's Jerome again. She thinks, *I can't talk to him tonight.* She's wiped out and keeps seeing the man in the dirty tee-shirt coming at Kate like a locomotive, the bat upraised. *Except I* have *to talk to him tonight, because I might know who the Surrogate Juror killer is.*

The shakes start up again.

"If that chair hadn't been there," she says.

Kate looks at her quizzically, head cocked. "*What* are you saying?"

"The chair. If it hadn't—"

Kate puts two fingers across Holly's lips. Very gently. She says, "It wasn't the chair. It was *you*."

Holly pushes away the glass of wine, which she has barely tasted. The bartender comes over. "Is there something wrong with that, Miss?"

"No. It's fine. But I have to make a call. You two should probably go to your rooms."

Kate gives a British-style salute, back of the hand to the brow, very pukka sahib. "Aye-aye, Cap'n."

Holly is not amused.

6

In her room, she calls Jerome and apologizes for not getting back to him sooner. "I was on the job."

"Everything okay there?"

"Fine."

"Did you figure out what was buggin me about that calendar page? I've been staring at it half the night."

That was most of your problem, Holly thinks. "I did."

"For reals?"

"For reals." Although self-doubt is one of her many default positions, she has no doubt about this.

"True?"

"Yes."

"Tell me!"

"First, tell me if you found anything out from Detective Atta."

"I did. Two of the jurors in the Duffrey case committed suicide. Ellis Finkel and Jabari Wentworth. They met during the trial and became lovers. Wentworth's wife kicked him out of the house when she found out he'd been sneaking around, and with a man. His family shunned him. That might have been a religious thing. Religion kinda sucks, don't you think?"

"No opinion," Holly says.

"Anyway, Finkel had AIDS, under control but a constant struggle for him. Short form, the police don't believe it had anything to do with guilt over what happened to Alan Duffrey."

"So terrible," Holly says. "A waste of two lives."

She finds herself close to tears, partially because of the pointlessness of those deaths, mostly because she's still dealing with the fact that Kate McKay almost got her head bashed in on her watch.

"Agreed," Jerome says. "Now tell me what I missed."

She tells him. There's silence on the other end.

"Jerome? Are you still there?"

"*Fuck*," he says. "Oh, *fuck*! Really? That simple? *Really?*"

She hasn't told him her second deduction, the one that rocked her back on her heels at the RiverCenter. She saves that for Izzy.

7

"Hey, Holly," Izzy says. She sounds half asleep. "Tom said to fill you in, and I will, but right now it's been a long day and I'm beat."

"Try to get un-beat. I might know who the killer is."

"What?" Izzy goes from fuzzy to wide awake. "Are you shitting me?"

"I'm not sure. Maybe. Jerome told me two of the jurors committed suicide, but he said it probably didn't have anything to do with the—"

"Yes. I mean no, it didn't. Holly, if you've got something, *give*!"

Holly doesn't need to look at the picture of the calendar page on her iPad; doesn't even need to close her eyes. She sees it, along with every name: BOB, FRANK M., KENNY D., CATHY 2-T. And BRIGGS. Only BRIGGS is different. Not much, just enough.

"Can you look at the picture of Reverend Rafferty's calendar? Do you have it?"

"Just a sec, I left my iPad in the kitchen."

Holly has never been in Izzy's apartment—at least not yet—but she imagines a narrow, easy-care kitchen and Izzy's purse on the counter. Maybe next to an empty wine glass. She imagines Izzy herself in flappy and comfy cotton pajamas.

"Okay, I've got the calendar page. What about it?"

"Let's start with Reverend Rafferty. I think he was nearsighted, but I think he was also vain. That's more a guess than a deduction, but did you find glasses?"

"There was a pair in his bedside table, yes. Probably for reading."

"Look at his appointments for May. Are you looking?"

"Yes. Get to it, *please.*"

Holly won't be hurried, because she's still explaining it to herself. "The names are all in caps, and slightly spread out." In her mind she sees it: not FRANK M. or CATHY 2-T, but F R A N K M. and C A T H Y 2 - T. "He could do that, because the boxes for days of the month are quite big."

"Yes. Seeing it."

"But BRIGGS is different. More squeezed together. Not a lot, but it's there. Jerome saw it, he just didn't understand what it meant. Are you looking? Do you see?"

"I guess . . . yeah, you're right."

"That's because Reverend Rafferty didn't make a *B*. He made a *T*. It was his killer who turned it into a *B*. Then, at the end of the name, he added a *GS*. He tried to make them look the same as Rafferty's capital letters and did a good job because capital letters are much easier to forge than cursive. What gives it away—"

"The last two letters are tighter," Izzy says. "Not much, but a little. And . . . yeah, that *B could* have started life as a *T*."

"It was never Briggs," Holly says. "Rafferty's appointment was with someone named Trig." Self-doubt won't be entirely denied. "I think."

"Yes! Fuck, *yes*! He must have used the pen that was next to the appointment book on the counter, because the ink matches perfectly."

"And he didn't just scratch out his name, because he thought the police lab might have some voodoo technique that could read it through the scratch-out." Holly considers. "He should have just taken the whole appointment book. He was too smart for his own good. And maybe paranoid. It was a hurry-up job, after all."

"The Bill Wilson name might also have been too smart for his own good," Izzy says. "You need to go back to your Program friend and ask if he's gone to AA or NA meetings with someone who calls himself Trig."

"Maybe I don't have to, and neither do you. I think Trig is Alan Duffrey's lawyer. Russell Grinsted."

"Not following. Help me out here."

"Do you have a pad and pen handy?"

"Sure, on the fridge. For shopping lists."

"Write down his last name. If you take out the *E*, the *N*, the *S*, and the *D*, what does that leave?"

"*G*, *R*, *I*, *T*. Grit?"

"Rearrange them, like you're playing Wordle."

"Wordle? I don't know what—"

"Never mind, just do it."

A pause while Izzy scribbles on her pad. Then: "Ah, fuck. Trig is buried in Grinsted. Isn't it? Tom was right about you, Holly. That's some real Agatha Christie shit right there."

It really is Agatha Christie shit, Holly thinks. It would work in a book as the big reveal in the last chapter, but does it work in real life? The essential unbelievability of the idea nags at her, it feels like a paper boat caught on a twig, but at the same time it's just so fracking *perfect*. And if Grinsted has decided he's some kind of criminal mastermind, like in a Batman movie . . . someone too smart for his own good . . .

"At the very least, you need to question Grinsted again," Holly says.

"No shit, and go at him hard," Izzy says. "First thing tomorrow. Early. But everyone involved thought he gave Duffrey's defense his best. How sure are you?"

"Not enough," Holly says fretfully. "I want to believe it, because it's so elegant, but it still feels shaky to me."

"Too perfect?"

"Yes." And Holly has come to believe that perfection will always be out of her reach. "I'm almost positive about the Trig part, though. He changed it to Briggs. I'll talk to my Program friend tomorrow. Right now you should go to bed."

Izzy laughs. "Thanks to you, I'm probably too wired to sleep."

8

Kate's stalker in Iowa City was Chris, but she's Chrissy tonight, wearing a shoulder-length dark wig and parked in her unobtrusive Kia outside the Country Inn & Suites. Her quarry is inside, in Room 302. Chrissy knows this because she was with the scrum waiting on Pershing Avenue. Holly's efforts at throwing the eBayers off are for the most part useless; the group Chrissy fell in with knows everything about Kate's stay in this particular quadrant of the Quad Cities.

Chrissy latched onto a scruffy-looking dude in a Hawaiian shirt who called himself Spacer. Spacer had several posters he hoped to get signed, plus some eight-by-ten glossies. He took Chrissy under his wing, probably hoping to take her to bed later on. Chrissy understood that even with her best makeup on she was no pin-up queen, but for guys like Spacer, still stippled with adolescent acne although he had to be at least thirty, beggars couldn't be choosers.

To the motley crew waiting outside the RiverCenter, Kate was prey and Spacer was one of the hunters. He called getting autographs "nailing the celebs" and explained to Chrissy that his group of fellow hunters had a text-and-phone network that included people (ratboys and ratgirls, in Spacer-lingo) at the town's four or five best hotels (good) and three of the RiverCenter ushers (better). The core group of celeb-nailers paid them either in cash or salable autographs.

"Kate's especially good, because someone might shoot her," Spacer told Chrissy. "If that happened her value would go way, way up. It's what happened when someone stabbed Salmon Rushiddy."

It takes her a moment to realize he's talking about Salman Rushdie. "What an awful idea."

"Yeah, tell me about it, but it's a contentious fuckin society, my darl . . . oh jeez, here she comes!" He raised his voice to a foghorn shout Chrissy could hardly believe came from that skinny body. *"Kate! Kate, over here! My sister is your biggest fan! She couldn't come, she's in a wheelchair!"*

The assembled autograph hunters began to converge on Kate . . . then, the unexpected. Chrissy and Spacer watched, amazed, as the big man with the bat came busting out of the crowd and went for Kate. Watched as the skinny older woman serving as Kate's security kicked a chair in front of the batman and sent him sprawling.

"Goal!" Spacer cried, and chortled.

The autograph wolves on Pershing got nothing signed—Kate and her assistant were gone in a flash—but Chrissy has no interest in valuable memorabilia. She got the actual room numbers from Spacer, and then ditched him.

Now Kate's room is dark, and so is 306, the assistant's room. In between, in 304, the skinny bodyguard has neglected to close her drapes. Chrissy can see her striding back and forth, gesturing, yanking at her hair, and jabbering away on her phone. Before tonight, Chrissy didn't see her as a problem, but the speed with which she reacted to the batman has caused Chrissy to rethink her assessment.

The skinny bodyguard ends the call. Closes the drapes. A few minutes later, her light also goes out. It's time for Chrissy to go back to her own place on the other side of town, a shacky collection of cabins called the Davenport Rest. Thanks to Andy Fallowes, she could afford better, but it's all she deserves.

As she pulls onto the gravel apron in front of Cabin 6, her phone chirps softly (Chris, with whom she shares the phone, has a far more masculine ring). It's Deacon Fallowes, calling from one of his endless supply of burners.

"How goes the hunt, dear one?" he asks.

"Well, let's put it this way," Chrissy says. Her voice is low, with a kind of Bonnie Tyler rasp. "She's breathing borrowed air."

"Where are you?"

"Davenport. She's going to Madison next. It's a day off. I'll sleep in a little, then follow. I may be able to take her there, but if I'm going to accomplish our goal without sacrificing myself, Buckeye City might be the best bet. Kate got shoved out of her date there by some singer, but they've rescheduled her for the night before. Singer gave up her final rehearsal, or sound check, or whatever they call it. I heard it tonight."

"How?"

"The cancelation and date change I got from McKay's website. The rest . . . I met some people tonight who know just about everything. Autograph hunters, but on steroids. I think I can find them in every city on her tour. Some of them even follow her from place to place." Then, belatedly: "Are we having a safe conversation, Deacon?"

"This phone is going into the river as soon as we're done talking." As always, Fallowes's voice is low and pleasant. "Your mission is taking longer than I expected."

"I got the wrong one in Reno, but that was just supposed to be a warning, anyway. In Omaha, the assistant intercepted the anthrax you sent. I vandalized her luggage. Left a message. Now they have a security woman, and she's pretty good."

Silence for a moment. Then Fallowes says, "This isn't a prayer situation but a real-world solution we're aiming for, and I can't emphasize how important it is." His voice rises and begins to take on that good old gospel pulpit rhythm. "The world must see there's a price to be paid for apostasy. This woman cannot be allowed to preach her witchcraft. Exodus 22, dear one—Exodus 22."

"Yes," Chrissy says. "I know it well."

"And remember if you should be caught—God will protect you, but Satan is wily—you did this on your own."

Chrissy feels a dull resentment at that, and perhaps Fallowes gets a sense of how she feels. He isn't the devil, but he *is* wily.

"I wish it could all be a simple case of black and white, like with Brenda's Bitches. Do you remember them?"

Chrissy smiles for the first time that night. "How could I forget? Those stupid scooters. That was quite a day, wasn't it?"

"Yes. Yes it was. A hallelujah day for sure. Get some rest. I'll call again."

But I can never call you, Chrissy thinks. *That would be risking your own precious butt, wouldn't it?*

She is horrified at such an ugly, resentful thought. It's a *Chris* thought, and although he resides inside her—in a real sense, he is her Siamese twin—she sometimes hates him. As, she supposes, he sometimes hates her.

No, we are two.

Our secret.

Cabin 6 consists of one room with an attached bathroom the size of a closet. The bed sags. The overhead light globe is filled with dead flies. The place reeks with the wet-socks aroma of advanced mildew. In one corner, a pallid and warty toadstool has oozed up between two boards.

She thinks: *Expiation.*

He thinks: *Soonest begun, soonest done.*

They think: *No, we are two. Separate and equal. Our secret.*

Sometimes she gets tired and thinks, *Why bother thinking about escape? Why bother when the expiation never ends? Why does God have to be so cruel?*

She wishes she . . . he . . . they . . . could throw those thoughts, that *apostasy*, in an incinerator and burn them. God isn't cruel, God is love. Her unhappiness . . . his . . . theirs . . . is nothing but sin-sickness, like a whiskey hangover. Their fault, not God's.

She opens the bathroom door and slips the fingers of her right hand into the opening on the hinged side. Slowly she pulls the door toward her.

"I repent my rebellious thoughts," she says.

The pain, first a pinch, becomes excruciating, but she continues to pull the door.

"I repent my fantasies."

The skin splits on the backs of her fingers. Blood begins to run down the paint-peeling wood.

"I will complete my mission. I will not suffer the witch to live."

She pulls tighter, and while she feels pain, she also feels the peace of expiation. She finally lets go of the door and pulls her throbbing fingers free. They will swell, but they're not broken, and that's good. She needs her good right hand, which she shares with her brother, to do the Lord's work.

Chapter 13

1

Holly sleeps badly, haunted by dreams of the big man with the bat. She doesn't kick the chair in these dreams, only freezes in place while the big man swats Kate's head off. She awakes with dawn just an orangey-pink line on the eastern horizon, pulls her iPad off the charger, and writes an email to Jerome.

> I hope you are busy with your book, and I hate to ask you to go back to work for me, especially after you got in touch with John Ackerly, but I have to. (Besides, I think you said you were looking for a distraction.) I believe the woman who is stalking Kate may be—is almost certainly—a religious zealot. Kate got a note in Spokane that said she who speaks lies shall perish, which is from the book of Proverbs. When the stalker dumped roadkill on Kate's luggage, she wrote Exodus 22 on the door. This is a long shot, J, but would you look online for churches that have been in trouble with the law for crimes having to do with abortion protests, women's rights, or LGBTQ+ rights or rallies. Start with Westboro Baptist Church in Topeka, and follow the breadcrumbs from there. I'm only interested in church protests that resulted in charges for gross trespassing, assault, criminal threatening, things like that.
>
> If you do this for me, not only will you be paid, you will also get

a free pass to call me "Hollyberry" three (3) times. Thank you, and if you are too busy, I understand.

Holly

She sends it off with a swoosh, then finds John Ackerly in her contacts and writes to him.

Dear John: If it will not violate your NA "anonymity clause," I wonder if you would ask around, not for Program people named BRIGGS but for someone named TRIG. I think that might be the killer's real name, or nickname. Thank you.

Holly

With that done, she goes back to bed, and manages to sleep for another two hours. This time there are no dreams.

2

Izzy Jaynes and Tom Atta arrive at the Grinsted home at quarter of nine on Sunday morning. A thin-faced woman in a quilted housecoat answers the door and looks at their badges. She doesn't ask why they've come, only tells them her husband is in the gazebo. She pronounces it *gaze*-bo. "Go through the kitchen," she says, and cocks with her thumb like a hitchhiker.

"Tell me something, Mrs. Grinsted," Izzy says. "Does Russell have a younger brother or sister?"

She doesn't ask why Izzy wants to know. "Only child. Raised to think of himself as the little prince." And rolls her eyes.

They go through the kitchen. Tom speaks low to Izzy. "I think there might be trouble in this particular valley." Izzy nods. Mrs. Grinsted struck her as a woman suffering a serious case of detachment.

Across a patio and in the middle of a good-sized patch of back lawn, a balding man in a red bathrobe and pajamas is sitting at a table in the gazebo, drinking coffee and reading the newspaper. He sees them coming and stands up, re-belting his robe. He doesn't ask to see their badges. He doesn't need to.

To both: "Cheezit, the cops." And to Izzy: "Atta I know from court. You I've never had the pleasure of deposing or cross-examining."

"Isabelle Jaynes," she says, and gives a brief shake to Grinsted's outstretched hand.

"What are you doing here bright and early on a Sunday morning? Don't tell me, let me guess. It concerns whoever is killing people and leaving the names of the Duffrey jurors in his victim's hands."

"That wouldn't be you, would it?" Tom asks pleasantly.

Russell Grinsted looks blank for a moment, then laughs. "Good one! Now what can this humble esquire help you with?"

Izzy and Tom don't reply. Grinsted looks from one to the other. "You're not joking."

"Not a bit," Tom says.

Grinsted turns and picks up his coffee cup and drains it. He speaks not to his visitors on this warm and charming spring morning, but to the empty cup, as if to a microphone. "Two city detectives show up at my house on Sunday morning while I've still got sleepy-dust in my eyes to ask if I'm killing people because of the late and lamented—by me, among others—Alan Duffrey. Who I just about tore my guts out defending. And they're not joking."

He turns to them, not laughing now but smiling. Tom will tell Izzy later that he remembers that smile from being cross-examined by Grinsted. Which was an unpleasant experience.

"And what has led you to that amazing idea, Officers?"

"Why don't you let us ask the questions, and then we'll let you get back to your Sunday morning," Izzy says. "Assuming the answers are satisfactory, that is. If they're not, you may have to accompany us downtown."

"Unbelievable. Un-fucking-believable. All right, ask away."

"Let's start with May third," Izzy says. "That was a Saturday. Where were you between the hours of, let's say five and seven PM?"

"Really?" Still with the smile, now accompanied by raised eyebrows. "Do *you* remember where you were on a Saturday three weeks ago?"

The kitchen door bangs open, and Mrs. Grinsted joins them. She has a coffee pot and two cups on a St. Pauli Girl tray. Also cream and sugar. "He was here, I should think. We watch *Antiques Roadshow* on Saturday afternoons or evenings. Streaming is convenient because you can watch any old time. Russ usually gets takeout. Whatever *he* feels like. I am rarely consulted. Coffee?"

"No, thank you," Tom says. "Of course, we usually expect spouses to offer alibis." He gives her his own smile, which is considerably more friendly than Grinsted's sharklike grin. "Just sayin."

Izzy: "What about the next afternoon? Sunday the fourth?" The day the winos were killed.

Grinsted says, "Oh my Jesus. Wait, I might actually have something on that." He goes into the house, tightening the belt of his robe and once again muttering, "Unbelievable."

"Do *you* have any memories of that Sunday?" Tom asks Mrs. Grinsted. "It was a chilly one, looked like rain, not like now."

"I went to church. I go every Sunday. Russ doesn't attend. I believe he was in his study, prepping a case or expecting somebody, but I can't really say."

"Does your husband own a firearm, Mrs. Grinsted?"

"Oh yes, we both have guns. I have a Ruger .45 and Russ has a Glock 17. They are for home protection. My husband is a criminal lawyer who often has bad people for clients. Sometimes he brings them home."

Both weapons are bigger than the gun used on Mike Rafferty, and *much* bigger than the gun used on the woman and the winos. But they will have to check those weapons, if Grinsted cannot provide any alibi stronger than a wife who doesn't seem especially crazy about him. Still, they have next to nothing . . . except for Holly Gibney's deductions, which Izzy trusts, and knows that Tom does, too. Up to a point, anyway.

Grinsted comes back with his own appointment book. He flaps it at them. "At two o'clock on that Sunday, Jimmy Sykes came over to fix my desktop computer. It kept crashing. I was hoping he could come on Saturday, but he was fully booked. Look."

Tom looks. Izzy writes down the name. "He's your IT guy?"

"Yes. He re-booted it or something, so I could do some casework."

"More like so you could play online blackjack," Mrs. Grinsted says.

Grinsted turns his thin smile away from Izzy and Tom and onto his wife. "Be that as it may, do you remember Jimmy coming in on Sunday?"

"Yes, but not which Sunday."

He taps the square for May 4th. "Here it is, dear one."

This provokes an eyeroll from Mrs. Grinsted.

Tom says, "You didn't just happen to jot that appointment down on that particular date before you came out here, did you?"

"I'd resent that if it wasn't so ridiculous."

"Here's an easy one," Izzy says. "May twentieth, last Tuesday. Let's say between six and ten PM. Home with your wife, I suppose. Maybe watching *Masterpiece Theatre*."

"I was playing poker. Not online, with friends." But for the first time, Russell Grinsted seems unsure.

His wife, however, doesn't. "He wasn't here, but he wasn't playing poker, either. If you ask him for the names of the men he was playing with, he'd be in real trouble, because they'd tell you he wasn't in the game. Russ isn't a killer, but he *is* a cheater. Last Tuesday night he was with his chippy."

Silence in the gazebo. Mrs. Grinsted puts the tray down. Her mouth grows a thin-lipped smile that is much like her husband's. *But is that surprising?* Izzy thinks. *Don't they say that men and women who've been married a long time grow to look like each other?*

"Her name is Jane Haggarty. She's a part-time legal secretary and ugly as a scarecrow in a melon patch. They've been seeing each other off and on for a little over a year." She turns to her husband. "Did you really think I didn't know? You are an *extremely* bad cheater, Russ."

Izzy hardly knows what to say next, mostly because Mrs. Grinsted—she still doesn't know the woman's first name—is so *calm*. Tom, however, has no problem. Grinsted, after all, once went at him on the stand.

"Will this Jane Haggarty confirm you were with her on the twentieth of May, Mr. Grinsted?"

"Erin, I . . ." Grinsted doesn't seem to know how to finish, but at least Izzy now knows Mrs. Grinsted's first name. Her first thought is *She looks too thin and too disappointed to be an Erin.*

"We'll discuss this later, after the police have gone," Erin Grinsted says. "For now just be happy I saved your bacon. For a lawyer, you certainly know how to talk yourself into trouble."

She leaves, disappearing into the kitchen without a backward glance. Grinsted sits down at the gazebo table. The belt of his robe, which he has been obsessively tightening, comes undone. The robe flops open. Underneath is a pajama jacket pooched out by a middle-aged potbelly.

"Thanks, assholes," he says without looking up.

"To coin a metaphor that may be apt in this case," Izzy says, "the jury is out on who's the asshole here. The question is whether this Jane Haggarty will confirm you were with her at the time when we believe Reverend Mike Rafferty was murdered." They will ask Grinsted for an alibi for the Sinclair murder if necessary. It may not be.

"She will." Still without looking up.

"Address?" Tom has his notebook out.

"4636 Fairlawn Court. She's married, but they're separated." He looks up at last. His eyes are tearless but glazed, like the eyes of a fighter who's just been the recipient of a hard right to the jaw. "Why in God's name would you think *I* was killing those people? I gave Alan Duffrey the best defense I could. Judge and jury got it wrong. Prosecutor has ambitions. End of story."

Izzy has no intention of bringing her private investigator friend into the discussion. Nor does she have to. She asks Grinsted if the name Claire Rademacher rings a bell.

"She worked at First Lake City," Grinsted says, sounding suspicious. "Chief cashier, if I remember rightly."

"You never called her to testify," Tom says.

"Had no reason to." Grinsted sounds more suspicious than ever. As a veteran litigator, he understands there's a trapdoor here somewhere; he just doesn't know where.

Tom Atta now tells Grinsted—with real satisfaction—about the *Plastic Man* comic books Cary Tolliver brought Alan Duffrey as a "congratulations on your promotion" present. There was no mention of this six-issue series in the court transcripts, nor of the Mylar bags. Izzy tries to tell herself she's not enjoying the look of dismayed understanding that dawns on Grinsted's face. Then she gives up. She *is* enjoying it.

Partly because Grinsted has been cheating on his wife, more because Grinsted thought his wife was too dumb to know, mostly just because she, like most police, dislikes defense attorneys. In theory, she understands their importance to the legal process. In practice, she thinks most of them suck. She reads Michael Connelly's Mickey Haller books, and roots for the Lincoln Lawyer to fall on his face.

"The fingerprints weren't on those kiddy-fiddler magazines?" Grinsted is still trying to get the enormity of his lapse into his head. "They were just on the bags?"

"That is correct," Tom says. "Maybe next time, Counselor, you should hire a private investigator instead of trying to hog the retainer and subsequent fees for yourself."

"Douglas Allen needs to be disbarred!" In his indignation, Grinsted seems to have forgotten he has big trouble on the home front.

"I think disciplinary revocation is the best you can hope for," Izzy says, "but that should put a pretty good-sized stick in his spokes. Disbarment is unlikely. Allen never *said* the fingerprints were on the magazines, he simply let you assume it. I doubt if you'll admit it, but I think you believed those magazines were Duffrey's all along, even though he denied it."

"Whatever I may have believed—and you aren't in my head, Detective Jaynes, so you don't really know—is immaterial to the defense I mounted for my client. I repeat, I pulled my guts out for that man."

"But you didn't pull them out enough to hire an investigator," Izzy says. She thinks—no, *knows*—that if Grinsted had hired Holly Gibney, Alan Duffrey would still be alive and free. So in all probability would McElroy, Epstein, Mitborough, and Sinclair. Also, an unknown woman with a juror's name in her dead hand. And Rafferty, him too.

Grinsted opens his mouth to offer a rebuttal, but Tom gets there first. "Even on your own, you should have figured out fingerprints that clear couldn't have been taken from the pulp stock those magazines were printed on."

"And *your* people didn't figure it out?" Grinsted asks. He pulls the belt of his robe tight again, as if trying to strangle the potbelly beneath. "Your forensics crew? They *must* have known, but nobody came forward! No one!"

This is something Izzy hasn't even considered, and it hits home.

"Our job isn't to do *your* job." She knows it's specious logic, but it's the best she can do on short notice. "You could have deposed Rademacher, but you didn't. You didn't even interview her."

"Doug Allen got Alan Duffrey killed," Grinsted says. He seems to be talking to himself. "With an assist from the police."

"Oh, I think you also played a part," Tom says. "Wouldn't you say so, Counselor? Or should I call you Trig?"

There's no guilty reaction to the calculated use of the nickname. No reaction at all. Grinsted just seems lost in thought. Perhaps realizing that this is just Confrontation 1, to be followed by Confrontation 2, after Izzy and Tom leave.

At this moment, Izzy realizes that Holly's deduction—which Holly herself found a bit shaky—is wrong. The anagram was a coincidence; what mystery writers in the old days would call a red herring.

"We'll be checking Jane Haggarty," Tom says, closing his notebook. "You have a nice day now, Mr. Grinsted."

Grinsted, whose day is shaping up to be anything but nice, makes no response. Izzy and Tom go back to the house. Mrs. Grinsted is in the kitchen, drinking her own cup of joe. Judging by the bottle of Wild Turkey on the counter, she has fortified her Folgers.

"Are you done with him?"

"For the time being, yes," Tom says. "Your turn."

If he expected a smile at this sally, he's disappointed.

"How long have you known about Haggarty?" Izzy asks. It has no bearing on their case, but she's curious . . . as she knows Holly would be.

"A year? Maybe sixteen months." Mrs. Grinsted shrugs, as if the topic doesn't interest her much. "Her perfume on his skin. Texts. Hangups a couple of times when Russ left his phone on the counter or on top of the TV and I answered. He didn't try to hide it very much. I suppose he thought I was stupid. Maybe I am."

"Maybe you were scared," Izzy says.

Erin Grinsted sips her fortified coffee. "Maybe I was. Maybe I still am."

"Does your husband go to AA or NA?"

"No. If he needs one of those anonymous programs, it would be the one for gamblers. Or sex addicts. Or both."

"Mrs. Grinsted, do you call your husband Trig?"

"No. I call him Russ. Most people do. Alan Duffrey did."

"Does *anyone* call him Trig?"

She looks up at Izzy and does the eyeroll thing again. "Why would they?"

Why indeed, Izzy thinks. *Back to square one.*

They leave her to discuss various matters with her husband.

3

While Izzy and Tom are talking to Russell Grinsted, Trig—the *real* Trig—is in Cowslip County, a hundred miles from the city. It's the least populated county in the state, and the kids whose bad karma it is to live there call it—of course—Cowshit County.

Trig cruises along Route 121, passing the occasional farm and barn, but mostly just woods and fields. There's little traffic; 121 has been rendered all but obsolete by the interstate, which runs through more populated areas to the south. He doesn't even kid himself about what he's doing out here. Although meeting Annette McElroy and her dog on the Buckeye Trail was only weeks ago, it seems like something that happened in another life.

When I was normal.

At first he tries to push that idea away, but gives up. Because it's not an idea, it's a fact. More and more what's happening reminds him of how he became an alcoholic . . . and why not? It doesn't matter if it's booze, dope, food, gambling, or obsessive-compulsive behavior, at bottom it's always the disease of addiction. He could blame his father (and sometimes does), but addiction—antisocial behavior, in shrink-speak—isn't caused by childhood trauma or stress or social pressure; it's just a glitch in the software that causes destructive behavior to repeat and repeat and repeat.

There's a saying he's heard in meetings: "First the man takes a drink, then the drink takes a drink, and then the drink takes the man." It's true. Somewhere in his twenties, not long after his sometimes loving, often destructive father died, a switch got flipped. One day he was drinking like a quote-unquote *normal person*, and the next he was an alcoholic. Boom. Over done with gone.

Trig has discovered that murder is pretty much the same. He thinks that after McElroy, he could have stopped. In the legal sense he'd crossed a red line, sure, but in his own head? Probably not. He doesn't think it was Epstein and Mitborough that tipped him over, either. He thinks—he's not sure, but he *thinks*—that it was Big Book Mike that flipped the switch. All he knows for certain is the next one, Sinclair, relieved a certain building pressure that had little (maybe nothing) to do with his original mission.

He passes through the tiny community of Rosscomb, consisting of a market, a gas station, and the Rosscomb United Baptist Church. Then he's out in the country again. Four miles further on, he sees a man driving a big old highpockets tractor and pulling a disc mower. It's too early for hay, the grass is still green, so maybe the farmer is going to sow some crop here. Beans or corn, likely.

Trig pulls over onto the shoulder and gets out. The Taurus .22 is in his pocket. He's not a bit nervous. Excited. Anticipating. He waits until the old tractor swings close and gives the man driving it a big semaphore wave and a grin. A truck passes, headed south.

That driver may remember a Toyota pulled over at the side of the road, and a man waving down the farmer.

He should back off, maybe just ask for directions and then drive on, but the girl he left at the shelter in Crooked Creek has whetted his appetite the way the first drink used to do. *Just a quick one after work*, he'd tell himself . . . then drink all the way home, even though his rational mind knew that getting picked up for DUI might crash his entire life. As those awful pictures and magazines had crashed Alan Duffrey's life . . . or so everyone thought, judge and jury included.

The farmer brings his tractor to a stop, but even idling, the old International Harvester makes a hellacious racket. He's as old as his tractor, with a tanned and weatherbeaten face under a big straw hat. Trig walks to one of the tractor's big mud-caked wheels, wearing a smile to which the farmer responds with a smile of his own.

"Help you, fella?" the farmer shouts over the racket of the tractor and the spinning mower blades. "You lost?"

"Yes!" Trig shouts back. "I'm lost!"

He takes the Taurus from his pocket and shoots the farmer twice in the chest. The sound of the gunshots is all but lost in the roar of the tractor. The farmer rears back as if beestung. Trig gets ready to shoot him again, but then he slumps forward. His hat falls off. Thinning gray hair blows in a light breeze, reminding Trig of milkweed puffs.

A car goes by on the highway. It slows. Trig gives the car a wave without turning around—*all okay here*—and it speeds up again. Trig takes the leather folder from his pocket and thumbs through the thinning collection of slips inside. He feels no sense of worry, just as he never worried in the old days when he'd drive home sipping from a handle of Smirnoff between his spread thighs. There is a sense of perfect rightness about this encounter, and oh God, such relief. The need will come again, but for the moment all is well.

I need MA instead of AA, he thinks, and actually laughs.

From his folder he takes the slip of paper with Brad Lowry printed on it. Lowry was Juror 12 in the Duffrey case. Trig picks up the farmer's straw hat and puts Lowry's name in it. Not hurrying, he also puts the slips for Jabari Wentworth (Juror 3) and Ellis Finkel (Juror 5) into the hat. The farmer has welded a handy step-up onto the side of the peakseat. Trig uses it and pushes the farmer back into an upright position, being careful not to joggle the transmission and start the tractor moving. Then he jams the hat down on the farmer's head. Eventually, someone will take the hat off. Eventually, the slips of paper will be found, and will be understood.

A farm truck full of equipment passes. Trig stands where he is, as if conversing with the farmer. The truck passes. He goes back to his car and drives away.

I'm going to be caught.

Not a guess but a stone-cold fact. He's remembering something that happened near the end of his drinking, the thing that got him to his first AA meeting. Three blocks from his house, drunk as a skunk with that handle of vodka resting against his crotch, he saw blue lights go off in his rearview mirror. Calmly, he had screwed the cap on the bottle, put it in the passenger footwell, and pulled over, telling himself the cop wouldn't be able to smell vodka on his breath like gin or whiskey, at the same time knowing that was a myth.

The cop flashed his light in Trig's window and asked for his license and registration. Trig handed them over, getting the registration from his Toyota's glove compartment—a different Toyota, but similar to the one he was now driving. The cop put his light on them, then went back to his cruiser. Trig tried to put the bottle of vodka in the glove compartment. It was too big to fit. Under the passenger seat. Also too big. He thought, *I may or may not spend tonight in the city drunk tank, but for sure my name will be in the paper's Police Beat column tomorrow.*

The cop started back. Trig returned the big bottle of vodka to the passenger footwell. It was the best he could do. A sense of fatalism washed over him.

"Have you been drinking, sir?"

"I had a couple after work, but that was hours ago." Not slurring. Or hardly at all.

"I see by your license that you're close to home."

Trig had agreed that was so.

"I suggest you go there, sir, and not get behind the wheel again until you are sober."

He then shone his light into the passenger footwell, spotting it on the three-quarters-empty bottle of vodka.

"If I see you weaving again, sir, you will go to jail."

So nothing in writing, just a verbal warning. That would not happen after killing seven people.

I should have taken the Rev's calendar instead of just changing the name. That was what Daddy would have called "too clever by half," probably punctuated by a clip to the side of the head. And what about the vehicles that passed while you were "talking" to the farmer? What if one of them saw the old guy slumped forward and thought it was peculiar? What if one of them jotted down your license plate?

He doesn't believe anyone did that, but the calendar is a different matter. That will have been gone over by experts, and they may already have decided that he has altered TRIG to BRIGGS. It's true that Trig is only a nickname, and nothing like his real one, but he *has* used it at AA and NA meetings. Almost always out of town, it's true, but he has attended the Straight Circle meeting on Buell Street a few times. What if someone in that meeting knows him in what alkies and druggies call "the other life"? He doesn't *think* that's likely—most of those at Straight Circle are low-bottom alkies and homeless drug fiends—but it's possible. One thing is sure: he won't be going to Buell Street again.

And look on the bright side, he tells himself. *I've name-checked eight of the twelve jurors. I might even get them all.*

In his rearview mirror, he sees a State Police cruiser coming up fast, and flashes back to that night when he saw blue lights in his rearview. That same sense of fatalism comes, as comforting as a blanket on a cold night. He touches the .22 in his pocket, slows down, pulls over. He'll shoot the cop, put a name in his hand, and then—maybe, maybe not—shoot himself. The cop car sweeps by him, speeding on down Route 121 toward Rosscomb.

"No," Trig says, letting go of the gun. "Not done, Daddy. Not done yet."

He turns on the radio, but he's too far from the city to pick up the news station, so he settles for some old-time rock and roll instead. Soon he's singing along.

Chapter 14

1

Holly is preparing to leave for Madison, the next stop on Kate's tour, when Izzy calls and tells her Russell Grinsted isn't Trig. "His alibis for Rafferty and Sinclair both check out. His gun and his wife's are the wrong caliber. Bottom line, the guy wasn't scared to see us, just pissed off." As an afterthought she adds (not without satisfaction), "Our visit may have tipped his marriage over. It was teetering anyway. He's been cheating on his wife."

Holly hardly hears that part. She can feel her cheeks heating with the kind of flush that would look feverish rather than pretty if she looked in a mirror (so she doesn't). "I sent you on a wild goose chase. I'm sorry, Isabelle."

"Don't be. It was a good deduction, just off-base. It happens. You were right about the other thing. We've got a forensics guy who's also an amateur graphologist. He spent part of his Saturday night looking at an enlarged photo of Reverend Rafferty's calendar under magnification. You were right. It's TRIG, not BRIGGS. *T* into *B* was the giveaway, he said. No question in his mind. If the Bill Wilson alias means the guy has been going to meetings, we have a real chance of finding out who he is. Trig isn't like Dave or Bill. It stands out."

"I'm really sorry, Iz. I went too far out on a limb and it broke off."

"Quit with the sorry," Izzy says. "Number one, we had to re-interview Grinsted anyway. Number two, we have a potentially valuable lead and that's down to you. Number three, you're always too hard on yourself. Give yourself some fucking credit, Hols."

Holly almost says, *I'm sorry, I'll try*, then chokes it off. "Thanks, Izzy, that's kind. I reached out to my guy in the recovery program. If he knows a Trig, he'll let me know and I'll let you know."

"I'll be doubling down on that," Izzy says. "This will come as a shock to you, but there are a lot of cops who have substance abuse problems and some of them go to recovery meetings. I'll circulate a memo that asks about Trig and guarantees anonymity for any cop who has info. You concentrate on taking care of that woman you're bodyguarding. They're saying nasty things about her on that so-called news station. The Big Bob."

"I'll do my best," Holly says, and ends the call. She goes into the bathroom and splashes cold water on her burning cheeks. She understands that Izzy is right; all her life she has dwelled on her failures while discounting her successes as coincidence or pure luck. Some of this was no doubt the result of growing up in the shadow (no; under the thumb) of Charlotte Gibney, but she suspects some of it is just the way she's built.

I need my own program, she thinks. *Call it SEA. Self-Esteem Anonymous.*

Her phone chirps. It's Corrie Anderson, telling Holly she and Kate are saddling up for the drive to Wisconsin.

"I'll be half an hour behind you," Holly says. "Keep on the main-traveled roads and watch out for cars that seem like they're sticking with you."

"Not easy," Corrie says. "After Iowa City, we've picked up the usual tail of Kate fans."

"Watch for a woman on her own." She almost adds, *Probably wearing dark glasses*, but that's stupid. On a sunny morning like this, most drivers will be wearing them.

"Roger that." Corrie sounds insouciant, unconcerned. Holly doesn't like it. "Hold on. Kate wants to talk to you."

There's a rustle, and then Holly's boss is on the phone. "I just want to thank you again for what you did last night. I was frozen in place. So was Corrie and everyone else. You, however, were not."

Holly starts to say something about how she didn't even think, just reacted. Then she thinks of Izzy saying, *Give yourself some fucking credit, Hols*. What she says is, "You're very welcome." Saying that is difficult but not impossible.

She ends the call feeling good about herself again. Well . . . no. Holly never feels exactly good about herself, but she *does* feel better, and decides to treat herself to a breakfast pastry before getting on the road.

Her phone rings again as she's going out the door. It's Jerome. He says he'll be happy to research fundamentalist churches that have gotten in trouble with the law.

"I know it's a big ask," Holly says, tossing her suitcase into the backseat of the Chrysler (the luxury of which she is coming to enjoy). "I'm sorry to take you away from your book."

"I told you, I hit a roadblock on it. I'll finish it eventually—it's how I was raised—but I guess I wasn't made for fiction. Research, though . . . I love that shit."

"Well, do what you can, but don't let your novel go cold on my account. My idea will probably come to nothing, anyway. I've already pulled one boner on the Surrogate Juror thing." Leaning against her car in the mellow morning sunshine, she tells Jerome how she thought Trig might have been a nickname for Russell Grinsted.

"Don't let it get you down," he says. "Even Aaron Judge strikes out once in awhile. Actually quite a lot."

"Thanks, J."

"Don't mention it, Hollyberry."

"That's one," she says, and can't keep the smile out of her voice. "You get two more."

He laughs, then says, "I'll hoard those. Stay safe, Hols."

"That's the plan."

2

It was Chrissy who went to sleep in Cabin 6 of the Davenport Rest, but it's Chris who wakes up, yawns, stretches, and gets into the rusty, coffin-sized shower. He doesn't need coffee; as a person that grew up in the Real Christ Holy Church of Baraboo Junction, he has never used it. Or alcohol. Or drugs, including aspirin.

He's in a good mood. Deacon Fallowes mentioned Brenda's Bitches last night, and Chris woke up thinking about them this morning. Pastor Jim (also Andy Fallowes) likes to say that "the Way of the Cross is a hard way," and it's true, but that makes every victory sweeter. The day the church bested Brenda's Bitches was a sweet day indeed. It's true that Mama didn't care for what happened, but as the Book of Titus says, women should not be argumentative, but submissive.

Not that she argued much that day; just a few words was all. As Isaiah says, "The ox knows its owner."

The bathroom's one towel is little more than a rag, but Chris doesn't care; he's having a pleasant walk down Memory Lane to Rawcliffe, Pennsylvania, and the Rawcliffe Women's Center.

That day he was all Chris.

3

Women's Center, indeed! Like Pastor Jim and Deacon Andy, Chris has always been amused by how the godless find sanitary terms for their evil. A women's center, not an abortion mill. Pro-choice instead of pro-murder.

At least, he thinks as he dresses in jeans and a tee-shirt from the blue suitcase, *Brenda's Bitches had the balls to call themselves something honest. They were bitches and proud of it.*

This was a year before *Dobbs v. Jackson*. Chris found out later, after they got back to Wisconsin, that the Bitches got to know one another—wait for it, wait for it—at the Rawcliffe PTA, Rawcliffe being a small and prosperous city not far from Hershey. By the time the Bitches got organized, Real Christ Holy had been picketing the Women's Center for almost five months, sometimes joined by like-minded local protestors but usually going it alone on days when it rained or snowed. As Pastor Jim liked to say, "Deal with it, brothers and sisters, and remember it's always sunny in heaven."

Funded by Hot Flash Electric money (Harold Stewart, Chris's father, religious and completely naïve, had no idea that the name of his company had a certain female implication), Real Christ Holy might pick a target in any part of the country, but once they picked it, they stuck with it.

There were women in the Rawcliffe PTA who approved of the protests, if not always of the signs the Real Christers carried (dismembered fetuses, bloodstained doctors' smocks, ABORTION PROVIDERS BURN IN HELL), but there were a dozen or more who did not. These ladies met at the home of Brenda Blevins, who was particularly incensed by the sign Pastor Jim was carrying. This was after an abortion doctor, Henry Tremont, was shot and killed by a religious martyr named Taylor Verecker as Tremont was coming out of church. Pastor Jim's sign read TAYLOR VERECKER WAS SENT TO DO GOD'S WORK.

The Blevins woman had an idea for a counter-protest, one that would generate plenty of headlines, and some of her friends, furious at the Real Christ Holy interlopers, went along with it. Also, it was funny. Chris was willing to admit it. No one ever said godless libtards lacked a sense of humor.

Blevins, partial heir to a chocolate fortune, had plenty of money—probably not as much as Chris's father, who had donated almost his entire fortune to Real Christ Holy, but she was wealthy enough to purchase nine motor scooters and nine leather jackets, all as pink as Barbie's Dreamhouse. On the back of the jackets: BRENDA'S BITCHES.

The nine women picked a drizzly day when Real Christ Holy only had a few local protestors helping them out. They formed up in a V-shape on Fourth Street, Blevins at the forefront. They rode their scooters at the protestors at about twenty miles an hour, singing a version of "We Shall Overcome" that rhymed *overcome* with *God-bothering scum.*

The Real Christers scattered before them. News photogs and TV cameras—all alerted by the resourceful Ms. Blevins—caught everything on film. The murder factory was in a strip mall at the end of Fourth. There was plenty of parking lot there for the counter-protestors to swing around in and return to the street. The Real Christ Holy protestors scattered again when they did. Signs were dropped and run over. Still singing, having a whale of a good time, the pink motor scooter drivers put-putted a couple of hundred yards up Fourth Street, circled, and returned yet again, singing and slinging such epithets as "Run, you self-righteous assholes!"

The Real Christ Holy men and women were cold, damp, and in too much disarray to be immediately angry. They were used to being shouted and jeered at, but not *driven* at. Most just looked bewildered. Chris's mother was rubbing her arm. The rightside mirror of a scooter had clipped her on its way by. Her sign, GOD SENDS KILLER DOCS TO HELL, lay at her feet. Chris was infuriated to see his mom looking sad and damp and beaten, with her no-color hair (women in Real Christ Holy did not dye) pasted against her cheeks.

Jamie Fallowes, Andy's son, grabbed Chris. He shouted, "I've got an idea! Come on!"

The two young men beat feet to the 7-Eleven at the far end of the strip mall. There they bought all the cooking oil and olive oil on the shelves. Jamie waited impatiently for Chris to pay with the Hot Flash credit card (Real Christ Holy did not believe in plastic, which was a tool of the deep state), then the two of them returned to the Women's Center, young men who were excited and laughing their heads off. Brenda's Bitches were back on Fourth Street, swinging around for another bombing run.

"Help us!" Jamie shouted to the other protestors. "Come on, you guys!"

Only Pastor Jim stood back (but smiling) as bottles of cooking oil were passed around, opened, and emptied across the parking lot the Bitches were using as their turnaround point.

"What are you doing?" Gwen Stewart asked her son. She had picked up her sign but refused to take a bottle of Wesson oil. "That's dangerous!"

Women from the center, some wearing nurses' uniforms—how grotesque was that—had come out to watch and cheer on the Bitches.

The scooters came back, Brenda in the lead, bent over her handlebars. A few of the Real Christ Holy protestors were still spreading oil, but most just stood aside with Pastor Jim and Deacon Andy. The scooters swept into the parking lot. "*Bitches rule!*" one shouted as she went by.

They reached the turnaround point. The asphalt was wet as well as oily, and every single one of them spun out. The singing and shouting were replaced by screams of surprise and pain. Most of the pink scooters slid all the way to the storefronts. One jumped the curb and struck the show window of Richard Chemel's Pawn & Loan. The glass shattered. Guitars rained down.

There was a moment of shocked silence from the little crowd gathered outside of the Women's Center, and then they ran for the scattered, moaning Bitches. One of the women, a nurse, slipped in the oily wet and went on her ass. Jamie whooped and clapped Chris on the shoulder.

The Bitches were all wearing helmets—Brenda had insisted on that—and the news reports about the incident said that, plus their low speed of travel, saved them from serious injury. Probably true, but there was plenty of road-rash, one broken arm, and a couple of sprained shoulders. Five or six of the felled Bitches were lying on the pavement in shock; a couple of others staggered to their feet; Brenda Blevins herself was on all fours with blood gushing from her nose.

Nurses and aides—plus a couple of young women who'd come in for the procedure—began helping the downed women to their feet. One of the nurses, wearing a smock printed all over with bluebirds (something cheerful for the mommies to look at while their babies were being sucked away in pieces), approached Jamie, who was grinning. She was trembling with outrage. *"How low can you go?"* she screamed. *"How rotten can you be to hurt a bunch of women?"*

Chris stepped between them before Bluebird Nurse could punch Jamie in the nose, which she seemed ready to do. "You're killing babies," Chris said. "How rotten is that?"

Bluebird Nurse looked at him, cheeks burning, mouth open. Then she spread her arms wide and actually laughed. "I've got a pregnant rape victim in there today, but I can't talk to you about that or anything else. Can I? You're lost. The whole fucking bunch of you, lost. It's the Great American Divide. At least you'll go to jail." She wheeled around and repeated, *"The whole fucking bunch of you!"*

But no one went to jail. Not Brenda's Bitches, not the Real Christ Holy protestors. Pastor Jim had a local lawyer—one of the good ones—on call, and the lawyer pointed out it was the Bitches who had started it. The security footage from the Women's Center cameras confirmed this. And while the cooking oil trick *was* sort of low, the Real Christ Holy group had been observing the buffer zone decreed by FACE, the Freedom of Access to Clinic Entrances Act. Also, several of Pastor Jim's crew exhibited bruises from passing scooters, almost all of them created after the fact. The one authentic bruise was on Gwen Stewart's arm, and she refused to show it to the police when they came. When Pastor Jim asked her—in his gentlest voice—why not, she only shook her head and wouldn't meet his eyes. "I might have already had it," she said. "I bruise easily these days."

4

Chris's good moods (which almost always happen when he *is* Chris) are as fragile as an overinflated balloon, and this one pops as he's putting his suitcases into the Kia's hatchback. It's that memory of Mama saying, *I might have already had it. I bruise easily these days*. Mama who said, *Our secret*. Mama who stood up for her twins when their own father was ready to throw them out of the church . . . and possibly out of their home. Mama had been nobody's ox that day.

She *didn't* already have a bruise, Chris saw the scooter's mirror clip her himself, but it was true that she bruised easily. Because, it turned out, she had leukemia. Six months after the Rawcliffe protest, she was dead. Once the initial diagnosis was made, there were no doctors and certainly no hospitals. Prayer was Pastor Jim's prescription, and all six hundred members of Real Christ Holy prayed for Gwendolyn Stewart without ceasing. In the end, God's will was done. When Andy Fallowes found Chrissy crying behind the house the day after the burying, wearing pedal pushers, makeup so ineptly applied it was clownish, and a wig all askew, he did not condemn her. He only said, "What could doctors have given her except one more year of suffering?"

It was cold comfort, but better than no comfort at all.

5

Holly is in Rockford, Illinois, Kate's truck about sixty miles ahead, when she gets a call from Izzy. She pulls into a Circle K and returns the call. Izzy is brief and bitter: "The son of a bitch got another one. Elderly farmer upstate in Rosscomb. Name of George Carville. A neighbor saw him sitting slumped over the wheel of his tractor and got concerned. The notes were in his fucking *hat*. Brad Lowry, plus Finkel and Wentworth."

"Did anybody see—"

"We're still checking, but so far nothing."

"Is it your—"

"Our case? No, it still belongs to the State Police and the Cowslip County Sheriff, but Tom and I are going up there and I have what you like to call Holly hope. It's rural. People take note of strangers. It was either carelessness or pure arrogance."

"Maybe both. Keep me informed when you can. And again, I'm sorry about—"

"I will, and *stop apologizing*." With that, Izzy is gone.

Before pulling back onto the highway, she gets a call from Corrie. They have arrived in Madison. "Kate wants you to join us for lunch, if that's okay."

"I'll be there soon."

6

When the women see Holly come through the door of the hotel restaurant, they exchange a look, then burst into gales of laughter. For a moment all of Holly's insecurities, never far from the surface, come rushing back. She thinks about high school. Laughter directed her way *always* makes her think of high school. Her left hand flies to the zipper of her slacks to make sure it's pulled up all the way. Then Corrie is waving to her. "You have to see this! It's too crazy!"

Holly comes to the table. Her breakfast Danish was hours ago and she was planning on a hearty brunch, but now she's not sure if she's still hungry.

"Corrie is a hero," Kate says solemnly. "She saved the day." Then she starts laughing again and holds up this morning's *Quad-City Times*. Holly takes it, not sure what Kate is talking about but at least sure (*pretty* sure) that she's not the butt of the joke.

The headline of the story below the fold reads WOMAN POWER ADVOCATE ATTACKED AT RIVERCENTER. Holly can't remember any news people among the eBayers (funny how that word sticks), but the accompanying photo looks a little too pro to have been taken with a phone. The Incredible Hulk, identified as Victor DeLong, 46, of Moline, Illinois, is sprawled facedown on the pavement. The baseball bat is in the gutter. The folding chair lies close by, legs up. In the foreground, turned toward the camera, looking extremely startled and extremely pretty, is Corrie Anderson. According to the news, it was Corrie who kicked the chair and tripped the would-be assailant.

"I'll call and have them print a correction," Corrie says.

Holly gets on that one posthaste. "Don't you dare. I like it just the way it is." Her mother's firm dictum about women in print is never far from her mind: *A lady's name should be in the newspaper only three times—birth, marriage, death.*

Of course for Holly, that ship has sailed.

"Corrie getting in the paper for her heroic efforts is only half of our happiness," Kate says. "We're at the Mingo on Friday night, and life is good."

"The last holdup was an insurance issue," Corrie says. "Sista's band will have a lot of equipment onstage. Insurance company was moderately crappy about that."

"Of course it was," Holly says. She's thinking of the donkey with the big teeth. It doesn't haunt her dreams, at least not yet, but give it time.

"Instruments and monitors, lots of power cords, plus Sista Bessie's cyclorama, which I'm told is famous soul singers from the old days. Kate had to sign a waiver."

"Of course she did," Holly says. "Insurance companies are *so* poopy."

The women laugh at that, although Holly doesn't consider insurance companies like Global funny. She says it's great news . . . although she was hoping to see Sista Bessie sing the National Anthem at Dingley Park. Plus Izzy pitching for the police team, of course.

Holly likes to think she can root with the best of them.

7

Barbara is in her small (but cozy) study over her parents' garage that Sunday morning, trying to write a poem. It's not going very well, because thoughts of her "Lowtown Jazz" poem—now a song—keep intruding. Time and time again she finds herself staring off into space, trying to think of words that rhyme with *jazz* without resorting to her rhyming dictionary. So far all she's come up with is *spazz* (not exactly politically correct) and *Alcatraz*. It's a relief when her phone rings, and a pleasure when she sees who's calling.

"No rehearsals today," Betty says. "You busy?"

Barbara looks at her scratchings and crossouts. "Not very."

"Come on to the hotel and get me. Show me something in this town that's *fun*. You up for that?"

"Sure, but what kind of things do you like?"

"Surprise me."

8

Betty is waiting in the lobby of the Garden City Plaza, looking frumpy and anonymous in a shin-length skirt, bobby sox, kerchief, and wrap-around shades. They go out the way Barbara came in, through the parking garage. They emerge in an alley behind the hotel.

"Where are we going?" Betty asks.

"You'll see. Are you up for a walk?"

"Walk sounds good." Betty slaps one meaty buttock. "I need to bust some calories."

"Judging from the way you're moving onstage, I'd say you're busting plenty."

They walk down Clancy Street and eventually come out on the waterfront. A block further along they come to Lakewood, the small amusement park with the Wonderland Pier at its far end. By then the two of them are chatting like old friends instead of new ones.

"Don't know if you like amusements," Barbara says. "This place just got going for the summer, and it doesn't look like much stuff is open yet—"

Betty grabs Barbara's hand and swings it. "*Somethin's* open, because I smell cotton candy."

Betty buys two cones, and they sit on a bench, eating pink clouds. "Every bite tastes like childhood," Barbara says.

"Same," Betty says. "You thought any more about touring with us?"

"I think . . . I ought to stay here. Try to write some poems. The music . . . I don't know . . . it kind of gets in my way."

"Cock-blocks the muse?"

Barbara bursts out laughing. "Never thought about it that way, but you're not wrong."

Betty trashcans her cone—she's vacuumed it up—and points across the boardwalk, which eventually leads to the pier. "*That's* open, too. Come on."

Barbara looks at the Dodgem Cars and bursts into giggles. "Are you serious?"

"Girl, I'm going to mess you up."

Betty buys tickets at the booth and crams herself into one of the cars. Barbara gets into another one and they race around, cranking their child-sized steering wheels, the poles on their cars spitting sparks and smelling like model train transformers. Barbara hits Betty first, spinning her into one of the padded rails. Betty shrieks with laughter and rams a twelve-year-old out of her way, chasing Barbara. By the time the overhead power dies and the cars drift to a stop, they have had several collisions and teamed to run a couple of teenagers into a corner, where they battered the kids relentlessly.

Barbara is laughing hard, and so is Betty.

"He'p me out of this thing, Barbara, I'm fucking stuck!"

Barbara takes one arm. One of the teenagers, bearing no animus, takes the other. They pull Betty out of the little car's cockpit.

"Like a cork out of a wine bottle," Betty says. "Thank you, Barb. Thank you, son."

"No prob," the boy says.

"Let's find the restroom before I piss my pants," Betty says.

They have the women's bathroom to themselves. Betty asks if Barbara has a boyfriend.

"No one steady," Barbara says. "I try em but don't buy em. How about you?"

"Girl, I'm too old for that."

"Never too old," Barbara says, hoping for both their sakes that it's true.

"I was married, but that didn't work. He was into dope and I was into booze. Was a wonder we didn't kill each other."

"I'm scared to drink," Barbara confesses. "Both grandfathers, paternal and maternal, were alcoholics."

"I haven't had brown liquor in seven years," Betty says. "You go on and stay scared. It won't hurt you none."

They ride the Ferris wheel, and when it stops at the top, with endless miles of lake disappearing into the morning haze, Betty takes off her kerchief and holds it up, letting it unfurl like a banner. She opens her hand and lets it fly away. They watch it go, a red streak against blue sky. Betty puts an arm around Barbara and gives her a hug, brief but strong. "This is the nicest time I've had in awhile."

"Me too," Barbara says.

"Listen, now, because I'm speaking truth. That title poem in your book, 'Faces Change,' it scared the hell out of me."

"Me too," Barbara says.

"Was it a true thing? Did you maybe see something?"

"I did." The Ferris wheel starts to move, bringing the real world up to meet them. "I'd like to tell myself it wasn't real, but I think it was."

Betty nods with perfect understanding. Which is a relief. She doesn't ask questions, which is a greater one. "Like a dog howling in the moonlight at what it can see and you can't."

"Exactly like that."

They buy ice cream and walk to the end of the pier. The sun is warm, but the breeze coming off the lake is cool. It's somehow the perfect combination.

"You sing with the Crystals next Saturday night," Betty says, looking out at the water. "Sing with me. Hear that audience go crazy . . . because they're gonna. *Then* you decide. But no matter what, you and I are going to stay tight. That work for you?"

"Yes," Barbara says, and knows that some day, maybe soon, she'll tell Betty about what happened in the elevator when Chet Ondowsky showed his real face. Underneath was nothing human. Not even close. Nobody knows about that but Holly and Jerome, but she's pretty sure Betty—who knows about dogs howling in the moonlight at what only they can see—would understand.

"Good."

"Can I ask you something, Betty?"

"Anything."

"What rhymes with jazz?"

Betty thinks about it, then holds up the remains of her ice cream. "Häagen-Dazs," she says, and they both shriek with laughter.

9

There's some sort of mix-up about the DoubleTree reservations in Madison, so after brunch the three women have to wait for awhile in the lobby while their rooms are made ready. Kate isn't happy about that but says nothing. At least not then.

That afternoon Corrie spots her boss in the pool and makes calls while Kate swims her endless laps. Holly goes back to her room and looks at the threats Kate's stalker has sent. There's the note Corrie picked up at the hotel desk in Spokane—accompanied by a photo showing Kate and Corrie laughing—and photographs of the anthrax card, outside and in.

Spokane: *You only get 1 warning, so receive it well. Next time it will be you and it will be for real. She who speaks lies shall perish.*

Omaha: A BASIC CARD FOR BASIC BITCHES on the outside. On the inside: HELL AWAITS THE DECEIVER. Carefully printed. Holly is surer than ever that their stalker is a religious crazy. In the case of Izzy's killer, maybe not religious (except in the AA/NA sense) but just as crazy.

Oh, and the picture titled LESBIANS. Which makes Holly think of Al Pacino in *Scarface*.

Holly goes back to the email she sent to Izzy, before signing on to Kate McKay's Magical Mystery Tour.

Nicely turned phrases. Perfect punctuation. Lawyer, or possibly . . . judge? As in Judge Witterson, who sent Duffrey to prison?

She's already goofed up once, suggesting Russell Grinsted might be Trig. She won't do that again. She goes to the website for Buckeye County District Court and finds a photo of Judge Irving Witterson. He looks to be in his late sixties or early seventies, which makes him an unlikely choice for Trig. Nevertheless, she sends the picture to John Ackerly, with a brief note attached, asking if he's seen this guy at meetings, calling himself Irv . . . or Irving . . . or Trig.

Enough. It's not your case. Get out of this room and breathe some fresh air. Take a walk, clear your head.

It's a good idea. It never occurs to her to swim in the hotel pool; she knows how to breaststroke and backstroke, her father taught her as a child, but besides worrying about yeast infections, she has none of Kate's body confidence, and the idea of being seen in public wearing a bathing suit makes her wince.

She doesn't even get as far as the parking lot. Corrie is sitting outside her room in the sun and crying. When she sees Holly coming, she puts on a smile.

"Hi, Holly!" Trying for chirpy.

Holly steals a chair from in front of the adjoining room and sits down beside her. "What's wrong?"

Corrie tries to widen her smile and succeeds in turning it into a grimace. "Nothing. Really."

"It doesn't look like nothing."

"But it is." Corrie scrubs a palm up her cheek in a furtive tears-be-gone gesture that Holly knows well. She was once Corrie's age, and not very well prepared for the world. The dirty truth is that she wasn't prepared at all. "It's just that Kate ripped me a new one once we were alone. Wasn't the first time, won't be the last. She can be generous, and she can be harsh."

"What was it?"

"About having to sit in the lobby. Because I forgot to call ahead and arrange early check-in. I forgot to do it because the rooms were in your name. There were people outside waving autograph books. She hates being gawked at."

Also hates not getting the Class A glide, Holly thinks. *Hates being treated like the rest of the peons.*

Holly says, "I should have done it."

Corrie shakes her head. "You have your job, I have mine. It's just . . . there's so much to keep track of."

Holly is surprised by how angry this behavior makes her, even though she can admire Kate for her courage and plain speaking. Part of it is because she's been treated as Corrie was this morning—John would say she can *identify*—but it's also simple unfairness. This young woman had bleach thrown in her face, and except for her own quick wits, could have inhaled anthrax dust. All Kate has suffered is having blood and guts dumped over her luggage; she didn't even have to replace the clothes *in* the luggage. Corrie has stuck with her through everything, all to get a scolding for not arranging early check-in at the hotel.

She says, "That's unfair."

Corrie glances at her, and something in Holly's expression clearly alarms her. "Don't say anything to her! Don't you dare get me in trouble! I understand how stressful things are for Kate. I really do."

What Corrie *doesn't* understand is that Holly would be incapable of going face to face and toe-to-toe with Kate McKay about this, anyway. Incapable of saying, *You treated your personal assistant badly and that is not acceptable.*

Holly has faced a loaded gun; on at least two occasions she has faced creatures for which there is no scientific explanation. It's not courage she lacks, it's the fundamental self-worth necessary to call someone out on their hurtful behavior. She may never be a person who can do that. It's a deeper character flaw than not wanting to be seen in a swimsuit, and she doesn't know how to fix it.

Never mind, she tells herself. *After all, I'm just another employee.* And immediately dislikes herself for thinking that way.

"I won't say anything, Corrie. But it's poopy behavior." And, sadly, the best she can muster: "Very disappointing."

Corrie puts a hand on Holly's wrist. "You have to think of the pressure she's under. *Been* under for years, starting with quitting the Pittsburgh City Council over that vote to get books about the so-called homosexual agenda out of the elementary school libraries—"

"I know about that," Holly says. "I've read her books, Corrie."

"But it was the Supreme Court decision—Dobbs—that turned most of her focus to the abortion thing. When they kicked it back to the states." Corrie is looking at Holly earnestly. "It's become a state-by-state crusade for her. Mobilizing the vote. Calling out men in power who have barely masked religious agendas. Is she a little insane on the subject? Sure. Maybe all super-dedicated people are. And how they hate her. Headlines like THE BITCH IS BACK in *Breitbart*, with a little asterisk replacing the *I*, so the Karens who read it won't be offended."

Holly hates that *Karen* pejorative, thinks it's not much different than *kike* or *dago*, a label that says don't think, just hate. She doesn't say so. Corrie is on a roll, so let her roll.

"Social media is even worse. Memes of Kate's face crossfading into a watermelon being blown apart by a .410 shotgun. Kate giving the Nazi salute. She's been accused of enticing underage girls to Epstein's Island. Of taking sheep-gland shots in her vagina to keep looking young. People who used to shoot at targets with Osama bin Laden's face on them now shoot at ones with Kate's face. Every night when she goes out, she knows her enemies will be there, booing and cursing. But she faces them. Faces them and stops them cold with humor and bravery."

"I know. I saw."

"It's not just this stalker. That guy with the baseball bat would have put her in the hospital or actually *killed* her, if you hadn't kicked that chair in his way and tripped him."

Holly knows this, and she knows something else, as well: Kate just stood there. Her face in the newspaper photograph says it all: *This cannot happen to me. I'm too special.*

"It's no wonder she blows off steam once in awhile. That's all I'm saying."

Holly makes no reply.

Corrie says, "You don't like her, do you?"

Holly thinks about how to answer. Finally she says, "I respect her." This much is true, but she still thinks that Corrie deserved better.

Deserves.

10

Trig is in his home office. The radio is tuned to the Big Bob, as it usually is, but he's hardly hearing it. Some local yokel is killing Sunday afternoon with a call-in show that mixes buy-sell-or-trade items with politics. Meanwhile, Trig has got insurance forms to fill out, three sets for three separate entities. What a word that is! Only an insurance company with a spokes-ass named Buster would call people entities.

This would be a busy week even if I wasn't killing people, he thinks . . . and then has to laugh. Thank God he still has a funnybone. He only has a few attachments to the real world since Annette McElroy, and that's one of them.

Sensayuma, he hears his father's ghost voice. *Where's your sensayuma, Triggy ole Trigger?*

Giving him an affectionate squeeze, or maybe—if he was drinking or in a pissy mood—thumping him alongside the head. Sometimes at the Holman Rink, when the other team was on a power play, his father would grip Trig's arm so hard he left bruises, only letting up when the power play expired. And if he showed Daddy those bruises later, would Daddy say, *Where's your sensayuma, Trig?* Of course he would. And for Mom? *Gone*. It was just Daddy and Trig. *She left us, buddy. Went walkabout.*

Well.

Maybe.

He looks at the Global Insurance papers without seeing them. Listens to the radio, where some call-in dinkleballs is trying to sell a power mower, without hearing it. He's thinking of Daddy. He does it more and more. Thinking of Daddy and thinking in Daddy's voice.

You're going to be caught, Trigger, where's your sensayuma about that? What you did today was so fucking risky I can't even tell you. Do you want *to be caught?*

Maybe part of him does. What most of him wants is to do it again and again and again. There are still jurors left to wear the guilt, plus Judge Witterson. Might he add him? Sure, if there was world enough and time. Why not? Finkel and Wentworth killed themselves and

God hit Cary Tolliver with the cancer stick. How many can *he* get? His dead father assures him that time is short, and Trig knows that's true . . . but why stop at thirteen or fourteen?

From the radio, the guy with the power mower for sale is telling the host that the "rhymes-with-witch" is going to be doing her gig in Buckeye City after all. He calls her Kate McSlay. Trig pushes back from the elderly home computer he keeps meaning to replace and listens.

"You're talking about the motormouth feminazi," the host says.

"Right!" the call-in guy says. "Real Americans will be at Dingley Park, watching the cops and firemen play softball for charity—"

"Not to mention Sista Bessie singing the National Anthem," the host interjects. "That's a big deal."

"Yeah, some Black lady," the caller says dismissively. "But the fake Americans will be at Mingo, listening to McSlay talk about killing babies and how it's all right to let their kids grow up queer."

"You mean gay," the host says, laughing.

"Gay, fag, queer, call it what you wanna. And taking guns away! What I think is someone should use a gun on *her*. One in the head and zip-zap, problem solved."

"Here at the Bob, we don't condone violence," the host says, still laughing, "but what you do on your own time is your own business. Let's go back to that mower. Is it a Lawn-Boy?"

"Yeah, and hardly been—"

Trig turns off the radio. He thinks, as he did at the dentist's office, that seven at a blow would be too many. But what if he could get the two fame-hags? Maybe with their assistants? If he can hold out until Friday night, it might be possible. He can't put slips of paper in their hands, not if he burns down the rink with them inside it, but he can still show their names, and in letters four feet high. Trig leans back in his chair, folds his hands over his slight paunch, and chuckles.

Hasn't lost his sensayuma after all, it seems.

Chapter 15

1

Isabelle Jaynes sometimes thinks that she would like to inhabit the world the cops inhabit on the various *Law & Order* programs. Those shows are nominally set in New York City but actually seem to exist in some TV wonderland where the detectives only have to deal with one case at a time and the connections appear like magic.

She and Tom spend the morning at one of the low-rises in Breezy Point, investigating a domestic double stabbing. The missus is in Kiner Memorial, critical but expected to pull through; the mister is dead as dirt on the kitchen floor, wearing nothing but one sock and a pair of bloodstained Jockey shorts.

Izzy and Tom split up, questioning the inhabitants of the other two apartments on the fourth floor and the two directly above and below. Although it's Monday, the start of another work and school week, everybody seems to be home, kids included. Izzy and Tom draw certain conclusions about that—they are, after all, detectives—but keep those to themselves. Meanwhile, the forensics team is doing its usual forensicky things. The stories the law-and-order team of Jaynes & Atta get from the neighbors are familiar in one way (the Greers were always fighting, lots of yelling, thumps, and thrown objects) and unique in another: Janelle and Norville Greer had the bad luck to snap at the same time and in exactly the wrong place.

"Most accidents happen in the bathroom," Tom says.

"Yes."

"Most murders, however, happen in the kitchen."

"Yes."

"So many sharp objects."

"Plus the toaster," Izzy says. "She brained him with the toaster even though he was probably dead already and she was bleeding like a stuck pig."

"Domestic bliss," Tom says.

"Happily ever after."

When they head back to the Murrow Building to file their reports, Tom says the only good thing about the Surrogate Juror case is that the State Police, with Lt. Ralph Ganzinger heading the posse, have pretty much taken it over, because only the murders of Mitborough and Epstein happened inside the Buckeye City limits.

Izzy doesn't argue, but she's not happy. To her, "pretty much taken it over" is the wrong phrase. To her, they have pretty much *hogged* the case. When they get back to the cop shop, things don't improve. Patti in Dispatch gives her a message to see Lew Warwick ASAP.

She finds her lieutenant in a familiar position, tilted back in the ergonomic chair Izzy lusts for, hands clasped on his middle, one foot on the corner of his desk. He straightens up and speaks the usual incantation: "Welcome to my lair."

She's in no mood for it after carefully tiptoeing her way around the Greer apartment on Pine Street, trying not to track in what seemed like gallons of spilled blood, which would both pollute the evidence and ruin her new (new*ish*, anyway) Salvas sneakers. "What can I do for you, Lewis?"

"You can report to Dingley Park from three to five every day this week, wearing your new blue shorts and your new blue tee-shirt, which comes with the Guns logo on the breast. There you and I will enjoy the sunshine, eat a hotdog or two, and practice, practice, practice."

"What?" Izzy drops into the far less comfortable chair on the other side of Warwick's desk. "Are you *kidding* me? With this guy Trig running around and killing people?"

"The Staties have taken over that case, and I understand the Feebs are also showing an interest." But his eyes slip away from hers. "And you're on regular duty the rest of the time. Until Friday, of course. Then you'll be at Dingley until the game is over. As will I."

"I'll be there until I get my ass handed to me in front of a thousand people, you mean." She puts her hands on her head, as if fearing it might explode. "I can't believe we're going to spend time getting ready for a *game* when there's a serial on the loose. In case you forgot, I actually *talked* to the guy!"

"You talked to someone who *said* he was the guy."

"He sent me a picture of Corinna Ashford's name in the hand of a dead woman!"

"You *think* she was dead. No body has been found. It could have been a prank."

"It wasn't," Izzy says flatly. "I know it wasn't."

Warwick runs his hands down his cheeks, pulling a long and lugubrious face. "These orders to practice for the game don't come from me, Iz. I'm just passing them on. I'm captaining the Guns team, but I'm not the Chief. If you know what I mean."

"Patmore?"

"She says it's all about the charities. In point of fact, she's still pissed about Crutchfield."

"The motor patrol guy who got the broken arm."

"Leg, actually. And there *is* the charity angle. Patmore can see herself in front of a roomful of media, handing a giant check to the Head of Pediatrics at Kiner. Cops helping kiddies! Great publicity for the department."

"Also for her." Izzy is still steaming, but also resigned. It is what it is, and it ain't *Law & Order*. Also, she'd be lying to herself if she didn't admit she feels a small but bright gleam of competition.

"There's also you and Pill," Lewis says, as if reading her mind.

"The fireman asshole who called me little lady."

"That's the one. The newspaper is sticking with the charity stuff, but Buckeye Brandon is all over the grudge-match angle on his podcast. He's calling you Beauty and Pill the Beast."

Izzy rolls her eyes.

"I know, but it's going to put butts on the bleachers, and Patmore likes that." Lewis stands up on his side of the desk, Izzy on hers. "I'm just the messenger, Iz."

"And the message has been received. I'll be there for practice, blue shorts and all. You and I can play long toss. Now may I be excused to do some actual work?"

"Absolutely. What's up with the Trig case?"

"Ask Ganzinger."

"I'm asking you."

"We haven't identified him. Staties, either, and the Feebs make three. Going through aliases—the computer guys are on that—and also spinning through the voter registration rolls. We've found Trigano, Trigelgas, Trigwell, Trigham . . . I won't bore you, there's sixty or seventy more, many of them Greek. I'm sure the State Police are duplicating our work."

"What about recovery meetings?"

"It's hard getting a handle there because of the anonymity thing, but I've found two cops who go to meetings, and Tom has got another one. So far, no one has heard of a Trig. Or Briggs, for that matter."

"Keep me informed."

"Sure. When I'm not busy finding out if I can still throw a dropball."

Lewis lets her have the last word, and she leaves, feeling a little better. Afternoons at the park, chili dogs, spring sunshine. Good-looking cops (some of them, at least). What could possibly go wrong?

2

While Izzy Jaynes (dressed in her new blue shorts and new blue tee) is playing long toss at Dingley Park, John Ackerly is attending the afternoon Straight Circle meeting in the basement of the Buell Street Methodist Church. It's always good to get a meeting, but he has another purpose this afternoon. He listens closely as the attendees identify themselves. No one calls himself Trig, but John could swear that someone *did*, not too long ago, and maybe at this very meeting. And maybe talking to Big Book Mike afterward? It's hard to be sure if it's a real memory or a false one. He goes to meetings all over the city, and there's certainly no face to go with the name.

He usually skips The Flame coffee shop—what alkies and druggies call the meeting after the meeting—but today he goes down there. A scrawny older man is leaning against the bricks outside, smoking a cigarette.

"Telescope!" John says.

"How ya doon, Johnny?"

"Hanging in there. Good meeting, wasn't it?"

"You know what they say, the worst meeting I ever went to was fuckin great." Telescope gives a phlegmy laugh.

"Shame about what happened to the Rev."

"Oh, man—I saw him just last month. Had a good convo. Last month was April, right? About how to handle my brother. Fuckin Jimmy's always comin over, trine to get me to go out drinkin with him. Like in the old days, you know. I needed some tips on how to handle him. And then someone offed him! The Rev, I mean, not my brother. How fucked up is that?"

"Totally."

"You know what they say: Only the good die young. Billy Idol even wrote a song about it."

John doesn't bother telling him he's got the wrong Billy. "Have a question for you. Ever been in meetings with someone calling himself Trig?"

Telescope squints one eye in an effort to remember, then shakes his head. John isn't surprised; Telly isn't even positive last month was April, after all. "Ask 2-Tone, why don't you? She's in there havin a coffee. Hey, you wouldn't buy me one, would you? I'm a little light this week."

"Sure." He gives Telescope a couple of bucks and goes inside. The woman he's looking for is sitting at the counter, sipping coffee. Her hair is now back to its original brown, but she still IDs herself in meetings as Cathy 2-Tone. He sits down next to her and they talk for awhile about the Rev.

2-Tone says she also saw the Rev for counseling in April (at least she's sure of the month), but doesn't tell John what she wanted counseling about, which is okay with him. That's not what he's after.

"I'm curious if you know a guy named Trig who goes to meetings."

"Why's that?" She brushes hair back from her face.

"I just want to get with him. Need some advice."

"Can't be advice about coke," Cathy 2-Tone says. "Trig's an alkie."

A lead! A lead! He hopes his face doesn't show his excitement. "You know him?"

"Don't *know* him, know him. Saw him a couple of times at Straight Circle and once at that closed meeting in Upsala last year, you know the woo-woo one where they turn off the lights and spark up candles?"

"Sure," John says. He's never been at any meeting where they light candles, but so what. "Don't know his last name, do you?"

"Man, I don't even know his *first* name, unless it's Trig. That would be a fucked-up first name, wouldn't it?" She laughs. "What's the deal, John?"

He sees Telescope come in, holding the two bucks John gave him in one arthritis-twisted hand. It gives him an idea. "Oh, you know, he owes me ten. What's he look like?"

"You loaned him ten bucks and you don't even know what he *looks* like?"

Jesus, John thinks, *it's like pulling teeth*. And Holly does this for a living?

"It was awhile ago."

2-Tone shrugs. "He looks like anybody. Medium tall, glasses, dressed kinda Mr. Businessman."

"White?"

She swivels toward him on her stool. "You loaned him ten and you don't even know if he's white? Come on, what's the deal?"

"Want a piece of pie to go with your coffee?"

"Could do."

"*Was* he white?"

"Course he was fuckin white."

"How old?"

"I don't know, maybe your age, more or less."

John is thirty-four. He slides a fivespot to her coffee cup. "Remember anything else about him?"

She considers it, then says, "He got a scar along the side of his jaw. Said in that Upsala meeting that his father gave it to him when he was drunk. That's the only reason I remember him at all. Did he do something to you, John? Is that why you want to find him? Tell the fuckin truth, Ruth."

He smiles. "I'm not Ruth."

She only looks at him.

"He maybe did something to someone." He grabs a napkin from the dispenser and writes down his phone number. "Will you call me if you see him again? There'd be fifty in it for you."

"Man, how bad did he fuck you?"

"Get some pie, Cathy." He pats her on the shoulder and leaves. Outside he sits on a bus bench and calls Holly.

3

Jerome googles Westboro Baptist Church and sees their motto is *God hates fags and all proud sinners*. This is attributed to Psalm 5, verse 5. Out of curiosity, he chases down the psalm in question and sees it says nothing about homosexuality, just "workers of iniquity."

He goes back to the Westboro Wikipedia page and finds a link to "churches accused of assault and disorderly conduct." He draws a yellow legal pad to him and begins to jot down notes. Before he knows it, he has fourteen churches. Two hours have passed, and he's still only skimming the surface. He wants to chase this some more. The thought-processes of these groups are fascinating, not to mention the way they twist the scripture to align with their whackdoodle beliefs. He reads about three churches—not one, not two, but *three*—that have engaged in female sexual mutilation, justifying the practice with a verse from Proverbs: "Her feet go down to death, her steps take hold on hell." *In other words*, Jerome thinks, *FGM is doing them a favor*.

One church in Wisconsin espouses hormone therapy for "men and boys with sinful female urges." What that seems to mean is chemical castration when praying the gay away doesn't work.

This is far more interesting than his lame private eye novel, which is full of crash-and-bash and nothing like the investigative work he's done for Finders Keepers. This stuff is real. Nutso but real. Beside his desktop computer is his two-hundred-page manuscript of *The Jade Killers*. Slowly, and with little regret, he pushes it to the edge of his desk, then off and into the wastebasket. *Flump*, and gone. Of course it's still on his computer, but it's the gesture that counts (or so he tells himself). With that taken care of, he returns to his research. Holly's interest is being overshadowed by his own, and he's wondering how many of these churches he might actually be able to visit before he starts writing something he really cares about.

4

"Thank you, Madison! You've been great!"

The audience is on its feet, applauding like crazy. Except for the boo-birds, of course.

Holly's phone, clipped to her waistband, rings. She ignores it, standing on tiptoe next to Corrie like a runner about to sprint. She *is* ready to run from the wings at stage left if she needs to. Because instead of walking briskly offstage with a final tip of her Wisconsin Badgers cap, Kate goes to the lip of the apron and begins to shake waving, outstretched hands. This is new, and Holly hates it. Any one of those hands could seize Kate, pull her off the stage, a beating could follow, a knife could flash . . .

Oough, I hate this job.

Her head is starting to pound. Earlier John Ackerly called her and relayed what he'd learned from Cathy 2-Tone: white and medium height, mid-thirties (maybe), spectacles. The only interesting things are the scar on Trig's jaw and the thing about the "woo-woo meeting" in Upsala. Because of the anonymity issue (Holly finds this more and more annoying, not to say poopy), she doesn't ask John to pass this on to Izzy Jaynes, but she asks him if he'd mind attending a meeting or two in Upsala. John agrees.

After twenty or thirty seconds that feel much longer, Kate stands back from the edge of the stage. She sticks the microphone into its sleeve on the podium and makes her *come on, come on, come on* gesture with her fingers. The audience is on its feet, roaring its approval.

"You came here, now go to the polls! TELL THE MOSSBACKS THAT THE OPPOSITE OF WOKE IS FAST ASLEEP!"

She strides off with plenty of hip-sway. Corrie is festooned with bags, mostly souvenirs and tee-shirts from the bookstore. Holly says, "Let's get out of here. This time we're going to ditch the eBayers."

Of that she's confident. From the venue's downstairs offices, a service tunnel leads under the street to a city museum—now closed—on the other side. Holly hurries down the stairs, Kate and Corrie behind her.

Kate is asking what she always asks—*Was it good tonight?*—and Corrie responds as usual, assuring her it was.

They walk through the tunnel and climb a set of stairs. A museum security guard is waiting for them. "There's quite a few people out there," he says apologetically.

Holly looks. Quite a few? Easily a hundred, all of them eBayers with posters, glossies, even—who the frack knew there were such things—Kate McKay bobbleheads and Funko toys. A woman in a Chicago Bears sweatshirt is waving an oversized *Breitbart* printout, the one with the headline reading THE B*TCH IS BACK. *As if Kate would sign that*, Holly thinks . . . then realizes she really might; it fits Kate's chin-out persona.

"How do they *know*?" Holly asks.

Corrie sighs with her lower lip out, blowing hair off her fringe. "I don't know. It's a mystery. We slipped them once, but now—"

Kate says, "Come on, come on, come on," and pushes through the door, head down, walking to the waiting car. Holly hurries to catch up, hand in her purse clutching her pepper spray, head throbbing. Brady Hartsfield and Morris Bellamy were bad, but the eBayers are somehow worse.

5

Later that Monday night.

In Dingley Park, the Guns and Hoses teams have finished their practices, with some good-natured trash talk from both squads (and some not so good-natured).

In Madison, Holly finally talks to Izzy, making sure Iz got her earlier message. Izzy did, and says she'll pass it on to the State Police team of four detectives that has been ginned up to investigate the Surrogate Juror Murders. Holly is tempted to hold back the part about the Upsala candlelight meeting, wanting to give John a chance to check it out, but passes it on (reluctantly). Izzy asks for Holly's source, and Holly tells her she'll need to check with said source before giving Iz a name.

"This anonymity thing sucks like an Electrolux," Izzy says, and Holly agrees. She thinks John will agree to talk to Izzy, but will be reluctant to give up *his* source, or sources.

She ends the call and lies down, but ramrod straight. Adrenaline is still buzzing around her body. She keeps seeing Kate walk to the apron and start shaking those waving hands. Kate's confidence, especially in light of all that's happened, is terrifying. They're off to Chicago bright and early tomorrow, a two-hour drive through steadily thickening traffic. Holly needs her rest but knows it will be a long time before she sleeps.

6

In Buckeye City, Trig parks in a public lot near the bus station and walks down to Dearborn Street, also known as Saloon Row. Four or five of the real dives have been closed down during urban renewal over the last few years, but a few are still open and doing good business even on a Monday night. The evening is chilly, with a strong breeze off the lake, and Trig is wearing his duffle coat. The Taurus .22 is in his pocket. He knows that what he's thinking of doing is crazy, but he knew driving with an open bottle of vodka was crazy, too, and it never stopped him.

Behind the Chatterbox he sees two men making out with two women. No good.

Behind the Lions Lair he sees a man in cook's whites alone, sitting on a plastic crate and smoking a cigarette. Trig starts to approach, hand sweating on the butt of the Taurus, but sheers off when another guy comes out and tells the guy in cook's whites to come on back inside.

His last stop is the Hoosier Bar, the closest thing the city has to a honky-tonk. The back door is open. The sound of George Strait singing "Adalida" comes out, and a drunken man in a cowboy shirt is dancing by himself up and down in front of a pair of dumpsters. Trig approaches him, heart thundering in his chest. His eyes feel like they're throbbing in their sockets.

The drunken man sees him and says, "Dance with me, asshole." Trig nods, moves in close, takes a couple of dance steps, and shoots the drunken man in the eye. The drunk falls between the dumpsters, legs kicking. Trig bends down, sticks the Taurus under the drunken man's chin, and shoots him again. The drunk's back hair flips. Blood splats on bricks.

A man comes out the back door. "Curt? You out here?"

Trig crouches between the dumpsters, throat dry, mouth tasting coppery. *He'll smell the gunsmoke!*

"Curtis?"

I'll shoot him, too. Have to, have to.

"Fuck ya, buddy," the man says, "there's a draft. Walk around." He goes inside and slams the door. Into the dead dancer's hand, Trig puts the name of Andrew Groves, Juror 1 in the Duffrey trial.

Daddy: *You're crazy. Out of control.*

It's true. "But I didn't flinch," he whispers. "No flinching, Daddy."

He leaves the alley and walks back to where he left his car. Only then, too late to do any good, does he think about security cameras overlooking the honor lot. There's only one, and it's dangling at the end of its cord, clearly broken. He's in luck again, but his luck will run out eventually. He thinks again that part of him wants to be caught. It's probably true. No, *certainly* true.

Give me a little longer, he thinks as he drives away. *Just a little.*

7

Holly got some sleep after all, and while she doesn't feel tip-top on her Tuesday drive to the Windy City, she doesn't feel bad, either. Music helps to keep her perky. She's got her phone mated with the Chrysler's

Bluetooth and is singing along, a thing she only does when she's alone. Abba's greatest hits give way to Marvin Gaye's. She's matching Marvelous Marvin note for note on "I Heard It Through the Grapevine" (a little off-key, but who's listening) when the music is interrupted by a call. She sees it's from Izzy and breaks her ironclad rule about never talking on the phone while she's driving. Not without some guilt.

"Did you catch him? Tell me you caught him!"

"No," Izzy says, sounding harried. "And he got another one."

Holly is confused. "You told me. The farmer. Carville."

"Not him, you're a murder behind. This one was a barfly named Aubrey Dill. Killed behind the Hoosier Bar. It's a place downtown, near the bus station."

"I know where it is," Holly says. She once collared a runaway at the Hoosier. "Saloon Row."

"A friend of his came out looking for him, didn't see him, then found him later when the bar closed. The friend said he smelled, I quote, 'something shooty' the first time he came out. Said he thought someone had been lighting off firecrackers or something. I think the guy was still there. If so, the friend is lucky to be alive."

"Did he leave a juror's name?"

"He did. Andrew Groves. That's eight of them. Five or six still on his kill-list. And do you know what?" Izzy's voice cracks with outrage. *"I'm still supposed to be practicing for that fucking charity softball game!"*

"I'm sorry, Iz."

"Even though this is another one killed in the city, Lew Warwick says it's still a state case. And the County Mounties are supposed to be covering the city the night of the Guns and Hoses game. Well, fuck that. I need to know who your source is in the Program, Holly. Can you give it to me?"

"I think so. I'll have to call you back."

"If this Trig goes to meetings, we have to ID him fast."

"You said you have some cops who are in recovery."

"We do, and they've started asking questions. That in itself is a problem. You see why, right?"

Holly does, and when she talks to John Ackerly (once again breaking her rule about talking on the phone while driving), he does, too.

"Bad enough I talked to Telescope and Cathy 2-Tone, having cops ask questions in meetings is even worse. News travels fast in AA and NA. Once this guy hears, he'll stop going. If he hasn't already."

"Someone *must* know him."

"Not necessarily. Lots of meetings, lots of addicts. And there's another possibility. He may have gone out."

"What do you mean?"

"*Out*. Drinking again. When alcoholics relapse, they avoid meetings like the plague."

Holly thinks a drunk would already have been caught but doesn't say so.

"Continue to ask questions, John, but be careful. This guy is dangerous."

"Don't I know it."

"Will you talk to Detective Jaynes?"

"Yes."

"Thank you. I have to hang up now. I'm coming into Chicago and the traffic is quite gnarly."

She ends the call and concentrates on her driving, reminding herself again that it's not her case. She has women to look after, and one of them seems to think she's so famous she's indestructible.

8

The first full rehearsal for the Sista Bessie Revival Tour happens at ten AM on Tuesday, May 27th. Barbara is okay with the arrival of the four-man horn section, even exhilarated by it. She's also okay dressing as one of the Dixie Crystals, in a high-necked white silk blouse and black leather pants; it's fun being one of the girls, and in uniform. She's okay until Frieda Ames joins them, then it becomes real. Because Frieda Ames is a *choreographer*.

Tess, Laverne, and Jem have worked with her before, and take Frieda's fine-tuning as a matter of course. For Barbara it's different. Before, the idea of performing with a superstar in front of five thousand concertgoers (and a hometown crowd, at that) was strictly academic.

Frieda coaching her on how to move with the Crystals as they sing backup brings it home in a practical way. The seats of the Mingo Auditorium are all empty this morning, but Barbara is hit with stage fright just the same.

"I'm not sure I can do this," she tells Frieda.

"You *can*, girl," Jem Albright says. "The steps are simple. Show her, Dance."

Frieda "Dance" Ames is older than the Crystals, eighty if she's a day, but she moves with the grace of a twenty-year-old. She points to the Tupelo Horns, which now includes Red Jones on sax, and tells them to "do the disco thang."

They start playing the intro to KC and the Sunshine Band's "Boogie Shoes," which will be the kickoff number of Sista Bessie's first show.

Frieda grabs a mic to be heard over the horns and begins to sway her hips. She points stage left. "You girls come on from there to center stage. Applause-applause-applause, yeah?"

Barbara nods along with Tess, Laverne, and Jem.

"Show plenty of strut-n-wiggle. Barb, you're last. Right foot, and *cross*. Left foot, and *cross*. At center stage, hands up, like a ref sayin the kick is good."

They all put their hands up.

"Now swing your arms left . . . and clap. Swing your arms right . . . and snap your fingers. Keep the footwork going."

The band is still playing that intro: *Bump-BAH-BAH-bump, bump-BAH-BAH-bump, bump-BAH-BAH-bump*.

"Sista Bessie comes on from stage right, doing her moves. Applause-applause-applause. Screaming. Standing O. She slaps hands with each of you girls. You just keep on. Left foot, right foot, swing left and clap, swing right and snap. Move those hips. Back up to give her the stage . . . *turn* . . . slap your asses . . . turn again. Come on, let's see it."

Feeling like she's in a dream, Barbara backs up with the other "girls," clapping and snapping and turning and slapping. The Dixie Crystals have good-sized boots to slap, Barbara not so much.

"One more turn, then *go get it*."

Tess, Laverne, and Jem sing the intro.

"Barbara?" Frieda asks, still on the mic. The horns continue to repeat the intro: *Bump-BAH-BAH-bump.* "Cat got your tongue, girl?"

They sing it together this time, and all at once something hits Barbara. Something good. She feels, God help her, like a Crystal.

"Stop!" Frieda shouts, and the horns quit. "Let's do it again and put some fucking *soul* into it. Go to your number ones!"

Barbara follows the Crystals to stage left. Her anxiety has been replaced by a kind of nervy anticipation. All at once she wants to do this. Like the song says, she wants to do it til the sun comes up. At stage right she can see Betty talking and laughing with Don Gibson, the Mingo's Program Director.

"Ready?" Frieda asks.

Tess gives her a thumbs-up.

"Okay, let's see those hips! And . . . *band*!"

The horns start up, *Bump-BAH-BAH-bump*, and the Dixie Crystals—now four of them—strut onstage, face the empty seats, and raise their hands over their heads. *They will applaud*, Barbara thinks, *and it will be cool. Very.*

She expects Frieda will tell the band to quit and command "the girls" to do it again, but instead Betty comes from stage right, and although she's wearing her mom jeans, a smock top, and sloppy loafers, when she slip-slides and does a twirl to center stage, she's Sista Bessie. She grabs the mic Frieda was using, falls in perfect step with the Crystals behind her, and begins to sing the lead.

By the time the song is done, Barbara knows two powerful things. One is that this is not her world; poetry is her world. The other is that she wishes she could be a Dixie Crystal forever. She gave Betty Brady her poems; Sista Bessie gave her a gift that's both precious and ephemeral.

The two things make something new and powerful; the two things also cancel each other out.

9

Trig is eating lunch in his office, an egg salad sandwich in one hand and a can of iced tea in the other. The radio is tuned to WBOB. Usually from eleven AM to one PM it's the Glenn Beck show, but today Glenn has been pre-empted by a news conference coming from the Murrow Building. The occasion is the Surrogate Juror Murders (the authorities have given in and started calling them that, as well). Present at the microphones are Buckeye City Chief of Police Alice Patmore and State Police Lieutenant Ganzinger. Trig knows the names of the BCPD police detectives assigned to the case, has actually met Jaynes and Atta, but neither of them are present at this meet-the-press event. The State Police have taken over the case, it seems.

Trig has worked for most of his life in positions where he has to deal with powerful people, and although he's listening for his life and freedom, he still must admire the deftness with which Chief Patmore has passed this ugly, squalling baby on to another organization. Which will therefore be blamed if there's more murders.

Not if, he thinks. *When*.

After a brief synopsis of what they know about the most recent murder, Ganzinger says, "We have an important new piece of information about the perpetrator of these crimes. We believe the name he goes by, probably a nickname, is Trig. That's *T-R-I-G*."

Trig freezes with his sandwich in front of his mouth. Then he bites into it. Did he know this was coming? Yes, of course he did.

Chief Patmore throws in her two cents' worth. "Given the Bill Wilson alias he used in his first threatening communication with our department, we think this individual may—I emphasize *may*—be a member of the recovery community, probably Alcoholics Anonymous or Narcotics Anonymous. If anyone in one of those programs knows an individual calling himself Trig, we hope you will come forward. Your anonymity will be protected."

Worse and worse . . . but also expected. The question is why he used the Bill Wilson name in his letter to Warwick, the head of the city's detective unit, and to Chief Patmore. At the time, it seemed natural and perfectly right; why else was he doing this except to make amends? And weren't amends central to the program of recovery that Bill Wilson had founded?

You didn't do it for that reason. You did it because you wanted to be caught. Maybe that's why you wrote those letters in the first place.

That's his father, and he rejects that. He wrote the letters because he wanted the guilty parties to feel their guilt. They *needed* to feel guilt.

Patmore and Ganzinger throw the press conference open to questions. The first: "Do you have a description of this Bill Wilson, also known as Trig?"

Trig's hand goes to the scar on his jaw and traces its short length. It only took seven stitches to close, but it *is* noticeable all these years later.

"So far we do not," Lieutenant Ganzinger says. It's comforting, but only if it's true. What if they know about the scar? Trig has watched his share of crime shows and knows the police have a way of holding things back. The way they may be holding back any passing witness who saw him standing on the tractor step and pretending to talk to the farmer he just killed.

Chief Patmore adds, "All we know for sure is that this individual is calculating but mentally unbalanced."

Trig thinks, *That's fair*.

Someone asks, "Can you tell us the name of the Duffrey trial juror that was left in Mr. Dill's hand?"

Patmore: "I see no purpose in giving that name, or any juror's name. They are not the ones being targeted."

The same reporter: "But in a way, they are, isn't that true?"

Ganzinger, sounding stoic: "These killings are entirely random, as far as we can tell. That makes the man perpetrating the crimes particularly hard to apprehend."

That same pesky reporter: "But how are the jurors coping with it? The purpose of the killings seems to be to make them feel culpable in the death of Alan Duf—"

Chief Patmore: "Let me stop you right there. The death of Alan Duffrey—the *murder* of Alan Duffrey—was the work of a State Prison inmate who has yet to be identified . . . but who will be found and punished. The jurors in the Duffrey trial have nothing to feel guilty about. Repeat, *nothing*."

Trig, sitting at his desk and looking at his half-eaten sandwich, mutters, "You are so full of shit you squeak." He takes another bite, chewing slowly.

"The Duffrey jurors did their duty as American citizens and citizens of this city, based on the facts at hand."

Pesky reporter: "But Mr. Wentworth and Mr. Finkel—"

This time it's Ganzinger who stops him. "Those suicides had nothing to do with the Duffrey trial, let me assure you."

Trig doesn't believe that. Not for a moment. He *drove* them to suicide, beat them to it like beating a recalcitrant cow into a killing chute, and if he could drive the others to it, he would consider it a job well done.

Trig recognizes the voice of the next questioner. It's that podcasting, truth-telling, scandal-mongering Hero of the People, Buckeye Brandon. "In light of these murders, Chief Patmore, how do you justify going on with the Guns and Hoses charity game at Dingley Park?"

Trig pauses in the act of taking another bite. He doesn't want them to cancel that game. That game is part of his plan.

Alice Patmore's response is smooth and uninterrupted by *ers*, *ah*s, or *ums*. As someone who has been in his share of high-pressure meetings—and dealt with his share of ego—Trig knows a prepared answer when he hears it.

"This cowardly murderer will not get to rob two deserving charities, Kiner Pediatrics and Muscular Dystrophy, of the money this Friday's softball game will bring in. The *considerable* money. City police, the County Sheriff's Department, and the State Police will blanket the city with officers on Friday afternoon and evening—"

"Many in plain clothes," Ganzinger puts in.

"Many in plain clothes," Patmore agrees. "And I'd encourage everyone with an interest in the game—or in hearing Sista Bessie sing our National Anthem *live*—to come on out, because it will be good fun and on Friday night, a crowd of fellow Buckeye City rooters will be the safest place to be."

It will *be safe*, Trig thinks, turning off the radio. *What* won't *be is at the far side of the park.*

If, that is, he gets another four days. They know the name he uses at meetings, but do they know his real name? He thinks they don't. *Hopes* they don't. And that version of Trig had a beard (one that covered the scar) and wore contact lenses. After his picture was in the paper in connection with the Duffrey trial, he shaved and went back to glasses.

He needs four more days. Until then, he'll stand down. No more killing. Then, two more.

Two at least.

Chapter 16

1

Holly catches up with Kate's truck at Sharko's BBQ on Route 59 in DuPage County. They eat, then push on together.

For public consumption, Kate's three-person party is registered at the Waldorf Astoria in Chicago, on East Walton Street. In actual fact, Holly has reserved a suite and two connecting rooms in her own name at the Peninsula, on East Superior. This has worked before but doesn't this time, and not just because Kate has been followed from Madison by an ever-lengthening comet tail of eBayers. Some of these autograph-hungry pilgrims from Madison and points west have gotten in touch with Chicago eBayers, and some of those must have had contact with the anti-Kate brigade, because they're also waiting and ready to be, in the words of one protestor, "Chicago nasty."

Cops are keeping them on the other side of the street, but when Kate and Corrie get out of Kate's F-150, they are greeted by a shower of babydolls soaked in fake blood. Most fall short, but one hits Corrie Anderson in the shoulder, leaving a red smear on her white blouse. She looks at it, surprised, then, on autopilot, bends to pick it up.

"Don't," Holly says. She has pulled her Chrysler in so close behind Kate's truck at the loading/unloading zone that the bumpers are actually touching. She takes Corrie's arm and hurries her under the canopy. Kate has already gone inside without looking back.

"*The new Holocaust!*" a woman screams. She sounds like she's crying. The eBayers leave, realizing their target of opportunity has departed, but the rest of the protestors pick up the crying woman's word and turn it into a chant: "*Holocaust! Holocaust! Holocaust!*"

This is their welcome to Chicago, that toddlin' town.

In her suite, Kate tells Corrie that the press should come here instead of doing the afternoon Q-and-A at the Waldorf. Turning her attention to Holly, she says, "It wasn't this way on my other tours."

Someone wasn't trying to kill you on your other tours, Holly doesn't say.

"Fuck it, I'm tired of hiding from a bunch of *Handmaid's Tale* propaganda-bots."

What rises to Holly's lips is *It's your funeral*, which of course she also doesn't say. What she says is, "You hired me to protect you, Kate. I'm doing my best. I have no idea how those . . . those autograph speculators are always ahead of us."

"Don't worry about the speculators, just throw yourself in front of me if you see someone pointing a gun," Kate says. She sees something on Holly's face that makes her add, "I'm joking, woman! Joking!"

Holly can feel blood rising in her cheeks. "It's no joke. Does the name Lauri Carleton ring a bell?"

It's been almost two years since the Carleton woman was shot dead by a man who was offended by her gay pride flag, but Kate knows the name. Of course she does. "What do you expect me to do, Holly? Back down? Show yellow? That's what they want!"

Holly sighs. "I know you can't do that, and I understand that having the press conference at the Waldorf doesn't make sense, at least not now, but . . ."

"But what?" Kate with her legs planted apart, fists on slim hips. "But *what*?"

"You might consider canceling it."

"Not at all," Kate says. Then adds, "Never."

Corrie scurries into her connecting room to make calls and get away from any verbal fireworks, but there are none. Holly Gibney is not made to argue, especially with clients. What she's made to do is her best. So she says she understands, and goes to her own room.

She has two texts, the first from Corrie, the second from Jerome Robinson.

Corrie: **I thought U 2 were really going to get into it.**

Holly: **No.**

Corrie: **I'm going to the venue. Cadillac Palace Theatre. Have 2 take care of biz. Will be back for an early dinner. Can U get K to her presser?**

Holly: **Yes. Stay alert.** To this she adds an eyes emoji.

She doesn't like to think of Corrie—who has taken the most abuse from their stalker—going to the venue solo, but there's only one Holly and her job is Kate. She opens the other text.

Jerome: **Just getting started & I've already run down 8 churches of the holy rolling type that have been in trouble with the law because of protests that ended w/ arrests. Most common was trespassing, but some protests turned violent. Went back 10 years. More every year, worse since the pandemic. Found an actual "Hate Map." True! Check email. Know U R busy but if anything stands out let me know.**

Busy? Holly thinks. *You don't know the half of it, J.*

She opens the email, which is titled—talk about impolitic—*Nutball Churches*. The attachment is a list of the eight churches, with thumbnail descriptions of what got each one in trouble. Two are in Idaho, one in Wisconsin, two in Alabama, two in Tennessee, and one in upstate New York. Before she can read the thumbnails, another text arrives, this one from Kate.

Presser in 45 mins. B there or B square.

I'm square and don't care, Holly thinks. She checks her bag for pepper spray, rape siren, and—little does she like it—Bill's revolver that's now *her* revolver. All anti-nutball equipment present and accounted for.

She thinks about calling John Ackerly to see if he's located the elusive Trig, but he would have called or texted if he'd found Trig, or even a lead to him. Besides, Izzy's case is Izzy's case . . . although this week it seems that Izzy's priority is a charity softball game.

Still, she can't help thinking about Trig as she checks her hair and lipstick in the bathroom mirror. The late Bill Hodges used to tell her that most cases were easy because most people who did dirt were lazy and stupid. In the few instances where the doers were a little smarter, Bill told her to stop, think, and isolate the central question in each case. Answer that and presto, case solved.

So what's the central question with Trig? That he's in AA? It must *be AA, because that 2-Tone woman told John he was a drinker, not a drugger.*

Does she need a little eyeshadow? No, not for a press conference at four PM; her late mother would faint. Just a little concealer, and by the way, *is* Trig's reason for attending AA the central question? Is *that* the mystery of the thing? No. The central question, Holly realizes, is much simpler, and might be the key to everything.

To her own face in the mirror, she asks it aloud: "Why does he care enough about Alan Duffrey to kill people?"

2

Chrissy is nearing Chicago, can actually see the skyline, when she makes a sudden decision to change course. She goes south on I-57, and at Gilman will turn east. Unlike Holly, Chrissy has no problem using her phone while driving. She calls Deacon Andy. He answers on the first ring and asks two questions: Is everything all right, and is Chris on a burner?

Chrissy answers yes to both, not bothering to tell Andy that today he's using the wrong name. For Fallowes, the person he's talking to will always be male. That's okay with Chrissy (who would never consider using new-age pronouns like "they" or "them"), because both she and Deacon Andy share the common goal of ending Kate McKay's reign of blood and terror.

"Chicago is out," Chrissy says. "Too many cops, plus her damn bodyguard. That bitch is good at her job."

"But it was the assistant who stopped that guy in Davenport," Fallowes objects.

He's obviously been following the news, but not closely enough. "It *wasn't* Anderson, it was Gibney. The press got it wrong, as they often do. But Buckeye City is Gibney's hometown, and I'm guessing—hoping—that once they get there, she'll let her guard down and relax a little. Also, the cops there are chasing some crazy guy who's killing people. That's got to take their focus off *our* troublemaker."

"Fine, your call as long as you keep the church out of it. What do you need from me?"

"The town is going to be crowded, because it's not just McKay. That Black soul singer is starting her comeback tour there on Saturday. It's a big deal. McKay is now on for Friday, got her date switched. Seven PM. The bodyguard has had them changing hotels, but that won't work in Buckeye City, because the hotels are booked solid. I want you to find out where they're staying and get me a room there. Can you do that?"

"I can," Deacon Fallowes says. No waffling. Like the Gibney woman, he's good at his job.

"Okay," Chrissy says. "One way or the other, this ends in Buckeye City. I'll be damned if I trail her all the way to Maine."

She ends the call. An hour later, Andy Fallowes texts her.

KM party reserved at the Garden City Plaza in Buckeye City. Rooms 1109-1110-1111. I got you a single 2 floors down, 919. Room reserved on Hot Flash Ltd. credit card, but use your own card and make sure they delete Hot Flash info. You know why. Also delete this text.

They can't entirely erase the digital trail leading back to Real Christ Holy, but they can at least obscure it. That matters because Chrissy may very well be caught or killed. The only pain in the ass is the need to make a stop along the way and become Christopher again. Christine has one photo ID, a Wisconsin driver's license, but no credit card.

It's the male half of his dual nature who has the Visa.

3

Jerome is continuing his research into radical-fundamentalist churches involved in violent protests (including some events that can only be called terrorism), when his phone rings. The area code is 818, which he recognizes as Los Angeles. Imitation being the sincerest form of flattery, he answers the way Holly does.

"Hello, this is Jerome, how can I help?"

"I'm Anthony Kelly, Sista Bessie's tour manager. I got your number from your sister. We all love Barbara."

"Me too, at least when she's not being a booger. What can I do for you, Mr. Kelly?"

"Call me Tones. I'm hoping you'll work for the tour, however briefly. At your mayor's invitation, Betty is going to sing the National Anthem Friday night at a charity softball game. Someplace called Dingo Park?"

Jerome grins. "Dingley Park."

"Right-right-right. She needs security from the venue to the hotel, then to the field, then back to the hotel again. It's for the insurance. Your sister suggested you. She says you've worked part-time with a local investigation agency."

"Finders Keepers. As it so happens, the woman I work for is doing her own security work right now."

"Barbara says she's with the women's libber."

Based on what Holly has told him, Jerome thinks Kate would prefer the term *political activist*, but doesn't say so. "What kind of time commitment are we talking about, Mr. Kelly? Tones?"

"Just four hours or so. You meet her at the Mingo Auditorium around five-thirty PM, where she'll be discussing clothes with her dresser—Alberta Wing. You then take her to the Garden City Plaza Hotel. Alberta has her own transpo. You have a car, right?"

"Sure."

"Company car?"

"No, mine."

"Fully insured, though? Collision, liability? Sorry to have to ask, but Global Insurance has got a huge policy on her. Fucking money-grubbers. Pardon my mouth."

"No need. My boss feels the same, and we're insured up the wazoo, both personal and company coverage. My boss gets a rate. Ours happens to be Progressive, not the Talking Donkey."

"Yeah, I hate that donkey, all those big teeth. At the hotel, Betty will shower and change out of her rehearsal slops while you wait in our hospitality suite down the hall. At 6:15 or 6:20, you escort her downstairs. A car will be waiting. Alonzo Estevez, the hotel manager, has agreed to drive her to Dingley Park. You ride with her to the field, where I understand that a private dressing room has been set aside. She won't be changing again, just wants some privacy before she does her thing. You with me so far?"

"Yes."

"A little before seven PM, Red—her sax player—will accompany her to the pitcher's mound. Red plays, she sings. You escort her back to the hotel, job done. What do you think?"

"Wouldn't a cop be a better choice?"

"A cop is exactly what she *doesn't* want. What she wants is Barbara's book-writing brother, who—according to Bets—happens to be Black and beautiful. I haven't met you so I'm taking her word for the beautiful part. Sista B Concerts Ltd. will pay you six hundred dollars for your time."

Jerome thinks about it, but not too long. "Okay, sounds good. May bring a colleague, if okay."

"Sure, but I'm only authorized to pay for one. Are you and your, um, colleague coming to the show Saturday night?"

"That's the plan. And I'll be there with my folks. They can't wait to see Barb on the big stage. Me too."

"I'll have seats for you in the third row," Tones says. "First is too close, your ears will get blasted and your necks will get stiff from looking up. Only three? I've got the whole row reserved. The women's libber's party is coming, too."

Jerome considers. He's smiling. This is actually pretty cool. "Better make it eight. Barb's aunts and their husbands will come from Cleveland if there are seats for them."

"Family reunion, I like it, consider it done. Backstage passes, too. Get them at the Will Call window."

"Thanks."

"No, thank *you*. I won't see you Friday. I'll be checking the sound and making sure the women's libber doesn't screw up our equipment once she's done talking. The lady says she can work around the amps and mics no problem, but I'm from Missouri."

Jerome has no idea what that means, so he just repeats his instructions—as Holly insists when working for Finders Keepers—and ends the call. He immediately makes another one.

"This is Happy," John says. "Hey, J, what do you say?"

"I say I may not be able to do the whole game on Friday night," Jerome tells him, "but to make up for it, how would you like to be part of Sista Bessie's security detail?"

"Dude, are you kidding me? I pissed my didies dancing to her music, back in the day!"

"I'm not kidding. Plus comp tickets to her show on Saturday night, and backstagers. I'm getting six hundred and I'll split it with you. What do you think?"

"What do you think I think? I am so there. Gimme the deets."

Jerome fills him in, thinking *Three hundred each for four hours' work. Seems almost too easy.*

As it turns out, he doesn't know the half of it.

4

Kate comes onstage that Tuesday night wearing a Chicago Cubs cap and a White Sox jersey with her name on the back. The crowd loves her for that, and for every word out of her mouth. Holly has seen it all before, and she knows that in deep blue Chicago Kate is preaching to the choir (only a small contingent of boo-birds), but her eloquence is still mesmerizing. Back and forth she goes, exhorting, pleading, joking, angry, heartfelt, outraged, hopeful. Holly has discovered Kate can be petty and insecure. That night in Chicago it doesn't matter. That night she gives a performance for the ages.

"I want to close tonight by asking you to remember the words of John the Apostle. He said, 'If any man loves the world, the love of God the Father is not in him.' But theology as practiced by Christian fundamentalists is *all about* the world. Mixing religion with politics is dangerous. Not the road to Calvary but the one that leads to fascism."

From the audience, someone screams, "*YOU LIE!*"

"Check your Bible," Kate says. "First John, chapter 2, verse 15."

"*HELL AWAITS THE LIAR!*" the screamer responds. Ushers are moving toward him, but he's standing on a walker and they are reluctant to approach, lest they be accused of manhandling a disabled person.

"I will take my chances on hell," Kate says, "but Chicago has been heaven for this woman. You've been a wonderful audience. Thank you from the bottom of my heart."

She is called back three times by a seemingly endless wave of applause and comes offstage crackling with energy. She sweeps Holly into a hug. Holly, who often shrinks from physical contact, hugs her back.

"It was good tonight, wasn't it?" Kate murmurs.

"Better than good," Holly says, and a cold thought—*This woman is begging to be assassinated*—makes her hug Kate tighter. "It was *great*."

5

Holly is up early on Wednesday morning for the four-hour drive from Chicago to Toledo. She gets out of the shower to find texts from John Ackerly and Jerome.

John: **I may have seen your boy Trig, but I think he looked different and was going under a different name. Wish I could remember.**

Holly: **Try.**

John: **Trying.**

Jerome: **I have gotten my own bodyguard gig. Sista Bessie, Friday night. She's singing the N'tl Anthem at Dingley. Barbara recommended me.**

Holly: **Good luck. I know you'll do a great job. I find bodyguarding rather unpleasant. Your opinion may differ.**

Jerome: **I have tix to Sista Bessie's concert on Sat. nite. Can U come? Watch Barb onstage?**

Holly: **I would love to but we are moving on to Cincinnati. Send vid. Come to hotel if you can. Garden City Plaza.**

Jerome: **Roger that.**

Marching dots suggest Jerome has something more to say, but Holly can't wait for it. She's about to turn off her phone and toss her suitcase in the Chrysler when it comes.

Jerome: **Hollyberry. And I still have one left.**

This is followed by a laughing-to-tears emoji. Holly has to laugh herself.

6

The trip to Toledo is uneventful and by mid-afternoon, Holly is once more spotting her client in another hotel pool. Back and forth Kate goes, churning and burning in her red suit. Corrie comes down at quarter to three and tells Kate she might want to get out of the water. Bad news, she says.

"Just tell me," Kate says. Gasps, really. "I want to get in four more laps."

"I don't think you'll want to hear this while you're swimming."

Kate leg-kicks to the edge of the pool and puts her arms on the curbing. Her hair is plastered to the sides of her face. "Spill it."

"We're canceled tonight."

"What?"

"Anonymous caller says that if you speak, an outfit called DOOM—Defense Of Our Mothers—is going to storm the building with automatic weapons and grenades. Caller said mass casualties will result."

Kate doesn't so much climb out of the pool as erupt from it. Holly holds out a towel, which Kate ignores. "They're shutting us down over a fucking *swat* call?"

"The call *I* got came from the Chief of Police himse—"

"I don't care if it came from the Pope of Rome! Killing my date over a goddam anonymous call? Trying to shut me up?" Kate whirls on Holly. "Can they do it?"

"They can. Public safety issue."

"But if they can do it here, they can do it anywhere! You see that, right? Some dingdong makes one call and that's all it takes to muzzle me? Bullshit! *Bull . . . SHIT!*"

Holly says, "When is your press conference?"

Corrie answers. "Four."

"Make that point," Holly says. "Suggest the police are capitulating to—"

"Suggest it? I'll come right out and say it!"

Of course you will, Holly thinks. And she knows Kate is almost certainly right; there may be doom, but there is no DOOM. Some

Kate faces Corrie. Holly always thought that stuff about blazing eyes was so much romance novel dookie, but Kate's actually do seem to blaze. "Get going, Cor. We're going to spin this motherfucker until it catches fire."

7

Trig leaves work early, passing a word with Jerry Allison, the building's elderly janitor, then going to Dingley Park. From the park's far side, beyond the trees, comes the tink of aluminum bats and the sounds of men yelling and hooting as the cops and firemen practice. He tells himself he's not there to find another surrogate juror (or possibly a surrogate judge), but only to make sure the druggie girl's body hasn't been discovered . . . but he's got the Taurus in one pocket of his sport-coat, and a hypo loaded with pentobarbital—purchased by mail for just forty-five dollars—in the other. If someone happens along, he could shoot or OD them and stash the body with that of the druggie girl. If female, he could leave the name of Amy Gottschalk, Juror 4. If male, the name of Judge Irving Witterson, that haughty son of a bitch who first denied Duffrey bail and then sentenced him to the max.

He's also thinking of games he went to with his father here, how he loved and dreaded them. When the long-gone Buckeye Bullets would score, his father would rub his head and give him a hug. He loved those hugs. After a win, there would be ice cream at Dutchy's. No ice cream when the Bullets lost, and after those games Trig had to be careful what he said, lest he be slapped, punched, or pushed into the kitchen counter again. Oh, the blood that time! Daddy sopping it up with a dishtowel and saying, *Ah, you baby, a few stitches will close that. Tell em that you stumbled over your own clumsy feet, you hear me?* And of course that was what he did.

Where was Mom in all of this? *Gone.*

So said his father on the few occasions when Trig dared to ask (and by the time he was ten, she was at best just a hazy recollection, not a real mother but only the idea of one). *She quit the family and we don't talk about quitters, so why don't you just go on and shut the fuck up.*

Trig gets a Coke at Frankie's Fabulous Fish Wagon and walks around the Holman Rink, which looks completely deserted. He sniffs for any aroma of decomposing druggie, but there's nothing. At least so far as he can tell.

Around to the front again, heading for his car, and presto, *another* druggie girl shows up. In that dirty halter top and tattered jeans, she can be nothing else. It's as if he's ordered her! Trig gives her a smile and slides his hand into the pocket of his sportcoat. He can already see himself putting Amy Gottschalk's name in this loser's dead hand. But then a young man emerges from the pine grove behind her. He's as scruffy as she is but wearing an Army shirt with cutoff sleeves, and he's built like a brick shithouse.

"Wait up, Mary," he says. Then, to Trig: "Hey, man—you got an extra couple of bucks for a couple of vets? Get us a coffee or something?"

Trig takes his hand off the capped hypodermic, gives him a five, then heads to his car, hoping the scruffy guy won't close in from behind and mug him. That would be a joke on old Trigger, wouldn't it?

Chapter 17

1

It's early Thursday morning—*very* early—but everything is ready to roll. Holly has always considered herself an organized person, but she's in awe of Corrie Anderson, not least because the woman is so young; her learning curve must have been zero to overdrive in a matter of weeks. Some of the credit has to go to Kate, of course. She picked exactly the right person.

Holly drives her employer around to three local radio stations before the sun is up. Kate drinks coffee in amounts Holly finds frankly terrifying—she herself would be bouncing around the room and climbing the walls.

Because Holly can't drive a standard shift (Uncle Henry offered to teach her, but as a teenager she was far too anxious to even try), she takes Kate around Toledo in her Chrysler, using her trusty GPS to get her from station to station. At each one, Kate makes the same points: DOOM is obviously bogus, the local powers that be, including the police, *know* it's bogus, but they've canceled her event anyway. Why? To shut her up. And if they can do it in Toledo, they can do it anywhere. To anyone.

The morning shows really *are* zoos, but Kate excels at the high-pressure banter these shock jocks specialize in. When one female caller (the morning shows also specialize in callers-in) accuses Kate of putting her own audiences at risk, Kate says, "Maybe they'd rather risk back-alley abortions? Risk their kids getting suspended from school because they come in wearing hightop fades or Mohawks? Risk having books the fundamentalist God-botherers don't like banned? Maybe let *them* decide what's risky, what do you think, caller?" And when the caller ventures the opinion that Kate is a high-riding bitch, Kate ventures her own opinion that the caller should put on her big-girl underpants and quit making decisions for other people.

In other words, it's all Kate, all the time.

2

Back at the hotel, Corrie has a list of phone interviews, almost two dozen in all. She suggests that Kate should do the in-depth ones—*Huffington Post*, NPR, PBS, *Slate*—before they get on the road to Buckeye City.

"Once we're rolling," she says, "you talk while I drive. You should be able to knock off the nine I've starred. Ten minutes each, ninety minutes *in toto*."

"Are you sure I can do them while we're on the road? I fucking hate it when the service drops out. You'd think, if we could put a man on the moon—"

"Coverage should be five bars all the way. I checked."

Holly's admiration for Corrie continues to go up.

"Make your points and move on. 'They're trying to muzzle me, to flush my First Amendment rights, let the people decide if they want to go, quit the bullpucky.' Hammer on those. Don't get sidetracked. Every time I poke you in the arm, wind it up."

Kate looks at Holly. "When I'm Madam President, this woman is going to be my chief of staff."

Corrie blushes. "I just want to protect your tour."

"*Our* tour. The Three Female Musketeers. Right, Holly?"

"True, Boo," Holly says.

Corrie: "We're still registered at the Garden City Plaza."

Kate: "And still in my name?"

"Yes. Holly said it would be best, given what's happened, if you don't look like you're ducking and covering."

"Goddam right."

"You can do the rest of the calls from there." Corrie shakes her fists in the air. "This could work."

Kate takes Corrie's list and starts making calls. Her energy seems unabated. Holly goes back to her own room, takes three minutes to finish packing, then starts going through Jerome's list of activist churches. He's added more details overnight. Kate's stalker may not be here, but she might well be.

Jerome writes that some of these churches have organized under the collective banner of AOG, standing for the Army of God. Three of them—two churches in Tennessee and the one in Alabama—warranted police involvement because of FACE violations, the Freedom of Access to Clinic Entrances. Protesting was fine; shouting insults at the women entering was also fine (although in Holly's opinion it shouldn't be); pictures of dismembered fetuses were okay; blocking the entrances and showers of blood, fake or otherwise, were not. Following various links embedded in the news stories, Holly discovers that since *Dobbs v. Jackson Women's Health*, those three clinics have been shuttered anyway, so she supposes the pro-lifers can chalk that up as a win.

In Idaho, members of Christ the Everlasting Redeemer lay down in front of a drag parade, while other members "blessed" the parade marchers with seltzer water. Instead of calling the seltzer water "blessings," the judge called it "third-degree assault." Also in Idaho, just a month later, members of the same little church were arrested for vandalizing a library that was rumored to be a meeting place for pedophiles belonging to the Q organization. In upstate New York, a women's clinic was firebombed. No one died, but two patients and a nurse were badly burned. The investigation ongoing, so far no arrests made.

Jerome's note about the Wisconsin church is brief: *Real Christ Holy, Baraboo Junction, Wisconsin. Google Brenda's Bitches*. Because Kate is still on her third call—Holly can hear her through the open door—she does just that.

The most informative article Holly finds is on a website called *Religion Good & Bad*. The story concerns a melee involving twenty or so demonstrators from Real Christ Holy, and a dozen or so women—Brenda's Bitches—who counter-protested on motor scooters. Holly notes that, although Real Christ Holy is based in northern Wisconsin, the protest occurred in Pennsylvania. Holly's deduction is that the church either has a wealthy patron or a number of rich congregants.

The *Daily Kos* article she goes to next has a jaded "this is the right-wing America we live in" tone that Holly doesn't care for. She starts to turn her iPad off, then decides to google the Real Christ Holy Church of Baraboo Junction a little further. She gets *beaucoup* hits, starting with Wikipedia.

It turns out that the unaffiliated church was bankrolled by Harold Stewart, the late president of Hot Flash Electronics and holder of several valuable patents. Those patents are now the property of Real Christ Holy, an AOG-affiliated church. The members of Real Christ Holy have protested in plenty of states on Stewart's money, not just Pennsylvania. In one case, four members of the church *were* arrested and charged with assault while protesting at a clinic in Florida. This was a year before the kerfuffle with Brenda's Bitches. Holly finds an article about it in the *Pensacola News Journal*. There's a paywall, but the headline is enough for her to cough up $6.99 for the introductory offer.

4 CHARGED IN FAKE ACID ATTACK AT SARA WATERS CLINIC

She mutters a very un-Holly-like "Holy shit."

Before reading the article, she looks at the accompanying photograph. It shows three men and one woman, arms linked in solidarity, mounting the courthouse steps, and looking defiantly up at the photographer. Two of the men are identified as Pastor James Mellors and First Deacon Andrew Fallowes, of the Real Christ Holy Church. The woman is Denise Mellors, the pastor's wife. The third man, much younger, is Christopher Stewart. The article doesn't say he's Harold Stewart's son, but Holly thinks it likely; he's certainly the right age.

Kate's voice goes away. Thoughts of the next stop—her own hometown—go away. She's having one of those moments she lives for: the hard click of things coming together. *It was a woman in Reno, not a man, but . . . what did Corrie say? "Bright red hair that couldn't be natural." And later the police found the wig.*

Corrie pokes her head in the door. "Kate's finished. With this round, at least. Are you ready to go?"

"What exactly did the woman in Reno say to you? Can you remember?"

"I'll never forget it because I thought I'd be blind for the rest of my life. She said, 'Here's what you have coming.' Then something from the Bible about not usurping the authority of the man."

"Come here a second."

"She's waiting, Holly, we really have to—"

"This is important. Come here."

Corrie comes. Holly shows her the article. "This crime in Florida—felony assault downgraded to a misdemeanor—fits the MO of the woman who threw fake acid at you. If it *was* a woman." She spreads her fingers to make the photo of the quartet going up the courthouse steps bigger. She taps Christopher Stewart. "Could this be the person who attacked you in Reno?"

Corrie looks for a long time, then shakes her head. "I don't know. It happened so fast, it was raining, and if it was this man, he was wearing women's clothes as well as a wig. A skirt, or maybe it was a dress. So I can't—"

Kate comes in. "Want to get going, ladies. Come on, come on, come on."

"Holly thinks she might have found the woman stalking us. Only if she's right, it's a man."

"Which wouldn't surprise me," Kate says. "They're usually the dangerous ones." She takes a quick look at the picture on Holly's tablet, then says, "Not bad-looking."

"Think back and look again, Corrie."

Corrie looks, then shakes her head. "I can't tell. I wish I could, Holly, but—"

"We have to roll," Kate says. "Do your sleuthing in the Buckeye, Hols. If this dodo is after me, he might already be there."

3

On the way to Buckeye City, Holly has a flash of inspiration. She pulls into the parking lot of a Shoney's and calls Jerome. He answers, but in the background she hears loud, echoing music. Lots of honking brass.

"I'm at the Mingo!" he shouts. *"Met Sista Bessie! They're rehearsing 'Twist and Shout!' Fantastic! Barb's singing with the group! It's—"* He's interrupted by a flurry of drums.

"What?"

"I said you won't believe how good she is! They all are! I'll send you a video!"

"Okay, but I need you to do something for me! Can you go somewhere quiet?"

"What?"

"CAN YOU GO SOMEWHERE QUIET?"

A few seconds later, the music is muted. "Is that better?" Jerome asks.

"Yes." She tells him what she needs, and Jerome says he'll see what he can do.

"And send me that video. I want to see Barbara doing the Twist."

4

Holly would dearly love to stop by her cozy little apartment and throw her road clothes in the washer. Put some fresh ones in her suitcase. Perhaps drink an espresso at her kitchen table in a bar of sunshine. Continue to research the Real Christ Holy Church of Baraboo Junction, Wisconsin, and possibly watch a video of Barbara onstage at the Mingo, dancing and singing.

Mostly she'd like to be by herself.

On the drive from Toledo, she finally gave in to the conscious acknowledgement that she doesn't like Kate much, Kate with her one-track mind and her somehow tiresome zealotry. She still admires Kate's courage, energy, and charm (the latter mostly deployed when she needs something or someone), but on that two-hour drive she also faced the fact that Kate is her employer rather than her client. *I hold her towel*, Holly thought, and what a miserable thought it was.

Instead of her apartment, she goes directly to the Garden City Plaza, pulling up at the check-in curb behind Kate's truck. The autograph-and-souvenir speculators have for the time being been crowded out by Kate supporters and Sista Bessie fans. The supporters line the other side of the street, holding up a banner that reads WELCOME KATE McKAY! WOMAN POWER FOREVER!

Kate approaches them and Holly, getting out of her boat of a Chrysler and hurrying to her side, thinks, *Here we go again.*

Kate makes her *come on, come on, come on* gesture. The supporters cheer and the few right-to-lifers in attendance boo heartily.

What will Holly do if someone flashes a gun? Pull Kate down? Yes, probably. Throw herself in front of her, a human shield?

Good question.

Kate doesn't hesitate in the lobby, just goes directly into the bar to get out of sight. Holly joins Corrie at the desk to do the check-in dance.

5

Chris arrives in Buckeye City at three PM. The Garden City Plaza has valet parking, but mindful of Deacon Fallowes's instruction to leave as faint a digital trail as possible, he parks in a public lot two blocks away, paying cash at the booth for three days . . . although he fully expects to be either dead or in jail after tomorrow night.

He totes his two suitcases, the blue and the pink, to the hotel, and sets them down outside the revolving door long enough to rest his arms and shoulders. The doorman asks if he can help with them and Chris tells him he's okay, thanks. He happens to look into the lobby, which is lucky, because McKay's assistant and the bodyguard bitch are at the desk, talking with one of the clerks. A party of middle-aged women standing in line behind them are wearing Sista Bessie shirts that show a much younger Betty Brady and feature the slogan GIVE ME SOME OF THAT OLD SISTA SOUL.

"Are you in town for the concert?" the doorman asks.

"Yes, if I can get a ticket."

"That might not be so easy. It's a sellout, and the scalpers are having a field day. I hope you have a reservation here, because the hotel is full up."

"I do."

Chris sees McKay join Anderson and Gibney at the desk, and they head for the elevators. The Sista Bessie fans move up to check in. Chris grabs his suitcases and goes inside. He gets his credit card out of his wallet, hesitates, then puts it back. He also has an Amex card, courtesy of Deacon Fallowes, in the name of William Ferguson. "Strictly for emergencies and good up to two thousand dollars," Fallowes said. "Use it only if they know who you are."

So far as he knows they don't, but some intuition, very strong, tells him to use the Ferguson card, and so he does. He tells the clerk that Mr. Stewart couldn't make it, so he's stepping in. "You can delete him from your check-in."

"Very good, Mr. Ferguson."

Room 919 is the sort of small box that hotel staff call a "ha-ha room," but Chris supposes it was all Deacon Fallowes could get on short notice. It's next to the elevators, and a busy chambermaids' closet is across the hall. The only view is of a brick wall on the other side of an alley. Still, it's nicer than most of the sleaze palaces where Chris and Chrissy have been staying. Nice enough to make him uneasy, thinking it's better than he deserves.

His arms and back are achy from lugging his suitcases to the hotel. Chris gets the aspirin from Chrissy's suitcase and takes a couple with a bottle of Poland Spring water from the little bar fridge. He lies down to wait for the pills to work.

Just fifteen minutes, he tells himself. *Then I'll find the auditorium where she's supposed to speak tomorrow night. Figure out a way to do it, and I better figure right, because there will only be one chance.*

But sleep has been hard to come by lately, and he falls into a light doze. Too often when his mind comes untethered—when it lets down its careful watch over the past, with its humiliations and hard decisions—he finds himself remembering his mother, who knew and accepted what she called his divided nature.

He never argued with her about that, but never believed there was anything divided about it. When he was Chris, he was Chris. When he was Chrissy, he was Chrissy. Mother bought Chrissy's clothes for her at Outlets at the Dells, which was far enough away to keep what she called "our little family secret." Those clothes were kept in the bottom drawers of Chris's bureau under his bluejeans and tee-shirts, along with a Glitter Girls doll Chrissy named Eudora. Although Daddy knew about his son's twin, Chris was forbidden to dress as Chrissy or sleep with Eudora until Harold Stewart had come in to ask if Chris had said his prayers and to kiss him goodnight. After that he could take Eudora from her confinement and become Chrissy.

His mother found acceptance easy. His father took refuge in ignorance.

Deacon Fallowes found his own way to acceptance, partly because he wanted to use the Stewart twins at some point (God would tell him when the time was right), but also because deeply religious people in every sect or faith can always find justification for what they want to do in one holy book or another. Deacon Andy found his in the Gospel of Matthew, chapter 19, verse 12: *For there are some eunuchs, which were so born from their mother's womb: and there are some eunuchs, which were made eunuchs of men: and there be eunuchs, which have made themselves eunuchs for the kingdom of heaven's sake. He that is able to receive it, let him receive it.*

"Do you understand that verse, Chris?"

He shook his head. "I'm no eunuch. I still have my . . ." He thought of how to say it without giving offense. "My manly parts."

"Suppose we think of eunuchs as those who are both male and female. Do you understand if it's put that way?"

Chris, then sixteen, said he did. He didn't, really—it was so much simpler than that, no tortured syntax needed—but he wanted Deacon Andy to be happy with him . . . or as happy as he could be. If that meant wringing some necessary meaning out of the Bible, so be it.

Fallowes put his hands on Chris's shoulders, strong and warm. Unlike Chris's father, then dead for two years, Fallowes really seemed to understand. Not his mother's understanding, which was kind, but in a fashion that suggested there might be a way to thread the needle.

"Tell me how the verse applies to you, assuming we make that one little change . . . which is, after all, just a slight modernizing of the King James."

"Does it mean some have made themselves both male and female for the kingdom of heaven's sake?"

"Yes! Very good." Deacon Andy gave his shoulders a slight squeeze. "And he that is able to receive God's Holy Word, let him receive it. Let me hear you say it."

"He that is able to receive God's Holy Word, let him receive it."

"And *she*."

"She that is able to receive God's Holy Word, let her receive it."

"Yes. Do what your heart tells you that you must receive. I will help you in that regard."

"I know you will, Deacon Andy."

"We'll talk more about what God wants of you." He paused. "And your sister, of course."

6

Before his doze can deepen into real sleep, he sits up, goes into the bathroom, and splashes cold water on his face. Then he sets off to scout the Mingo Auditorium. There's a crowd in front of the hotel. Some are wearing Sista Bessie Soul Power shirts. Some are carrying pro-life signs and waiting for an opportunity to jeer at Kate McKay. Chris knows jeering won't stop her.

Nothing will stop her but a bullet.

7

Why does it have to be the Holman Rink?

The question keeps recurring to Trig, interrupting the work of his real life, which now seems more and more like a dream to him. His computer is on and there are contracts that need to be filled out and emailed to various companies; there are insurance forms and various indemnifications to be printed, signed, and sent off. But this month—the *last* month—his real work has been murder, as drinking was his real work before he joined AA. And, say! Did he ever really believe he could make the jurors feel guilty? Or that smug ADA? Or the stiffnecked, self-righteous judge?

It's late in the game, too late to continue fooling himself, which is what he has been doing. There are jurors—maybe Gottschalk, or Finkel, especially Belinda Jones—who undoubtedly felt regret when Alan Duffrey was murdered in the prison-yard, and more regret when it turned out he had been imprisoned for a crime he hadn't committed. But did they feel actual guilt, the kind you lose sleep over?

No.

Why does it have to be the Holman?

Because the Holman was alpha, and it's only right that it should be omega. After his mother left—after she was *gone*, put it that way—some of the best and worst times he ever spent with his father

(*alpha/omega*)

had been in that rink, watching the Buckeye Bullets skate, and never mind that he couldn't say anything right after a Bullets loss. Never mind that there had been that night when he had tried to comfort Daddy about the terrible referee that cost them the game and his father had pushed him into the counter, Daddy mopping up the blood afterward and saying, *Ah, you baby, a few stitches will close that.* His father, so sure about everything, never apologized. Never explained. When Trig dared—only once or twice—to ask about his mother, Daddy said, *She's gone, left us, that's all you have to know, now shut up about it if you don't want your ass busted.*

Maisie knocks on his office door and pokes her head in. "You have a call on line one, Don."

For a moment he doesn't respond because Don is his real-life name, and more and more during these last days of the last month he thinks of himself as Trig. He supposes that even before Duffrey was killed and Cary Tolliver came forward, he must have been planning something like this, a *spree*, without letting his conscious mind know. It was certainly that way with the drinking. Once you meant to do it, you couldn't let your conscious mind in on the secret. In AA they said *slip* stood for *something lousy I planned.*

"Don?" It's Maisie, but she's far away. Far, far away.

There's a ceramic horse on his desk. He uses it for a paperweight. He touches it now, caresses it. His mother gave it to him when he was very young. He liked that old horsey. Loved it, really. Took it to bed with him (much as Chrissy took her Glitter Girl, Eudora, to bed with her). It was a horse with no name until his father said, *Call it Trigger, because it looks like the one Roy Rogers used to ride.* Daddy said, Roy Rogers was an old-time cowboy. So the ceramic horse became Trigger and Daddy started calling him Trig. Mommy never did, Mommy called him her little Donnie, but then she was *gone.*

"Don? Line one?"

He snaps to. "Thanks, Maisie. Off in the clouds today."

She gives him a noncommittal smile that might say *not just today*, and withdraws.

He looks at the blinking light on his phone and wonders how his caller would respond if he picked up the handset and said, *Hello, this is Trig, also known as Donald, also known as Juror Nine.*

"Quit it," he says, then takes the call. "Hi, this is Don Gibson."

"Hi, Mr. Gibson, this is Corrie Anderson. Kate McKay's assistant? We've spoken before."

"Indeed we have," Trig says, putting on his friendly Program Director's voice.

"Thanks for getting us in tomorrow. A lot of Kate's supporters will appreciate it."

"Thank Sista Bessie, not me," Trig says. "She was kind enough to cancel her last pre-show rehearsal."

"You thank her for me, would you do that?"

"Happy to."

"Kate is fine with working around Sista Bessie's equipment. As for me, I just have a few questions about the logistics of her lecture tomorrow evening."

"Happy to answer them, but first I have a question of my own. Could you come in tomorrow and sign a few papers? One of them is pretty important. It's a Global Insurance form, and considering Ms. McKay's . . . mmm . . . controversial stance on some issues . . . it should be executed before Ms. McKay goes onstage."

"I have to be at the auditorium to take a delivery of Kate's most recent book tomorrow at two. Twenty cartons, actually. Would two be okay?"

Actually, it wouldn't. Too many people around.

"I was hoping you could come in around noon, because I have an appointment at two."

The appointment is a lie, but Maisie will be gone to lunch at noon, and with Sista Bessie and her band having the day off, the auditorium will be empty. There was a delivery scheduled, but he canceled it. He also told Margaret, the kitchen lady, and Jerry, the janitor, to take the day off.

"Would that be possible?" He gives an embarrassed little laugh. "I don't mean to be a pain in the butt, but no signature means no insurance, and no insurance means no lecture. I'm kind of out on a limb here, Ms. Anderson, because if Kate McKay gets canceled, who is going to get blamed?"

"Me, actually," Corrie says, and laughs. "But I guess you would, too. Am I allowed to sign? Because if you need Kate's signature, I better come over right now and bring her the—"

"No, no, your signature will be fine," Trig says smoothly. Actually, as the Mingo's Program Director, he can sign most insurance papers himself, and in this case there *are* no papers.

"I can do noon," Corrie says.

"I suggest you park behind the auditorium. I can meet you there and take you in through the service entrance."

"I'll be Ubering. Not risking Kate's new truck in a city I don't know."

"Thanks," Trig says. "It's a load off my mind."

And if she brings McKay's bodyguard along, so much the better.

Chapter 18

1

Holly watches the video Jerome has sent three times, and can't stop smiling. Because it was recorded on his iPhone, the sound is blurry and echoey, overwhelming the voices of Sista Bessie singing lead and the Dixie Crystals singing backup, but the images are crisp and clear. Betty Brady is wearing a headwrap, a shapeless muumuu-type dress, and red canvas hightops, but the Crystals—Barbara included—are trying out what Holly assumes are their show clothes: black high-waisted pants and silk-shimmery white shirts. Although she guesses the three original Crystals are three times Barbara's age (or close to it), Barbara is in perfect step with them, doing the call-and-response to Betty's lead, adding an in-harmony *Ooooo* to each *Shake it up, baby*. Barbara looks like she's having the time of her life, and Holly—who hated the few press conferences she was forced to attend and could never in her wildest dreams muster the courage to get up onstage herself—is delighted for her.

There's a knock on her door as she's starting a fourth viewing of the video. She expects Corrie or Kate, but it's Jerome, with his man-bag (which Holly gave him last Christmas) slung over one shoulder. She didn't realize how homesick she was until she sees him, and she's also still overwhelmed with happiness for Barbara. The two things combine and Holly, ordinarily the least demonstrative of women, throws her arms around Jerome and hugs him tight-tight-tight.

"Whoa, girl, I love you, too." But he hugs her back, lifting her hundred and fifteen pounds and swinging her from side to side before setting her back on her feet. "You saw the vid, I take it."

"Yes! It's wonderful! She looks so . . . I don't know . . . so . . . so *something*."

"Natural? Happy?"

"Yes!"

Jerome grins. "Just hope she doesn't get stage fright once she's in front of an audience."

"Will she?"

"I don't think so," Jerome says. "She wants to do this at least once, and she and Betty have really bonded. I mean, they're tight."

"Is Barb going on the rest of the tour?"

"Hasn't said, and she's drawn to the idea, but I'd guess in the end she'll probably stay home and stick to writing."

"Shoemaker, stick to thy last," Holly murmurs.

"What?"

"Never mind. But it's exciting, isn't it?"

"Yes."

"And you'll be taking care of Ms. . . . Sista . . . when she sings the National Anthem at Dingley Park?"

"Yep. That's exciting, too. I don't expect problems, because people are crazy about her coming out of retirement." He lowers his voice. "Speaking of problems, where's yours?"

Holly hastily assures Jerome that Ms. McKay is no problem (although she guesses Jerome might know better). "Kate's next door, on the right. She's got the suite. Corrie Anderson—her assistant—is on the left. Kate likes to swim, and I'll have to go down to the pool with her pretty soon. Did you have any luck with what I asked you about?"

"Plenty. Research is my métier. You woke me up, Hols. I trashed my novel—"

"Jerome, no!"

"Jerome yes. I'm going to write about these crazy-pants churches instead. The stuff you asked for is just the tip of the iceberg. This is some scary shit. I could tell you some of the things I've already found, but that's for another time. Right now I've got the pictures you asked for. One still is from a brief court hearing in Rawcliffe, Pennsylvania, all charges dismissed. The other is from the Macbride in Iowa City. I had them blown up as eight-by-ten glossies."

He unships his man-bag and removes two pictures. The one from Rawcliffe isn't great, but good enough for Holly to identify Fallowes, one of the Real Christ Holy deacons, and the young man who has to be Christopher Stewart. In the photo he's got his head down and his hair, which is long for a churchgoing boy of the fundamentalist sort, is obscuring part of his face.

The picture from the Macbride in Iowa City is far better. He's in the third row, his hair combed back, his face upturned, his arm raised.

"Looks like he's having a come-to-Jesus moment," Jerome says.

"That's not it," Holly says. She's excited. "In the early part of her appearances, Kate asks all the men in the audience to raise their hands, and only keep them up if they've had an abortion."

"Not exactly a trick question," Jerome says, "but I guess that'd be the point."

Kate gives a courtesy knock and pokes her head in. She's wearing a hotel robe over her red bathing suit. "Time to swim, Holly. And who, pray tell, is this handsome hunk of man?"

"My Finders Keepers associate, Jerome Robinson," Holly says, wondering what Kate would think if some man said of her, *Who is this good-looking, curvaceous chickadee?*

"He found another picture of the man—not a woman but a man—who has almost certainly been stalking you. Christopher Stewart."

Kate comes into the room. Her robe is open, and Holly sees Jerome give her the sort of quick onceover that she assumes is a heterosexual male reflex . . . although not the longer, almost clinical inspection that's become notorious as "the male gaze."

Kate either doesn't notice or doesn't care. She bends over the Macbride photo. A smile dawns on her face. "You know what, I actually remember this guy. He forgot to put his hand down with the rest of the men, and I made some crack about him being the XY chromosome version of the Virgin Mary. The audience laughed—with him, not at him—and gave him a hand. He blushed. Now that you know who he is, what are you going to do about him?"

"Tell the police," Holly says, "but they are otherwise occupied with a serial killer—"

"The Surrogate Juror nut," Kate says. "He's all over the news."

"Yes." The police in general and Izzy in particular are also occupied with a charity softball game, but that's so stupid (at least in Holly's opinion) that she doesn't like to mention it. "We're also going to keep our eyes wide, aren't we?"

"Yes," Kate says, but she's got her phone to her ear. "Corrie? Are you still here? Good, can you come to Holly's room?" She lowers the phone. "She'll be right in."

Jerome says, "Can I make a suggestion?"

"Of course," Kate says to him, and without first glancing at Holly. Which Holly finds irritating, interesting, and amusing . . . all at the same time.

"I bet Holly already knows," Jerome says, which Holly considers *très galant.*

Holly does. "We need to check all the hotels and motels for a Christopher Stewart, either reserved or already here. Including this one."

"I'll ask Tom Atta," Jerome says. "He's only a sub in the big game tomorrow, claims he's got a hamstring pull, so he should be able to do it."

"What game?" Kate asks, but before Jerome can answer, Corrie comes in with her head bent over her laptop.

"There's a problem with Cincinnati, Kate, but I'm handling it. Elmira is okay, the weather isn't going to be a problem after all. I have to go in to the Mingo tomorrow at noon to sign some dumb insurance papers—"

"Never mind all that for now, look at this picture from Iowa City," Kate says. "It's a lot better than the one in the Florida paper. Is this the female impersonator from Reno?"

"I told you, I only got a glimpse—"

There's a Sharpie in the side pocket of Corrie's slacks, perfect for signing autographs, and also perfect for drawing on glossy photos. Holly plucks it out and draws bangs on the upturned face of the man who was sitting in the third row of the Macbride a week ago.

Corrie looks long and hard. Then she turns to Holly. "That's him. Her. Whatever. I'm almost positive."

Holly says, "As well as the police, we need to make sure the press knows about this guy. And social media. The Macbride picture is good. We might not be able to get it in the print edition of the paper tomorrow, but on Twitter and Facebook, in the online edition of the—"

Kate clamps down her shoulder, and hard. "Are you crazy?"

"What do you mean?" Holly is bewildered.

"Bad enough you want to tell the cops. I guess I have to allow that because the guy might be a threat to others, but *no press, no Twitter.* They canceled me in Toledo. If you give the politicians an excuse to cancel me here, they'll take it."

Holly grips Kate's hand and detaches it—gently—from her shoulder. Later she'll see the bruises of Kate's fingers there. "This man wants to kill you, Kate. Do you understand that?"

"Every time I go onstage someone wants to kill me, and it's probably just a matter of time before someone tries it. Do *you* understand *that*?" Kate's smile is positively feral. Holly is speechless. So is Corrie.

At last, Jerome says, "What about circulating the picture to the Mingo personnel as well as to the cops?"

"And to the other venues we'll be at," Corrie adds.

Kate nods. To Holly she says, "*Will* the cops try to cancel me?"

Holly gives Kate her own smile, not feral—she can't *do* feral—but thin and without humor. "I don't think so," she says. "If any of them can be spared from their charity softball game, I think they'll see you as bait."

2

Jerome buzzes off to Staples, where he makes two hundred copies of the picture from the Macbride audience-cam. He takes four dozen to Dingley Park and gives them to Tom Atta, who looks huge and athletic in his blue shorts and tee. Except for the elastic bandage wrapped around one knee and calf, that is.

"So it's not bad enough that we've got a serial killer on the loose while the cops are practicing to play softball," Tom says. "Now we've got to be on the lookout for this cuckoo-bird, too."

"Will you pass those out? Here and to the radio cars?"

"Sure. Guy looks like a normal American."

"So did Ted Bundy. What about checking hotels and motels?"

"Do you think this guy will have checked in under his own name?" Tom asks, then answers himself before Jerome has time to. "He might, if he doesn't know we're onto him."

Jerome likes that *we*.

Tom says, "The Surrogate Juror nut is now a State Police case, guy named Ganzinger. That makes the Chief happy, but I'd love it if the home team could take down at least one bad guy. So yeah, I'll have Dispatch call around. And speaking of the home team . . ."

He nods at the field, where Izzy is walking to the pitcher's mound, looking impossibly long-legged in her police team shorts. Her catcher, a squat fireplug with COSLAW on the back of his shirt, walks beside her. On the third-base side, the Hoses squad comes alive, giving whistles, catcalls, and a sarcastic cheer.

"Gonna light you up, Red!" one of them yells. He's a tall drink of water, with knees almost up to his chin. "Light you up like a Roman candle!"

"That's the guy that talked trash to Iz at the softball press conference," Tom says. "They kind of got into it."

Izzy stows the softball she's been holding in the pocket of her glove so she can give him the finger.

Tom nods at the tall Hoses player. "His name, oh so appropriate, is Pill."

"Got into it for real or for show?"

"It was supposed to be for show, but he got under her skin, so she got under his."

Coslaw crouches behind home plate and pounds his catcher's mitt. Izzy does a herky-jerky windup, bends, and throws. The ball arcs over the catcher, bounces off the top of the backstop, and comes down on Coslaw's head. The Hoses players howl. One is laughing so hard he falls off the bench, kicking his legs at the bright blue sky.

"*You tryin to hit the Skylab?*" George Pill bellows.

The catcher picks up the ball and flicks it back to Izzy. Even from Jerome's place on the bench next to Tom, he can see Izzy's cheeks have gone bright red.

"She ain't even supposed to be pitching," Tom says. "Got drafted because she pitched in college back in the day. Our regular guy got in a bar fight and broke his stupid hand."

"SKYLAB, SKYLAB!" The Hoses players seem to like that one, although that particular object fell out of orbit decades ago. *"RED-HEAD'S TRYIN TO HIT THE SKYYYLAB!"*

Izzy's next pitch falls short, plopping into the dirt in front of home plate. The Hoses players are killing themselves now, trash-talking up a storm.

"Um, she could have a problem," Jerome says.

"Izzy'll get it together," Tom says, although he doesn't sound altogether convinced. "You should take some of those pictures to the Mingo, where Holly's lady is going to speak. Give them out to the ushers and such."

"That's my next stop," Jerome says.

"And pass them out to any hotels or motels you pass along the way."

On the mound, Izzy is throwing more smoothly now, although Jerome hopes she'll be able to put a little more mustard on her pitches when the actual game starts. Right now she's throwing batting practice stuff, every pitch begging *clobber me.*

He stands up and hollers, "Bring it, Iz!"

She gives him a smile and touches the brim of her cap.

3

Kate is turning laps in the Garden City Plaza pool. Holly is once again sitting poolside with a towel at the ready, but she also has her tablet and phone. She uses PeopleFinders to get Andrew Fallowes's phone numbers—there are two of them. Being an experienced investigator, Holly deduces that one is probably his church office and one is his home. It's two-thirty PM in Wisconsin, so Holly tries the church number first. A robot wishes her a blessed day, and gives her five choices. Holly pushes the one for Administrative Services, wondering how rich a church in northern Wisconsin must be to have five choices.

After two rings, she gets an actual human being. "This is Lois, and God loves you!" the actual human being almost sings. "How may I help you?"

"My name is Holly Gibney, and I'd like to speak with Mr. Fallowes."

"May I ask how Deacon Fallowes can help you today, Holly?"

Holly has a dislike for people who use her first name on short notice; they usually want to sell her something. Insurance, maybe. "It's of a personal nature," she says. "Be sure to tell him my name." Which may mean nothing to him, or a great deal.

"I'll just put you on hold for a moment, Holly, if I may."

"You may," Holly says.

She waits. Back and forth Kate goes in the pool; red suit, blue water.

After thirty seconds or so, a rich baritone voice says, "This is Deacon Fallowes, Miss Gibley. How may I help?"

Sometimes, when she least expects it, Holly finds herself capable of an almost divine sensitivity, flashes of subconscious understanding she calls, with her usual (and seemingly intractable) self-deprecation, "my crazy intuitions." She has such a flash now. Fallowes hasn't misheard her name; he has deliberately mispronounced it. He knows who she is, and if he knows that, he almost certainly knows the mentally unstable person who has been stalking Kate McKay. Does he know what Stewart is doing? Holly isn't sure, but she thinks he very well might.

"I'm calling about one of your parishioners," she says. "A young man named Christopher Stewart."

After the minutest pause, Fallowes says, "Oh, I know Chris. Know him very well. Harold's boy. Fine young man. What about him, Miss Gibley?" He pauses a bit longer, then adds: "And where are you calling from?"

You know very well where I'm calling from, Holly thinks, *but here's a question: Did you wind Stewart up and set him on this course, or did he do it himself?*

"Mr. Fallowes . . . Deacon . . . I have reason to believe that Christopher Stewart has been stalking my employer, a woman named Kate McKay. I'm guessing you know that name, as well."

"Of course I do." A chill has entered Fallowes's voice. "The baby killer."

"You can call her whatever you want," Holly says. "Stewart threw bleach in her assistant's face, thinking it was Ms. McKay. That's assault. He delivered a deadly poison backstage at one of Ms. McKay's lectures. That's assault with intent to kill. I have reason to believe—"

"You *believe*. Do you have any proof?"

"He has attended several of her lectures, maybe all of them. I have a clear picture of him from Iowa City. He was in the third row with his hand up. I think he's in this city or soon will be. He is a danger to others and also to himself."

"I reject your premise and have no idea where Chris might be," Fallowes says, and she knows he's lying about either one. Probably both.

"For your sake and the sake of your church, Deacon Fallowes, I hope that's true. Because if he hurts Kate, or someone close to her, or even some innocent bystander or bystanders, the results will be grave. In a phrase I'm sure you're familiar with, there will be hell to pay."

"I resent your insinuations, Miss Gibney. They are accusatory."

Finally got my name right, didn't you?

In the pool, Kate is finally slowing down. Soon she'll want her towel. Holly will give it to her, well satisfied with her progress.

"Mr. Fallowes? Deacon?"

Silence . . . but he's listening.

"If you know where he is, call him off. Because the trail will lead back to your church. And to you."

"I've heard quite enough," Fallowes says, and ends the call.

Kate swims to the side of the pool. "Press conference dead ahead. Towel?"

Holly gives her a smile. "Right here." And holds it out.

4

Chris is walking to the lot where he left his car when his phone rings. It's Deacon Fallowes. "Do you have another phone?"

Meaning does he have a burner. He has several, but they're all in the Kia, under the back compartment where the temporary tire is kept. He starts to tell Andy that, but he interrupts.

"Call me on another one. Get rid of yours." With that he hangs up.

So it's serious. Chris's plan to check out the Mingo will have to wait until he finds out what bee Deacon Andy has in his bonnet.

When he gets to the parking lot, he changes phones and calls back. The news is about as bad as it can be.

"They know who you are." Andy's voice is as rich and mellow as ever, but Chris is an expert when it comes to fear, he's felt plenty since the morning he woke up and saw his sister's dangling hand, and he senses panic just below the surface of Deacon Andy's mellow-fellow voice. "You have to break off and come back."

Chris walks to the edge of the lot and stares at the traffic on Buckeye Avenue. Just another Thursday afternoon in the Second Mistake on the Lake. People with their own piddling concerns. Chris has his own concerns, and they aren't piddling.

"No."

"What?"

"I'm not breaking off. I'm going to get her, and I'm going to get her *here*. Enough tiptoeing around."

"Christopher, as your deacon and a church elder, I'm ordering you to come back. If you continue, you'll be doing the church irreparable harm."

You mean I'll be doing you *irreparable harm*, Chris thinks. Suppressed resentment rises inside him, like a hot spring that means to break free one way or the other.

"If I'm caught, I'll tell them I did it on my own." He has no intention of being caught. At least not alive.

"Christopher, listen to me. They won't believe that. We're on the deep state's radar, have been for years. Just like Waco. And Ruby Ridge."

Chris tries to set aside the resentment. And the anger. It's hard. Would he be in this position—this *fix*—if it wasn't for the church? Only his mother understood his pain, but except for her ultimatum about Chrissy, she was too gentle to stand against the church's iron Old Testament beliefs.

"They have your picture from the McKay woman's lecture in Iowa City. It will be circulated to every policeman in the city. If it hasn't been already."

"They are going to be otherwise occupied." On his walk from the hotel, Chris has seen Guns and Hoses fliers on just about every building and power pole. "They have a serial killer and a big charity game to deal with. Looking for the McKay woman's stalker will be a very low priority."

Fallowes seems not to have heard. "Every hotel and motel, too. Including *yours*."

It's something he hasn't thought of, and it sets him back on his heels.

"Come home, Christopher. We can work this out as long as they can't identify you from Reno or Omaha."

I don't think they can. I was Chrissy in both places. That gives him an idea. If he can get back to his hotel without being spotted as McKay's stalker, everything may still be well.

"I need you to help me," Chris says. "I need you to find me a place where my sister can stay unseen until McKay goes onstage tomorrow night at seven. Go on the internet and search for abandoned buildings close to the Garden City Plaza Hotel."

"Christopher, I won't do that."

The anger bursts free. "You will, though. You better. If you don't, I'll tell them all this was your idea. Yours and Pastor Jim's."

Fallowes makes a sound that's half sigh and half moan. "If you did that, you would kill this church, son."

"I'm not your son," Chris says. Then, without knowing he means to do it, he screams, "*She can't kill babies! Bad enough that God can!*"

He looks around to see if anyone heard, but the parking lot is his alone under the beating-down afternoon sun.

"Dammit, son . . . Chris, I mean . . ."

"Find me a place where I can disappear, Deacon Andy."

"Any abandoned buildings I find will be locked—"

"I'll get in." *At least as long as it's not alarmed.*

"Chris—"

"I'll get rid of my phone and hold onto this burner until you call. After, I'll get rid of this one, too. I want at least four abandoned buildings, so I have a choice. No, make that five."

"The internet isn't reliable, Chris. I may find a building that is *supposed* to be abandoned, but in *reality* it might not—"

"That's why I want a choice," Chris says, and has to restrain himself from adding what would have been unthinkable when he started on this crusade: *You dumbbell.*

"Chris—"

He hangs up.

5

Chris walks back to the hotel with his head down and his John Deere cap pulled low. As he approaches he sneaks a look up and sees the assistant, Corrie Anderson, getting out of an Uber. A close one! He waits until she's inside, and gives her a little extra time to get to the elevators. He has a bad minute passing the doorman, but that goes okay. At least he thinks so. Hopes so.

In Room 919, Chris dons a lavender pants suit—she thinks of it as her Kamala Harris suit—earrings, makeup (including a bright slash of lipstick), and becomes Chrissy. Her purse is in the pink suitcase, along with two wigs. She left on this pilgrimage with three, but got rid of the red one in Reno. One of the remaining wigs is blond, but she doesn't want to wear that, because her own hair is blond. She dons the black one, fluffs out the bangs, and adds an Alice band that matches the lipstick.

She slings her purse over her shoulder, picks up the pink suitcase, and leaves the room. She's praying she doesn't meet the bodyguard from McKay's party in the elevator or the lobby. She doesn't know for sure, but thinks the Gibney woman was probably the one who put the fear of God into Andy Fallowes.

The lobby has cleared out for the time being. One of the female desk clerks gives Chrissy a look of casual contempt as she goes out. Chrissy doesn't understand it at first, then does. The clerk thinks she's looking at a hooker that's just finished providing a client with a little afternoon delight.

Outside the hotel she turns right for no other reason than that the doorman is looking left. She has no idea where to go and wait for Andy Fallowes's call. A block down, she asks a passerby if there's a place outside in the sunshine where a gal can rest her feet, maybe even get a bite to eat.

"How about Dingley Park?" he says, and points in the direction she's going. "Six or eight blocks, plenty of benches, plenty of shade, and the food trucks will be open."

"Isn't that where the charity game is going to be played tomorrow?"

"Yeah, but that's way on the other side of the park."

"Thank you, sir."

"Always a pleasure to help a pretty girl," the passerby says.

He goes on his way and Chrissy, feeling flattered, goes on hers.

6

Kate does her press conference from four to five in the hotel's Lake Room. She looks fresh and blooming following her exercise and a quick *après*-pool shower. Holly stands at the back, unnoticed even though this is her hometown and she's made a few headlines here herself. Small and graying, rather plain in the face but well-groomed, she has a talent for being slightly *dim*. She keeps her hand in her purse, touching but not grasping her pepper spray. She recognizes most of the local news people, also national TV news demi-celebs Clarissa Ward, Lauren Simonetti, and Trevor Ault. Corrie got her wish; being shut down in Toledo has turned Kate's tour into a crusade.

All the reporters have Christopher Stewart's Iowa City picture; Jerome gave a stack to Holly before buzzing off to talk to Tom Atta at Dingley Park. She asked the hotel's chief of security to hand them out. Buckeye Brandon, the city's demi-celeb podcaster, is sitting in the front row wearing his old-fashioned newshawk's fedora, and with his old-fashioned tape deck slung over his shoulder on a leather strap. He tilts his mic (definitely newfangled) toward himself long enough to ask the first question.

"Ms. McKay, there's a psycho—the so-called Surrogate Juror Killer—at large in this town, and now a purportedly dangerous stalker is after you. And yet the city police force is pushing ahead with their annual Guns and Hoses softball game tomorrow night."

Kate says, "Do you have a question, sir, or did you just want to give a sermon?"

There's a ripple of laughter from the rest of the press pool, but Buckeye Brandon is undeterred. "I was laying down the background, because you're an outsider in our fair city. The question is how do you justify the risk not only to yourself but to your audience?"

For Kate, this is a fat pitch. "Since the *Dobbs versus Jackson Women's Health* decision in June of 2022, over one hundred women's clinics have closed nationwide. These organizations—"

Buckeye Brandon interrupts with a smile. "Do you have an answer, ma'am, or did you just want to give a sermon?"

This brings more laughter, and for once Kate looks a little off her game. "Those closed centers provided many services other than abortion—pap smears, birth control, mammograms, adoption services. How do you justify *that*?"

Buckeye Brandon is unfazed. "You haven't answered my question."

Holly expects Kate to challenge this—she's a woman who likes to have the last word—and is relieved when for once Kate backs off, just saying that the security measures at the Mingo will be sufficient, and to say more would compromise those measures.

The press conference moves on to other subjects, only returning to Christopher Stewart at the end. A reporter from the AP asks Kate if Stewart is connected to any terrorist organization, such as ISIS or the Army of God.

"So far as we know now, he's only connected to a church in Wisconsin called Real Christ Holy. You'd have to ask them about terrorist ties."

Deacon Fallowes will be fielding some requests for comment tonight and tomorrow, Holly thinks, and not without satisfaction.

The last question comes from Peter Upfield, of *The Western Clarion*. It's delivered in a grating, accusatory voice. "How will you respond, Ms. McKay, if there is an attack by this Stewart person tomorrow, and people are killed?"

Kate gives him a razor-thin smile. "That's like asking a man if he's still beating his wife, isn't it? No matter how that sort of question is answered, it gives the accusation credence. It's what I'd expect from someone who works for a rag like the *Clarion.* Thank you, ladies and gentlemen."

Kate walks up the center aisle, and when she reaches Holly, a murmur arises from a few of the local reporters, who have finally recognized her. Buckeye Brandon shouts, "How long have you been working for Kate, Holly?"

She doesn't answer, and doesn't relax until Kate is safely back in her suite.

7

Corrie is in her room, making calls to local radio stations, spiking the current rumor going around that Sista Bessie is going to introduce Kate tomorrow night. Corrie tells them the Sista will be otherwise engaged, singing the National Anthem at a charity softball game twelve blocks away. Any further questions should be addressed to Sista Bessie's press representative, and no, Corrie doesn't know who that would be.

Kate, for the time being at loose ends, asks Holly if she'd like to have a room service dinner with her. Holly agrees and they sit together on the couch, looking over the menu. The prices are terrifying, but Kate tells Holly to knock herself out.

"I only let people order what they want if they save me from getting my brains bashed in."

While they wait for the food, Izzy calls. Holly excuses herself and takes it in her room. Izzy begins by congratulating Holly on identifying the unstable young man who has been dogging Kate McKay's tour.

"Way back when this began, I told Lew Warwick that if he wanted an ace detective, he should call you."

"Izzy, that's really not—"

"I was righter than I knew. You're amazing, Holly."

As always when complimented, Holly wants to change the subject. In the background, she can hear men yelling and the chink of metal bats hitting balls. "You're at Dingley Park, right?"

"Yes indeed. Have been for most of the day."

"At Kate's press conference, Buckeye Brandon asked about why the police were going on with the game when the Surrogate Juror Killer is still on the loose."

"Yeah, we've taken a certain amount of chong from the tong about that." Before Holly can decide if that's racist, Izzy pushes on. "I understand and sympathize, but I understand Chief Patmore's point, too. The game brings in well over a hundred thousand dollars for the Kiner Pedes unit and Muscular Dystrophy. Cancel it, the charities lose and the bad guy wins. Plus, people are apt to be safe in a crowd, and we're expecting a big one."

"Are you having any fun?"

"Actually I am. I can still throw a dropball." She lowers her voice. "Trying to keep it a secret from the firehouse boys."

"The pitch you threw in the gym, right?"

"Yeah. The softball version of a sinker. If I don't lose the actual knack when I'm under pressure, I'll get strikeouts and a lot of ground balls. For the grounders, it's up to my fielders."

"Well, good luck," Holly says. "I wish I could be there."

"Haven't had any insights on *our* case, I don't suppose. Although the Trig catch was brilliant."

"I've thought about it a lot," Holly says. "No leads?"

"We've almost certainly ID'd the car the killer was driving when he killed George Carville—the farmer—as a Toyota Corolla or Avalon, but what good is that?"

"Not much, I suppose. They are very common."

"And the guy has been very lucky. It's Ralph Ganzinger's case, which is probably just as well for us, but if you think of anything, let me know."

"Are you sure Alan Duffrey had no friends that would take up his cause in this extreme way?"

"Colleagues, but no real friends since he left the Army in 2016."

"Never married?"

"No, but we—Tom and I, that is—have reason to believe he was about as hetero as they come. A deep dive on his computer turned up a couple of high-end escort services he may have used, credit card receipts tend to verify that, and he was an occasional Pornhub visitor."

"What kind of Pornhub visits? Young girls? Or boys?"

Izzy laughs. "On Pornhub, most of them look young. Have you never been there? Even for a scouting expedition?"

"No," Holly says. She has on a few occasions visited a site called Passionate Kisses, but that at least has a wrapping of romance on the sexy stuff. Kind of like the novels of Colleen Hoover, which Holly enjoys.

"Pornhub's actually a little sad," Izzy says, "and Duffrey never went for the pretend schoolgirl stuff. Or the schoolboy stuff, once you discount the pix Cary Tolliver slipped onto his computer. Pretty much straight-up boffing. Grinsted pointed that out, and the prosecutor—Allen—countered by saying Duffrey probably erased all the nasty stuff . . . except for the stuff Duffrey thought was safely hidden. Which, it turns out, he never had anything to do with."

"But someone cared enough to start this vendetta in Duffrey's name," Holly says.

"Tom thinks it's just a crazy person."

"I like Tom, but I think he's wrong. I keep asking myself who cared enough to start killing people as a result of that trial. Who felt guilty enough himself to do that?"

"Well, if you think of anyone, let me know."

"No friends who might be out for revenge? You're sure?"

"Not that we know of."

From outside, Holly hears the rattle of a room service trolley. Kate calls, "Dinner's here, Holly! Don't let it get cold!"

"I have to go, Izzy—time to eat. I'm having hundred-dollar lamb chops."

"What the fuck, are they dusted in gold?"

Holly laughs, ends the call, goes into the suite, and eats her expensive dinner. Kate makes conversation by asking about Holly's work as an investigator. Holly opens up a little . . . although not about her more *outré* cases. She rarely talks about those.

8

After dinner, Holly gets a call from Tom Atta, who is at Dingley but ineligible for the big game because of the hamstring pull. He tells her that he also called the Real Christ Holy Church administrative extension. "Got someone named Lois."

"Did she sound like she was singing?"

Tom laughs. "Actually, she sorta did. Said Fallowes wasn't there, and when I asked about Chris Stewart, she got all cagey and said she wasn't free to divulge the names of parishioners."

"They know him," Holly says. "Lois may not know what he's up to, but I'd bet my house and lot that Fallowes does."

"Do you *have* a house and lot, Holly?"

"Actually I don't, but I do have a condo."

"After I got *bupkes* from the church, I called the Baraboo Junction Town Office, which, given the population, is probably the size of a trailer. They were just closing, but I got a clerk willing to chat with an officer of the law. She ID'd Chris Stewart as a member of the Real Christ Holy Church."

"I already knew—"

"Here's something you might not know. This chatty clerk said there was some big kerfuffle in the church a few years ago. She told me Chris Stewart was kind of a black sheep in Real Christ Holy because he got caught wearing girls' clothes as a kid, but this clerk said the church prayed it away."

"Maybe they didn't quite succeed," Holly says.

Chapter 19

1

Chrissy has almost given up on Deacon Andy when her burner finally comes to life. She's sitting at one of the picnic tables near the Dingley Park food wagons, with her suitcase safely placed between her feet (which are clad in sensible but stylish Vionic flats). The lights have just gone on around the playing field, where the men from the Police and Fire Departments are still practicing. Chrissy would like to be on the well-lighted bleachers over there—here on the park's darker side she's already been hit on twice—but doesn't dare. The chances of being recognized are too great. Here on the edge of the trees is safer, and the two guys who approached her were pretty hesitant. She even toted her suitcase to Taco Joe's food wagon and got a burrito. She knew it was a risk, but her stomach had gone beyond growling and was actually roaring.

She answers the phone on the first ring.

"You really need to come home," Andy Fallowes says. He sounds put out and scared. "I got a call from a city detective as well as that bodyguard person. This is *serious*, Christopher."

"I'm Chrissy."

Andy pauses, then gives a longsuffering sigh. "Chrissy, then."

"Not coming home. Finishing what I started. If I can do that, I'll keep you out of it. If you don't help me, I won't."

"Pastor Jim says—"

"I don't care what that old man says. Do you have a list of some places where I can disappear until tomorrow, or don't you?"

Another sigh. "There are two empty warehouses on Bincey Lane. That's near the lake. There's an empty Sam's Club out by the airport—"

"Too far," Chrissy says. "I don't dare go back to my car."

"There's also an abandoned hockey rink in a place called Dingley Park. It's awaiting demolition—"

"What?"

"I said . . ."

But Chrissy barely hears the rest of it. She's looking at the conical, paint-peeling roof poking over the tops of the surrounding fir trees. She thought it was some kind of storage shed.

She thinks, *Who says God doesn't help those in need?*

2

Chrissy makes a slow, ambling circle of the condemned building, pink suitcase in hand, keeping an eye out for anyone drifting around on this side of the park, probably those looking for drugs or blowjobs. She sees no one, but catches a strange and unpleasant aroma, which she thinks is probably improperly stowed garbage from behind one of the food trucks, most likely the one selling fish.

When she comes back to the double doors, she sets her suitcase down and examines the keypad. Before Chris's father became rich as an inventor of inverters, voltage regulators, and smart circuits, Harold Stewart was a humble electrician, one who knew many tricks of the trade . . . some of which Donald "Trig" Gibson would have remembered from his own father's sermons in this very building.

Put things on the floor. They can't fall any further.

Never go back to your van empty-handed.

Use a potato peeler to strip wires.

If you can't get into a building with a keypad, try the Plumber's Code.

Chrissy looks around, just as Trig did before her. She pulls off the keypad's cover, just as Trig did before her. She reads the Plumber's Code on the inside of the cover—9721—just as Trig did before her. She pushes the numbers. The light on the keypad turns green, and she hears a clunk as the locking bar releases. She snaps the cover back onto the keypad and goes inside, ready to run if she hears the *meep-meep-meep* of a burglar alarm. There's nothing. She closes the door.

Safe! Good God almighty, she's safe.

She's glad she didn't toss the burner down a sewer grate. It's a flashlight-equipped Nokia Flip. She takes it from the jacket pocket of the pants suit, turns on the light, and shines it around. She's in a lobby. There are a couple of dust-covered ticket windows on the right and on the left there's a snackbar denuded of snacks. The smell in here is stronger, and she no longer thinks it's trash from the fish wagon. That's a decomposing animal.

Chrissy goes into the rink, phone in one hand, suitcase in the other, shoes gritting on the dusty concrete. The floor, once a-shimmer with ice, is now just cracked concrete crisscrossed with beams that look like railroad ties. For all she knows, that's what they are. From high above, where the last daylight is still leaking through cracks in the roof, she can hear the soft coo and flutter of pigeons.

There's something draped across the beams at the center of the rink. She believes it's the source of that smell, and too big to be a dog. She thinks it could be a person, and as she walks toward it, stepping from one beam to the next, she sees that it is.

Chrissy examines the decaying body and murmurs, "Oh, you poor thing. I'm so sorry."

She kneels down, although this close, the stench of decay is almost unbearable. It's a girl. Chrissy can only be sure of that because of the scraggly hair and the nubs of breasts. The fiends and fuckers have mostly been kept out, but there's no way to keep the rats and insects at bay, and they have picked away at the dead girl's face until there is little face left; the eyes are empty sockets that stare sightlessly up at the roof with an expression of outraged shock.

There is something in the girl's right hand. Chrissy spreads the fingers and brings the phone down close. Two words: CORINNA ASHFORD. Probably her name.

"Until tomorrow night, it's just you and me, Corinna," Chrissy says. "I hope you don't mind the company."

Chrissy stands up and beam-walks back to the snackbar. She feels terribly sorry for the dead girl, no doubt killed and left here by some sex maniac. But Chrissy isn't sorry enough to sit with her.

Corinna is just too smelly.

3

Back in her connecting room, while Holly is trying to decide if seven-thirty is too early to get into her pj's, her phone rings. It's Barbara. She sounds out of breath and happy. Her phone call telling Holly she'd won tickets to the Sista Bessie show seems like years ago instead of weeks. Since then she's become an honorary Dixie Crystal and has established a firm friendship with the woman she now calls Betty.

Holly listens to what Barbara is proposing and says she will if she can; she has to check with the woman she's protecting. She doesn't want to call Kate her boss, probably because that is exactly what Kate is.

Kate is sitting on the sofa in her suite, watching a panel of politicians or politician wannabes (Holly isn't sure there's a difference) discuss the latest cultural hot-button issue.

"Holly, you should sit down and listen to this shit. You won't believe it."

"I'm sure it's interesting," Holly says, "but if you're set for the night, I'm going out for an hour or two."

Kate turns from the TV and gives her a wide smile. "Hot date?"

"No, just going to see my friend Barbara. She's going to be singing at the shows here in town with Sista Bessie. Including one song, which was originally a poem, that she wrote herself."

"No shit!" Kate jumps up. "How totally cool! She won that poetry prize, didn't you say?"

"Yes, the Penley." Holly knows (courtesy of Charlotte Gibney, from whom all wisdom of the bummer type flowed) that pride goeth before a fall, but she feels pride, anyway. Is almost bursting with it. "Her book has been published and is selling pretty well." This is a white lie, but Holly feels that wishful thinking makes it hardly a lie at all.

"Then get with her, for God's sake!" Kate goes to Holly, puts her hands on her shoulders, and gives her a friendly shake. "Take some video, if she sings and if they'll allow it. I'll send Corrie out to get her book tomorrow. I want to read it."

"If I can get over to my apartment, I'll give you a copy," Holly says. "I've got an extra." Actually she has ten, purchased from Appletree Books in Cleveland.

"Fantastic." Kate grabs the remote and zaps off the TV. "When I was a kid, I idolized Avril Lavigne and Rihanna. I used to fantasize about being onstage in a glittery low-cut gown, singing something bouncy and fast, like that song 'We Got the Beat.' Do you remember that one?"

"Yes."

"Instead, I wound up doing . . . this." She looks around at her new suitcases and stacks of her latest book, waiting to be signed. "It's good, I wouldn't change it, but dreams . . . sometimes dreams, they . . ."

She shakes her head, as if to clear it.

"Go on. Visit your young friend. Tell her we'll be in the audience Saturday night, clapping and cheering her on. Also tell her Katie McKay envies the *hell* out of her chance to sing with Sista Bessie."

There's a knock on the door. Holly checks the peephole, then lets Corrie in with an armload of Woman Power tee-shirts for Kate to sign. Kate groans, but good-naturedly.

"I'm going out for awhile," Holly tells them. "Keep the door locked, okay?"

"I doubt very much if this guy Stewart could get upstairs," Kate says. "His picture is *everywhere*."

"Just the same. And remember he might look like a she."

Kate puts one stocking-clad foot behind her and does a deep curtsey that would look perfectly acceptable in the Court of St. James's. "Yes, boss."

No, Holly thinks. *That's you*.

4

Barbara said to use the service entrance, which Holly knows from the old days, when Bill Hodges was still alive. This is how they came in on the night when Brady Hartsfield tried to blow the fracking place sky-high.

Holly parks in the small employees' lot beside a white Transit van with MINGO AUDITORIUM on the side. Beneath it is a motto: *JUST THE GOOD STUFF!*™ The service door to the little kitchen is open. Two men are standing beside it, a bald guy in jeans and a Sista Bessie tee, the other in a sportcoat and tie. From inside comes the booming, echoing sound of a rock-and-soul band in full flight.

The man in jeans comes to her, hand held out. "I'm Tones Kelly, Sista's tour manager. And you must be Barbara's friend Holly."

"I am," Holly says. "Very nice to meet you."

"We love Barbara," Tones says. "Sista especially. She read Barbara's book of poems, and they just clicked."

"And now she's in the band!" Holly says. Marvels, actually.

Tones laughs. "She sings, she dances, she plays the tambo on the beat, she writes poems . . . what can't she do? A star is born!"

The other man comes forward. "Hello, Ms. Gibney. I'm Donald Gibson, the Mingo's Program Director."

"You're going to be a busy bee this weekend," Holly says, shaking his hand. Two years ago she would have offered her elbow to both men, but times have changed enough for her to resume the old practice. She still keeps a bottle of hand sanitizer in her purse, though. Some would call her a hypochondriac, but so far she's avoided even a mild case of Covid, and she wants to keep it that way.

Donald Gibson leads the way down a short corridor. As they go, Holly recognizes the song the band is playing as an old Al Green tune, "Let's Stay Together." Sista Bessie (Holly can't think of her as plain old Betty, at least not yet) is singing in a low, sweet voice that channels Mavis Staples so clearly that Holly gets a run of gooseflesh on the back of her neck. The music stops in mid-verse, and as they step into the elevator, the band starts up some other song, one Holly doesn't recognize.

"They are doing a bump rehearsal, because your Ms. McKay has the hall tomorrow night," Tones says. "Betty thought Ms. McKay might want it tomorrow day to do a sound check."

"That will ease her assistant's mind," Holly says. "What's a bump rehearsal?"

"They do a little bit of every song on Sista's set list," Tones says. "To make sure the band and Ross—he's our sound guy—are on the same wavelength. The settings change between rave-ups and ballads. So do the lights and the cyc, but I let Kitty Sandoval worry about that. I just need to make sure the sound is right."

"You also have to make sure the band stays in the same key from song to song, right?" Gibson asks. He pushes his glasses up on his nose.

"Right," Kelly says.

There's something familiar about Gibson, but before Holly can begin to think of what it might be or where she might have seen him before, the elevator doors open backstage and the band wallops them: the intro to "Land of 1000 Dances."

Gibson takes Holly's hand—she doesn't like it, but allows it because it's dark back here—and leads her to stage left, the exact post she expects to be occupying tomorrow night when Kate speaks. She's hardly aware of Gibson letting go and stepping back, because she's totally absorbed by what's going on at center stage. Entranced, really.

Barbara is wearing black pants and a shimmery white shirt. She's banging a tambourine with the heel of her hand, swinging her hips, stepping in time with the other three Dixie Crystals, and looking young—so young and sexy and beautiful. It's a dance-craze song from yesteryear, and she segues from the Pony, to the Frug, to the Watusi, to the Mashed Potato. Even the Twist. And she *shines*.

The band cuts out. Barbara sees Holly and runs across the stage, leaping over the power cords. She hurls herself into Holly's arms, almost knocking her over. Her cheeks are high with color; tiny drops of sweat nestle in the hollows of her temples.

"You came! I'm so glad!"

Sista Bessie joins them. "You are Barbara's friend, Holly."

"I am. And I'm sure you hear this all the time, but I'm a big fan of your songs. I remember your gospel days."

"Long ago," Betty says, and laughs. "Long time gone. Barbara is some kind of special, as I'm sure you know."

"I do," Holly says.

"We are just finishing up. We have three more bumps, then the show closer, which you may recognize. It's called 'Lowtown Jazz.'"

"I know it very well, Sista Bessie."

"Call me Betty. The Sista is strictly show-and-blow. Come on, Barb, let's get this done so we can all go home and I can rest my weary dogs." To the band she hollers, *"No work tomorrow, guys and dolls!"* They cheer that.

Holly watches, mesmerized, Tones Kelly and Donald Gibson forgotten, as the band launches into "Dear Mister," one of Sista Bessie's early hits, then "Sit Down, Servant," and then a verse of her biggest hit, "Let's Stay Together."

A roadie flips Betty a towel. She mops her broad, makeup-free (tonight, at least) face with it, then addresses the band again. "In honor of our special guest, Barbara's friend Miss Holly, we are going to do 'Lowtown Jazz' reet and complete. I want you to make that mutha *strut*!" She turns to Barbara. "Get out front, girl, and count us off!"

This time the chills go all the way up Holly's body, from her heels to the nape of her neck as Barbara—who she can still remember as a gawky teenager just out of braces—faces the empty seats. She raises her fisted hands and pops up a finger from each. *"One . . . two . . . you know what to do!"*

The drums start, a tom-tom beat low and steady. The bass kicks in, then the brass. Barbara does a Michael Jackson slide back to Sista Bessie as the Crystals, now a trio again, start singing, *"Jazz, jazz, bring that shazz, do it, do it, show me how you move it, get on down and groove it, do that Lowtown jazz."* Sista Bessie and Barbara sing the verses together, dancing in perfect step, trading the mic, singing words that Holly knows not just from Barbara's published book but from a coffee-stained legal pad where the first draft was jotted.

The song goes on for almost five minutes, a show closer for sure, and Holly is mesmerized, especially by the end, where everyone in the band falls out except for the driving drums.

"Let me hear you, Buckeye City!" Sista Bessie exhorts the empty seats. On Saturday night, Holly knows, five thousand people will be on their feet, singing, *Jazz, jazz, bring that shazz, do that Lowtown jazz.* Singing her friend Barbara's words. Holly feels like she's dreaming awake, the sweetest dream ever, and when the drums stop, she doesn't want to wake up.

Onstage, Betty and Barbara embrace.

"She really loves that girl," Tones says.

"She certainly does," Donald Gibson says, almost dreamily. "My, my, my. She certainly does."

5

Chrissy totes her suitcase behind the snackbar and sits on it, because she doesn't want to get the seat of her Kamala suit dirty. She has four bars on her Nokia burner. Most of the local news outlets are paywalled, but one indie site, operated by someone calling himself Buckeye Brandon, is free. There's a transcript for each of his podcasts. Chrissy selects the one for "The Surrogate Juror Murders: What We Know So Far," and reads it with great interest.

It confirms what she was already quite sure of, based on news reports she's listened to while traveling from Davenport to Buckeye City: she has, by either fate or pure accident, stumbled upon one of the Surrogate Murderer's victims. Buckeye Brandon's recap includes the names of the judge, the defense attorney, the prosecutor, and all the jurors—the twelve who actually decided Alan Duffrey's fate, plus two alternates. One of the primaries was Corinna Ashford, which is the name Chrissy found in the poor dead girl's hand. Buckeye Brandon doesn't seem to know that someone has been murdered in Ashford's name, probably because the police don't know or because they're holding it back.

Chrissy thinks the Surrogate Juror Murderer may be tempted to use the rink again. Possibly to gloat over his kill, possibly as a place to dump another body. *Because*, Chrissy thinks, *the trees around this place would be the perfect hunting ground for someone like this monster. Lots of homeless people dumpster-diving behind the food wagons, probably addicted to drugs and always looking for more. For all I know, cruising for drugs is how the dead girl in the old rink ran into her killer. What better place to put another kill than a condemned building? Did he send the police a picture of Corinna Ashford's name in that poor girl's hand?*

"I bet he did," Chrissy murmurs.

She can't be sure the Surrogate Murderer will be back, but he might be. All Chrissy knows is that she herself intends to stay here until

Kate McKay's lecture tomorrow night. If the man who killed that girl should return to the scene of the crime before then . . .

She unzips her purse. Inside are cosmetics, lotion, a mirror, a wallet with pictures of her mother inside (but no credit cards; Christine Stewart has none), safety pins, bobby pins, a little writing pad, a snack-sized bag of Doritos, and a .32 ACP. It's fully loaded, and that should be enough to take down Kate McKay. Plus the assistant and the bodyguard if necessary . . . but only if necessary. The last shot she's been saving for herself.

Now the gun has another purpose. It may be possible for her to serve the Lord not only by killing the female monster who advocates the murder of helpless babies; she may also be able to kill the crazy person who is murdering innocent strangers. She thinks that crazy person will come. *Must* come.

She thinks God put her here for more than one purpose.

6

The band has left, the star and the backup singers have left, the roadies and the techies are gone, the stage is dark. Only Trig remains, and he means to go back to his trailer-park home soon. *In all probability for my last night*, he thinks. There's some sadness in the thought, but no real regret. More and more he believes that he was lying to himself all along. It was never about creating guilt in those that caused Alan Duffrey's death; that was just an excuse. It was killing for the sake of killing, and since there is no Murderers Anonymous, there's only one way he can stop. And he will, after finishing the job . . . or at least as much of it as he can manage.

But the world must know.

He sits at his desk, bouncing the ceramic horse—Trigger—up and down, thinking about how to proceed. Then he puts it back in its place and opens an app on his desktop. It's titled MINGO SIGNBOARDS and controls the digital readout over the lobby doors and the huge signboard out front on Main Street, where passersby can read the current schedule. Right now those signs read FRIDAY MAY 30 7 PM KATE McKAY and SATURDAY-SUNDAY MAY 31 AND JUNE 1 SISTA BESSIE **SOLD OUT**.

The computer is asking him NEW SIGNBOARD? Y N.

Trig clicks on Y. A new field appears.

He types: AMY GOTTSCHALK JUROR 4 (KATE McKAY) BELINDA JONES JUROR 10 (SISTA BESSIE) DOUGLAS ALLEN PROSECUTOR (CORRIE ANDERSON) IRVING WITTERSON JUDGE (BARBARA ROBINSON) ALL GUILTY. He pauses, then adds: DONALD "TRIG" GIBSON JUROR 9 GUILTIEST OF ALL.

DONE? Y N.

He clicks on Y.

POST NOW N OR HOLD H?

He clicks H.

When the next field appears, the one for the time the signboards will change, he thinks carefully. The National Anthem at the charity game is key. If Sista Bessie sings it, all may go as planned.

He has no real belief that everything will work as he would like it to work—too many moving parts, too much unpredictability—but murder has made him a fatalist. He must move ahead and take what he gets.

He googles *How long on the average is the National Anthem at baseball games?* The answer is one minute and thirty seconds. He can't ask google if the softball game will start on time, but unless it gets going very late, it shouldn't matter. For all he knows (*too many moving parts, too much unpredictability*), Sista Bessie will slip in the shower, get a migraine, come down with Covid, get bopped on the head by an enthusiastic fan, *anything*, and be unable to sing at all.

With a sense of crossing his own bloody Rubicon, he types MAY 30 7:17 PM for the time his final signboard will replace the current one. The computer asks him to confirm, which he does.

If all goes as he hopes, tomorrow evening at 7:17 there will be a crowd milling in and around the Mingo, wondering where their idol is. Then someone will see the electronic signs change, and they will understand.

7

It isn't too hard for John Ackerly to locate "the woo-woo meeting where they turn off the lights and spark up candles." It's called the Twilight Hour, and convenes in the basement of a church in Upsala. He takes a drive out there, expecting nothing but hoping for any scrap of info he can pass along to Holly. If nothing else, he can get a shot of sobriety—"claim his chair," as they say in the various recovery programs.

It's a good meeting. John listens, but mostly he looks around, picking out half a dozen oldtimers. He speaks to several after the meeting, asking if they remember someone who identified as Trig. Two of them do, both vaguely; one of the old chestnuts passed around at meetings is that alkies and drug fiends have "a built-in forgetter," and it's true.

"Sure, I remember him," says Robbie M. "Bearded fella, but then I think he shaved. Mighta moved away." Robbie is on a pair of canes. He makes his way—slowly, painfully—into the church kitchen, where he pours himself a final paper cup of coffee. John shudders to think how strong the stuff must be at the bottom of the four-gallon urn.

"Anything about him stand out?"

"Nope. White, middle-aged—more or less—your size. Why you interested?"

"Just trying to track him down for a friend."

"Well, I can't help you. Big Book Mike might be able to, but he's dead."

I know, John doesn't say. *I found him*.

John is sure Holly would have more questions to ask, but he can't think of a single one. He thanks Robbie and heads for the door.

"Usually called himself Trig, but sometimes Trigger. Like the horse."

John turns back. "What horse?"

"Roy Rogers's horse. You wouldn't remember, too young. Couple of times, this was years ago, he ID'd himself by his real name."

"What real name?"

"Told you, it was years ago. Does it even matter?"

"It might. It might matter a lot."

"Could have been John. Like you." Robbie sips from his paper cup, frowning. "Although it might have been Ron." He scratches his wattled neck. Then, as a question: "Could have been Vaughn?"

John takes a napkin from beside the coffee urn and writes his number on it. "If you think of anything else about the guy, give me a call. Would you do that?"

Robbie drops him a wink. "He owe your friend money? Is that it?"

"Something like that. You take care, Robbie." He watches the old guy tuck the napkin into the back pocket of his timeworn Dickies workpants, where it will undoubtedly be forgotten.

8

Jerome is watching a late basketball game on TV when he gets a text from his sister.

Barbara: **Can you get Betty at the Mingo tomorrow? She wants to check show clothes/costumes with her dresser.**

Jerome: **Sure, already on the schedule.**

Barbara: **Pick her up there at 5:30 she said and bring her to the Garden City Plaza. She's got a special ride to Dingley Park in some fancy convertible. I think with the mayor. She says you should come with! ☺**

Jerome: **OK. BTW you look great in those tight pants.**

Barbara: **Shut up. 😊**

Jerome texts John Ackerly, asking if he's still up.

John: **Sure. Went to a meeting. Now watching the Cavs.**

Jerome: **Me too. Game sucks.**

John: **Totally.**

Jerome: **Can I pick you up at 5 PM tomorrow? Then U drive my car to the field?**

John: **OK, I'm there. Pick me up at Happy.**

The Cavs are getting their shit handed to them on the West Coast. Jerome turns off the TV and goes to bed.

Chapter 20

1

5:30 AM.

Holly doesn't sleep well unless she's in her own bed, and the stress of being Kate's security has further unbalanced her sleep cycle. She's awake before dawn but forces herself to lie quiet and do her morning meditations before getting up. When those are finished, she checks her phone and finds two new texts.

John: **I went to a meeting in Upsala last night. 2 old guys remembered Trig. No descriptions worth beans. Guy was white, had a beard, shaved it at some point. Called himself Trig or sometimes Trigger, like Roy Rogers's horse (?). A few times, maybe early in sobriety, he might have called himself by his real name, which could have been John. Or Ron. Or Don. Or maybe Lon as in Chaney bwa-ha-ha. I'll try again next week.**

Izzy: **Praying for rain so game will be canceled.**

Holly goes to the window and pulls open the drapes. The sun is coming up and there isn't a cloud in the sky. She texts **Thank you keep me informed** to John Ackerly. To Izzy: **Looks like you're out of luck.**

This turns out to be so true, Boo.

2

There's a Starbucks down the street from the hotel. Holly gets a caffè Americano and a breakfast sandwich. She loves the way coffee brings the morning world into focus. Loves mornings, period. It's when she feels most herself. She walks the seven blocks to Dingley Park to look at the field where her friend will find either glory or shame tonight (probably an exaggeration, but she's full of coffee). The bleachers now are empty, the foul lines scuffed almost to invisibility. She sits on the bottom bleacher for awhile, feeling the first sun warm her face, digging the day. A young man in a headscarf and tattered jeans bops up to her and asks if she has any spare change. Holly gives him a fivespot. He tells her thanks, ma'am, and gives her a soul shake before she can protest. When he's gone, she uses her hand sanitizer, sits awhile longer, and strolls back to the hotel, stopping on the way back to pick up—O rare luxury—an actual print newspaper.

This is the best part of the day, she thinks. *Hold onto it a little.* Except, of course, it's like the poet says: nothing gold can stay. As a seasoned investigator, she knows this.

3

In her room, she checks for fresh messages (none), reads her newspaper, and brews another cup of coffee (not as good as Starbucks but passable). At eight-thirty she knocks lightly on the door of Kate's suite. Both women are there. Kate is making notes for a speech she won't, as it happens, be giving. Corrie is on the phone in the suite's bedroom, working out logistics for Pittsburgh, the next stop on the tour. Kate is scheduled to speak at the Carnegie Library Lecture Hall, but given the way things have snowballed, that venue's now too small, and the PPG Paints Arena, which seats almost twenty thousand, is too big. Corrie tells whoever she's talking to that she doesn't want Kate to see a lot of empty seats. Listening to her, Holly thinks she really might be a presidential-level chief of staff someday.

"I'm going over to the Mingo to look around," Holly tells Kate. "Scope the place out. Do you need anything?"

"Nope."

"Please stay in the room until I come back. A few eBayers and right-to-lifers have already arrived."

"Yes, Mom," Kate says without looking up, and Holly realizes—with a kind of comic despair—that Kate will do exactly what she wants.

Holly pilots her Chrysler to the Mingo Auditorium and parks next to the Transit van. She has phoned ahead, and the Program Director's assistant, Maisie Rogan, is there to let her in.

"The boss isn't here yet, but I expect him by ten or so."

"Don't need him," Holly says. "Just want a look around."

"Before you ask, the entire staff has either gotten pictures of this Christopher Stewart dingbat or will get them as soon as they come in."

"Excellent, but there's something you should be aware of. He may be dressed as a woman and wearing a wig."

Maisie looks troubled. "Then how are we supposed to—"

"I know, it's a problem. You'll just have to do the best you can."

They take the elevator up to stage level, where Maisie shows her the video set-up. It's very good. Many cameras, many angles, few blind spots. The stage itself is littered with amps, monitors, mics, and music stands. Holly takes pictures so Kate will see what she has to work around. They go down a few steps at stage left and enter the auditorium. Holly is happy—no, delighted—to see that eventgoers will have to pass through metal detectors to enter the auditorium. Maisie shows Holly the various exits.

"We need to get out with as little fuss as possible," Holly says. She has no hope of dodging all the eBayers, but if Stewart is here ("the dingbat," she likes that), they may be able to dodge him. "Do you have any ideas?"

"I might," Maisie says. "It worked for Neil Diamond when he was here."

They take the elevator down to the break room, where a dozen or so employees are grazing at a buffet consisting of coffee, fruit, yogurt, and hardboiled eggs. On one wall is a sign reading REMEMBER YOU ARE DEALING WITH THE PUBLIC, SO SMILE! Below this are framed pictures of staff members, including not one, not two, but *three* stage managers.

"Why so many managers?" Holly asks.

"They rotate in and out. Mostly because our big shows are keyed around holidays. Those guys all work when we put on *The Nutcracker*. What a horror show that is, runny-nosed kids everywhere, don't get me started. Come on back."

She leads Holly past the buffet and back into the small kitchen. There's a door between the stove and the fridge that gives on the far end of the employees' parking lot.

"This is your escape route," Maisie says.

Holly takes pictures. "I'll tell Kate's assistant. And do me a favor?"

"I will if I can."

"Don't tell anyone we're going out this way." She says this with no real belief they can fool the eBayers, but as always, she has Holly hope.

4

11:15 AM.

Corrie spends five minutes on hold, all the time worrying she'll be late for her scheduled meeting with Donald Gibson at the Mingo. She's about to kill the call when the program coordinator at the North Hills Event Center breaks into the hold music and confirms (finally!) Kate at the venue for Tuesday, June 3rd, eight PM. It's just twelve minutes from downtown Pittsburgh, the seating capacity is ten thousand, and the Event Center's fee is reasonable.

She hangs up, lifts fisted hands over her head, and murmurs, "Anderson shoots, Anderson scores."

She hurries down to the second-floor fitness center to tell Kate, who is swimming early today. Holly is sitting by the pool, holding Kate's towel and reading about the Real Christ Holy Church on her iPad. Kate herself is churning tirelessly in her red bathing suit. Corrie tells Kate about the favorable change of venue in Pittsburgh. Kate gives her a thumbs-up, barely losing a stroke.

"I sat on hold forever, waiting to nail down that venue, and all I get is a quick attagirl," Corrie grumbles.

Holly gives her a smile. "Some poet or other said, 'They also serve who only stand and wait.' Or in our case, make phone calls and hold towels."

"That wasn't just 'some poet or other,' that was John Milton, the original cool-daddy versifier."

"If you say so."

"Have you heard anything more about Chris Stewart?"

"If you mean has he been arrested, I wish I could say yes, but he hasn't."

"What about the other man? The one who's killing jurors?"

"Not jurors, innocent people who *stand* for jurors, at least in this dingbat's mind. That's actually Isabelle Jaynes's case."

"But you're interested, right? Sent out one of your minions to investigate?"

Holly thinks of the little yellow creatures in *Despicable Me* and laughs. "John's not a minion, he's a bartender."

"Nothing from him?"

"Unfortunately, no."

"Okay. A girl can hope. I'm off to the Mingo to sign some insurance papers."

Holly frowns. "Really? I thought all that was done in advance."

"So did I, but the paperwork never seems to end. It's seventy per cent of my job. Make that eighty. I might stop at a couple of stores on the way back for a skirt and a pair of jeans. I also need pantyhose."

"Be careful."

"I'll be fine," Corrie says, and cocks a thumb at Kate. "She's the one you have to look out for."

5

11:30 AM.

While Corrie is in the hotel lobby waiting for an Uber, Izzy Jaynes is at Dingley Park's softball field and getting her game face on. She would much rather be doing police work, but since she has to be here, she means to do the best job she can. In part because the ceaseless razzing is slowly but surely making its way under her skin.

The firemen have ceded the field to the cops, but they're hanging out in the bleachers, snarking up hotdogs and fish tacos, amusing themselves with trash talk. Because she's slow-pitching batting practice for her PD guys, most of it is aimed at her. Some of it's harmless, but a lot of it is unpleasant sexist bullshit. Nothing she hasn't heard before—George Pill wants to know if those legs go all the way up—but that doesn't make it any better.

Izzy was a competitor in college, and a competitor on the cops. She's smart, but it was mostly that competitive streak that caused her to rise in a mere ten years from a police academy grad with a newbie short haircut to her current position in the detective squad. She may not be up to Holly Gibney's deductive skills—knows it, actually—but she also knows she's better than Tom Atta and most of the others on the detective squad. Lew Warwick knows it, too. It's why he called her in to look at the letter from Bill Wilson, aka Trig, aka who knows.

Let them think this is how I'll throw once the game starts, Izzy thinks. *Let them just think that.*

She can't throw as hard as Dean Miter, who last year held the FD team hitless for three innings, but she has that dropball, her secret weapon, and she has no intention of throwing it in front of Pill and the rest of the Hoses hosers.

Her phone vibrates twice in the pocket of her shorts, but she ignores it until everyone on the PD team—those who are here; more will arrive when their shifts are over—has had a chance to hit. The Surrogate Juror Murders are important, but the State Police have that for the time being. Keeping the peace in Buckeye City is important, but the County Sheriff's Department is supposed to be handling most of that tonight. She's worried about Kate McKay, too, but she has faith in Holly to keep the McKay woman safe.

All these things matter. The game tonight does not . . . except to Izzy it now does. She may not be able to no-hit the firemen as Dean Miter did for three innings last year, but she intends to stand up for the team and for herself. She intends to stuff some of that FD trash talk right down their smoke-eating throats. Her job has, for the time being, taken a backseat.

That would never happen with Gibney, she thinks as she totes a bucket of balls back to the PD dugout. *She'd keep her eyes on the prize.* And surprise-surprise, both of her missed calls are from Holly, who says she's in the hotel fitness center.

"Improving our skinny little bods, are we?"

"Watching my boss improve hers," Holly says. "I think she's almost done. Have you found out anything about anything?"

"Nope," Izzy says, hoping the guilt she feels doesn't show in her voice. The fact is, she hasn't even checked with Ken Larchmont, back at the station. Ken won't be playing softball tonight. He has to go two-fifty, and is nearing retirement.

"Nothing on Trig from any of the cops who go to meetings. Nothing on Stewart, either. Detective Larchmont is calling around at hotels, motels, and b-and-b's, double-checking, but so far, *nada*."

Feeling more guilty than ever, Izzy checks her phone to make sure Ken *hasn't* called her in the interim.

Holly says, "Stewart's gone to ground somewhere. Take it to the bank."

"Sounds about right."

"You're at the field?"

"Guilty as charged."

"Don't feel guilty. It's for a good cause, Izzy, and I have faith in you. You'll do well."

"Doing well would be nice," Izzy says. On the field, some of the firemen are heaving a ball around while the rest take batting practice. George Pill looks at Izzy, puts his hands on his hips, and does a comic bump and grind.

Keep laughing, shithead, Izzy thinks. *Wait until I get you in the batter's box.*

Be careful what you wish for.

6

12:00 PM.

The Anderson woman, Kate's assistant, shows up on the dot, which Trig appreciates. He's expecting to have an *extremely* busy day, but there's an upside: once it's over, he can rest in eternal darkness. He has "a god of his understanding," because the AA program insisted it would help to keep him sober, and it has, but he doesn't expect heaven or hell. The god of his understanding is a selfish being who assigns humans to oblivion and keeps eternal life all to itself.

He's waiting at the service entrance for her. He knew she probably wouldn't send the Uber driver away, as she's only expecting to sign a few papers, and he's prepared for that. He gives her a wave with one hand. The other remains in the pocket of his sportcoat jacket, touching a hypodermic needle loaded with 200 milligrams of pentobarbital.

Corrie waves back and he stands aside, extending a hand to usher her into the little kitchen. Once she's past him, he grasps her around the waist good and tight, kicks the door shut, and injects her in the soft spot at the base of her neck, just above the collarbone. Corrie's struggles are mercifully short. She collapses limply forward over his arm. He drags her to the L-shaped counter and props her against it. Her eyes are open but rolled up to whites. She's standing, but her chest doesn't appear to be moving.

Has he killed her? Even with this modest dose? Does it even matter? Because it might—if McKay's smart, she will demand proof of life—Trig slaps her across the face. Not with all his strength, but plenty hard. She takes a gasping, whooping breath. Trig finds the other hypo, ready to give her another, smaller dose, but Corrie slides sideways until her cheek rests on the counter. Her eyes are still open, one iris now showing, the other still gone. Drool trickles from the corner of her mouth, but she's breathing again on her own. Her knees buckle. Trig helps her down to the floor. He decides she can be left for a short time. *Very* short.

He goes out to the employees' lot and taps on the window of the Uber driver's car. "She's decided to stay a little longer."

Once the driver is gone, happy with his hefty cash tip, Trig opens the Transit van's back doors. He tries to lift Corrie in his arms and can barely manage. She's slim but muscular. He gets her under the arms instead and drags her to the service entrance door. Looks around. Sees no one in the sunstruck back parking lot. Well, maybe the ghost of his father. A joke but not a joke.

"Fuck you, Dad. Not flinching."

He takes two deep breaths, psyching himself up, and heaves her into the back of the van. Her lolling head bonks on the floor and rolls to one side. She makes a fuzzy interrogative sound, then begins snoring.

In the van, everything is prepared. He rolls her on her side—which will help in case she vomits—and binds her ankles together with gaffer tape he takes from a reusable Giant Eagle shopping bag. He puts her hands behind her and binds them to the small of her back, winding long strips of tape around her waist and cinching it tight. He would like to tape her mouth closed so if she wakes up she won't be able to scream, but there's the chance of her choking to death if she does vomit, and the internet says that can happen after a dose of pento.

He's sweating like a pig.

Trig has no more than slammed the Transit van's door when *another* car shows up, this one a black Lincoln sedan with GC PLAZA HOTEL COURTESY CAR on the turned-down visor. Getting out is Sista Bessie, looking as big as a battleship in a madras caftan. With her is another woman so skinny she's little more than a stuffed string.

"This is the boss of the venue," Sista Bessie says to her skinny companion. "I don't remember your name, sir."

He almost says Trig.

"Donald Gibson, Ms. Brady." And to the skinny woman: "Program Director."

What if she wakes up now? Wakes up and starts yelling?

"We are just going to look at some costumes and see if they need to be let out," Sista Bessie says. "I have put on a pound or three since starting rehearsals."

"More like ten," the skinny woman says. "Once you start singin, you a pig for your food." Her snow-white afro looks like a dandelion puff.

"This is Alberta Wing, my costumer and dresser," Sista says. "And I don't need to tell you she got a mouth on her."

"I say what I mean," Alberta Wing responds.

Trig smiles politely, thinking, *Go in go in GO THE FUCK IN!*

The hotel's courtesy car starts to pull away, but Sista Bessie yells, "*Wait up, now! Wait up!*"

The driver has got the windows closed so the air conditioning can get traction, but the Sista has got a set of lungs on her, and he hears. The taillights go on, then the backup lights. The driver's window rolls down. Sista takes a bulging wallet from her purse and extracts a bill. "For your trouble," she says.

"Oh, ma'am, you don't have to do that. It's part of the hotel's—"

"I insist," she says, holding the bill out.

"Isn't it just powerful warm," Alberta Wing says to Trig.

Is she waking up yet? Does she hear us?

"It surely is."

"This kind of weather is just boogery. No other word for it. What do you think, Mr. Gibson?"

"It is."

She nods. "Yes indeed it is. You sweatin *hard.*"

The black Lincoln glides away. Sista Bessie comes back. "You are nice to wait by the door for us," she says. "I'll probably spend most of the afternoon."

Is that a thump from inside the van? Or his imagination? Trig has a crazy yet vivid memory of "The Tell-Tale Heart," where the sound came from beneath the floorboards. *Like a watch wrapped in cotton*, Poe wrote, and how can he remember that from freshman year in high school? And why now?

Because all my plans can be undone by one cry from that van. Like a billion-dollar SpaceX rocket blowing up on the launching pad.

"I may even take a nap," Sista says. "Wonderful dressing room. Big long couch. I've stayed in some real dumps in my time."

"Lord, yes," Alberta Wing says. "Remember Wild Bill's in Memphis?"

"*That* place!" Sista laughs. "I was singin away and this fella in the front row ejected his night's worth of beer in his own lap. Never got up at all!"

That *was* a thump. He's sure of it.

"Let's go in, ladies, out of the hot sun." He ushers them into the kitchen and sees one of Corrie Anderson's loafers lying on the linoleum. He kicks it aside, into the shadow of the door. "You know to take the elevator to three, Ms. Brady, right?"

"Oh, I know my way," she says. "Two facts of show business: Know your way around the hall you're singin at, and never lose track of your purse. Come on, Albie, through this little coffee bar."

"I have to run an errand across town," Trig says. "Don't let anyone steal the silverware while I'm gone."

Sista Bessie laughs. Alberta Wing doesn't. Even in his distracted state, Trig thinks she's a woman who doesn't laugh much, and so what? All that matters is that they're on their way. Out of his hair.

Back outside, he hears muffled yells from the back of the van. He opens one of the doors and sees the troublesome woman rolling from side to side, trying to get free, and yes, she has vomited. It's on one cheek and in her hair.

He gets in back, shuts the doors, reaches into the pillowcase, and takes out the Taurus .22. He digs the muzzle into her breast. "I can stop you making noise this second. No one will hear the shot. Do you want that?"

She stills immediately, eyes wide and full of tears. "What do you want?" Slurry.

"You can live through this," he says, which is a lie. "But you must be still." He puts the gun in the pocket of his sportcoat and pulls a strip of tape from the roll.

She sees what he means to do and turns her head aside. "No! Please! My nose is clogged from throwing up! If you put that over my mouth I'll suffocate!"

He takes the spare hypodermic out (there are others, fully loaded, in his desk drawer). Hypo in one hand, tape in the other. "Which do you prefer? Always assuming you want to go on living, that is."

What if Sista Bessie comes out while he's dealing with this troublesome woman? Sista Bessie wanting something else? Stars *always* want something else. Bottles of water, fresh fruit, M&M's, a fucking *masseuse*.

Corrie nods at the tape. "But poke a hole in it."

Not knowing why he even gave her a choice (but feeling obscurely glad he did), Trig punches a hole in the strip of tape with the tip of the hypo and plasters it across her mouth. Only then does he realize he's forgotten something.

"Listen to me. Are you listening?" So much to remember!

This will never work. It's crazy. I'm *crazy. Daddy would laugh. Laugh and go upside my head.* "Gone," *Daddy said. At the Holman Rink he said that, during one of the eighteen-minute intermissions.*

"When he said that I knew," he tells Corrie. "It was in his voice." She only looks at him, eyes wide and brimming with tears. She doesn't know what he's talking about. *He* doesn't know, either.

So he tells himself.

"Never mind that. I need to know your phone's passcode. I'll say numbers from zero to nine. Each time I get the right number, nod your head. Understand me?"

She nods.

"Give me the wrong code and you'll be punished. Do you understand *that?*"

Of course she does.

Shouldn't have done it here, you dummy, Daddy says. *Should have waited. What if the Black singer comes out wanting you to get her a sandwich or a bottle of beer?*

Too late now. He takes the pen, says numbers, and one by one writes down the four-digit code.

7

12:20 PM.

Holly finally feels it's okay to stop by her apartment. Corrie's at the Mingo, with a bit of shopping to follow, and Kate is Zooming in her suite—a CNN interview followed by a taped sparring match for *The Five* on Fox News.

As a rule she's no fan of country music, but she happened on an Alan Jackson song that so struck her that she loaded it onto her phone and tablet. The song is called "Little Bitty," and she can (as she's sure they say in John Ackerly's AA program) *relate.* Her apartment is a version of that song: little-bitty washing machine, little-bitty drier,

mouth. It's Corrine Anderson, Kate McKay's assistant. Corrie sees Chrissy as well. Her eyes widen. Chrissy pulls back before the man can follow his prisoner's gaze—so she hopes—and runs lightfooted back to the snackbar.

Has he seen her? She doesn't know. If he has, she really will have to shoot him, but she no longer wants to do that unless she has to.

The man finally returns. She hears his footfalls approaching as he walks from one of the beams to the next, then the gritting of his shoes on the dusty lobby floor. She waits, gun clasped in her hands.

Look for his shadow, she tells herself, but the lobby is gloomy and there may *be* no shadow. *Listen, then, just listen.*

The gritting steps don't approach the snackbar, nor do they pause. The man goes back to the double doors instead. For a moment the lobby brightens as he steps out, then the gloom returns. There's a clunk as he uses the keypad to lock the door. Ears straining, she hears an engine start up, then dwindle.

He's gone.

9

12:55 PM.

Midday custom is slow at Happy, because there's no juke, no TV over the bar showing sports highlights, and they don't serve food other than peanuts and chips until evening, when it's only hotdogs. John Ackerly is taking advantage of the lull to load glassware into the dishwasher when his phone rings.

"Hey, is this John?" It's the voice of an old man who's spent most of his life smoking two packs a day. There is a juke wherever his caller is; John can hear Bonnie Tyler telling the world about her total eclipse of the heart.

"Yeah, this is John. Who've I got?"

"Robbie! Robbie M., from the Upsala meetin? I'm at the Sober Club in Breezy Point. Borrowed Billy Top's phone. You know Billy Top?"

"Seen him at meetings," John says. "Crewcut. Sells cars."

"That's him, right. Billy Top."

A Mr. Businessman type bellies up to the otherwise empty bar. He's red of eye and pale of face. To John's eye he looks like trouble. Mr. Businessman yells for a Scotch, no rocks. John serves him with a practiced pour.

"What can I do for you, Robbie?"

"I still can't member the name that guy used a couple of times instead of Trig, but I do member something he said at that Upsala meeting, had to've been more'n a year ago, but it stuck in my head because it was so fuckin funny. Got a big laugh from the group."

Mr. Businessman tosses back his Scotch and calls for another. John is good at reading people—as a bartender it's a survival skill—and besides being trouble (or because of it), this guy has the look of a man who just got bad news. *I'll be pouring him out of here around three o'clock*, he thinks, but the guy is still relatively sober, so John pours him another drink but tells him to slow down.

"What?" Robbie asks.

"Wasn't talking to you. What did John or Ron say that was so funny?"

"He said, 'Have you ever tried to hire someone to clean up elephant shit at ten in the morning?' Got a big laugh."

"Thanks, Robbie." Thinking, *For nothing*. "If you think of his name, call me back."

"I'll do that, and if your friend gets some money, push a few bucks my way."

"I don't—"

Just then Mr. Businessman picks up his glass, rears back, and throws it at the backbar mirror, which shatters and knocks several bottles of booze—not well pours, either, the expensive stuff—off the shelf. He then bursts into tears and puts his hands over his face.

"Gotta go, Robbie. Trouble in the valley."

"What kind of tr—"

John ends the call and dials 911. Mr. Businessman puts his face down on the bar and begins sobbing. John goes around the bar and gives him a squeeze on the shoulder. "Whatever it is, buddy, it'll pass."

10

In the Breezy Point Sober Club, Bonnie Tyler has been replaced by Chrissie Hynde talking about life on the chaingang. Billy Top is holding out his hand for his phone. Robbie hands it over.

"That guy didn't call himself Ron or John," Robbie says. "It was Don. It just come to me. Out of the blue, like."

"That always happens when you stop trying to think of sumpin," Billy Top says. "Rises up to the top of your mind. Want to play box hockey?"

"You're on," Robbie says, and five minutes later he's forgotten all about the guy who needed elephant shit cleaned up at ten in the morning.

Chapter 21

1

1:00 PM.

Someone is walking toward Corrie, stepping carefully across the beams laid on the concrete floor. She turns her head as far as the tape around her neck will allow, which isn't far. She's not quite choking, but it's like breathing through a tube. It makes the headache from whatever Gibson dosed her with that much worse. She can't believe this has happened to her. And that it happened so fast.

It's a dark-haired woman in a pants suit, but the rink is so shadowy that Corrie can't make out her face at first . . . but when she speaks, Corrie recognizes that low, slightly husky voice. She heard it once before, in Reno. Telling her to suffer not a woman to usurp the authority of man. *First Timothy, bitch.*

"Hello, Corrie Anderson. This time I know who you are. And I bet you know who I am."

Corrie does. It's Christopher Stewart.

Stewart drops to one knee in front of the penalty box and stares at her the way a scientist might study a test animal that will soon be sacrificed to the greater good. Which is exactly what Corrie feels like. Her terror is overlaid by surrealism. She could almost believe she's having a terribly vivid nightmare, because how likely is it that she should be drugged and taken prisoner by one obviously crazy man only to be confronted by another?

"He didn't kill you," says the man in the wig. "He killed the other one, but not you."

Stewart half-turns and holds out his hand like a game-show host displaying tonight's big prize. Corrie sees a shape lying on the criss-crossing beams at what was once center ice. Almost *melting* there. She realizes with growing horror that it's a dead body, and further realizes that what she's smelling isn't just the residue of whatever this lunatic drugged her with.

As if reading her mind, Stewart says, "The poor girl is starting to stink, isn't she? I could even smell it outside."

Please let me go, I'm not the one you want, Corrie tries to say, but of course nothing comes out through the hole in the tape but muffled sounds that bear no resemblance to actual words.

"Killed the other one, but not you," Stewart repeats. "And I think I know why."

Even with her headache and still woozy from the shot, Corrie thinks she also knows why. Stewart says it for both of them.

"You're *bait*."

2

1:15 PM.

Trig returns to the Mingo and backs the Transit van up to the service entrance door. He goes inside the little kitchen, sees Corrie's shoe, and stuffs it deep in the trash. She won't be needing it again.

He takes the stairs, not wanting the Black singer and her dressing person to hear the elevator, know he's back, and come down with annoying requests. He's got his own business to attend to, his own plan. Which is crazy, of course. He knows that. He's read that the odds of winning two dollars on a one-buck scratchoff ticket are four to one. He thinks the odds of this scheme working are considerably higher. Not astronomical, human nature being what it is, but high. Maybe fifteen to one.

I'll get some of them, no matter what. If I could talk a potentially hung jury into convicting Alan Duffrey, I can get at least some of them.

"I was positive he was guilty," Trig says as he reaches the top of the stairs. *"Positive."* But there was plenty of blame to go around. Plenty of fault. They should have had the courage of their convictions. They shouldn't have buckled. Shouldn't have flinched.

Lowry saying let's vote again, I'm losing business at my store, and that time he finally voted guilty. That just left Bunny. How did I do it? How did I talk them around?

"I just channeled my father," he says. "It was easy."

He can hear women's laughter from the third floor. Sista Bessie and the skinny one, Alberta what's-her-face. He goes into his office. He pats his sportcoat pocket to make sure he's got Corrie's phone. He has a call to make on it, but that's for later. Right now he checks his computer for the numbers of Sista's band and support staff. Barbara Robinson's name and number were a late add, but as his daddy used to say, better late is gooder than never.

Trig picks up the ceramic horse. Caresses it. It's sort of a good luck charm. Daddy said Trigger was a palomino. Expensive horses to buy, and Daddy also said that Roy Rogers had Trigger stuffed when he died, which somehow seems like *bad* luck, but never mind that.

Trig calls Barbara, and Robinson answers on the second ring. In the background he can hear laughing voices, shouts, and the *tink* sound of metal bats on balls. He deduces she's spending her off day at Dingley Park.

Trig has thought of and rejected half a dozen pretexts to bring Barbara Robinson back to the Mingo before realizing that he doesn't need one, not really. He just has to sound suitably serious.

"Hi, Ms. Robinson. This is Don Gibson, the Mingo Program Director?"

"Hi. What can I do for you?"

"Well . . . Ms. Brady is asking for you. She's here at the Mingo."

"What does she want?" The sounds from the ballfield are fading as she walks away from them. She's caught his sober tone. Good.

"I don't know," Trig says. "She won't tell me. She's in her dressing room, and it sounds to me like she's crying."

Barbara says, "I'll be there as fast as I can."

"Thank you," Trig says. "I think that would be best. I'll wait for you at the service entrance and let you in."

Easy as that.

He ends the call, opens his desk drawer, and removes a slim black leather case. In it are six more hypodermic needles loaded with pentobarbital. He doesn't expect to need all of them, but always safe, never sorry. He plucks out one of the capped-for-safety needles and stows the case in his pocket.

3

1:35 PM.

Holly is entering the lobby of the Garden City Plaza Hotel, having made her way through the growing crowd outside—fans of Sista Bessie, fans of Kate, people hating on Kate. No one pays any attention to Holly, which is just the way she likes it.

Halfway across the lobby her phone rings. It's John Ackerly. "Hey, Holly, how are you?"

"Fine. And you?"

"It's been an exciting day at Happy."

"What happened?"

"Obstreperous drunk. He did some damage—to the bar, not to me—and the cops took him away."

"I'm sorry to hear that."

"Not the first time for something like that, won't be the last. I called because I talked to an old guy named Robbie at a meeting last night, and again just before the shit hit the fan. He said the guy you're looking for—"

"That *Izzy's* looking for," Holly says.

John laughs. "Calling bullcrap on that. I know how you roll—once you start, you don't quit."

Holly doesn't dispute this. "Go on."

"Robbie remembered something the guy said. 'Try to get someone to clean up elephant shit at ten in the morning.' Or words to that effect. It was at a meeting and got a big laugh. Does *that* mean anything to you?"

"No." And it doesn't. Except it makes her recall her trip to the auditorium the night before. Why, she doesn't know. She thinks of pulling up in the employees' parking lot in her boat of a Chrysler. Sista Bessie's tour manager and the Mingo's Program Director waiting to meet her.

For a moment she almost has whatever has been eluding her, but before she can grasp it, she's back on how great it was to watch Barbara dance and sing while the band got its groove on . . . and it's gone.

"Well, I told you what I heard," John says. "All I can do. I'm leaving the bar early and meeting up with Jerome. We're bringing Sista Bessie to the hotel. Don't hate me for hanging out with the stars."

"I'll try not to," Holly says.

"Jerome's riding with her to Dingley Park. Doing the bodyguard thing."

"Bodyguards everywhere," Holly says. "We are busy people."

"But nobody has to clean up elephant poop," John says, and again she almost has it . . . has something, anyway . . . but it slips away again. *Give it time*, she thinks. *Give it time and it'll float to the surface.*

Then she thinks that's what they say about drowning victims.

4

1:50 PM.

To Trig it's like the second performance of a play. This one goes a little smoother, as second performances tend to. Barbara arrives in an Uber but sends it away, which solves one problem. She speed-walks to the service door, gives him a quick smile, and hurries inside. He grasps her around the waist and shoots her up—*déjà vu* all over again. She struggles, then sags into unconsciousness.

Trig bundles her into the Transit van and binds her as he bound Corrie, only this time also duct-taping her to a side stanchion so she can't roll around and kick the side of the van when she comes to, perhaps attracting attention. He pops her purse into the Giant Eagle bag along with Corrie's phone, more rolls of duct tape, and a large can of Kingsford charcoal lighter fluid.

Trig thinks of his father saying *Practice makes perfect.* He used to say that when they were facing off in the driveway, Trig with his own little hockey stick. His father would flick the puck at him and thump him a good one on the arm every time he flinched away.

Practice makes perfect.

And: *Gone. That's all you need to know.*

"And I *did* know," Trig says.

The young woman's eyes flutter but don't open. The breathing through her nose is snotty but regular. Trig drives to the Holman Rink.

Two down, two to go.

The big ones.

5

1:55 PM.

Holly has just downloaded an article to her laptop when there's a light knock on her door. It's Kate. "No press conference this afternoon. I'm holding my fire for tonight. What are you up to?"

"Backgrounding Christopher Stewart. And his church. It may help."

"Background leads to foreground? Is that it?"

"Something like that. Do you need me?"

"No. I'm going to put the DO NOT DISTURB on my door and take a power nap. Corrie's still out shopping. Poor girl can use a break. I've been running her ass off."

Not exactly the way Holly would have put it, but accurate enough. "Do you want me to give you a wake-up?"

"No need, I'll set my phone." She bends over Holly's shoulder to look at the screen. "Is that them? The Church of One Hundred Per Cent Jesus, or whatever they call themselves?"

"Yes. This one's from the *Lakeland Times*, in Minocqua, Wisconsin."

The headline reads, BARABOO JUNCTION CHURCH HOLDS PRAYER VIGIL AT NORMA KLEINFELD CLINIC. The accompanying photo shows two dozen people kneeling in the rain. Lined up behind them on the sidewalk are placards showing bloody fetuses and slogans like I ONLY WANTED TO LIVE and WHY DID YOU KILL ME?

Holly taps the screen. "This is Christopher Stewart, your stalker. The man next to him is the one I talked to while you were swimming. Andrew Fallowes. I don't know for sure if he wound Stewart up like a little clockwork toy, but I think he did."

She turns and is surprised to see tears in Kate's eyes.

"No one wants to kill babies." Kate's voice is hoarse and unsteady. "No one in their right mind, anyway."

"Are you sure you don't want to put a hold on your appearances until Stewart is caught?"

Kate shakes her head. "We keep on." She wipes her eyes in a fast, angry gesture. "And you didn't see that."

"See what?"

Kate grins and gives Holly's shoulder a light squeeze. "That's the right attitude. Hold onto it. I'll be up by four-thirty. Five at the latest."

"All right." Holly turns back to her laptop. *Background leads to foreground*. She likes that.

"Holly?"

She turns. Kate is in the doorway.

"It's not easy being the bad bitch. The devil-dog. Do you know that?"

"Yes," Holly says.

Kate goes out.

6

2:15 PM.

Sportcoat Man returns. He brings in another one, also young and barely conscious.

Once he's in the arena, Chrissy returns to the doorway. She knows it's dangerous, but she has to see. She watches as Sportcoat Man binds the new one to the penalty box's other post. He then takes a picture of Corrie Anderson with one phone and the new arrival with another. When he straightens up, pocketing the phones and saying something to the new one, Chrissy catfoots back to her hiding place behind the snackbar.

Once Chrissy is sure Sportcoat Man is gone, she walks into the arena and goes to one knee in front of the new one.

"I have nothing against you. I want you to know that."

The young woman's mouth is taped shut, but her eyes are easy enough to read: *Then let me go!*

"I can't free you. Not yet. Eventually I may be able to." She repeats, "I have nothing against you," and walks back into the lobby to wait for the one she wants. The one that God, working through the agency of Sportcoat Man, is going to deliver to her. Chrissy is sure of it.

The two women can't even look at each other; the tape around their necks is cruelly tight. Barbara can press her shoulder against that of the other woman. And the other woman presses back. It's not much in the way of comfort . . . but it's something.

7

2:30 PM.

Trig has barely returned to his office at the Mingo when the scrawny Black woman, Alberta what's-her-face, gives a token rap on the door and then walks in uninvited. She's got a sparkly dress over her arm.

"Betty nappin," she says. "Wants you to wake her up around four-thirty. I got to let this dress out back at the hotel. She gettin so *fat*."

"Do you need me to call a—"

"A ride? Already got one, he should be waitin. Damn well better be, cause time is *tight*. Four-thirty, mind. Don't forget."

Ordinarily Trig would be irritated at being treated like a flunky, especially by someone who's a flunky herself, but this afternoon it doesn't bother him. Too many things to do, too many balls in the air.

What if they get free somehow?

That's stupid, the kind of thing that only happens on TV shows. They're trussed up like turkeys.

"Grocery day?" the scrawny Black woman asks. She flashes many white teeth in an alligator grin.

"What?"

"I ast if it's grocery day." She points beside his desk, and he sees he's brought in the Giant Eagle bag. Wasn't even aware of it.

"Oh . . . no. Just a few things. Personal things."

"Few *scanty* things?" The alligator grin widens and she waggles her eyebrows like Groucho Marx. What is she implying? He has no idea. Then the grin winks off like a neon sign. "Just kiddin witcha. Don't forget my gal Betty."

"I won't."

The Black woman leaves. He hears the whine of the elevator going down. Sista Bessie is snoozing in her dressing room. That's good. *Very* good. And he'll wake her up, all right. Yes indeed, she'll get the wake-up of her life. He could do her right now, the place is empty and no one would hear the shot, but she needs to sing the National Anthem. It will be her swan song. The signboard needs to change at 7:17, while the game is going on at Dingley and at the Mingo the crowds are wondering where the hell Kate is.

In a weird echo of Chrissy Stewart, Trig says, "I have nothing against any of you. You're just . . ." What? What are they? The right words come to him. "You're stand-ins. Proxies. *Surrogates*."

The murders have to happen at the Holman Rink, because that was where Daddy told Trig that his mother was gone, which meant never coming back, which meant dead, which meant Daddy killed her. The Holman Rink was where Trig finally understood that fact. Did not run off, as Daddy told the police.

It would be nice to believe that it was Daddy who made Trig an alcoholic. That made him a murderer. That made him the one who had badgered the three holdouts on the Duffrey jury to give in and vote to convict.

None of those things are true. He was a drunk from the first drink and a serial killer from the first murder. Finding out that Duffrey had been falsely convicted, then murdered in prison . . . that was like the first drink. A pretext. He has a character flaw, it is intractable, and will only end with the death of the guiltiest one of all. Which is him.

But it still must end at the Holman Rink, and it must end—*will* end—in fire. The next call will go to Kate McKay, but not for a little while. Let tonight's big game on the other side of the park get closer. And let him think of exactly what he will say to her to make her come . . . and make her keep her mouth shut. He suspects these things may turn out to be quite easy. He has seen YouTube vids of her in action, and knows her for what she is—a woman used to doing things herself, and used to getting her way.

C'mon, Trig thinks. *C'mon, c'mon, c'mon.*

8

3 PM.

In Dingley Park, off-duty cops and firemen are bringing in beer in coolers and nips in the pockets of cargo shorts. PD and FD who *are* on duty are also drinking. The carny atmosphere spreads under the warm sunshine, and the trash talk grows thorns.

Izzy gets a soda and makes some calls, hoping that either Bill Wilson (aka Trig) or Christopher Stewart has been apprehended. No luck. She looks around for Barbara, but Barbara has left. She *does* see George Pill, who points at her, then grabs his crotch. *Stay classy, George*, Izzy thinks.

In her hotel room, Holly has given up on research—Real Christ Holy is just too depressing—and stands looking out the window. She has *seen* something . . . or *heard* something . . . and until she can recall it (and hopefully dismiss it), it's driving her buggy.

I drove to the Mingo. I parked in the service area beside a white van. I went to the door. The bald man, the tour manager, said we all love Barbara. He said she sings, she dances, she plays the tambo on the beat, she writes poems . . . what can't she do? He said a star is born. What does that mean? What *can* it mean? Holly knocks her knuckles on the side of her head. "What am I missing?"

In the large third-floor dressing room of the Mingo, Betty Brady is asleep on the couch and dreaming of her childhood in Georgia: bare feet, red dirt, a dime bottle of Co'-Cola.

Arriving at the Garden City Plaza Hotel, Alberta Wing surveys the growing number of pro-life protestors on the far side of the street and wonders how many of the neatly groomed white women in that crowd would be willing to give birth to a stone-blind baby amid the trash and discarded liquor bottles behind the Dilly Delight Smokehouse in Selma, Alabama. Before setting to work on the dress Betty will wear tomorrow night, she lets out the sequined bellbottoms her old friend and homegirl will wear to sing the National Anthem in a few hours. *Your booty gets much bigger, you won't be able to get it through the door*, she thinks, and laughs. She puts the bellbottoms on a hanger along with the starry sash Betty means to wear around her middle. Once the song is sung, Bets will duck into her dressing room—a little cubicle set aside for her in the equipment shed—and put on some jeans and a hoodie, which Alberta also puts on a hanger. She thinks of the white Program Director's guilty expression when he looked at the grocery bag, and wonders what he had in there. She has to laugh.

At Happy, John Ackerly is ready to turn things over to his stand-in, Ginger Brackley. Across the broken backbar mirror he's tacked a checked tablecloth and written on it with a Sharpie: WE HAD A SLIGHT ACCIDENT. "I'm doing this for you, so you better get her autograph for me," Ginger says, and John says he'll try.

In his apartment, Jerome puts on his best black pants, a nice blue cotton shirt, a thin gold chain, and black hightop Converse sneakers (a bold touch). He puts some shea in his hair—just a bit—and is ready two hours early, but too excited to even think about writing or researching Army of God churches. He tries Barbara, but her phone boinks immediately to do not disturb. When invited to leave a message, he tells her to turn her damn phone back on because he wants to meet her at the game.

In the Holman Hockey Rink, two bound women wait on hands and knees as the minutes crawl by.

Behind the snackbar, Chrissy is also waiting. She knows who the kidnapper is. The media even has a name for him: the Surrogate Juror

Killer. Sportcoat Man is also God's servant, although he doesn't know it. If he comes back with Kate McKay, this can end. Chrissy thinks she might even be able to get away. Surely it's not wrong to hope.

9

3:50 PM.

A long time ago, in a galaxy far far away—actually the Gibson driveway in the early 1990s—Daddy would flick a hockey puck at his little Trigger, who would be dressed in a child-sized Buckeye Bullets uniform, complete with goaltender's helmet . . . and Daddy would flick it *hard.* If Mommy saw, she'd shout out the kitchen window, *You stop that, Daniel!* Called him Dan or Danny most of the time, Daniel only when she was mad at him. Which happened more and more often. Once she was *gone*, there was nobody to make Daddy stop. Practice was hell, and hell went on. *Practice makes perfect*, Daddy would say, and every time Trig shrank from the puck, Daddy would yell, *Don't flinch! Don't you flinch, Trigger! You're a goaltender just like Cujo, just like Curtis Joseph, so don't you flinch!* And when Trig couldn't help it, Daddy would give him a look of disgust and say, *Get after it, Useless. That's another goal for the bad guys.* And Trig would have to go out in the street to get the puck.

"Don't flinch," he murmurs to himself as he takes Corrie Anderson's phone from the grocery bag. "Don't you flinch."

If the McKay woman calls the cops . . . or tells her skinny little bodyguard, who will probably *convince* her to call the cops . . . everything will collapse. No way around it. But there is a certain grim irony in what he's about to do, which he appreciates. Making the Duffrey jurors feel guilty was only a pretext (he realizes that now), and probably useless, but now everything depends on more convincing, and inducing a very real sense of guilt. He thinks: *Only guilt can make this work.*

The puck is flying. It may hit him in the mouth, but he will not flinch.

He makes the call.

10

3:55 PM.

Kate has her phone silenced, with three exceptions: Holly, Corrie, and her mother. Her ringtone wakes her from paper-thin sleep and a dream of plucking daisy petals with her mother as a child: *loves me, loves me not*. Kate gropes for the phone, thinking, *It's Mom, she's worse. As long as she's not dead.* Roselle McKay, so young and beautiful in her dream, is now elderly and bald and sick from a combination of chemo and radiation.

Kate struggles to a sitting position and sees it's not Mom, which is a relief. It's Corrie. But when she answers, it's not Corrie who speaks to her.

"Hello, Ms. McKay." A strange male voice. "You need to listen to me very careful—"

"Where's Corrie? Why have you got her phone? Is she all right?"

"Shut up and listen."

Politicians and pundits across America could testify on how hard it is to silence Kate McKay, but the imperative in those four words—the *savage* imperative—does it.

"I have your Ms. Anderson. She's tied up and gagged but unhurt and alive. Whether or not she remains alive depends entirely on you."

"What—"

"Shut up. Listen to me."

"It's you, isn't it? Christopher Stewart."

"Ms. McKay, I can't waste time telling you to shut up, so the next time you get off the subject at hand, I'm going to put a bullet in Ms. Anderson's knee and she'll never walk straight again even if she lives. Do you understand me?"

For once in her life Kate has no idea what to say, but Holly (were she there) would recognize the deer-in-the-headlights expression Kate was wearing when the man holding the baseball bat came at her.

With what might be a certain dry humor (how grotesque), her caller says, "If you understand, you can say yes."

"Yes."

"I'll send you a picture of Ms. Anderson so you know she's all right. So far. You will come to the Holman Hockey Rink, in Dingley Park. By the time you arrive, there will be people coming into the park from Buckeye Avenue and Dingley Plaza to attend a charity softball game to be played there tonight, but the Holman Rink is on the other side of the park, abandoned and condemned. Take Service Road A. Your GPS will show it to you."

She chances an interruption. "Sir . . . Mr. Stewart . . . there are tons of people in front of the hotel who know what I look like."

"That's your problem, Ms. McKay. Solve it. Use the brain God gave you. I want you at the rink between five-fifteen and five-thirty. That fifteen-minute window is the key to Ms. Anderson's survival. Get there earlier or later, and she dies. Tell anyone, *anyone at all*, and she dies. If you come, and come alone, you both will live."

"Are you—"

"Shut up. If you ask me even one more question, I won't bother with putting a bullet in her knee, I'll kill her right now. Do you understand that?"

"Y-Yes."

When was the last time she stuttered? College? High school?

"Let me recap. Holman Rink, between five-fifteen and five-thirty, which is approximately seventy-five minutes from now. If you don't show up, she dies. If you tell anyone and I find out—I have my ways—she dies. Show up accompanied by someone else, she dies. Understood?"

"Yes." She's awake now, all the interior lights on and turned up to bright. *Is* this Stewart? She can't understand why it would be anyone else, but he sounds older than the man looks in Holly's photographs.

It must be him.

"Show up according to my instructions, and you both walk away unharmed."

Sure, Kate thinks, *and we won in Vietnam.*

The phone goes dead, but six seconds later it vibrates as a text comes in. She opens it and sees Corrie duct-taped, almost mummified, to a steel post coated with peeling yellow paint. Her eyes are wide and full of tears. Her mouth has been sealed with duct tape wound around the back of her head and Kate thinks—funny how random thoughts intrude—that the tape will pull out chunks of her hair when it comes free. That will hurt . . . but only if she's alive to feel it.

Now she begins to feel anger. She thinks of Holly, then rejects the idea, and not just because her caller *has his ways*. Holly is good at her job—the speed with which she kicked the folding chair in front of that rampaging bull of a man confirmed that—but this particular monstrosity would be beyond her. She looks like a strong gust of wind would blow her away, she's rather timid, and—face it—she's getting on in years.

Besides, Kate wants to handle it herself.

She wishes she *had* bought guns for her and Corrie; this might not have happened if she had insisted that Corrie carry a piece, but in the onrush of events she never even tried. What she *does* have is the Sabre Red Pepper Spray Holly supplied her with.

She looks long and hard at the picture Christopher Stewart has sent her (because it must be him, who else). Corrie taped to a steel pole like an insect caught in flypaper. A breathing-hole punched in the tape over her mouth. Corrie, who has already had bleach thrown in her face and could have inhaled a deadly poison, except for her own quick wits. Corrie looking like a horror movie actress about to be sacrificed to a horror movie killer—not the Final Girl but the Second-to-Final Girl, the one who gets fourth billing in the credits.

She writes a brief note to Holly and sticks it on the suite's bedroom door with one of the Dr. Scholl's callus pads she keeps in her purse. Then she picks up the hotel phone, identifies herself, and asks for the hotel manager. When he's on the line, she says: "How can I get out of here without being seen?"

Chapter 22

1

4 PM.

Trig's office is on the second floor of the Mingo Auditorium. The dressing rooms are on the third. Talking to Kate McKay on the phone was all well and good, but with Sista Bessie, facetime would be better. He needs to think about it, and very carefully.

He decides a little shock therapy might be in order.

2

4:05 PM.

Holly has called Jerome and asked him if cleaning up elephant poop at ten AM means anything to him. Jerome said it didn't. She tried Barbara to ask the same question and her call went straight to voicemail. Holly guessed she was either in the shower or practicing her dance moves as an honorary Dixie Crystal.

She decides to take advantage of a no–press conference day by lying down and having her own power nap, but she's too wired to even doze. She missed something that should be too big and obvious to miss . . . and yet she *is* missing it.

An idea comes to her, maybe brilliant. She sits up, grabs her phone, and calls a person who probably knows as much about Buckeye City as anyone: her recently retired partner, Pete Huntley.

3

4:10 PM.

There's a star decaled onto the door of Sista Bessie's dressing room, and a taped sign that says, KNOCK BEFORE ENTERING. Trig simply barges in. The woman is sprawled on the pull-out couch and fast asleep. Dressed in her slop-around clothes, she doesn't look famous, and lying still instead of doing various rock-and-soul moves around the stage, mic in hand, she looks ginormous.

She hears him come in and sits up, first rubbing her eyes and then looking at her watch—not a Patek Philippe or even a Rolex, but a plain old Swatch. "I told Alberta I could sleep until four-thirty, but since you're here—"

She starts to get up. Trig advances two steps, puts his spread fingers into the top-swell of one breast, and pushes her back down on her fat ass. This gives him surprising pleasure. He's seen a lot of famous people come and go, and in his heart of hearts, he's always wanted to do that. They all think they are God's anointed because they can attract a crowd, but they put their pants on one leg at a time just like anyone else.

Meanwhile, time is fleeting and the puck is flying. Too late to turn around. Too late to flinch.

She stares at him from the edge of the couch. "What in the *hail* do you think you're doin, Mr. Gibson?"

He pulls over the chair in front of the makeup mirror and sits on it backwards, cowboy-style. "Making sure you're fully awake and aware. Listen to me, Sista whatever-your-real-name-is. Very closely."

"Name's Betty Brady." She is fully awake and aware now, and looking at him with narrowed eyes. "But since you seen fit to push me, why don't you go on and call me ma'am."

He has to smile at that. She's got some sand. She makes him think of Belinda "just call me Bunny" Jones in the jury room. She had some sand, too. Once Lowry gave in, Bunny was the last holdout. But he wore her down, didn't he?

He says, "Okay, ma'am, that's fine with me. You'll be leaving here soon, I understand you're planning to go back to the hotel and change clothes for your appearance at Dingley Park, and I won't stop you from doing that. With me so far?"

"With you, yes I am. Cain't wait to see where this is goin." Sounding almost pleasant, but also sounding more southern, and looking at him with those same narrowed eyes.

"Once you leave, you can do whatever you want, it's your decision, but you should look at this before you make it."

He holds up Barbara Robinson's phone and shows Sista Bessie—his ma'am—the picture of Barbara bound to one of the penalty box poles.

Betty puts her hand to the wattles below her throat. "Mother of God, what . . . what—"

"My partner has a gun on her." Trig produces this lie smoothly. "If you tell the cops, if you tell *anybody*, she's going to die. Got it?"

Betty says nothing, but her expression of dismay is all Trig could have hoped for. The singer has been a weak point all along. (Well, there are actually *lots* of weak points, it's an extremely rickety plan, but this is one of the weakest.) How much does this woman, this *star*, care for her new friend? He listens; *keeps his ear to the ground*, as they say. So, for that matter, does Maisie, who is all about famous people. They've heard enough to know Sista Bessie has taken the girl under her wing. Enough to always keep the girl's book of poems close and to have included her in the band, at least for this first gig. Enough—this to Trig's mind is the convincer—to have adapted one of the girl's poems into a song important enough to be the show closer.

Enough for him to take the chance.

"If you've got it . . . ma'am . . . give me a nod."

Betty nods without taking her eyes from the picture of Barbara. It's as if she's hypnotized by it, the way a bird can supposedly be hypnotized by a snake, and for the first time Trig really believes this rocket will fly.

"For the next three hours or so, can you act as if nothing is wrong? Go through with singing the National Anthem before that game?"

She thinks about it, then says, "Back in the day, I once played Giants Stadium with intestinal flu in front of eighty-two thousand people. Didn't want to disappoint em, so I wore Depends. Threw up at intermission and nobody but the boys in the band ever knew. I can do it, but only if you convince me you mean to let her go."

"I mean to let *both* of you go. But let's not get ahead of ourselves. Once you finish the Anthem, I'll give you a call and tell you where to come and get her. It's not far."

She gives him a goggly-eyed look, then laughs. Actually *laughs*. "You are one crazy white man and you are also one *dumb* white man."

"Enlighten me."

"I sing the song. Not eighty-two thousand watchin me do it, but as many as that park'll hold. I go back to change my clothes in the little room they got set aside for me, and when I come out, there's going to be two, maybe three hundred people standin outside and hopin to get my autograph or at least a picture. You think I can just slip away? Shi-*yit*."

Trig hasn't considered this. He expects the other one, McKay, will find a solution, because hotels—the good ones, at least—usually have a way or even two ways by which celebrities can make a quick and quiet escape. But from a makeshift dressing room in the cinderblock equipment building at the softball field? To coin a phrase, that's a very different ballgame.

But because the plan depends on it, he says what he said to Kate McKay. "Find a way."

"Let's say I do. Do you expect me to believe you're goan let her and me go? I was born at night but it wasn't *last* night, and I have an idea who you are. You been killin people in this town, Mr. Gibson. So like I say, convince me."

Lies work best when the person being lied to wants to believe. They also work best when they are combined with the truth. Trig employs both strategies now.

"I was on the jury that convicted an innocent man named Alan Duffrey. I had help from an ambitious, self-righteous prosecutor and from the man who framed him, but that's no excuse for what I did, which was browbeating three jurors who felt that Duffrey was telling the truth when he testified in his own defense. If not for me, that jury would have hung. And do you know what happened to Alan Duffrey?"

"Nothing good, I'm guessin."

"Killed in prison before the truth came out. The load of guilt I've been carrying since . . ."

He shakes his head as if this were actually true, but he no longer believes it is, or ever was. His mother used to say—before she was *gone*—that popcorn is just an excuse to eat butter. He now believes that the guilt he hoped to load onto his fellow jurors was just an excuse to commit murder.

But she's giving him a look like she understands. Of course that might be what he thinks of as the Celebrity Sincere Face. Most of them are good at it.

"I've decided to show mercy," he says. "You and the young woman—Barbara—can walk away from this. There's another pair of women who may not be so lucky. Or perhaps they will be. I haven't decided."

He's decided *everything*.

"If you show your love for this Barbara by speaking to no one and then showing up at the place I'll tell you—no matter how difficult getting out unseen may be—I *will* let you go. That's my promise to you. If you *don't* love her enough to show up, you will still live, but she dies. Do you understand the choice I'm offering you? *Ma'am?*"

Betty nods.

Trig gets up from his chair. "I'm leaving now. You have a decision to make. Don't you?"

Betty nods again.

"Make the right one," Trig says, and leaves.

When he's gone, Betty puts her hands over her face and begins to cry. When the tears let up she gets down on her knees, closes her eyes, and asks God what she should do. Either God speaks to her, or her secret heart does. Maybe those things are even the same. She makes a call and asks an old friend if he took the bus to the city.

"You know me, Bets. I don't like to fly. I would have taken a Greyhound to England that time we went if I could've."

"But that's not the only reason you take the bus, is it, Red?"

4

4:20 PM.

Alberta Wing said time is tight, but Holly doesn't know that; she thinks she has at least an hour before Kate will want to go to the Mingo, maybe even longer, so she and Pete spend some time catching up: her cases, his fishing exploits. He tells her again that she should come down to Boca Raton, and she tells him again that she will . . . and maybe this time she actually means it. God knows she could use some time to unwind once this current job is over.

Pete only has one coughing fit, very brief, so maybe he's finally overcoming his case of long-haul Covid. When the coughing lets up, he says, "Great talking with you, Hols, but I doubt if you called just to bat the breeze."

"I did have another reason, but I'm almost embarrassed to tell you. And it's really Izzy's case, not mine, but she's got other priorities this weekend. At least she does tonight."

"Yeah, the softball game. I keep up on all the hometown doins, especially the ones about the police. After what happened to Emil Crutchfield last year, I hope she beans one of those firemen. Is this about the Surrogate Juror thing? Almost has to be, right?"

"It is. I have reason to think the killer said something at an AA meeting about elephants."

"Elephants." Pete sounds bemused. "Packy-derms."

"Right. What this guy supposedly said was, 'Have you ever tried to hire someone to clean up elephant shit at ten in the morning.' Does that mean anything to you?"

Silence.

"Pete? Are you there?"

"I'm here and it rings a bell. Just can't catch hold of why."

"I can relate to that," Holly says.

"Can I call you back?"

Holly checks her watch. It's going on quarter to five. Kate will be up by now, getting ready to roll. "Yes, but if it's not in the next twenty or thirty minutes, my phone will be off until nine-thirty or so."

"Working?"

"Working."

"Sometimes I wish I still was," Pete says. "I'll give you a call if anything occurs."

"Thanks, Pete. I miss you."

"Miss you, too, Hols."

She ends the call, peeks her head out into the corridor, and sees the DO NOT DISTURB sign still hanging on Kate's door. Holly's sure she's up, but guesses she might be taking a quick shower.

5

5 PM.

There's a minor traffic jam near Dingley Park, people already headed for the ballfield, but Trig honks his way through, fixated on getting to the Holman Rink before the McKay woman. A yellow flier for the charity game lies on the passenger seat, seeming to mock him. Everything has to go off on time, and not just the game. If McKay is early getting to the rink, it could spoil everything. *Would* spoil everything. Once he's on Service Road A, the crowds streaming to the field on the other side of the park are left behind. He parks the Transit van, grabs his grocery bag, and uses the Plumber's Code to let himself in. He trots across the lobby and into the arena to make sure his prisoners are still his prisoners. He relaxes when he sees them. There's plenty of gaffer tape in his bag, but there's no room for his next expected guest in the penalty box, so he'll have to secure her to the bleachers. Assuming she's tractable. He would like to kill all four of them at once—five, counting himself—but if McKay makes a fuss, she'll have to go right away. If he makes that clear, self-interest may ensure her cooperation. He touches the Taurus in the pocket of his sportcoat, making sure it's still there.

Across town, John Ackerly is standing in front of Happy, looking natty in his own sportcoat and tailored slacks. Jerome swings to the curb and John climbs in. "Exciting times, bro," John says, and Jerome gives him a fist-bump.

With the connivance of the manager, Kate gets an Uber at the Garden City Plaza's utility-and-supplies exit behind the hotel. Her ride is also stuck in Dingley Park traffic, the driver inching ahead by fits and starts while Kate's phone seems to be racing past 5:05 to 5:10 and then to 5:15. If she can't get to the abandoned hockey building before five-thirty, will Stewart make good on his threat to kill Corrie? Kate thinks the chances of that are good. Too good.

"Can't you get around these people?" she asks, sitting forward. The driver lifts his hands in a Gallic gesture that says, *You see the situation as well as I*. Kate has her phone in her hand and her handbag slung over her shoulder. As the time on her phone changes from 5:15 to 5:16, she dips into the bag, brings out three tens, and flings them into the front seat. She gets out, cuts through the crowd to the sidewalk, and calls up the Maps app on her phone. She sees her destination is twenty minutes away if she's walking, so she doesn't walk. She runs.

6

5:17 PM.

Holly pokes her head out of her room again and sees the DO NOT DISTURB card still hanging from the doorknob of Kate's suite. This is a little worrying. What's perhaps more worrying is that there's still no sign of Corrie, who is—like Holly herself—a compulsive early bird. Before she can decide if she should use the key cards she has to check their rooms, her phone rings. It's Pete. She considers dismissing the call, then takes it.

"I knew I remembered something about packy-derms. The Calloway Family Circus was in town. Few years ago, this was. Rinky-dink outfit, just one ring instead of three, next door to fly-by-night, gone now. The Calloway had a trio of packy-derms they called Mama, Papa, and Baby. You know, like in 'Goldilocks'? If the girl had found a house in the woods where elephants lived instead of bears, that is. Which is ridiculous, but is it more ridiculous than a bears' house with beds and a stove? Probably also a fucking TV, pardon my *française*? I think not."

Get to the point, Holly restrains herself from saying. She pokes her head out again, hoping the DO NOT DISTURB sign will be gone from Kate's door, but it's still there. Also no sign of Corrie, burdened with shopping bags, hurrying down the hall from the elevator.

"Anyhoo," Pete says (after another brief coughing fit), "the Calloway Circus, in every town they went to they'd do some free advertising by inviting all the grammar school kiddos to a local venue so they could see some of the acts, and actually pet Baby's trunk. In Buckeye City, the kids got to see some of the show—and Baby—at the Mingo. What I remembered was a picture of Baby onstage, wearing a little sunhat."

Holly has been standing in the doorway. Now she staggers back a step as if physically struck. She realizes what has been troubling her, what was too big to miss . . . only she *did* miss it, didn't she? The phone sags away from her ear and she hears Pete say, tinny and distant, "Holly? Are you there?"

She says, "I have to go, Pete," and ends the call before Pete can reply.

Last night at the Mingo. Pulling up beside a white Transit van in the employees' parking lot. Two men waiting for her outside, one in a Sista Bessie tee, the other in a sportcoat and tie. The former was Sista Bessie's tour manager. The latter . . .

Hello, Ms. Gibney. I'm Donald Gibson.

Donald Gibson, the Mingo's Program Director.

Donald Gibson, who was also on the jury that convicted Alan Duffrey.

Can't be him. Can't be.

Only what if it is?

Holly's first impulse is to call Izzy. Her finger is hovering over the favorites button when she reconsiders, and not just because her call will almost certainly go to voicemail if Izzy is on the softball field, getting ready for the game that starts in less than two hours. She told Pete it was Izzy's case, but it no longer is. The Surrogate Juror Murders now belong to the State Police.

She should get in touch with SP Detective Ralph Ganzinger, but won't. She's already made one embarrassing mistake by telling Izzy that she thought Russell Grinsted, Alan Duffrey's lawyer, was Trig. Calling Ganzinger could be another, even bigger mistake. Is she supposed to tell Ganzinger, who she doesn't know from Adam, that she thinks the killer is Donald Gibson because he once said something about elephant shit? *Might* have said? That he might have said it at an AA meeting, and the alias the killer's using is Bill Wilson, the founder of AA? That he calls himself not Briggs but Trig? Would anyone but her follow that winding train of logic? Would it matter if she said, *I know it, I feel it*? It would to the late Bill Hodges, and it might to Izzy, but to anyone else? No. And what if it's like her brainwave about Grinsted? What if she's wrong again?

The mother who lives in her head speaks up: *Of course you're wrong, Holly. Why, you couldn't even remember your library book when you got off the schoolbus!*

She looks at her watch and sees it's 5:22. First things first; it's time to collect her famous employer and go to the Mingo. In fact they'll have to beat feet not to be late. *Kate* is her job, not Bill Wilson, aka Trig (and possibly aka Donald Gibson). Also—and this idea causes a wave of relief to wash through her—she can ask Kate what *she* thinks. *A woman who believes in herself*, Holly thinks. *One not cursed with terminal insecurity.*

The mother in her head is telling her she's passing the buck and only weak people do that, but Holly ignores her. She goes next door and uses the key card to let herself into Kate's suite.

"Kate? Where are you? We have to go!"

No answer. The bedroom door is closed. There's a note. Holly pulls it off the door and reads it.

7

5:23 PM.

Jerome and John Ackerly park near the service entrance behind the Mingo. Jerome says, "I hope she won't be embarrassed to ride to the hotel in a Subaru."

"Don't be an ass," John says.

Jerome uses the code his sister gave him to open the door, and they hurry through the little kitchen.

"Her dressing room is on the third floor," Jerome says, but Sista Bessie is waiting for them in the break room, reading from Barbara's book of poems. Jerome is struck by how much she looks like his Aunt Gertrude. This leads to a second thought, which should be elementary but somehow isn't: this is just another human being. A fellow rider on the journey from cradle to coffin. That leads to a third thought, which he will try to hold onto: unless and until it's used, talent is just an illusion.

Sista Bessie stands up and smiles. It looks strained to Jerome, and he wonders if she feels a little off, maybe coming down with something. "Young Man Jerome," she says. "Thank you for the ride."

"You're more than welcome," he says, and takes her outstretched hand. "This is my friend, John Ackerly."

Although that's his cue, John doesn't immediately turn to Sista. He's staring at a line of framed pictures on the wall below a message to the staff that reads, REMEMBER YOU ARE DEALING WITH THE PUBLIC, SO SMILE!

"John?"

He seems to wake up and turns to his friend and the elderly woman. "Big fan," he says. "Can't wait to hear you sing."

"Thank you, son. I think we better get going. Don't want to be late."

"Yes," Jerome says, but John walks to the framed pictures below the REMEMBER TO SMILE memo. He's looking at the photo of a smiling bearded man.

8

Holly: Christopher Stewart has taken Corrie. He says that if anyone tells the police, he will kill her. I believe him. If you call your cop friend and Corrie dies, it will be your fault. I got her into this. I'm going to get her out of it. K.

Hardly aware of what she's doing, Holly crumples the note in her fist and strikes herself in the forehead twice, and hard. She feels like a woman who has run up to the edge of a precipice and almost fallen over. If she had called Izzy, as she first intended, or got in touch with the State Police detective, she could have been signing Corrie Anderson's death warrant . . . and possibly Kate's, as well.

And what is she supposed to do now? Just what the frack is she supposed to do?

The GPS tracker on her truck!

She picks up the phone, calls the front desk, and after what seems like an eternity is connected with the parking garage. She identifies herself as Kate's security woman and the attendant tells her that Kate's F-150 is still parked in the garage. Holly's heart sinks. She's about to hang up when the attendant says, "She took an Uber. Went out the utility exit. Just like Lady Gaga did when she played the Mingo."

Holly thanks him and sinks down on the sofa, Kate's note still crumpled in her hand. Much later, she'll see the bloody crescents her fingernails have cut into her palm.

What now? What the hell am I supposed to do now?

Her phone rings. She grabs it out of her pocket, hoping it's Kate. It's John Ackerly.

"John, I can't talk to you now. I've got a situation here, and I need to think."

"Okay, but wait one. I'm coming to the hotel with Jerome and Sista Bessie, but I thought you'd want to know this right away. I think I know who Trig is! The guy I saw at the Buell Street Straight Circle meeting! This was years ago and he had a beard then. Now he's clean-shaven and wears glasses! His picture is on the wall at the Mingo! He's the Program Director!"

"Donald Gibson," Holly says.

"Ah, dookie," John says. "You already knew. Do I call the cops, or what?"

"No!"

"Are you sure?"

She's *not* sure, that's the pure hell of it; Holly is rarely sure about anything. But she's *close* to sure. Kate thinks Christopher Stewart has

Corrie, but logic suggests Kate is wrong. How could Stewart have taken Corrie, when his name and picture are everywhere? Gibson, on the other hand, could have taken her easily, because she was going to the Mingo to sign—*supposedly* sign—insurance papers.

"I'm sure. You have to keep it to yourself, John. Promise me."

"All right. You know best."

If only, Holly thinks. *What can I do? Depend on Kate to rescue Corrie?*

It would be nice if she could even half-believe that, but she keeps thinking of how Kate froze when the man with the bat came at her. This is no pundits' forum on CNN or MSNBC; this is a crazy man who is luring her in. If Kate had taken her truck, Holly might be able to track her to wherever Corrie was being held, but she *didn't* take her truck.

Think, she tells herself. *Think, you stupid ineffectual bitch*, think! But the only thing that comes to mind is a thing Bill Hodges used to say: *Sometimes the universe throws you a rope.*

If ever she needed a rope, it's now.

9

5:30 PM.

Kate sprints through a small lot for park employees, past a white Transit van, and up a cracked and frost-heaved sidewalk to an old wooden building with faded hockey players flanking the double doors. She's breathing hard, but not gasping; years of swimming have conditioned her for this hard run from Dingley Boulevard, which skirts the park, to Service Road A. One hand is in her purse, gripping the can of pepper spray.

As she reaches the doors, she risks a glance at her watch and sees it's 5:31. What if she's too late?

She hammers on the door with her free hand. "I'm here! I'm here, goddammit, don't you kill her, Stewart! *Don't you*—"

The door opens. Trig's right arm is cocked back like a rifle bolt, his right hand fisted. Before Kate can get her hand out of her purse, he punches her in the face. There's a crunch as her nose breaks. The pain is enormous. A red mist, not blood but shock, clouds her vision as she stumbles backward and goes down on her butt. She holds onto the cannister of spray in her purse while she's falling, but when she lands, her hand is jarred loose. The strap of her purse slides down to her elbow.

Trig bends, trying to shake the pain out of his hand. He grabs her forearm, yanks her to her feet, punches her in the face again. Kate is distantly aware that warmth is flooding over her mouth and chin. *Blood*, she thinks, *that's my bl—*

"*NO!*" someone shouts. *"NO, SHE'S MINE!"*

The hand gripping her arm lets go. There's a gunshot, and Kate is vaguely aware of something buzzing close by her ear. She plunges her hand back into her purse as someone—a woman with dark hair—rushes at the man who's grabbed her. The woman has a pistol in her hand, but before she can level it for a second shot, the man grabs her wrist and twists it. The woman screams. The man pulls her, turns her, and uses her forward momentum to hurl her into Kate, who is still struggling to get the pepper spray out of her purse. They both go down, the woman on top of Kate.

This close, face to face like lovers in bed, Kate can see speckles of stubble on the woman's face, and realizes it's a man. The one in the picture Holly showed her. Christopher Stewart.

The man in the sportcoat bends over Stewart and grabs his head in both hands. He twists it, and Kate hears a muffled crack as Stewart's neck fractures, or—oh God—actually breaks. Kate finally gets the can out of her purse.

"Hey, you fucking piece of shit."

The sportcoat man looks at her and Kate gives him a faceful of Sabre Red Pepper. He screams and claps his hands to his eyes. Kate struggles to get out from beneath Stewart's dead weight. She looks around for somebody, *anybody*, and sees no one. On the far side of the park there are hundreds, maybe even thousands, of people, but nobody here. Not a soul. She can hear John Fogerty's "Centerfield" blaring from the softball field's speakers, the sound tinny with distance.

"Help!" she tries to scream, but all that comes out is a wheezy whisper. It's not the run; it's the shock of being punched, then having Christopher Stewart land on top of her.

She struggles to her knees, but before she can get away, a hand closes around her ankle. It's Stewart. Foam is drizzling from his mouth, his wig has come askew, and he seems to be grinning. He gasps, "Baby . . . killer."

Kate kicks him in the throat. Stewart's hand loosens, then lets go. Kate staggers to her feet, only to be knocked sprawling again by a hard blow to the center of her back. She turns her head and sees the man in the sportcoat. His eyes are fiery red and spouting tears, but he's seeing her. She tries to get to her feet again and he kicks her. There's a flare of pain as something in her left side breaks.

The man in the sportcoat stumbles over Stewart, flails for balance, gets it, and grabs her arm. He jerks her to her feet again, backs up, and falls over Stewart, who is spasming weakly. Kate lands on top of the sportcoat man and rams her forehead into his mouth.

"Ow! Fuck, that hurts! Stop it, bitch!"

She rams down again, and feels Mr. Sportcoat's lips squash against his teeth. Before she can do it a third time, something clubs her on the temple. The red mist returns. Then darkens to black.

10

5:33 PM.

Holly decides she'll have to call the police after all—there's no other option. She's reaching for her phone when she remembers something from Iowa City: Kate holding up the keys to her truck and her seaside home in Carmel. "They need their own bodyguard," she said. "I'm always losing track of these puppies."

So Holly, wiser in the ways of computer-assisted living than Kate McKay, had attached an Apple AirTag to Kate's keyring.

She grabs her phone, drops it (her hands are shaking), snatches it off the carpet, and opens the Find My app on her phone. *Please, universe*, she thinks. *Throw me a rope.*

The universe obliges. The app shows her KATE'S KEYS, and locates them in what looks like Dingley Park, 1.8 miles away.

Holly goes back to her room and gets Bill Hodges's gun out of the safe in the closet. She puts it in her purse and heads for the elevator.

Kate and Corrie.

Her responsibility.

11

Trig looks around with streaming eyes and sees they still have the Holman Rink to themselves. His mouth is throbbing and he keeps swallowing blood. The music continues to blare from the speakers at the softball field. He can actually *taste* the stuff the bitch sprayed him with, and his sinuses feel like they're swelling. He needs to flush both eyes and sinuses, but has no idea if the faucets in the restrooms are still working.

Never mind that now.

He grabs the McKay woman by the hair and drags her into the foyer caveman-style. Her feet pedal and she makes a fuzzy protesting sound. He's tempted to kick her again for what she did to him—God, how his eyes *burn*! She wasn't supposed to fight back!

Never mind, never mind.

Trig grabs the man in the woman's pants suit—Stewart—and drags him into the foyer. Trig knows this is the guy who has been stalking Kate McKay. Any doubt he might have had on that score was put to rest by what the man screamed as he tried to shoot Trig: *She's mine!*

Stewart is trying to talk. His hands are twitching, but he can't seem to turn his head. A huge lump has arisen on the nape of his neck where some vertebrae have either been dislocated or snapped.

Trig goes back outside. He picks up the black wig the man was wearing, and the can of pepper spray he clouted McKay with, finally knocking her out before the witch could head-butt him again. His lips are swelling.

You deserved it, his dead father says. Trig can see him now through his watering eyes. A wavery ghost. *You flinched.*

"Did not, Daddy. Never did."

He goes back in, shuts the doors, and kicks away the gun McKay's would-be stalker tried to kill him with. He kneels on the floor beside the man in the pants suit. From his pocket he takes the Taurus .22. The would-be stalker rolls his visible eye to look at it.

"I couldn't put your name on the Mingo signboard, because I didn't know you'd be here," Trig says, "but that's okay. You can be a stand-in for Russell Grinsted. Do you know who that is?"

The would-be stalker makes a rusty gargling sound. It might be *Jesus*.

"Not Jesus, my friend, Alan Duffrey's lawyer. I wasn't going to kill somebody in his name, but since you're here . . ."

He puts the Taurus against the man's temple. Chrissy Stewart makes a few more inarticulate sounds, perhaps the beginning of a plea for mercy, perhaps wanting a word with Jesus, but Trig shoots him before he can get much out.

Trig says, "You can talk to Jesus in person. And as for Grinsted, I'm sure he could have done a better job."

His eyes still burn and his sinuses still throb, but his vision is clearing. Kate McKay is starting to come around. Trig hauls her to her feet. How many times has he done that? He can't remember, only knows he's getting tired of doing it. She's no lightweight. And they're not supposed to fight back, dammit.

"Do you want me to hit you again? Knock you out? Maybe fracture your jaw? Or I could shoot you in the gut. Would you like me to shoot you in the gut? You wouldn't die, at least not for awhile, but it would hurt like hell. Want that?"

Kate shakes her head. Her lower face is covered with blood. Her front teeth, top and bottom, are broken off.

"That's a good call. *Ma'am*." He escorts her, stumble-stepping and dazed, into the rink. "Step over the boards. Wouldn't want you to trip. Here's your friend Corrie, and a new friend, Barbara. They can't say hello, but I'm sure they're happy to see you. Over here by the bleachers, you troublesome bitch. We have to wait for one more, then we can finish up."

Chapter 23

1

5:45 PM.

Holly rides down in the elevator with competing scenarios running through her mind like overlapping images from different projectors aimed at the same screen. One basic thought comes through all of them, a unifying drumbeat: *My responsibility, my responsibility*.

The Charlotte Gibney who lives in her head tries to add, *My fault, my fault*, but Holly refuses to swallow that particular poison pill. Her boss has mistaken Trig for Stewart, but that isn't Kate's biggest mistake. The real error—hopefully not fatal—is her belief that she can talk Corrie's kidnapper into seeing sense. This isn't a cable news debate where logic and quick, cutting comebacks will carry the day. Holly thinks Kate McKay's arrogance is the worst kind. It doesn't recognize itself.

The hotel elevators open on a short hallway around the corner from the lobby. When Holly steps out, she hears an excited babble of voices accompanied by a spatter of applause. She walks to the end of the hall and sees Sista Bessie—broad-shouldered, deep-bosomed, big-legged—in the lobby. Betty stops to sign a quick autograph for a star-struck desk clerk in a hotel blazer, and offers a token smile for the clerk's iPhone. Standing beside her, looking crazy-handsome in his blue shirt, is Jerome Robinson. Holly feels an almost insurmountable urge to rush to him and enlist his help in what she has to do (whatever *that* is).

Others want autographs, but Jerome shakes his head and points to his watch, miming *we're late*. He escorts Sista—Betty to her besties—toward the elevators. Holly has only seconds to make a decision, and instead of standing where she is so they'll see her, she steps into the newsstand and turns her back. It's an instinctive move, as thoughtless on the conscious level as taking the next breath. She only realizes why she avoided Jerome while she's looking at the magazines without seeing them. Jerome has his own security job to do this evening. He would let that go in a moment if Holly asked him, but she won't ask him to desert his post. Or put him in harm's way. How would she ever explain to his parents or to Barbara if she got him hurt or, God forbid, killed? That *would* be her fault.

She crosses the lobby to the revolving doors, Find My app open on her phone.

2

5:50 PM.

The late Christopher Stewart got a ha-ha room; the best Corrie could wangle for her boss was a junior suite; three floors up, Betty Brady got the Presidential. Jerome escorts her inside. Sitting in the living room in front of the TV are two people, one male and one female, both old and skinny. The man is wearing a showy red suit and a black turtleneck with a peace sign on a gold chain. Short snakeskin boots adorn his feet. Betty introduces them to Jerome as Alberta Wing and Red Jones and says Red will be accompanying her on sax when she sings the Anthem.

"Your outfit is on the bed," Alberta says. "I had to let out the ass of the pants to the limit. You gettin so *big*, girl."

It's clear that Alberta expects a zesty comeback—Jerome does, too, it's how his aunts and mother do when they get together—but Betty just gives another of those token smiles and tells Red to come with her. He picks up a blue travel bag and leaves his saxophone case by his chair. The two of them go into the bedroom and Betty closes the door.

Alberta says, "This song she's doin tonight is a freebie, and those the ones that always cause trouble. You ever hear that old sayin, no good deed goes unpunished?"

Jerome says he has.

"It's true. Huh, lookit you, like the cat that got the cream." She waves a dismissive hand. "You think you gettin close to a big star is all this is, somethin to tell your friends and your kids about later on, but I'm sayin you must take this serious. Hear me?"

"I do."

"You goan take care of her? Keep anyone from gettin nasty with her?"

"That's the plan."

"You make sure the plan works, then." Alberta shakes her head. "Somethin weighin on her. She ain't right."

3

In the bedroom, Betty strips off her shirt, displaying a truly mighty bra and a mightier midsection. The mom jeans come next, exposing an acre of cotton underpants. Red takes a glance, then turns his attention out the window to the skyline.

Although burdened, Betty isn't entirely devoid of humor. "You can look, Ernest," she says. "It's not like you haven't seen me with my clothes off before."

"True," he says, still looking out, "but the last time you was a double-D."

"Triple," she says, shimmying on the sequined bellbottoms and a pink silk smock that falls to her thighs. She cinches it with the starry sash. "Now I'm a goddam F, but ne'mine my bra size. Did you bring it?"

"Yes I did, and why you want it I don't know."

"Nor do you need to. Give it over."

For nearly twenty-five years, since 9/11 tightened up inspections and restrictions at airports, Red has traveled by bus. He never liked to fly in the first place. He's afraid of being hijacked, he hates the turbulence and the crowding, says the food isn't fit for sick dogs. He says trains are better, but he favors a good old Greyhound because he says it gives him a chance to watch at least three movies and unpack his thoughts. Sometimes he even entertains fellow travelers with a tune or two, like "Yakety Sax" or "Baker Street." Also, he can bring along "his good pal," which he now takes out of his ancient Pan Am flight bag. It's an elderly Smith & Wesson J-Frame revolver. The worn wood grip has been wrapped in a layer of white tape.

He hands it to her with clear misgivings. "Five-shot cylinder, .38 slugs, fully loaded. Would put Mike Tyson down, so for Christ's sake don't shoot yourself with it. Remember there's no safety."

She puts it in her purse. "Thank you, Red. We been the miles together, haven't we?"

"And more to go, I do hope," he says. "Don't you want to tell me what you want that for?"

She shakes her head. Which is what he expected.

4

5:55 PM.

The crowd across the street from the hotel has grown exponentially. There are still plenty of pro- and anti-Kate demonstrators, but the majority of the crowd, which stretches up and down the block, seems to be made up of Sista Bessie fans hoping to get a glimpse of her . . . and to take the all-important photo, of course.

Parked in the turnaround is a powder blue Thunderbird with the hotel's manager standing beside it. Mr. Estevez is stroking the side with a proprietary air that can only mean this is his baby. Parked behind it and looking rather dowdy in comparison is a red Subaru that Holly recognizes. She also recognizes the man leaning against the driver's side.

Her bartender friend sees her and waves. "Holly! Did you see Jerome?"

"I did," she says, not adding that she made sure Jerome didn't see her.

"We're escorting the star to the game. Well . . . Jerome is. I'm just following. Never mind that, is it him? Is Gibson the guy you're looking for?" And before she can answer: "I *know* it's him. I'd send his picture to Cathy 2-Tone to get a backup confirmation, but I don't have her number."

"It's him."

"Have you told the police?"

"No. And I don't want you to, either, but keep your phone on. If you don't hear from me by . . . say nine o'clock, call the cops and ask for either Isabelle Jaynes or Tom Atta. Tell them Trig is Donald Gibson, from the Mingo. Remind them he was on the Duffrey jury. If you can't get either of them because the game is still going on, call Ralph Ganzinger of the State Police. Got it?"

"This sounds serious, Holly. Are you going to get in trouble? Some kind of jackpot?"

Come with me, John, Holly thinks. Then: *My responsibility, my responsibility*.

"Just keep your phone on. Wait for my call."

"I will," he says, but he won't. John Ackerly is going to have his own problems not long hence.

He cocks a thumb at the T-Bird. "The mayor was going to come, but she canceled. Probably thought going to a softball game while a serial killer's on the loose wouldn't be a good look come election time."

That the game is being played at all while a serial killer is on the loose is crazy, Holly thinks, but doesn't say. What she says is, "Take care of yourself, John," and sets out for Dingley Park, joining the throngs of people headed that way.

5

6 PM.

"Who *are* you?" Trig shouts at the dead man, and delivers a kick to the corpse's midsection.

Of course he knows who the dead man is, knows perfectly well, and not just from Buckeye Brandon; the entire staff of the Mingo has this asshole's picture. Other copies of the photo have been posted backstage, in the ticket booths, in the elevators for the staff and public, and on the bulletin boards in the men's and women's bathrooms. It's the McKay woman's stalker.

Still, he asks it again: "Who the fuck *are* you?"

In his head an earworm awakes and he hears the song by The Who that serves as *CSI*'s theme. What he actually means—somewhere in the back of his mind he understands this—is *Who are you to try and stop me from finishing my job?*

He trussed McKay to one of the supporting bleacher stanchions near the other two women, then dropped Stewart's gun into the inner pocket of his sportcoat. Now he kicks the body again and asks again who he is.

Don't be a fool. You know who he is, Trigger.

Daddy's right there, leaning in the doorway, wearing his lucky #19 Buckeye Bullets shirt.

"Shut up, Daddy. Shut your fucking trap."

Never would have dared say something like that when I was alive.

"Well, I don't have to worry about that, do I? You deserved that heart attack. I wish I could have done *this* after you had it." He kicks Christopher Stewart's body hard enough to lift it briefly from the dusty foyer floor. "And *this*. And *this*."

The ghost standing in the doorway laughs. *You worthless fucking flincher. Mr. Useless, that's you.*

"*MOTHER-KILLER!*" Trig shrieks. *"YOU'RE A MOTHER-KILLER! ADMIT IT, ADMIT IT!"*

In the old days before AA, there was a part of him—the barest kernel—that always stayed sober no matter how much he drank. That time the cop stopped him three blocks from his house, he had known to be polite. Polite and coherent. Dignified. No yelling. No slurring. While most of his mind was racing and raging and terrified of what a DUI arrest would mean to his job at the Mingo, a job that was essentially a mixture of public relations and keeping the celebs happy, that kernel of sobriety kept him courteous and reasonable and the cop had let him go with a warning. Nevertheless, he understood that driving while so drunk, and with an open handle of vodka close by, meant that kernel of sobriety—of *sanity*—was shrinking. His descent into chaos was close, and so he had sought help in the Program.

This was like that, only worse. With each murder he had grown bolder and less sane. Now he's kicking a corpse and talking to his dead father. *Seeing* his dead father. Crazy. On the other hand, so what? He has an hour before the Black singer shows up—assuming she is able to show up at all—and this *idiot*, this surrogate for Duffrey's lawyer, had actually tried to *kill* him! Had just missed!

"*Who ARE you?*" he screams, and it is good to scream. It's *great* to scream. He kicks the body again.

Stop it, you little idiot. The ghost leaning in the doorway is now munching popcorn.

"Shut up, Daddy. I'm not afraid of you."

He leaves the body and begins to snatch the old posters off the walls. The hockey players he and his daddy had rooted for. He snatches them and crumples them, shouting as he does it. "Bobby Simoy, *fuck you*! Evzenek Beran, the Czech Wonder Boy, *fuck you*! Charlie Moulton, *fuck you*!"

An armload of paper. Hockey players from his terrified childhood. Hockey players long *gone*, like his mother. He looks at the armload of paper he is holding to his chest and whispers, "Who *are* you guys?"

6

6:05 PM.

Barbara Robinson understands that she is going to die. Once upon a time, not too long ago, she faced a creature from beyond rational understanding, a creature whose human face dripped and ran into something that was living insanity. She hadn't thought then that she was going to die—not that she could recall, at least—because she had been too horrified. But Mr. Gibson is no creature from outside the known universe, he's a human being. Yet like the thing that had been masquerading as Chet Ondowsky, he's a face-changer. She's seeing that other face now as he comes into the rink with an armload of paper, stepping from tie to tie and talking to a father who isn't there. She understands that extreme horror is, in its own way, merciful. It doesn't allow you to look ahead to the end.

No more poems. No more singing. No more spring nights and fall afternoons. No more kisses and lovemaking. All about to be burned away. And speaking of burning—

Mr. Gibson pushes his armload of paper into a square made by four of the crossties. Barbara wishes she were too horrified to know what that paper means. Then the other girl, the one he took first, bumps her shoulder repeatedly and makes muffled noises. The other girl knows what the paper means, too.

It's kindling.

7

6:15 PM.

It's almost two miles to Dingley Park, and the Thunderbird convertible bearing tonight's guest singer passes Holly, rolling at walking speed, while she's still half a mile away. An elderly Black man is in the backseat with Jerome, sitting comfortably with his arms widespread. Holly bends down and pretends to tie her shoe as the car goes by. Once it has, she resumes walking, phone in hand.

She can see the tops of the light standards that ring the playing field when she catches up to the blue T-Bird again. It's pulled over at the side of the road with the flashers going. The people who were walking toward the park, carrying coolers and blankets, now crowd around the car and its famous occupant. Mr. Estevez is behind the wheel, back ramrod straight, exuding ownership.

Holly stops and watches Sista Bessie get out and approach a family with young kids who squeal excitedly when they see her coming. Jerome vaults from the T-Bird's backseat and shadows her. *Good for you, Jerome,* Holly thinks. The kids look to be about eleven and nine and surely don't know Sista Bessie from Eve, but they are holding up signs in those rainbow colors only Crayolas can create: WE LOVE YOU SISTA B!

Betty hugs the children, and tells them something Holly can't hear. A crowd gathers, laughing and excited. Phones are raised. Sista smiles for pictures, but when someone offers her a pen and paper, she shakes her head. "Not startin that nonsense, so don't ask."

Holly slips in a little closer, fascinated in spite of her mission. The elderly black man in the red suit still sits easily in the back of the T-Bird, smiling as more and more people approach Sista Bessie. She's coming back to the car. Holly crosses the street so Jerome won't see her and continues on toward the park. The Wise Men had a star. Holly, not feeling wise at all, has her Find My app.

The blue T-Bird passes her again, and Holly again pretends to tie her shoe until the car is gone.

8

6:20 PM.

Jerome is amazed.

Word has spread—*Sista Bessie is on her way to the field in a big old blue convertible!*—and more and more people are falling in behind the T-Bird, which continues to roll along at a stately pace. People surround it, stand in front of it to snap pictures, then good-naturedly break away to allow it passage. There's no pushing, no anger, only an apolitical shower of good wishes for the Sista. Dingley Boulevard fills in from side to side with cheering people. Mr. Estevez continues to sit erect behind the wheel. Betty touches outstretched hands, waves, smiles for photos. Jerome thinks her smile looks strained. He gets out again, vaulting over the back deck, and walks behind the slow-rolling car, trying to keep people away from the blind side. He feels like a Secret Service agent. Someone gives him a flower. A large Black woman says, "Take care of her, honey, she a national treasure." He's thinking this might be what it would be like if Tupac came back, or—perhaps—Whitney. There are a few cries of *Stay strong* and *We love you, Sista* and *We'll be at your show, honey*, but many of the hundreds following and surrounding the car are silent and awestruck. Yet Jerome, who has never precisely believed (or not believed) in such things as telepathy or emotional transmission, can feel strong vibes of human kindness here: alive, strong, and well. From the tears in Betty's eyes as she turns from side to side, acknowledging the crowd that's walking with them, it seems that—whatever else might be bothering her—she feels it, too. He wonders briefly if Holly's Kate McKay, famous in her own way, has ever felt this sort of love, the kind that's untinctured by the hate her supporters feel for those on the other side of the political spectrum. He guesses probably not.

The T-Bird bears right. Ahead, bathed in bright white light, is the park. The crowd stops to let the car pass under the arched gate that says, GUNS AND HOSES TONIGHT. They begin to applaud. Then to cheer.

Those who follow stop to chuck money into a gigantic fireman's boot on the left or an equally gigantic plastic policeman's hat on the right. The crowd is laughing, happy. They have seen an authentic Talented Celebrity, the night is pleasant, and they are primed for a good time.

9

The doors of the Mingo Auditorium opened at 6 PM, and by 6:20 the seats are filling up. A pro-life contingent, wearing blue tee-shirts showing a baby *in utero* (although looking roughly four months old), takes up a bloc of seats in the middle of the first three rows, but pro-choice people fill in the aisle areas around the pro-lifers, isolating them. They are wearing red shirts that say, HANDS OFF MY BODY. One of the pro-lifers checks out one of the pro-choicers—a heavyset elderly woman with a scream of white hair—and says, "You couldn't pay me to put my hands on your body." The elderly woman replies, as she learned from her teenybop friends many years ago in junior high school: "If you don't like it, don't look."

From the speakers comes a medley of Sista Bessie's hits from back in the day, and the stage is littered with the band's equipment. In the middle of this is a podium for the star of tonight's show, who at this moment happens to be trussed up to a bleacher stanchion.

All the ushers have pictures of Christopher Stewart and check faces dutifully, but so far they have seen no one even close to his description . . . and it helps that tonight men, especially young men, are in a decided minority. There's also no sign of Don Gibson, the Program Director. That's not unheard-of; once arrangements for the night's gig are made, he sometimes shows up late or not at all.

The signs over the lobby doors and out front on Main Street still read FRIDAY MAY 30 7 PM KATE McKAY and SATURDAY-SUNDAY MAY 31 AND JUNE 1 SISTA BESSIE **SOLD OUT**.

They will continue to say that for another fifty-seven minutes.

10

6:25 PM.

Holly's progress is slow until she can veer away from the crowd. She would like to run, or at least jog, but doesn't dare. She doesn't want to attract attention from either the news crews filming the crowd or the cops, dressed in blue shorts and blue shirts with the Guns logo on them, who are directing traffic.

The flashing green dot takes her to the left, along a narrow street (made narrower by cars parked on both sides) called Dingley Place. Music from the field's PA rolls and echoes, currently Taylor Swift's "Hey Stephen." Holly walks through two parking lots that are crammed full. Beyond this is a narrow paved lane with signs reading SERVICE ROAD A and PARK SERVICE ONLY and ALL OTHERS WILL BE TOWED.

The app is telling her she's about three hundred yards from her destination, and it almost has to be the old condemned hockey rink. She had no idea this service road existed, even though the picnic area where she and Izzy had their lunches has to be nearby. (Those lunches now seem impossibly long ago.) With trees lining both sides of the road, the daylight is becoming an untrustworthy murk.

She comes out in another, smaller, parking lot meant for Park Service vehicles. According to the app, *YOU HAVE REACHED KATE'S*

KEYS. She turns her phone off and puts it in her pocket, mindful of its glow in the shadowy lot. Up ahead, parked with two wheels on the pavement and two on the grass, is a white Transit van. The fir trees are tall enough to block the light from the playing field stanchions here, but there's enough for Holly to read what's written on the van's side: MINGO AUDITORIUM and *JUST THE GOOD STUFF!*™

The truck is empty. Kate must be close, and, very likely, Corrie. Holly's mind flashes briefly to Barbara and Jerome. At least they are safe, and thank God for that. Lizzo drifts to Holly from the PA like something out of a dream.

She sees a wide paved path—frost-heaved and sprouting weeds from many cracks—leading to the dark hulk of the rink. Ghostly hockey players adorn the double doors. One day last fall, she and Izzy walked around this place as they munched fish tacos from Frankie's lunch wagon, and Holly knows there are no windows. She sits on the bumper of the Mingo van and tries to think how to proceed.

He may have already killed the women, in which case she's too late. But if he has, why is the van still here? That he left it and walked away strikes her as unlikely. There are a hundred cops nearby—hell, maybe two hundred—and she doesn't dare call them for fear of precipitating two murders, and, very likely, Gibson's suicide.

She checks the time and sees it's just gone 6:40. Could he be waiting for the game to begin? She can think of no reason why he would. But the game isn't the only thing happening at seven tonight. There's also Kate's lecture. Suppose he wants her crowd to gather, and wonder where she is? Wonder and worry? Gibson might even hope Christopher Stewart is drawn to the Mingo and can be captured. The irony of that happening might appeal to a crazy man; it has a comic-book Joker feel to it.

She tries to pray and can't. Now through the loudspeakers comes the sound of a cheer squad chanting, something about Mary and her little lamb.

Wait, the Charlotte Gibney in her head tells her. *It's all you can do. Because if he knows you're here, he'll shoot them both and it will be your fault.*

But she has another voice in her head, one that belongs to her late friend, Bill Hodges. *That's bullshit, Holly. Do you want to be standing around out here with your thumb up your butt when you hear gunshots?*

She does not.

Holly starts toward the doors, keeping to the side of the main walkway and in the thickening shadows of the trees. She reaches into her unzipped purse and touches the .38. It used to belong to Bill. Now, like it or not, it belongs to her.

Chapter 24

1

The bleachers are chock-full, and of course they face toward the field, so when the blue Thunderbird enters the park grounds, everyone on the third-base side stands and turns to watch it go by. Those on the first-base side, which includes the cops' dugout, don't get a good look at first, because the people across the field are blocking the view. There's applause and cheering.

"What's up?" Izzy asks.

Tom Atta climbs on top of the dugout and shades his eyes from the bank of lights. "Some old car touring the field. Vintage. Almost got to be Sista Bessie."

They don't have to wonder long, because Mr. Estevez takes the T-Bird on a complete circuit. Izzy and Tom trot down to the bullpen area reserved for the cops team, and get a good look when the T-Bird comes to their side. It rolls at a steady five miles an hour. A young man is now riding on the rear deck, black Converse sneakers parked on the back bumper. He looks bemused. Tom points and says, "That's Jerome. Holly's friend."

"I know."

Standing in the front, wearing a dark blue sash covered with stars, is Sista Bessie. She waves to the cheering crowd.

Izzy applauds like mad. "I remember her songs. They used to play on the radio all the time when I was a kid. Sweet voice."

The car disappears behind the cinderblock building. "Can't wait to hear her sing," Tom says.

"Neither can I."

2

The T-Bird pulls up to the equipment building on the other side of the centerfield fence. Well-wishers, autograph seekers, and eBayers gather, but Jerome and Mr. Estevez do their best to shoo them away, or at least keep them back, shouting, "Give the lady some privacy." John Ackerly has been allowed to park in the small VIP lot. He gets out of Jerome's Subaru and daps first Red, then Jerome. "All good?"

"Fine so far," Jerome says.

Two representatives of the opposing teams come around the corner of the building. The Guns rep is Lewis Warwick. He gives Jerome a nod, shakes hands with Red, then turns to Betty and tells her how honored they are to have her.

The Hoses greeter, Fire Chief Darby Dingley, is wearing too-short shorts that display his large can and knobby knees. "Very pleased to have you, Sista Bessie. Can't wait to hear you sing."

"Can't wait to do it," Betty says.

"If you'd do us one favor before you go into your dressing room?"

"Will if I can."

Dingley hands her a silver dollar. "We have to pick a home team. Would you flip that? Lieutenant Warwick can call it."

Betty flips the silver dollar high. Warwick calls heads. Betty snaps it out of the air, slaps it on a meaty wrist, and peeks. Looking at Warwick, she says, "Sorry, boss."

"Home team!" Dingley gloats. "We get our lasties! *Yesss!*"

Warwick offers congratulations which, when coupled with his sour look, don't sound terribly sincere.

Betty takes her after-show clothes into the equipment room, toting her purse. Between a bat-rack and a mowing machine she sees a door with her picture pasted on it (snipped from her pre-tour *People* magazine interview). She peeps inside.

"Not much," Lieutenant Warwick says, "but the best we could do on short notice."

"There's a toilet," Dingley says. "If you . . . you know . . . need to . . ."

"It's fine," Betty says, putting him out of his misery. All she wants is for them to go the fuck *away*. There's something she has to do, and it's important.

Warwick says, "We have a mic. Wireless. When it's time, you'll come straight to the pitcher's mound. Chief Dingley and I will walk you out, and I'll hand the mic to you. Or your accompanist." He glances at Red, who is reclining on a bench to the left of the door, back against the cinderblock, looking to Jerome as comfortable as old Tillie. He's got his sax case on his lap.

Betty says, "No need for a mic, it'd drown out Red's horn. I've got plenty of lungpower, believe me. No need to walk me out, either. I trust Young Man Jerome here to get me to where I'm supposed to do my thing." She comes back and squeezes Jerome's shoulder. "If he can write a book, he can escort me to the pitcher's booth, or whatever y'all call it."

Dingley says, "That'll be fine, ma'am, whatever you want." He turns his attention to Mr. Estevez, standing nearby with his hands neatly folded. "You can park beside that Subaru, and stand by. Take Ms. . . . Ms. Sista . . . back to her hotel after she sings."

Estevez nods.

Betty says, "I may stick around a bit, boys. Take in a little of the game. I'll let you know." Before anyone has a chance to say anything else, she goes into her makeshift dressing room and closes the door behind her.

"Take care of her," Warwick says to Jerome, and starts away without waiting for a response. Which would have been *Of course I will—her and Red, too.*

Jerome looks at the old man, who is looking back at him with troubled eyes and a frown. "Red? All right? Not feeling sick?"

Red seems about to say something, then makes a business of attaching a glittery strap to his instrument. When he looks up at Jerome, his face is serene again. "Never better. I love me a gig, even if it's only one song long."

3

6:45 PM.

The gun is now in Holly's right hand. She's careful to approach the doors from the side, but when she gets close she sees there is no peephole to worry about. There's a keypad, and the tiny red light glowing above the numbers tells her the doors are locked. Inside she hears two voices, a child and a man. This strikes her as weird. Very.

The child says, "I took down all the posters, all your favorite players, how do you like that?"

The man replies, "You wouldn't do it if I could get at you."

The child: "Fuck you!"

The man: "Don't talk to your daddy like that."

The child: "What did you do to her?"

The man: "Never mind. She's *gone*. That's all you need to know."

Holly realizes there *aren't* two people on the other side of the doors. The reason it's weird is because Donald Gibson is speaking in two voices, and he's got Kate and Corrie in there . . . unless they're already dead.

The man-voice shouts, "Who are you?" He laughs, then almost sings it, the words punctuated by grunts of effort: "*Hoooo . . . are . . . YOU?*"

There's a long pause, then the child-voice says, "We're going to wait, Daddy. Either she'll come or she won't." Laughter, cracked and high. "As many as I can get, as many as I can get, why not?"

Holly raises the gun, points it at the lock, then lowers it again. Shooting locks works in the movies, but would it in real life? Maybe all it would do is alert him, in which case he'd shoot his two hostages, as he's shot . . . how many others? Five? Six? Seven? In her current state of stress, Holly has lost count.

We're going to wait, Daddy. Either she'll come or she won't.

Is Gibson talking about a real person, or a phantasm? Holly doesn't know. All she's sure of is that the father—the Daddy—is make-believe. Gibson is like Norman Bates in *Psycho*, only talking in his father's voice instead of his mother's. Which fits, because Gibson *is* psycho. Maybe he thinks his mother is going to come. Or some girl he dated in high school. Or the Virgin Mary, riding down from heaven in a chariot to bless him and tell him he's not crackers but doing the absolute right thing.

All Holly knows for sure is that if someone comes, someone *real*, he'll have to open the door. Then she can shoot him.

Holly slides to the left, the .38 raised to shoulder level. Waiting is the best choice, she knows this, but if she hears gunshots from inside the deserted rink, she thinks she'll lose her mind.

The child: "I hate you, Daddy."

The man: "You can't even hold your liquor. Mr. Useless, that's you. Mr. Alcoholics Anonymous."

Then, screaming: "*WHO ARE YOU?*"

4

6:46 PM.

Betty is alone at last, and can take off her show face. She hangs up her clothes for after the song and puts her purse on the room's one shelf. She heaves a long, trembling sigh, and feels her pulse in the side of her neck. It's too fast and stumbling all over itself. There are pills in her bag. She slips one under her tongue, then adds a second. The taste is bitter but somehow comforting. She wipes a hand down her face, then gets kneebound. She folds her hands on top of the closed toilet seat. She begins her prayer as she did as a child, whispering the incantatory words "Jesus, mighty Jesus."

She pauses, gathering her thoughts.

"There's no way I can save that girl's life without your help, mighty Jesus, no way at all, but she's a good girl, I already just about love her like the child I gave up when I was seventeen, and I mean to try. I don't even know if that Mr. Gibson will call me like he said he would, because he's as crazy as a rabid dog. I think he might mean to kill us both. I hope if I shoot him with Red's gun you'll forgive me. Not if there's no other way to save her. Please help me to sing out there like there's nothing wrong, all right? I'm in the way of believing you can do all those things—as long as I do my part—but now I have to ask you for a miracle, mighty Jesus. There ain't no way I can get out of here without being seen, there will be all kinds of people waitin for me, because that is the curse of what I have become. I don't know what to do about that, which is why I need a miracle. I—"

Lewis Warwick taps on the door with her face on it. "Ma'am?" he says. "Sista? It's time."

She whispers, "I pray it in your name, mighty Jesus," then stands, reknots her starry sash, and comes out.

"Thank you again for doing this," Lewis says.

She nods distractedly. "Will my little bag be safe in there? I see there's no lock on the door." Her phone is in her purse, and so is Red's gun.

Warwick beckons Mr. Estevez, who is standing by the T-Bird. He asks Estevez to stay outside the door of Sista's dressing room and make sure nobody enters. Mr. Estevez says he'll be happy to do it.

"All right, then," Betty says. "Red? What do you say?"

Red stands up, sax around his neck, and when Betty extends her hand, he takes hold. "Let's git it."

Betty extends her other hand. "Come on, Young Man Jerome," she says. "I want you with me."

"That's my honor," he says, and takes her hand. It's warm in his. "You are quite a gal, Betty Brady."

She smiles, thinking, *I better be. I just better be.*

They walk onto the field, the three of them with their hands linked. When the gathered thousand or so in the bleachers—hundreds more are standing—see them heading toward the pitcher's mound, they get on their feet, applauding.

Two Black men, one old, one young. One sturdy-built Black woman between them. Their shadows, blacker than they are, walk beside them, crisp as cutouts. Red Jones whispers a question in Betty's ear, and she nods. She turns to Jerome and tells him about a slight change in plans; there's going to be a little additional music.

5

6:50 PM.

To the left of the Holman Rink doors, pressed against the splintery, gray-painted boards, Holly realizes she needs to pee, and badly. *Hold it*, she tells herself. *Just hold it*. But if she tries, she's going to wet her pants. She steps carefully into the bushes (hoping there's no snakes or poison ivy), lowers her jeans, and squats. The relief is enormous. She pulls up her pants and returns to her post as the mournful strains of a well-known tune, played on the saxophone, reach her.

In the foyer, Trig cocks his head listening. He can make out what the music is, and he smiles. He thinks, *How fitting*.

In the rink, Corrie and Barbara are waiting for what comes next, death being the most likely. They both understand this.

Kate has been afraid of death ever since she first saw shooting targets with her face on them for sale on the internet. That fear has been mostly academic, mitigated by the understanding that if it comes, her death will be a rallying cry. What she never expected was to be taken by some random crazy person with no political axe to grind, a man to whom she means nothing more than one more victim in a senseless killing spree. The pain in her face, exacerbated by the windings of tape around her head, is enormous. *If I get out of this*, she thinks, *I'll be buying some orthodontist a new Tesla . . . but I don't think I'll be getting out of it*. The crazy man has stopped arguing with himself. He's listening to the music.

In the rink, the three women who are going to die also listen.

6

6:52 PM.

On the field, the trio—Red and Jerome, and Betty (only now she's Sista)—stops at the pitcher's mound, where Izzy Jaynes will soon begin her night's work as the PD's hurler. Sista Bessie raises her hands for quiet, and the crowd stills.

Red steps forward and begins to play "Taps," each note its own tolling bell. There's a soft rustle as hats are removed. He plays slowly but doesn't drag it out—no schmaltz. Sista knows better than to give the audience time to applaud, not for "Taps."

When Red plays the last note—a C—she draws breath and sings *a capella* from her belly and diaphragm: "*O say can you see, by the dawn's early light . . .*"

Jerome feels chills and goosebumps race up and down his arms as Red joins in, segueing from C to G, not only playing under her but making a half-turn away from her so that her voice, even more beautiful than in those few rehearsals, is the star. She sings with her hands outstretched, slowly widening her arms as if to take in the entire audience.

As she reaches the penultimate line—*O say does that star-spangled banner yet wave*—Red counts off in his head: *One-two-three-four*, just as they rehearsed. Then she gives it everything she has, and so does he, blowing like Charlie Parker or Lester Young. Hands to the sky, Sista Bessie puts all her soul into it: "*O'er the land of the free, and the HOME of the BRAVE!*"

There is a moment of utter silence, and then the crowd goes bonkers, cheering and applauding. Hats are waved; hats are thrown onto the field. Sista Bessie and Red bow. Jerome beckons the audience—*give it up for her, c'mon, c'mon, c'mon*—and the noise redoubles.

Sista Bessie puts her hands to her mouth, kisses her fingers, and spreads her arms wide once more, giving the assembled crowd her love. Then the three of them walk back toward the equipment building. The applause and cheering continues as Betty, Jerome, and Red leave the field.

Red says, "However the game turns out, won't nothing beat that. You killed it, Bets."

"Totally amazing," Jerome says.

"Thank you. Thank you both."

"Are you all right, Ms. Brady? You look pale."

"Fine. Just a little double-tap from the old pump. I need to go in and get out of these duds. See if you can clear those lookie-loos out. They just want autographs. Tell em to go watch the game. And you call me Betty, just like your sister does."

"I will, and I'll see what I can do about those people." Jerome's face says he has little hope of moving the crowd, and Betty thinks, *Don't I know it. Those folks didn't come for the game, they came for me, and only mighty Jesus can clear em.*

She goes into her little dressing room, closes the door, changes out of her singing clothes, and waits for the phone to ring.

7

7:00 PM.

The Fire Department team runs onto the field to cheers from the third-base side and jeers from those on the first-base side. The loudspeakers broadcast Steven Tyler screaming "Take Me Out to the Ballgame."

The song reaches Holly as she circles the Holman Rink step by careful step, being quiet, looking for emergency exits. She finds two, both locked. At one point, as she nears the side of the building closest to the food wagons, she thinks she hears muffled sounds from inside the arena. They could be sounds of life or wishful thinking.

At the Mingo, almost every seat is filled. Maisie Rogan, the Assistant Program Director, is frantic, because tonight's speaker isn't here. After trying Don four times and getting voicemail four times, she checks all the dressing rooms again. No Kate. She tries McKay's assistant, and gets another dose of voicemail. At last she walks out to the podium at center stage, avoiding music stands and amps but almost tripping over a power cord. The audience applauds, sensing an introduction, but Maisie shakes her head and holds up her hands.

"There's going to be a slight delay in tonight's program," she says. The audience mutters about this. One of the pro-lifers yells, "What'd she do? Pussy out?" This prompts prompt replies of *Shut up* and *Save it for the chaplain* and *Pipe down*.

A woman yells, "Don't legislate my vajayjay!" This brings applause and hoots of approval. Maisie scuttles back to the comforting darkness at stage left and starts making more calls.

They all go to voicemail.

Betty hears "Take Me Out to the Ballgame" from her tiny dressing room, where she's sitting on the toilet with her phone in her hand. She's had worse dressing rooms when she was just a teenager starting out, places without running water and puke-smelling shithouses behind firetrap chicken shacks and juke joints like the Shuffle Board or the Dew Drop Inn, where the pay was five dollars a night plus tips and a pitcher of beer. At least you could get a little fresh air through the loose boards. This one, with its cinderblock walls and single flickery overhead fluorescent tube, looks like a jail cell in one of those southern towns. Nothing like the one she had at the Mingo.

This little room (at least it has a toilet and mirror) isn't her problem. Nor is Red's J-Frame revolver tucked into her bag. She's checked it twice, and it's fully loaded. Her problem is how to get away undetected. She suspects that Red and Jerome are still outside, sitting on that bench. The hotel manager, Estevez, and Jerome's friend John are probably with them. And the autograph hounds. How is she supposed to slip away? Fame has never felt like such a burden. They call this city the Second Mistake on the Lake. *Her* mistake, a big one, was ever coming here in the first place. What has happened to Barbara is all her fault.

"Mighty Jesus," she says. "Mighty Jesus, show me the way."

Her phone rings.

8

7:04 PM.

Trig goes back to the arena, stepping delicately along the ties. His prisoners are still all present and accounted for. *Squared away*, Daddy would have said. He calls the Black singer.

"You want to go east from the field," he tells her. "Your phone will point you the way. Cross the soccer field and the playground. You'll see some food trucks—"

"Mr. Gibson, there are forty-sixty-eighty people outside where I am, waitin to get my autograph."

Daddy says, *Didn't think of that, Mr. Useless, did you?*

"Shut up!"

"What?" She sounds confused, fearful. Good, that's good.

"Not talking to you," Trig says. "The people who want autographs are your problem, not mine. I ought to shoot your little Black friend right now for interrupting me with your nonsense."

"Don't do that, Mr. Gibson, please. You said about the food wagons?"

"Okay, right. Right. There are trees behind them. And picnic tables. You go through the trees and there's a big wooden building like a grain silo, only bigger around. You can probably see the roof of it from where you are. It's an old hockey rink. Condemned. That's where you come."

Trig looks at his watch. The signs at the Mingo will change in just twelve minutes. Give people some time to see them. To realize what he's done. Doing.

You aren't doing anything. You're Mr. Useless. You're Mr. Flincher.

"What I'm doing, Daddy! What I'm *doing*!"

"Who you talking to, Mr. Gibson? Your father?"

"Never mind him. I want you here at the Holman Rink at 7:40. Thirty-five minutes from now. Knock on the door. Say, 'It's me.' I'll let you in. If I don't hear a knock at 7:40, I'll shoot her. I'll shoot them all."

"Mr. Gibson—"

He ends the call. He points the .22 first at Kate, then at Barbara, then at Corrie. "You . . . and you . . . and you. If you're lucky, I *will* shoot you. If you're not . . ."

From the Giant Eagle grocery bag he takes the lighter fluid. He squirts it onto the crumpled posters in their nest of old creosoted wooden beams.

"They're gonna see this," he tells the three women. "Everyone at their stupid game. See it, see it, see it. You know what my daddy would have called it? A Viking funeral!"

He laughs, then goes back to the foyer and resumes kicking the body of Christopher Stewart. The son of a bitch actually tried to *stop* him! To *shoot* him!

9

7:06 PM.

Lewis Warwick (PD) and Darby Dingley (FD) don't care for each other, but they agreed on one thing: there must be no bitching and moaning this year about partisan umpires, as in years past. No "homing" for either side. There happens to be a big Babe Ruth League tournament coming up in Cincinnati in early June, and for three hundred dollars, Warwick and Dingley hired two umps from that squad—not kids but grown men. Since these two aren't from Buckeye City, they don't give a shit who wins.

The field umpire lowers himself, hands on knees. The home plate umpire pulls down his mask and crouches behind the catcher. Both sets of bleachers, filled to capacity, cheer. "*No batter, no batter, he's a whiffer!*" Darby Dingley shouts.

The first Guns hitter, Dick Draper, steps in and waggles his bat. He drives one to left. The FD fielder fades back and catches it easily.

Top of the first, one out.

The big game is underway.

10

7:10 PM.

The crowd at the Mingo Auditorium is getting antsy. One of the pro-lifers, a cheerleader at St. Ignatius before marriage and six children, starts chanting, "*Kate McSlay, Kate McSlay, chickened out and ran away!*" It's an immediate success. The other pro-lifers, outnumbered but game, take up the chant. The cheerleader stands and motions for the pro-lifers to get up and get loud.

"KATE McSLAY, KATE McSLAY, CHICKENED OUT AND RAN AWAY!"

Someone throws a can of peanuts and bops Cheerleader Mom on her bouffant. It bounces away harmlessly—all that hairspray—but one of the pro-life men lunges over the seat and grabs the woman he believes to be the culprit.

Fisticuffs follow.

It's on.

Chapter 25

1

7:11 PM.

Betty is starting to think she'll have no choice but to go to that old hockey building—she's called up a picture of it on her phone—with a comet-tail of autograph seekers trailing out behind her. They'll be around her, too, and probably in front as well, holding out their phones and their damned autograph books: *Just one, please, Sista, please.* It's not like she can run away from them. Once upon a time, maybe; fifty years and two hundred pounds ago.

Outside the Holman, Holly also hears cheering from the softball field. Inside, there's shouting, then silence, then more shouting. Gibson speaks in three voices: his own, the child he was, and a deep voice that she supposes is his daddy. So far there have been no gunshots, but she expects them at any time because the man is obviously as mad as a hatter.

Her indecision is driving *her* mad. Any move she makes could be the wrong one. Her dead mother is making it worse, shaking her head sadly and saying, *Bad decisions lead to grief instead of relief, I've always told you that.*

Holly thinks, *I'm fracked.* Then she decides that's too mild. *Far* too mild. *Fucked is what I am. And I really want a cigarette.*

At the Mingo, the fight is petering out. It wasn't much to begin with; these folks are more used to fighting their battles on social media.

Ushers are separating the outnumbered pro-lifers from the pro-choicers. Cheerleader Mom is weeping in her husband's arms, saying, "What's wrong with these people, what's wrong with them?"

On the softball field, the cops have gone down one-two-three, and Isabelle Jaynes takes her position on the mound for the first time since college. Her adrenaline is working overtime, and the first warm-up pitch she uncorks doesn't just go over her catcher's head; it goes over the backstop and into the overflow fans who are standing behind it. This produces laughter, hoots, and catcalls from the Hoses bench and their fans. Some leatherlung in the Hoses dugout revives an old favorite: "*She's tryin ta hit the SKYYYLAB!*" This jape produces more heckling from the FD fans and players, to a great degree fueled by beer.

The Guns catcher is a fourteen-year radio patrol car veteran named Milt Coslaw, six-five, a real moose. He's also the PD's cleanup hitter. In his blue shorts, his hairy legs look like pillars. He trots out to the mound. The leatherlung, realizing he has a hit on his hands, bellows, "*SKYYYLAB!*"

"You got that out of your system, Detective Jaynes?" Coslaw asks. He's grinning.

"God, I hope so," Izzy says. "I'm scared to fucking death, Cos. And call me Izzy. At least until I walk the park. Then you can call me shitbird."

"You're not going to walk the park," Cos says. "Shoot 'er easy while you warm up. Mellow and easy. Like you were throwing batting practice this morning. Were those assholes watching that? You know they were. Save the steam for when you're loose, because you ain't nineteen anymore. And whatever you do, don't show them that dropball until it's for real."

"Thanks, Cos."

"Sure. Let's get these jakes."

The big man has settled Izzy down, and she finishes warming up, hardly doing more than lobbing it in. *Save the steam*, she thinks. *Save the dropball*. She's not thinking about Bill Wilson, Sista Bessie, the dead surrogate jurors, or Holly. She's not thinking about her job. She's living with one thought and one thought only: *Show these jakes who we are.*

Betty barely hears the shouts from the ballfield, or the groans and cheers when the lead-off Hoses batter opens the bottom of the first by striking out on a perfectly thrown dropball. She has peeked out once, and saw Red and Jerome still on the bench outside, telling hopeful Sista Bessie fans with pads and cell phones to keep their distance. She thinks, *I'll never get out of here* and *I have to get out of here* and *mighty Jesus, mighty Jesus*.

In the penalty box, Kate McKay is thinking, *I need to prepare to die, but God, there's so much work still to be done!*

Nearby, Corrie and Barbara are thinking much simpler (and perhaps more practical) thoughts: *If I could live. If I could see my mom and dad again. If only this was a dream.*

2

7:17 PM.

Izzy dispatches the Hoses team easily, two strikeouts and a grounder. Her catcher, Coslaw, leads off the top of the second and on the first pitch pounds one over the centerfield fence, narrowly missing Mr. Estevez's vintage Thunderbird. Guns 1, Hoses 0. A Hoses fan throws a bottle at him as he rounds first. Coslaw bats it contemptuously aside.

Betty's phone suggests it's about a quarter of a mile from her current location to the old arena on the other side of the park. She can make it by 7:40, but her margin for error is melting away. She wonders if she could send Jerome in her place. Barbara is *his* sister, after all. But if—no, *when*—Gibson asks Betty to say something before he opens the door, Jerome is not going to sound anything like a soul singer in her mid-sixties. Also: What if he kills Barbara's brother?

At the back of the Mingo auditorium, two ushers come in and announce to an already unsettled crowd that there's something very weird going on with the signs over the lobby doors and out by the street. People begin leaving to look.

AMY GOTTSCHALK JUROR 4 (KATE MCKAY)
BELINDA JONES JUROR 10 (SISTA BESSIE)

DOUGLAS ALLEN PROSECUTOR (CORRIE ANDERSON) IRVING WITTERSON JUDGE (BARBARA ROBINSON) ALL GUILTY. DONALD "TRIG" GIBSON JUROR 9 GUILTIEST OF ALL.

Some of them don't understand. Many do. Jerry Allison, the Mingo's janitor since time out of mind, is one who does, and not just because he listens to Buckeye Brandon. He's noticed Don Gibson getting a little . . . call it *odd* . . . over the last few weeks. Plus, there's Gibson's paperweight, the ceramic horse. Jerry is of an age when he can remember *The Roy Rogers Show*, Roy's pal Gabby Hayes, and Roy's horse.

Trigger.

3

7:20 PM.

Sitting on the bench outside the equipment room, Red looks at Young Man Jerome and thinks, *I should tell him.* But then he thinks, *Bets can't get out of here unseen anyway, not with all these people congregated around. I don't need to tell.*

Which is a relief.

4

7:23 PM.

At the Mingo, the audience that came to see Kate McKay do her firebrand routine is instead gathered around the signboard over the lobby doors or the bigger one facing Main Street. Pro-choice and pro-life attendees are united in their puzzlement. The first State Police cruisers begin to arrive, with no way to know they're on the wrong side of town. An ecstatic Buckeye Brandon is filming everything and dreaming about his star turn on the cable news networks.

On the field, the game is moving briskly. The first FD batter in the home half of the second, a squirt named Brett Holman, steps in and waggles his bat. On the mound, Izzy takes a deep breath, telling herself to settle, settle. She winds and throws a perfect dropball. The squirt waves three inches above it. The PD fans cheer. The leatherlung on the FD side bawls, "*Show us your SKYYYYLAB pitch, honeybabe!*"

Not likely, Izzy thinks, and throws another perfect dropper. The squirt just about swings out of his shoes, to no result. Coslaw puts one finger between his legs, calling for a straight fast pitch. Izzy has her doubts, but throws it. This time the squirt, expecting the drop, swings *under* the pitch, actually digging up a puff of dirt with the head of his bat.

"*Siddown, bush!*" a fan on the PD side yells as the squirt trudges back to the bench. The FD fans boo. Middle fingers are displayed. The next Hoses batter steps in.

I can do this, Izzy thinks. She brushes her hair back and leans in for Coslaw's sign. *I can really do this.*

She winds and fires. A perfect dropball.

"*Strike one!*" the umpire calls.

In her dressing room, Betty Brady stands up. Fuck the autograph hounds. She can't just sit in here. She has to *go*.

Izzy throws another dropper. The batter lets it go past knee-high, but the umpire raises his fist. Darby Dingley leaps from the FD dugout and strides onto the grass, nearly transgressing the foul line, which would have gotten him tossed. His face is almost as red as his too-short shorts. "*You homer!*" he yells at the ump. *"That wasn't even close!"* Those on the Fire Department bleachers take up the cry. The PD fans beg to differ, telling the FD fans to shut the hell up. Good sportsmanship has taken a hike.

Holly—still indecisive, now back on the left of the rink doors, still with the revolver drawn and the barrel pointing toward the darkening sky—cocks her head, listening. Sounds are coming from the softball field. She thinks at first they're cheering, but then changes her mind. That's not cheering. It's *yelling*. Someone—no, a great many someones—sounds pissed off.

In the arena, Trig is also listening. "Daddy? What's that?"

But Daddy doesn't answer.

5

The audience is rapt, living and dying with every pitch. There's two down, both strikeouts, in the bottom of the second when George Pill, Izzy Jaynes's wiseass nemesis, steps into the batter's box. She doesn't fear him; is actually glad to see him. The dropball is working like a charm, and every time Milt Coslaw calls for the straight hard one, the Hoses have been foozled. *I can do this*, she tells herself. Her arm feels loose and warm and strong.

George Pill makes a gesture that's almost McKay-like: *C'mon, c'mon, c'mon, throw the fucking ball*, and then cocks the bat. Is he sneering at her? Good. Great. He can sneer all the way back to the dugout. She throws strike one.

"*She's cheating!*" the leatherlung calls. From the foul line, where he's still glowering, Darby Dingley adds his two cents' worth. "*Check the ball, ump!*"

Izzy throws the dropper. Pill flails and misses. The PD side cheers. Now all the FD fans are chanting along with Darby: "*Check the ball! Check the ball!*"

The ump waves them off. He knows the ball isn't the problem; he checked it himself before tossing it to Izzy to start the bottom half of the second. That sneaky drop pitch is the problem, and it's not *his* problem.

The PD fans chant, "*Strike him OUT! Strike him OUT!*"

Betty opens the door of her dressing room and steps into the equipment room.

Jerome, John, and Red get up from their bench and saunter to the corner of the building to see what all the shouting is about. All but the most dedicated autograph seekers—the eBayers, in it for money rather than love—do the same.

The leatherlung: "*She's cheating!*"

Dingley: "*Check the ball for grease, ump!*"

Lew Warwick, coming to his own foul line on the other side of the diamond: "*Sit down and shut up, Darby! Quit being a poor sport!*"

Dingley: "*Poor sport, my rosy red ass! She's throwing a fucking SPIT-BALL!*"

Izzy ignores all the noise. Takes a breath. Looks in for the sign. Cos has one finger down, wanting the straight fast one.

Izzy throws it, and everything goes to hell.

6

7:28 PM.

George Pill connects and hits a bouncer along the infield grass between first base and the pitcher's mound. For a moment Pill just stands at home plate, transfixed. Then he runs. The Hoses fans rise to their feet, anticipating their team's first hit.

The Guns first baseman is a young patrolman named Ray Darcy. He fades toward second and barehands the ball on the third bounce.

Izzy Jaynes knows that if the first baseman is pulled out of position, it's her job to cover the bag and take the throw. She's off at the *chink* sound of the aluminum bat and is standing on the first-base line to take the feed. Darcy's throw is on the money, and she spins to tag George Pill out, aware he may try to slide under her.

He doesn't. With a scowl on his face, Pill redoubles his speed, lowers his head, and crashes into Izzy, his shoulder digging into her breasts and his helmeted head into the socket of her shoulder. She hears a dull *crrack* as her shoulder parts company with her upper arm, and hers is the first shriek that everyone—here and at the Holman Rink—hears. The ball bounces out of her glove and Pill stands on first base, helmetless now, oblivious of the screaming woman on the ground. He's grinning and—incredibly—making the *safe* sign. He's still making it when Ray Darcy hits him with a flying tackle, straddles him, and begins punching his lights out.

The Guns and Hoses players sprint from their benches and light up a full-fledged, fists-flying donnybrook. The field ump tries to get between them and is flattened. The Guns fans begin erupting from the bleachers. On the Hoses side, Darby Dingley is waving his fists above his head and screaming, "*Get em, you firemen! Fucking GET EM!*"

Lew Warwick runs across the field, grabs Dingley, and shoves him onto his butt. "Don't be an asshole, quit throwing gas on the fire," he says, but the damage is done.

The Hoses fans pour down from their bleachers, ready to rumble. Some fall and get up, some fall and get stomped on. Gunners meet Hosers at midfield. The loudspeaker squawks and remonstrates before being cut off in a howl of feedback. Calls to reason wouldn't have mattered, anyway. The crowd, many of them fueled by beer, wine, and the harder stuff, begin to whale on each other. It's not like the pallid kerfuffle at the Mingo Auditorium; this is serious shit.

In foul territory, just south of first base, Izzy rolls back and forth, cradling her broken shoulder in agony, forgotten until Tom Atta scoops her up.

"Getting you out of here," he says, and to Ray Darcy, as he goes by: "Stop hitting that fireman, Officer. Fucking poor-sport dickbrain's unconscious."

A police car rolls slowly onto the field, jackpot lights flashing and siren gobbling. Hoses fans surround it, halting its progress. Other Hoses fans begin to rock it, and eventually turn it over on its side in left field.

Bedlam.

7

Betty Brady walks past piles of uniforms and soccer gear and peers out the door. She doesn't know what has happened and doesn't care. What matters is the way is suddenly clear. Mighty Jesus has heard her prayer. For the time being, even the autograph hounds seem to be gone, but she knows they'll be back. There isn't a second to waste.

She takes a last look around to make sure she's okay, then sets off at a lumbering jog for the round roof of the rink rising above the surrounding trees, holding her purse to her bosom with one hand. Trailing her is one final and extremely dedicated eBayer, a bespectacled man Holly would have recognized from Iowa City, Davenport, and Chicago. In one hand he's got a poster of a much younger Sista Bessie standing outside the Apollo Theater. He's calling to her: *Just one, just one.*

Betty can't hear him. The noise of the crowd—angry voices, terrified voices, cries of pain, a din of yelling men and women—redoubles. At the edge of the trees she stops and grabs her vial of heart pills out of her bag. She takes three, hoping they'll hold off the heart attack she's been dodging for the last eight or ten years of her life, at least until she does what needs doing.

Hold on, you old rattletrap, she tells her heart. *Hold on a little longer.* She takes Red's gun out of her purse.

"Sista Bessie!" the bespectacled eBayer calls. "I'm a huge fan! I couldn't get a ticket to your show! Would you sign—"

She turns, gun in hand, and although it's not pointing at him—not exactly—the bespectacled eBayer decides he's not such a huge fan, after all. He turns tail and runs. But holds onto the poster. Signed, on eBay or one of the other auction sites, it would fetch four hundred dollars.

Four hundred at *least*.

8

Before Jerome can enter the scrum (which now covers the whole field) and start pulling people apart, Red Jones grabs his arm. "Betty," he says. "If she's gone, I guess maybe you better go after her."

Jerome looks at him, frowning. "Why would she be gone? She's still in her dressing room, right?"

"I'd like to believe it, but I don't think so. She wanted my gun."

"What?"

John Ackerly staggers through the centerfield gate with blood gushing from his nose and mouth. "Fucking *drunks*!" he screams. "Some asshole sucker-punched me and laughed and ran the fuck away! I hate fucking *drunks*!"

Jerome ignores him. He takes Red by his skinny shoulders. "What gun? Why did she want it?"

"My .38. I don't know why. Something gone wrong with her. I should have told you sooner. Stupid old man couldn't make up his mind. I was gonna after the Anthem, then I thought, 'Shucks, all these people wantin pictures and autographs, she'll never be able to get out.' But now . . ." He shakes his head. "Stupid old man, gravy where my brains should be. That gun is loaded and I think she means to shoot somebody."

Jerome can't believe it. They go back to the equipment room, leaving the Guns and Hoses fans to sort themselves out. The dressing room door stands open. The sequined bellbottoms and starry sash are heaped on the floor. Betty is gone. *Then* he can believe it.

He backs out and sees a bespectacled man running toward the softball field, trailing a poster behind him like the tail of a kite. He looks from Red to Jerome and says, "I asked for an autograph and she pointed a *gun* at me! She's crazy!"

"Where is she?" Jerome asks.

The bespectacled eBayer points. "I know some celebs don't like autograph hunters, but a *gun*?"

Jerome runs for the trees. Once in them he sees Betty just ahead, sitting on the bench of a picnic table, head hanging down, looking pale and exhausted.

9

In the arena, Trig is sitting on the bleachers shoulder to shoulder with Kate McKay. The tape over her mouth is soaked with blood and has come loose, helped by her tongue.

"You know," he says, "you make some good points."

"Let them go," she says. Her voice comes out in a rough growl. She tries to nod in the direction of the two young women taped to the penalty booth. Her head is bound too tightly to move more than an inch or two, so she settles for casting her eyes in their direction. "I'm the one you want, the famous one, so let them go."

Trig has been lost in memories of how he sat on these very bleachers with Daddy. How Daddy would grip his arm hard enough to leave bruises. How he'd sometimes hug Trig during the intermissions. Kate's voice brings him back. He looks at her with surprise. "How did you get so conceited, woman? Did you grow into it, or were you born that way?"

"I just—"

"You're not the one I want, you were just *there*. This isn't about fame, it's about *guilt*. Which is what brought you here, right? Plus some half-assed notion of rescuing your buddy."

"But . . . you . . . I thought . . ."

"When I say you make good points, I think that's probably because my father killed my mother."

Kate stares at him.

Trig nods. "Said she was *gone*, but I know what I know."

"You need help, sir."

"And you need to shut up." He slaps the tape back across her mouth, but it won't stay.

"Please, if we could just talk about this—"

He puts the Taurus against the center of her forehead. "Do you want to live another few minutes? If you do, *shut up.*"

Kate shuts up. Trig looks at his watch. It's 7:38.

I don't think the Black singer's coming, Daddy. I'll have to be content with these three. Plus me, of course.

10

Jerome reaches Betty and drops to one knee beside her. A pistol with a taped handgrip lies on the bench next to her.

"Cain't," she says. "Thought I could but I cain't."

"Can't do what?" he asks. "What is it?"

She points at the round gray building, just visible through the trees. "Barbara."

Jerome tenses. "What about her?"

"In there. Crazy man got her. Gibson. From the Mingo. He said get there by 7:40 or he'd kill her, but I cain't . . . legs just give out."

He's up at once, but Betty grasps his wrist with surprising force. "You cain't, either. He wants me to knock and say, 'It's me.' If he hears a man, he'll kill her."

For a moment Jerome entertains the idea that this is all some crazy delusion on Betty's part, maybe even early-onset Alzheimer's, but it's

Barbara she's talking about, *Barbara*, and he can't allow himself that luxury.

Betty is saying something else, but he doesn't listen. Jerome takes the gun and runs for the Holman Rink.

11

7:40 PM.

Trig gets up and walks down to the penalty box. He points the .22 first at Corrie, then at Barbara. "Which of you is first?" he asks. "I think the white girl."

He puts the gun against Corrie's temple. Corrie closes her eyes and waits to see if there's anything on the other side of the known world. Then the pressure of the gun barrel is removed.

"All right, Daddy. If you say so."

Corrie opens her eyes. Trig is stepping over the wooden ties, heading back to the foyer. He speaks to them without turning around. "Daddy says give her five more minutes. Daddy says women are always late."

12

Holly can't believe what she's seeing: Jerome.

He comes running out of the trees with a little pistol in his hand. He sees her and stops, every bit as startled as Holly is herself. He's going to say or shout something—she can see him getting ready to do it—and so she puts a finger to her lips, shaking her head. She beckons to him, realizing as she does it that it's Kate's gesture: *C'mon, c'mon, c'mon*. As he starts toward her, she pushes both hands down in a *quiet* gesture.

Jerome reaches her and puts his lips to her ear. "You have to say, 'It's me.' I can't do it. And sound like her."

"Sound like who?" Holly whispers.

"Betty," he whispers back. "Sista Bessie."

"I can't—"

"*You have to*," he whispers. "Knock and say, 'It's me.' Or he'll kill Barbara."

Not just Barbara, Holly thinks.

Jerome points at his watch and whispers, "We're out of time."

13

7:43 PM.

He decides he doesn't want to shoot anyone but himself.

Trig goes back into the arena, stepping over the boards until he reaches the paper-stuffed square at center ice. He squirts on a little more of the Kingsford fluid, then takes out his Bic. As he kneels, preparing to strike a light, there's a hammering on the door. He freezes for a moment, not sure what to do.

Why choose, Mr. Useless? Daddy asks. *You can do both.*

Trig decides Daddy is right. He strikes a light and drops the Bic onto the crumpled posters. Fire blooms in the square of old dry wood. He looks at the bound women, their eyes wide with horror.

"Viking funeral," he says. "Better than my mother got. My mother is *gone*." And goes to answer the door.

14

Holly stands in front of those doors. Jerome stands nearby, his lips pressed together so tightly that his mouth has all but disappeared. It seems she waits a very long time before Gibson speaks on the other side, his voice low and confidential. "Is that you, Sista Bessie?"

Holly deepens her voice as much as she can and tries to imitate Betty's light southern accent. "Yeah, it's me," she says, and thinks she sounds horrible, a goony minstrel-show racist doing a caricature Black voice.

There's another pause. Then Gibson says, "Are you here because you're guilty?"

Holly looks toward Jerome. He nods at her.

"Yeah," Holly says in her deepest voice. "Guilty f'sure."

It's horrible. He'll never believe it.

Then, after an agonizing pause, the red light on the keypad turns green. Holly has that one moment, that one signal, to raise her gun before the door opens. Gibson stares at her extremely Caucasian face, eyes widening. He has his own gun, but Holly doesn't give him a chance to use it. She shoots him twice: center mass, just as Bill Hodges told her. Gibson staggers backward, pawing at his chest, eyes wide. He tries to raise his gun. Jerome shoulders Holly aside and shoots him again with Red's pistol.

Gibson utters one word—"Daddy!"—and falls forward.

Holly spares him only a glance before looking into the arena. "Fire," she says, and giant-steps over Gibson's body.

In the circular rink area, the crumpled posters are blazing and the crisscrossed ties surrounding it are catching, blue flames turning yellow and racing along their lengths. Two women are bound to the penalty box, a third—Kate—to a bleacher stanchion nearby.

Holly runs toward them, stumbles, goes down, and is barely aware of splinters jabbing into her palms. She gets up and goes to the women shoulder to shoulder in the penalty box. If she had a blade she could free them easily, but she doesn't.

"Jerome, help me! Put out the fire!"

Jerome runs back to the body of Donald Gibson, and yanks off Gibson's sportcoat. The man's arms come with it, and Jerome has to struggle. Although he's dead, Gibson won't give the coat up. His shoulders roll from side to side, head wagging like some grotesque ventriloquist's dummy. At last Jerome pulls the coat free and runs into the arena with the coat's silk lining ripped and trailing out behind him. Holly is unwinding the tape binding Barbara's arms to the yellow steel pole, but it's slow, slow.

Kate spits away the bloody tape over her mouth and shouts, "Faster!" in her growling voice. "Do it faster!"

Always the boss, Holly thinks. She grabs swatches of tape in both hands and pulls with all her strength. One of Barbara's arms comes free. She rips the tape off her mouth and says, "Corrie! Corrie! Do Corrie!"

"No," Holly says, because Barbara is her priority. Barbara is not just her friend but a loved one. Corrie will be second. The boss will come third . . . if at all. Holly's hands are slippery with blood from the splinters. She yanks the longest one out and goes to work on Barbara's other hand.

In the middle of the floor, by the stuttery glow of the two working battery-powered lights, Jerome throws Gibson's sportcoat over the fire and begins stomping on it—left-foot, right-foot, left-foot, right-foot—as if treading grapes. Sparks fly up in a cloud around him. Some burn through his shirt, stinging his skin. One of his pantlegs smolders, then catches fire. He bends and beats out the flames, vaguely aware that his snazzy Converse sneakers have begun to melt around his feet. *Athletic socks don't fail me now*, he thinks.

Holly manages to unwind the tape around Barbara's middle. Barbara tries to stand and can't, tries to piston her legs and can't. The tape binding her thighs to the seat of the penalty box is too tight.

"Your pants!" Holly shouts. "Can you slide out of them?"

Barbara pushes her trousers partway down, gets some slack in the tape, and tries to pump her legs again. This time she can. Her knees come up to her chest, then to her shoulders. She wriggles out of her pants and her legs are free.

Gibson's sportcoat is burning and flames are racing every whichway along the boards. Jerome gives up trying to smother the fire and comes to the penalty box, jumping from one crosstie to the next. He goes to work freeing Corrie. To Holly he says, "I slowed it down but it's on those ties. The sides will be next. Then the rafters."

The fire is indeed spreading. Jerome is doing his best to get Corrie loose, but she's been wound up even tighter than Barbara.

"Hey. Young Man Jerome. Take this."

He turns his head and sees Betty. Her afro is matted and her face shines with sweat, but she looks better than she did on the picnic bench. She's holding out a pocket knife with a worn wooden handle. "I always keep it in my purse. From when I was on the chicken circuit."

Jerome has no idea what a chicken circuit is, and doesn't care. He snatches the knife. It's sharp, and slices through the tape holding Corrie to the penalty box easily. He leaves her to finish freeing herself and moves on to Kate. The ceiling of the old arena is high, which helps with the growing billows of smoke, but it also acts as an open flue, feeding the fire.

"Help me," Jerome tells Holly. "It's getting a teeny bit hot in here."

But the heat on his back is nothing to the heat on his feet. His sneakers are now misshapen lumps. He hopes that when he takes them off—assuming they get out of this—the hightops will peel away his socks but not his skin. He's aware they may take some of both.

Holly helps as best she can. Barbara, now free but barefooted and bare-legged, tries to help finish freeing Kate.

"No, no, get out of here!" Jerome yells at her. "Help Betty, she's almost out on her feet! Go on!"

Barbara doesn't argue. She puts an arm around Betty's waist and together they make their slow, stumbling way over the railroad ties to the foyer.

Corrie stands up, then sags. "I can't walk. My legs are all needles and pins."

Jerome carries her, shambling along in the Frankenstein clumps of his sneakers but managing to stay on his feet. Flames are racing over the crisscrossed beams, making orange checkerboard patterns.

Kate is also unable to walk. She tries, then sags to her knees. Holly hooks a hand into her armpit and hauls her up, calling on strength she didn't know she had.

"You keep saving me," Kate says in her husky, growling voice. Her chin and shirt are a bib of blood. The glimpses of teeth Holly can see between her swelling lips are little more than fangs.

"It's what you hired me for. Help me."

They make their way, first to the foyer and then outside with the growing fire at their back. When they are in the blessed coolness of the May night, Jerome goes back in and seizes Donald Gibson's legs. He drags him out and says to Holly, "There's another one, just as dead. I don't think I can get him . . . or maybe it's her . . . until I get these off." He sits on the ground and begins pulling off one half-melted sneaker.

Holly goes in. The fire hasn't reached the foyer, but the arena itself will soon be engulfed and the heat is already baking. She grabs one of the legs of the person Gibson must have killed—Chris Stewart. Chrissy. She thinks, *I can't, too heavy*. Then Kate is there, and grabbing the other leg. "Haul," she croaks. Always the boss.

They pull Chrissy Stewart out into the thickening twilight. Barbara is sitting against the side of the Mingo van with her head on Betty's shoulder. Jerome has managed to pull his sneakers off. His feet are red, but only the left one is raising blisters.

Kate sits down hard, looking at the body they've just dragged out of the rink. "This is the bitch who's been stalking me," she says. "Stalking *us*."

"Yes. Kate, we have to get out of here. That building's going to go up like a torch."

"One minute. I need to get my breath, and she surely needs to get hers." She means Betty. "Good thing she had that knife, or we would have roasted like the chestnuts in that Christmas song."

Kate lifts Chrissy Stewart's arm, and examines it. "Cute outfit. Or was, before this. Did he want to be a girl and his church wouldn't let him? Is that what all this has been about?"

"I don't know." What Holly knows is they have to move soon. She goes to the van, and God is good: the keys are in the cupholder. She opens the driver's door, then turns to look at the others, who are brightly lit silhouettes in the orange glow of the fire.

"We're getting out of here," she says. "In this. Right now."

Barbara and Betty help each other to their feet. Jerome hobbles over with the help of Kate, who is taking as much of his weight as she can.

"What about them?" Jerome points to the corpses.

"Oh God, no," Corrie says, but she goes to Gibson and grabs him by one arm. She pulls him to the back of the van. "There's another one . . . a girl, but . . . burning now. *Cremating*." She moans.

Holly doesn't want anything to do with either of them. What she wants is to sleep for about twelve hours, then wake up to coffee, a jelly doughnut, and about a dozen cigarettes. But Kate is walking back to him . . . or her . . . the person in the pants suit. Holly joins her. They drag Stewart to the van, but neither of them have the strength to throw the bodies in. Jerome does that, grunting with pain as his injured feet take their weight. He shuts the doors, then staggers.

"You drive," he says to Holly. "I can't. My feet."

"*I'll* drive," Kate says, with a touch of her old certainty.

And she does.

Chapter 26

1

On a warm and sunny morning in late June, a few days after Dingley Park has reopened, Holly sits at the picnic table where she and Izzy often have lunch. It's the same one (she doesn't know this) where Betty Brady stopped, unable to go any further and convinced she had signed her new friend's death warrant thereby.

Holly is early; she's always early. The food trucks aren't open yet, but from the nearby playground, she can hear the shouts of children playing tag and climbing on the monkeybars. The equipment shed is still blocked off with yellow police tape. It was looted at the height of the riot and the stuff inside—uniforms, pads, balls, bats, shoes, even athletic supporters—was scattered across the converted softball field, along with broken bottles, torn-off red and blue shirts, even a few teeth. The bases were looted and carried off, perhaps as souvenirs. Holly can't understand why, but so much about human behavior (including her own) will always be a mystery to her.

Her friend John Ackerly suffered a broken jaw in the melee. He didn't realize it until the next morning, when he looked in the mirror and saw the lower half of his face swollen to the point where "I looked like Popeye in one of those old cartoons, only without the pipe." He was treated at the Kiner ER, waiting his turn among five dozen or so other walking wounded from the Guns and Hoses softball game. The doctor gave him a prescription for oxycodone tablets, which he used for three days and then flushed down the toilet. He told Holly that he liked those pills just a little too much.

She and Izzy used to be able to see the round roof of the Holman from this table, but it's gone now; nothing is left of the rink but blackened, smoking rubble cordoned off by police tape. Donald Gibson, aka Bill Wilson, aka Trig, apparently meant to burn his victims like seventeenth-century witches. State Police detectives searching Gibson's home at the Elm Grove Trailer Park have found a stack of notebooks, some labeled *Character Defects*, as in the AA program, and others labeled *Letters to Daddy*. The latter make it clear that Annette McElroy's murder was Gibson's first.

The Daddy Chronicles (so dubbed by Buckeye Brandon) also accuse Donald Gibson's father of murdering Bonita Gibson, who disappeared in 1998, when Donald was eight years old. Avery McMartin, a long-retired city detective, confirmed (on the Buckeye Brandon pod) that Mr. Gibson was a suspect in his wife's disappearance, but the woman's body was never found and the case of Bonita Gibson has long been consigned to the department's open-but-inactive file.

Kate McKay is now the most famous woman in America. Her picture—bloody mouth, disheveled hair, tape-burns on her face and neck—has been seen all around the world, including on the cover of *People* magazine. She refused to wash until that iconic photo was taken back at the hotel. The tour has been repurposed to much larger venues, where Kate's *c'mon, c'mon, c'mon* gesture brings roars of approval. Millions of women are wearing tee-shirts with Kate's face on them, some with bloody mouth, some without, always with the fingers spread in that gesture. More states, two of them deep red, have enacted laws that safeguard a woman's right to abort.

"Or not to abort," Kate always says. "Remember that. Life is *always* the preferred choice, but that choice belongs to the woman."

There have been rumors that she may run for office. Perhaps even the highest office. Holly finds the idea ridiculous. Kate's too focused on her own cause to ever be elected. She has tunnel vision. Or so Holly thinks.

Holly has resigned her post as Kate's security. Three ex-military women have taken her place. They are younger than Holly, and better looking (as the young tend to be). They call themselves the Bod Squad.

Corrie has gone back home to New Hampshire.

The Buckeye City Police and Fire Departments were and continue to be in a heap o' trouble. A commission has been created to study the causes of the riot, and to come up with sanctions for such behavior. Police Chief Alice Patmore and Fire Chief Darby Dingley have both resigned. Questions about the decision to play the charity game while a serial killer was on the loose continue to be asked. "Better belated than never," Buckeye Brandon says of those questions. *Crows*, actually.

The boys in blue and those in red hunker down, probably embarrassed by their behavior (maybe even shocked), but not too worried. Yes, the Softball Riot has become comedy fodder for late-night talk show hosts in their monologues, but that will pass. And really, how many cops and firemen can be suspended when there's crime to fight and blazing buildings to be put out? Half of the combatants claim they weren't even there, and the other half claim they were trying to stop it. Which Holly knows, from Tom Atta and Lew Warwick, is utter bullpoop.

Most members of the PD and FD will skate. There are two notable exceptions. Ray Darcy, the Guns first baseman, has been suspended for six months, the first three without pay. George Pill has had his ass canned from the Fire Department. From all that Holly has heard from Warwick and Izzy, that dismissal was better than the assault charge Pill so richly deserved. Izzy declined to press charges. Russell Grinsted tried to convince Izzy to sue Pill, but Izzy declined. She never wants to see George Pill's face again. Or Grinsted's, for that matter.

Jerome had his novel filed away on his desktop and has gone back to it. His close call—he hobbled on crutches for a week because of first-degree burns on his feet, and showed Holly the constellation of burn-holes in his shirt—seems to have delivered a needed jump-start to his creativity. He plans to work on the Army of God book when he's finished his private eye novel. He says nonfiction is where his heart lies. He stays in touch with Corrie, telling her that her bad dreams will pass. Corrie says she hopes he's right.

There were no Sista Bessie shows in Buckeye City, of course; even if Betty hadn't suffered a minor heart attack, the Mingo was a crime scene. It is currently closed, with a few June and July shows—George

Strait, Maroon 5, Dropkick Murphys—rescheduled to the fairgrounds. Others have been canceled.

The Mingo, with Maisie Rogan now at the helm, will reopen in August with a very special show.

2

Frankie's Fabulous Fish Wagon opens for business. Sitting and waiting for Izzy, hands folded neatly before her (she has finally stopped biting her nails), Holly thinks: *I have killed five people now, and do they keep me awake at night? They do not. With four, I was in fear of my own life. With Donald Gibson . . .*

"I was doing my duty as a bodyguard."

A job she will never, *ever*, do again.

Betty Brady, also known as Sista Bessie, has flown back to California in her private jet, and with Barbara Robinson to keep her company. They have grown very close, but Barbara stays in touch with her old friends, and will be back . . . at least for awhile. Holly FaceTimed with her just last night. It's Barbara's second close call with death, and she's suffering her own nightmares, but says that, on the whole, she's doing quite well, partly because she has a basis for comparison. She tells Holly that at least Donald "Trig" Gibson was an *ordinary* crazy, if there is such a thing; not like the other one. They don't refer to the other one by his name, Chet Ondowsky, but simply as the outsider.

She says she's writing poetry again, and poetry helps.

3

From behind her: "I'm hungry as hell, but you might have to help me with the food."

Holly looks around to see Isabelle Jaynes walking—with great care—toward their favorite table. Her arm is in a sling, and her shoulder is practically mummified. She clearly hasn't been to the beauty parlor since her injury; Holly can see two inches of gray growing out of her dye-enhanced red hair. But the eyes are the same; misty gray and good humored.

"And *get* the food, of course. Fish tacos for me."

Holly helps her sit down. "I want scallops, if he has them today. Do those pins in your shoulder hurt?"

"Everything hurts," Izzy says, "but I've got another ten days' worth of heavy-duty painkillers. Beyond that I'm not looking. Feed me, woman. I need vittles and a gallon of Coca-Cola."

Holly goes to the fish wagon and brings back the chow. She doesn't have to help her friend eat after all. Izzy's a righty, and it's her left arm and hand that are incapacitated.

Izzy turns her face up to the sky. "The sun feels good. I've been spending too much time indoors."

"Are you doing physical therapy?"

"Some. There'll be more once they unstrap me." Izzy makes a face. "Let's not talk about it." She starts on her second fish taco.

"Will you ever pitch again?"

"Fuck, no."

"Okay, next subject. Do you know anything about the Real Christ Holy Church?"

"Ah. As a matter of fact, I do know some stuff, and it's *dee*-lightful. Lew Warwick told me. You know he's acting Chief of Police now, right?"

"I heard that." From Buckeye Brandon, actually, who's always got the biggest scoop of the newest poop.

"It'll only be for a short while, until they bring in some hotshot from one of the bigger cities. He's okay with that. Lew got this from ATF. It's not public yet. Want to hear the story?"

"You know I do." Holly's eyes are sparkling.

"There was a woman in the church named Melody Martinek, okay?"

"Does she sound like she's singing when she answers the phone?"

"I've never talked to her. Just shut up and listen, okay? She was a close friend of Christopher Stewart's mother, and one of the few who knew Christopher liked to dress in female clothes. It was in honor of his sister. Or because he sometimes thought he *was* his sister, Martinek had no opinion on that. Eventually, after both his parents had died, it became general knowledge in their little cult. Martinek got disillusioned and left the church when Mrs. Stewart died. Said they wouldn't let Stewart go to the doctor because they were going to pray the cancer away."

"Like they probably tried to pray Christopher Stewart's female half away," Holly says.

"Yeah, probably. You know, Holly, I think the religions of the world are responsible for a shitpot of trouble."

"Finish your story."

"Martinek talked to the cops in Baraboo Junction. The local cops talked to the state cops, and the state cops talked to the ATF. ATF got a search warrant based on the Martinek woman's sworn statement and found a huge cache of weapons in the church basement. Big stuff, including rotary-barrel 50-caliber machine guns, M67 fragmentation grenades, mortars . . . you get the picture. Real Christ Holy was preparing for a Real Christ Holy War and has been shut down."

"What about Andrew Fallowes?"

"Not such good news there. He's all lawyered up. I mean a *platoon* of legal beagles. The lawyers say he knows nuttin about nuttin. Not about Chris Stewart, not about the weapons, either. I guess Fallowes thinks Gunnery Sergeant Jesus brought all them shootin irons down from heaven."

"The federals or the Wisconsin State Police or . . . or *anybody* . . . they have *nothing* on Fallowes concerning Christopher Stewart?"

"No."

Holly says, "That's crap! No, it's *shit*! Fallowes wound Stewart up. Set him in motion. I fracking *know* it."

"I'm sure you're right, but he's walking free and will probably continue to walk free. There's mucho megabucks behind that church, and you know how it goes, right? Money talks, truth walks."

Izzy fumbles a bottle of pills out of her jeans pocket and gives it to Holly. "Will you open that for me? It's a two-hand job. The blue ones are antibiotics. I'm supposed to take them with food. The white ones are painkillers. I'll take two of those after the food."

Holly gets them out and Izzy swallows a blue pill with Coke. She looks at the two white pills and says, "I can't wait."

"You don't want to get addicted."

"Right now the only thing I'm addicted to is pain. And fish tacos. Would you get me another one?"

Holly is happy to, because her friend has clearly lost weight. When she comes back, Izzy is grinning. "Is it true?"

"Is what true?"

"About Sista Bessie? She's going to open the Mingo with a show in August?"

"It's true."

"You're sure?"

"I'm sure. I got it from Barbara. She's staying in Betty's guest house, and she's agreed to be an honorary Dixie Crystal, at least once, and right here."

"Can you get me tickets?"

Holly smiles. She's radiant when she smiles. The years fall away and she's young again.

She says, "You bet I can. I've got friends in the band."

4

The janitor's cubicle and adjoining equipment room at the Mingo Auditorium is in the basement, and eventually Jerry Allison is allowed back in there. The Mingo was locked down by the cops, and forensics people in white Tyvek suits have been through it with their brushes, fingerprint powder, and their Luminol. Three videographers accompanied their every step, photographing it all, including Jerry's basement hidey-hole.

"Be careful of that," Jerry said when one of the Tyvek guys bent to examine the ceramic horse on Jerry's cluttered desk. "It's a family hair-loom."

Bullshit, of course. He filched it from Don Gibson's desk before the cops descended. He always liked that old horsey, that old Trigger.

On the day Holly and Izzy have their lunch in Dingley Park, on his way back to his room, nothing on his mind but the Baby Ruth in his pocket, Jerry stops outside the door. Someone inside says, low: "Where'd you bury her, Daddy?"

Heart beating so hard it thrums in his scrawny neck, Jerry goes into his cubbyhole-sized room. Which is empty. Only the ceramic horse on his desk.

Staring at him.

August 28, 2024

Afterword

This was a difficult book to write, partially because I had surgery to repair a damaged hip in late September 2023. *Never Flinch* has gone through multiple rewrites and three title changes. I'm finally happy with it. Or—let us be truthful—happy *enough*. It's never all I'd hope for, but there comes a point when you must let it go.

I have been helped along the way, most especially by Robin Furth, who does research, helps me avoid howlers, creates absolutely extraordinary timelines, and most of all is tremendously supportive. There were times, especially post-surgery, when this book might have died without her. A dedication is small recompense, but also necessary.

Liz Darhansoff is my agent, having replaced Chuck Verrill and never missing a beat even as she was dealing with her own grief about the loss of her longtime business partner. She has been a stalwart and supportive aide, especially in the cold months of November 2023 to February 2024, when I despaired of ever finishing.

Nan Graham is my longtime editor. The changes she suggested were all useful. Even more useful—and cheerful!—are the little penciled checkmarks in the margin that mean something hit home for her.

Chris Lotts does foreign rights and has a new kiddo—hooray for Hugo.

Katie Monaghan does publicity. She's always cheerful, always supportive, always smart about various PR opportunities—what's good, what's bad, and what's just plain butt-ugly. She also makes the world's best cookies.

Thanks are due to my friend Naresh Motwani, who coined the term *eBayers* for the autograph hunters that follow me around and gather outside hotels when I'm on tour. These aren't fans who want a signed book or two for their collections, but the speculators who feel their hounding is just another price celebrities pay for *being* celebrities. I tend to disagree, but that's just me . . . and *eBayers* describes them perfectly, because most of them do bay.

Thanks to Jon Leonard, who is a jack of all trades and master of every damn one. He's kept my computer computing, keeps the house from falling down around our ears, and has co-custody of Molly, aka the Thing of Evil. She just loves him to death, and vice-versa . . . but Jeez-Louise, why not? *Everyone* loves Molly.

Jaya Miceli has created some gorgeous cover concepts, including this one.

Christina Zarafonitis creates wonderful audiobook editions of my stuff and is ever patient as I stumble through various pronunciations on her voicemail.

Thanks to my wife, who read the first draft of this book and said, "You can do better." That was hard news to get, but eventually I heeded it because she was right (she usually is). I love you, Tabitha.

Last but hardly least, here is a list—sadly incomplete—of those supporters of women's right to choose who have been murdered for doing their duty.

Dr. David Gunn, murdered March 10, 1993, in Pensacola, Florida.

Dr. John Bayard Britton, murdered July 29, 1994, in Pensacola.

Clinic volunteer James H. Barrett, murdered July 29, 1994, in Pensacola.

Receptionist Shannon Lowney, murdered December 30, 1994, in Brookline, Massachusetts.

Receptionist Leanne Nichols, murdered December 30, 1994, in Brookline.

Security guard (and police officer) Robert Sanderson, murdered January 29, 1998, in Birmingham, Alabama.

Dr. Barnett Slepian, murdered October 23, 1998, in Amherst, New York.

Dr. George Tiller, murdered May 31, 2009, in Wichita, Kansas.

Officer Garrett Swasey, murdered November 27, 2015, in Colorado Springs, Colorado.

Jennifer Markovsky and Ke'Arre Marcell Stewart, murdered November 27, 2015, when they accompanied their friend to a Planned Parenthood clinic.

However you feel about abortion, one fact is indisputable: these people were murdered for their beliefs.